# Antares Victory

## (A Novel)

### By

## Michael McCollum

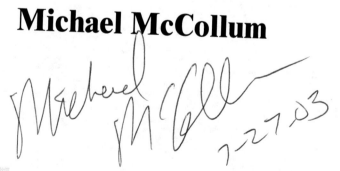

**SCI FI - ARIZONA**
A Virtual Science Fiction Bookstore and
Writer's Workshop on the INTERNET
**www.scifi-az.com**

ISBN 1-929381-09-3
350 pages
© 2002 by Michael McCollum

Michael McCollum
Proprietor
Sci Fi - Arizona
1931 East Libra Drive
Suite 101
Tempe, AZ 85283
mccollum@scifi-az.com

1-929381-09-3 Mod 1-37/20020922

# Table of Contents

# Antares and Spica Foldspace Clusters

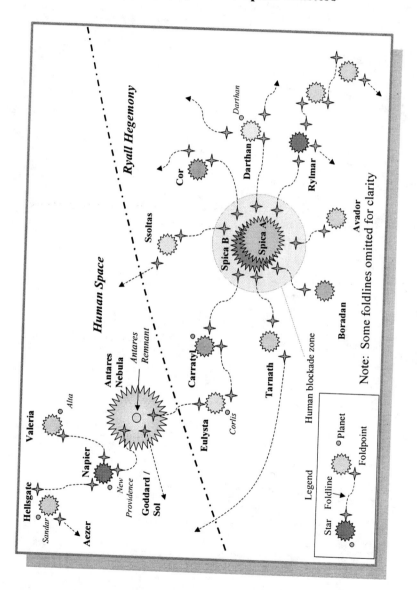

# Chapter 1

Admiral (First Rank) Richard Arthur Drake lay strapped in his acceleration couch aboard the orbit-to-orbit shuttle and gazed at the glowing apparition that covered half the ebon sky before him. Here in the Napier system, the Antares Nebula was a hundred times larger than it was in the night skies of home.

The nebula was a lustrous ball of gas and dust as beautiful as it was deadly. Its intricate network of swirls was a gossamer spider web suspended inside the shell of a shimmering cosmic egg. Save for its seemingly solid central core, the nebula's delicate filaments were nearly transparent until they approached its outer shell, where they again took on the hue of a fluorescent glow tube. The apparition was a reminder of the enormous cruel joke that God... or Mother Nature, or Saint Murphy, or someone... had played on Drake, his wife, humanity, and yes, even the Ryall.

Six years earlier, Antares had been the brightest star decorating the night sky of Drake's home planet, Alta. The baleful red spot had dominated the winter firmament ever since colonists first set foot on the blue-white world that was in many ways a virtual twin to Mother Earth. For four hundred and thirty winters, Antares had been the real-life version of the red stars with which Altan children decorated their *fala* bushes at Christmastime, an ochre beacon hovering low over the Colgate Mountain Range each evening after sunset. Then, at 17:30 hours on the night of Aquarius 16, 2637, the ruby star had undergone a breathtaking transformation. In a matter of minutes, the dying ember blossomed Phoenix-like to become the brightest star in the galaxy.

To those who observed the newborn electric spark high above the city of Homeport, there was no mystery as to what had happened. The cause of the transformation was obvious.

Antares had been well into its dotage long before human beings discovered star travel. For thousands of years, the red supergiant star had profligately consumed hydrogen, heedless of the day when that fuel must inevitably run out. That day came in 2512 (standard calendar). With nothing left to burn, the fusion reaction that had long powered Antares' inner engine flickered, and died.

With no internally generated heat to oppose the pull of gravity, the core of the red giant collapsed. Gigatons of star stuff gave up its energy of position as it slid down the gravity well, causing the surrounding temperature to jump more than a billion degrees in an instant. The release of so much energy in so short a time triggered new fusion, which generated yet more energy. The runaway reaction could not be contained.

Antares exploded into the largest supernova ever observed by human beings.

The universe is a very large place, especially when measured in terms of the veritable crawl that is light speed. The distance between Antares and Alta was such that it took the nova wave front 125 years to cross the gulf of space between them. When the first photons from the explosion finally reached the colony world, they burst forth in a phenomenon that quickly became known as Antares dawnlight. However, as impressive as the giant star's funeral pyre was during those first few weeks, in one important respect, its appearance had been anticlimactic.

Scientists have long known that the cataclysmic flash that marks a supernova is merely a minor side effect of what is really taking place. In addition to outshining all other stars in the galaxy, a supernova produces a titanic storm of particles across the subatomic spectrum. While these and many other effects are of interest only to astronomers, Antares' death had carried with it one consequence that affected the lives of everyone on Alta. In addition to vaporizing everything around it – including the hapless ships and crews then in transit across the Antares system – the supernova disrupted star travel throughout the region, cutting Alta off from the rest of human space.

The invisible pathways between the stars are the result of long lines of folded space that emanate from the gigantic black hole that inhabits the central core of the Milky Way Galaxy – and indeed, all spiral galaxies. These "foldlines" weave intricate webs of folded space as they sweep outward along the spiral arms, intersecting some stars while bypassing others. Where a foldline intersects a star, it is often focused by the star's gravity well to produce a "weak spot" in the vacuum of space. Such weak spots are called "foldpoints," and within their planet-sized volumes, it is possible to produce a hole in space-time. A ship that positions itself within a foldpoint and then generates a precisely formed energy field will effectively drop out of the universe and be flung instantly along the foldline to the next weak point, where it returns to normal space without having traversed the intervening distance.

For half a thousand years, humanity's ships had used foldlines to circumvent Einstein's universal speed limit. Foldlines were the superhighways to the stars, with most stars possessing at least two foldpoints, and sometimes as many as four. Antares, in the days before its fiery death, had been the champion foldpoint producer in human space. It possessed six of the gateways, making it the major interstellar transportation hub in the sector that bore its name.

Valeria, Alta's star, possessed but a single foldpoint, a deficiency that made the Val System an interstellar cul-de-sac. Of necessity, all traffic to and from Valeria passed through the Napier System, from which Alta was first colonized. That, at least, had been the situation before the Antares Supernova. The titanic explosion had disrupted the foldline running through the Val system, causing Alta's single foldpoint to vanish without a trace.

The loss of its sole gateway to the stars had plunged the Altan colony into a century of isolation. Nor had the Altan scientists any expectation that the sudden blossoming of the supernova in their sky twelve decades later would change the situation. In this, they proved less than prescient.

For when Valeria finally pricked the surface of the supernova's expanding bubble of radiation, the geometry of foldspace underwent a dramatic transformation. Having passed beyond the Val system, the supernova shockwave no longer intersected the foldline running between the two stars, allowing Alta's foldpoint to form once again high above the system's yellow dwarf primary.

The fact that Valeria was once more connected to the rest of human space might have gone unnoticed for several years had it not been for an anomalous event a few weeks after Antares flashed violet-white in Alta's sky. While studying the newly revealed supernova, an orbiting telescope picked up a mysterious ship materializing in the vicinity of the system's long-lost foldpoint. As astronomers watched openmouthed with amazement, the unidentified ship turned toward deep space and began thrusting as though the legions of hell were chasing it.

Drake had been a captain in the Altan Space Navy at the time. He had commanded *ASNS Discovery*, one of the three old interstellar cruisers that were stranded in the system when Antares exploded. Shortly after the appearance of the mysterious ship, the

Admiralty ordered Drake to intercept the interloper at maximum boost.

The chase was a difficult one conducted at high gravs the entire way. When they finally overhauled the intruder, they found a ghost ship. *TSNS Conqueror*, one of the terrestrial space navy's mightiest dreadnoughts, proved to be nothing more than an animated hulk manned by a dead crew, with no indication of what or who had killed them.

The discovery left the Altan government with a problem. On the one hand, the arrival of *Conqueror* announced that the way to the stars was once again open. On the other, its condition was mute testimony to dangerous circumstances somewhere beyond their local sky. If *Conqueror* could have destroyed the whole of the Altan Space Navy with little or no effort, yet had itself been battered to scrap metal by some unknown enemy, what of those who had destroyed it? Were they Alta's friends or were they its foes?

Having asked the question, the government decided to send Richard Drake to find the answer…

"Task Force coming into view, Admiral," the pilot of the shuttle said from beside Drake.

Drake shook off the reverie into which he had fallen. It was a nasty habit of his whenever he contemplated the Antares Nebula, brought on undoubtedly by the fact that his own life had been inextricably linked to the nebula ever since it blazed bright in Alta's night sky.

Alta was far away at the moment, as was his pregnant wife. He missed Bethany already, not that he'd had more than a few months to be with her these past three years. Building the largest invasion fleet in the history of interstellar war had monopolized his attention, giving him the opportunity for only a few brief visits home, and one glorious vacation that had lasted an entire week. Still, Bethany had usually been within comm range, and the two of them had spent many enjoyable hours talking face to face via comm screen into the wee hours. Now more than a hundred light years of vacuum separated them, a distance that could only grow as humankind launched its maximum effort to defeat an implacable alien foe.

#

Drake pulled himself aboard the Terrestrial Blastship *Victory*. In the suiting cubicle just inside the main ship lock, he found a Marine honor guard and a young man in the uniform of a commander in the Royal Sandarian Navy. *Victory* was in microgravity to ease the arrival of landing craft from the other ships in the fleet. The Marines stood rigidly at attention with their boots locked into the floor grid to keep them from floating away. The commander floated free, steadying himself with a guideline.

Drake paused just inside the inner airlock door as martial music emanated from the ship's bulkhead-mounted speakers. It was some tune that he had heard on Earth, but one that he could not name. The unfamiliar musical style indicated that the march must have been written after Alta was cut off from human space.

When the music ended, the saluting Marines all snapped their right hands down in unison. Drake pulled himself toward the officer, whom he recognized.

"Admiral Drake, it's good to see you," Phillip Walkirk exclaimed, extending his right hand while keeping hold of the guideline with his left.

"Your Highness, good to see you again," Drake replied as he grasped Walkirk's hand. "I see you have come up in the world. I remember when you were a lowly ensign."

Walkirk smiled. "It could be that I have connections at court."

That, Drake knew, was an understatement. Four years earlier, Phillip had been assigned aboard *Discovery* as an exchange officer. Drake had objected to the assignment when he first heard about it, not that he had anything personal against the young officer. The problem was that Phillip was not just any member of the Sandarian Navy. His father was John-Phillip Walkirk VI, hereditary king and ruler of Sandar, and Phillip would one day follow him on the throne. The thought that the heir-apparent might be injured, or even killed, while serving aboard an Altan cruiser had been enough to give Drake insomnia.

Walkirk had served well while aboard *Discovery*, and had even led the Marine boarding party that captured the Ryall freighter *Space Swimmer* in what proved to be a pivotal action for the human war effort. He had accompanied *Discovery* to Earth, where events had unfolded that led inevitably to this gathering of the fleet.

Phillip, he noted, had filled out in the last few years. He still had the jet-black hair, intense eyes, and the prominent nose that marked the Walkirk clan. His shoulders were broader than they had been and his voice lacked the youthful tremor that sometimes crept in when he was excited. His eyes had gained a few wrinkles at their corners, as well; but then, whose had not?

Drake was significantly grayer than he had been when the two of them first met and he had to work harder than ever at keeping his paunch under control. His green eyes tended to squint more, the result of countless hours spent in front of a computer screen working out the myriad details required for the impending invasion of Ryall space. He had not been alone in that task. Thousands of specialists across human space had worked out the plan on which they were about to bet the human race. Drake had a proprietary interest. The whole thing had originally been his idea.

At 41, he was getting to be an "old man" for a spacer, and the fact that he had been forced to leave his expectant wife a mere month before the birth of their first son had done nothing to improve his mood.

"How many are onboard?"

"Everyone, Admiral. You are the last to arrive. I am here to guide you to the briefing."

"Then guide away."

The young prince reversed his position and pulled himself along the guideline toward the hatch leading out of the hangar bay. Drake followed him. Soon the two of them were gliding through the corridors and passageways of the big terrestrial blastship. Unlike Drake's original command, which was a ring and cylinder design, *Victory* was an oversize cylinder, the better to utilize interior volume while retaining the ability to spin the ship for artificial gravity. It was an outrigger design, with many of its weapons and instruments in twin pods held stationary while the central body rotated, not unlike Drake's new flagship, *Conqueror II.* As he trailed Phillip through endless corridors and passageways, he wondered how the prince could have memorized the route in the short time he had been onboard.

Around them, serious-faced men and women moved with hurried purpose. If they recognized the insignia on the two colonial officers' shoulders, they made no sign. Besides, spacers maneuvering in micro gravity had need of both hands for locomotion and none left over for saluting.

After it seemed they had traversed the entire length of the big ship, Phillip guided him to a large compartment in which three hundred naval officers were crammed into every available cubic meter, placing a heavy strain on the blastship's environmental system. These were the captains and executive officers of the ships that had gathered in the Napier system in preparation for entering the Antares nebula. They did not, however, represent the whole of the invasion fleet, or even a majority of it. Task Force Spica would consist of eight major components, of which only two were represented aboard *Victory*. The fleets that made up the rest of the invasion force were assembling in half a dozen star systems across human space. They would rendezvous with the Altan and Sandarian fleets, and the sizeable Terrestrial Space Navy contingent that had been assigned to augment them, once all were inside the nebula.

Most of those present had strapped themselves into seats bolted to the curved deck, while several clumps of officers floated free to consult with one another. As Drake entered, acceleration alarms began to hoot and a disembodied voice announced the imminent return of spin gravity. Drake quickly used the "overhead" handholds to move to his position at the table that had been set up at the front of the compartment.

There he joined Grand Admiral Georges Terence Belton, who was already strapped into his seat. The admiral was reviewing his notes. At Drake's approach, he looked up and nodded gravely.

"Welcome, Drake. How was the trip from Alta?"

"Hurried, sir. I wish the lizards had given us another month to prepare."

"Hell, why not ask for another year?"

"No sense tempting the fates, sir. A month would have been sufficient."

Belton rubbed his chin, and then nodded. "You might be right. I know I would have been more prepared for this coming fight. Still, while we are wishing, we might want to ask for another hundred orbital fortresses."

"Just get us the ones we already have in time to do some good, sir."

G.T. Belton was in overall command of the Spica Operation, and Drake's boss, even though he would not be going within a hundred light years of the fleet's objective. Belton had done a brilliant job in bringing a billion disparate elements together to mount the invasion. However, like General Groves of the fabled Manhattan Project, Belton's skills were that of an organizer more than a warrior. Now that the time had come to put his planning into practice, he would continue in overall command – as much as a sop to the politicians of Earth as for military necessity – but a younger, more vigorous commander would take over direct operational responsibility for the invasion.

After a lengthy debate in which several of the better-known candidates had counterbalanced one another out of the job, a little-known colonial officer had been chosen for operational command of humanity's invasion fleet. That officer was Richard Drake, of the Altan Space Navy.

"Ready to give the lizards a swift kick in the tail?" Belton asked as he buckled in.

"Yes, sir," Drake replied. "And thank you for the trust you have shown in supporting me for this command."

"You may want to hold your appreciations until you have a few engagements under your belt. Being at the sharp end of the spear can be a thankless job, especially when you have to deal with REMFs."

"REMFs, sir?"

"Old terrestrial navy expression, Drake. Its roots are obscene. It refers to the assholes back at base who won't give the man in combat what he needs unless he asks in triplicate. You can rest assured, by the way, that so long as I am on the job, there will be a minimum of that sort of bullshit."

"I know that, sir. I also know how many senior officers were passed over for this assignment, and how much your opinion counted in the decision."

Belton lowered his voice until only Drake could hear him against the background noise. "Then you also know, Admiral, that there will be a thousand pairs of eyes watching your every move, waiting for you to screw up."

"Yes, sir."

"Are you interested to know what tilted the decision in your favor?"

"If you would care to tell me, sir."

"Because this invasion was your doing, Drake. You Altans arrived on Earth with a map of enemy foldspace, something no one else had managed to obtain in more than a century of war. Yet, even though you presented us with the key to victory on a silver platter, not one of us saw the implications until you forced us to see them. That shows an independence of thought that will be sorely needed in the coming campaign."

Belton spoke standard with an odd, but understandable, accent. He was a native of the legendary city of Rome, a fabled place that Altan children studied in school, but one that no Altan (to Drake's knowledge) had ever seen with his own eyes. Their first brief visit to Earth had been too hectic to visit the Eternal City, and his two trips since were consumed with planning for the invasion.

"I still appreciate the chance you are giving me, Admiral. I won't let you down."

"Appreciation noted," Belton said gruffly before raising his voice to his normal subdued bellow. It was a voice that projected an image at odds with Belton's short stature and thinning hair. "Now then, Admiral Drake, are you ready to get on with the war?"

"Yes, sir."

"Let us give the engineers five minutes to put some spin on this old bucket and then we start the briefing. I will keep my remarks short to give you more time for your spiel."

"That will be fine, sir."

While Drake led the bulk of humanity's offensive fleet into the heart of enemy space, Grand Admiral Belton would establish the bases and infrastructure needed to keep the fleet supplied. As Bethany, Drake's historian wife, had remarked when he told her of his appointment to operational command, Belton was to be General George C. Marshall to Drake's George Patton. Richard knew who General Patton had been, of course. One of the ships in the fleet was named *Patton*.

He had never heard of George C. Marshall.

#

"Officers of the Allied Forces of Humanity, welcome!" Admiral Belton roared when a few tenths-gee returned to the ship. As he spoke, the terrestrial admiral let his gaze sweep over his audience. His listeners wore the black-and-silver uniforms of the terrestrial navy, the ornate black-and-green of the Sandarians, the subdued, slightly quaint uniforms worn by the Altans, and a dozen more.

"You have all been briefed extensively as to your jobs during the coming mission, so I won't bore you by being repetitive. Rather, Admiral Drake and I have invited you here today because this will be our last chance to gather in person. We will not likely find ourselves within a few million kilometers of one another again any time soon. Indeed, even if things go as well as we have planned them, many of us will not be returning to human space for several years... and let us be honest, some of us will not be coming back at all. That is the way of war, a necessity we warriors accept as the price of service to our race.

"Events will move very quickly once we enter the nebula and there will be little time for consultation. Therefore, it is important that every fleet and subfleet commander, every ship captain, every first officer, every ordinary spacer, understand our grand strategy. So, let me give it to you without the usual diplomatic niceties.

"We will attack without warning, we will strike hard and swiftly, we will close with our enemy at every opportunity, we will pummel them without pause and respite. If we are audacious, we will have the advantage of surprise. Indeed, we *must* have it, for without surprise, we will lose the coming campaign. You have all seen the roster of ships taking part in this operation and must know what it has cost us to assemble this many combat units so far from home. If we lose, the human race will be on the defensive for years to come while our worlds rebuild what we will have lost.

"The stakes are high, ladies and gentleman, but the prize is worth it. After too many decades of fighting holding actions, we are striking into the very heart of our enemies' domain. There we will be outnumbered and outgunned. We can give no quarter in the coming action, nor can we seek any. Our foes are xenophobes who oppose the very idea that we exist. They cannot help it. The impulse is baked into their very genes. For that reason, we cannot give them a break. If this is to be a war of extinction, it is our job to see that the other side does most of the dying.

"As we go into danger, I would leave you with the following thought: We are not deploying this fleet merely to gain a narrow tactical edge. We do not seek a long-term strategic advantage. This time our goal is nothing less than total victory."

The admiral paused a few seconds to give his words time to sink in. He was gratified that he detected no false bravura or mindless smiles at the prospect of going into harm's way. The mood of the gathered officers seemed one of grim determination. He approved of their attitude. The coming days and weeks would be grim indeed, and they would require all the determination the human race could muster. He finished his scan of the audience with a nod toward Drake.

"I will now turn this briefing over to the man whose wild idea this operation originally was. Since no good deed ever goes unpunished, he will be in operational command of those of you who will engage in the initial assault.

"Ladies and gentlemen, Admiral Richard Drake, of the Altan Space Navy."

#

Drake climbed to his feet in the careful way people do in minimal gravity. Springing up too quickly would merely have caused him to bounce a couple of meters into the air, possibly to hit his head on the maze of bare piping that cluttered the overhead, most certainly to look foolish until he floated back down again. When he had achieved an erect posture, he moved carefully to the podium, not so much walking as gliding his feet like an ice skater across the deck plates.

He took a few moments to arrange his material and to check the order of his presentation, already loaded into *Victory*'s main computer. Then he looked up at the expectant crowd, took a deep breath, and launched into the plan that he and a few thousand others had spent the last three years perfecting.

"Good afternoon, ladies and gentlemen. Welcome to Task Force Spica. As you are well aware, the Antares Supernova of 2512 really messed up this section of space."

As Drake spoke, the holocube flashed to show the exploding star in its depths. Around it, etched dimly in glowing red paths that were not quite straight, were the foldlines of the Antares Foldspace Cluster. "When Antares blew, it changed the focus of foldlines all over the cluster and caused a new foldpoint to appear here in the Napier system. That foldpoint led directly into the heart of the Ryall Hegemony.

"You've all read books or seen holo-epics of that first encounter with the Ryall. You know how the Ryall fleet came boiling through the foldpoint to rain nuclear fire down on New Providence without provocation, even as its population was evacuating to escape the supernova's radiation. That was how we humans first learned of the Ryall, and of their xenophobia.

"It has been more than a century since that first clash, and for all of that time, humanity has been on the defensive. Even though we seem well matched in terms of technology and weaponry, we have been steadily losing this war for twelve decades now. Four years ago, we discovered the reason why."

Drake pressed a control on the podium and a diagram appeared. On it, the dimly glowing paths from Antares emanated like the strands of a spider web. One of these strands terminated in the Napier system, where the war had begun. Another pathway originated inside the Antares Nebula and arched across the screen to terminate in a star with the odd name of Eulysta.

It had been in the Eulysta system that Drake and the Altan-Sandarian military expedition had discovered the Ryall mining colony on Corlis, an otherwise uninhabited planet. It was there they had captured *Space Swimmer* with its astrogation computer intact. This, in turn, had given humankind its first good look at the geometry of Ryall space. Beyond Eulysta lay Carratyl, home system to one of the Ryall agricultural worlds. Beyond Carratyl lay Spica, the heart of the Ryall Hegemony.

"This is why the Ryall have been able to outfight us for a century. Spica is larger than Antares and possesses eight foldpoints. Just as Antares was a major hub for our commerce before it exploded, Spica is a major hub for Ryall interstellar commerce. In fact, it is their *only* such hub.

"Human space is strung out along the spiral arm of the galaxy, but Ryall space is a compact ball of stars, all of which are tied directly or indirectly to the central nexus at Spica. What this means is that no Ryall world is more than three foldspace jumps from Spica, which is a considerable improvement over the eight, ten, or even twelve jumps between the most widely separated human stars. Because of this arrangement, the Ryall enjoy interior lines of communication and can better utilize their navy. With fewer jumps between stars, they can always respond to our attacks more quickly than we can respond to theirs.

"If Spica is their strength, it is also their Achilles' heel. The ease with which they move goods from star to star has caused their economy to become differentiated. The worlds of the Ryall Hegemony tend to specialize. Some build weapons and ships, others build computers, still others grow the majority of their food. This arrangement makes considerable sense in a foldspace cluster where the stars are only a few jumps apart. However, it also makes them dependent on their interstellar commerce. Where our shipping largely consists of luxury goods and machinery intended to make our colonies self sufficient, theirs carries everyday necessities. Their worlds have become so specialized that the Ryall must trade to live.

"That, then, is where we are going to hit them. So long as the Ryall control Spica, they can coordinate their attacks better than we can defend against them. Our defenses are too spread out, our reaction times too sluggish. They, on the other hand, can bring their whole fleet to bear on a single objective in a matter of weeks.

"If, however, we blockade Spica, we will have gotten an iron wrecking bar into the gears of their well-oiled machine. With our ships in control of their primary transit system, it will be they who are hamstrung for a change. Denying them transit of Spica will break the hegemony into foldspace strings of just two or three stars each. They will not be able to communicate with one another, except by going the long way around the few series of foldspace transitions that bypass Spica.

"Instead of the well-coordinated, massive assaults they have launched in the past, isolated systems will be forced to launch uncoordinated attacks through foldpoints where we will be waiting to slaughter them as soon as they materialize. For once, we will have the interior lines of communication and the luxury of nearby support. Instead of facing the whole, massive Ryall fleet at once, we will defeat each uncoordinated attack in detail."

Drake let his gaze scan the surrounding faces.

"Make no mistake, ladies and gentlemen. It is going to be a long war. Yet, if we can hold on long enough, the Ryall economy will collapse from the disruptions caused by our blockade. It will be our job to hold on until that happens."

#

# Chapter 2

Varlan of the Scented Waters lay amid the unfamiliar green of alien plants, breathed the strange, but not unpleasant odor of them, and let a sun that was not her own warm her gray-green flanks and tail. She was physically comfortable, having pulled her six short legs up close to her body and stretched her long neck out across the green carpet of tiny plants that so reminded her of the *visoleth* fields of home. For some reason, her captors favored keeping the small plants chopped off to a uniform height. The machine that did the chopping was quietly at work in a distant section of the large green field and would not enter the section around Varlan until its sensors detected her departure.

Her physical comfort on this warm, sun-drenched day was in sharp contrast to her psychic turmoil. She lay amid the greenery with nictating membranes covering her eyes, and her long, mobile ears erect, as she considered the strange turn her life had taken since her capture by the two-legged-monsters.

She had been perfectly happy with her life as manager of the Corlis Raw Materials Extraction Facility, where she had spent her waking periods in comfortable routine worrying about production goals, personnel health, and equipment maintenance schedules. Her year had been governed not by Corlis's seasons — since the planet rode upright in its orbit, and thus lacked such — but by the semi-annual visits of the ore freighters that transported refined metals back to the home stars.

Her comfortable routine had been shattered one day when *Space Swimmer*, the ore carrier then in orbit about Corlis, reported the sudden appearance of strange ships in the interstellar gateway from the Evil Star. The development had been as frightening as it was unexpected. Her species' natural philosophers knew that the second gateway in the Eulysta system led into the heart of a supernova remnant. In fact, had it led anywhere useful, Corlis would have been colonized long since, rather than being the home of a single outlying mineral extraction facility.

She realized immediately that if the enemies of her species had developed ships capable of safely penetrating the Evil Star's maelstrom of high-energy particles, whipping magnetic fields, and searing radiations, then Those Who Rule must learn of it immediately. She dispatched *Space Swimmer* toward the normal interstellar gate to spread the alarm and then turned her attention to transforming the tunnels of her facility into a defensive fortress.

As he fled toward the gateway and the safety of home space, Ossfil, *Space Swimmer*'s commander, beamed the data captured by his ship's sensors back to Varlan on Corlis. Two alien ships quickly multiplied to more than a dozen. Almost as quickly as *Space Swimmer* spotted their arrival in the Eulysta system, the monsters detected the fleeing ore carrier and dispatched high-acceleration craft to intercept it.

The rest of the alien fleet left the alternate gateway and began boosting for Corlis. Having done all she could to warn Those Who Rule, Varlan settled down to making the coming assault on her facility as expensive as possible.

Her defensive preparations were completed about the time the swift ships of the enemy overtook *Space Swimmer*. Three mornings after the ore carrier's capture, armored bipeds attacked her facility. The fight had been sharp and quick, and the enemy everywhere victorious. Not even the defensive redoubt she established in Tunnel 3 held for very long. In the end, she and her surviving workers found themselves prisoners of an alien enemy.

Imprisonment was not as she had expected. The monsters treated her and her workers well. There was no torture or vivisections, nor were they deprived of food or a comfortable environment. However, the psychic strain of captivity had been great, especially after she learned the Monsters had captured *Space Swimmer*'s astrogation computer. The race had long guarded the secret of their interstellar portals like a mother hovering over a clutch of eggs. To lose such a database intact was a disaster beyond description.

It had only been much later that she learned just how great a disaster it was.

"Varlan, there you are!" the familiar voice called. She lifted her head and turned her supple neck until her snout pointed directly back along the line in which her tail was pointed. There she saw Bethany, once of the Lindquists, now of the Drakes, approaching across the green carpet.

Bethany was one of the most confusing aspects of Varlan's captivity. She was a two-legged-monster, true; yet, she considered herself Varlan's friend. More surprisingly, despite her built-in horror at the thought of a universe inhabited by two races of intelligent beings, Varlan could not help feeling kindly toward Bethany. Not only did she find companionship with the two-legged female, she actually felt concern over Bethany's well being, especially now.

All of the two-legged monsters seemed odd to Varlan's eyes, as though part of them was missing. However, she could see intellectually that the seemingly unstable bipedal form had its own functional elegance. When she had first met Bethany, the human had possessed a sleek form suitable for slicing through water. Even the various swells and curves that Varlan had learned were associated with Bethany's gender had a certain alien gracefulness to them. No longer.

Over the past two cycles, the abdomen of Varlan's companion-enemy-friend had become grossly distended and her sense of balance, always precarious in Varlan's eyes, had become even less reliable than usual. Her walk, which had once been flowing as she teetered from one of the long stilts she used for legs to the other, was now uncertain and hesitant. Her new walk showed a distinct unease, so much so that the monsters even had a word for it, a word that Varlan had only recently learned. Bethany no longer walked, she *waddled*.

"Hello, Bethany of the Drakes. I thought it a day to sun myself," Varlan called when Bethany had 'waddled' to where she lay. "I hope you did not become concerned about my absence."

"No, of course, not," Bethany said as she towered over Varlan's supine form. She looked uncomfortable, but her current physical condition did not allow her to sink to the carpet to rest. Had she done so, she probably could not have gotten up again.

"Are you uncomfortable?" Varlan asked.

"No more so than any other pregnant woman," Bethany replied with a laugh, "which is to say 'yes.'"

"It seems to me that laying eggs is more efficient," Varlan answered seriously. That, at least, was the way her species reproduced.

"You won't get any argument from me. I am afraid that I will have to interrupt your leisure, however. We have a delegation of xenologists from Earth who would like to meet you. I'm afraid there was some sort of mix-up with the schedule. They are here now."

Varlan did not groan. That was not the way her kind expressed exasperation. Instead, her ears went momentarily flat against her elliptical skull and her snout pitched perceptibly down, both gestures that Bethany had long since learned to read.

"I know. I would rather not go through another round of inane questions either. Just remember, that which cannot be cured..."

"... must be endured," Varlan finished the surprisingly Ryall-like thought. She hoisted herself to her feet and stretched her tail out to its full length. "Let us go meet the gentle scientists from Earth."

#

"Oh my, when is it due?" the white-haired woman who was the sole inhabitant of the conference room asked as they entered. In addition to a long table with the chairs all on one side, the room contained a raised dais on which a carpet of Altan river rushes had been spread for Varlan's use.

"Sometime between 'any moment now' to 'three weeks from yesterday.'"

"I certainly hope we can complete our business before the ambulance hauls you away. Boy or girl?"

"A little boy. He has his father's hair and my eyes and will be quite a little hellion if the geneticists have any clue as to what they are talking about."

"I had a little boy a long time ago," the woman said, her voice catching a bit. "You will have your hands full for a few years."

"How old is your son now?" Bethany asked.

"He would have been 43 this month had he lived. He was killed at the Battle of Archernar."

"Oh, I'm so sorry."

"No need to be. It has been more than a decade since his ship took a Ryall torpedo, and I am far from the only mother who has lost a son in this war. By the way, I am Doctor Olivia Southington, Department of Xenology, University of Buenos Aires."

Bethany took her extended hand. "I'm Bethany Drake, and this is Varlan of the Scented Waters."

"Yes. Varlan is the first Ryall I have seen close up — alive. We have had a few corpses to study, of course. Oh, pardon me. That comment must have seemed incredibly callous."

Varlan, who had been studying the interchange between the monster females... the human women, she automatically corrected herself... turned a curious eye toward this latest in a long line of interrogators.

"I do not understand, Doctor Southington," she said in nearly flawless standard, save for the slight hiss her vocal apparatus gave to the sibilants.

"I forgot that I was in the presence of one of your race, Varlan. It is impolite of me to speak so callously of your dead."

"My race does not put the same emphasis on the dead as does yours, Doctor," Varlan replied. "We are more interested in the living and especially the hatchlings."

"Yes, I have read that. In fact, that is one of the reasons I have come all this way. I would like to understand more about your species' beliefs and customs, especially from the viewpoint of a member of your managerial caste."

"I will, of course, place myself at your service," the Ryall responded smoothly. Since her capture, she had learned to imitate human verbal customs, even if she did not always understand them.

"Don't monopolize the poor beastie, Olivia," a male voice said from behind them. Varlan turned to look. A small, dark-haired man had entered the room, followed by a younger female — probably an administrative assistant, to judge from her manner as she followed the newcomer into the room.

"Bethany Drake. Varlan of the Scented Waters. May I introduce Jorge Santiago, my colleague, and Señorita Consuela Aragon, our assistant?"

"Santiago. Señorita Aragon," Bethany replied as she presented her hand first to the man, who kissed it, and then to the young woman, who shook it in the usual manner.

"Señor Santiago, Señorita Aragon," Varlan parroted.

Santiago put his hands on his hips and stared frankly. "My, you are a polite one. How long since you were captured?"

"Four of your years."

"How do you like it here?"

"How would you like to be held captive by your species' enemies?" Varlan responded smoothly.

"What...?" Santiago sputtered, then laughed. "Why, I don't suppose I would like it at all."

"Then we agree."

"Excuse me," Bethany said, "but what is it we can do for you Señor Santiago, Dr. Southington?"

"We have come to interrogate your prisoner."

"Guest," Bethany warned sharply.

"Fine, guest. We understand you have gotten farther with Varlan than any of the professional interrogators have gotten with the warrior caste prisoners that they hold."

"It depends on what you mean by 'farther.' Frankly, Varlan and I come closer to understanding one another than most people thought was possible for intelligent beings of divergent species. Isn't that right, Varlan?"

"Yes, Bethany. We have an understanding that even I would not have thought possible before meeting you." Sensing Bethany's irritation with the brusque Santiago, Varlan intentionally did not say 'before I was captured.'

"That is excellent," Olivia Southington replied, also sensing the tension and stepping deftly in to dissipate it. "Jorge and I have made it a point to study Ryall myths as a way to better understand them. I am afraid that we have gotten as far as we can from merely reviewing interrogation reports. We need to talk to someone who is intimately familiar with those myths, someone who actually believes them and knows their cultural context. And since so many ships were coming this way to support the invasion, well we thought we would drop by to see Varlan in the flesh."

"We will, of course, do everything we can to help you. Is there any myth in particular that you would like to explore?"

"One in particular. We would like to understand better about the Swift Eaters."

#

One hundred and fifty light-years from Alta, at a point where the Evil Star was a glowing gas cloud in the sky, another Ryall was frustrated. Periskay, of the Clan of the Distant Mountains in the Mist, was no captive, except of his assigned duty. An ex-student of Dolki, the master engineer-philosopher of the Ryall race, Periskay had been assigned to investigate the destruction of the mineral extraction facility on Corlis. What at first seemed a massive industrial accident was beginning to take on all of the mystical properties of the species' legends from the dim days before written history. Even with the facility wiped from the face of Corlis by a racing wall of water, there should have been clues to the cause of the disaster. Yet, Periskay was faced with a dearth of useable information.

The mystery began in an ordinary enough fashion. Those whose job it was to keep starships on schedule reported that an ore

cul-de-sac system, the only place where a ship could put in was at
the agricultural world that orbited Carratyl.

A ship sent to search for *Space Swimmer* had not found it in
the Carratyl system, and had proceeded to Eulysta to see if it was
still in orbit about Corlis. There they had found the mineral
extraction facility in ruins, its workforce missing, and no sign of the
ore carrier.

While terrible, the destruction of industrial facilities was not
unknown in the history of The Race. Therefore, to learn the cause,
Those Who Rule had dispatched an expedition to Corlis. Periskay,
although still young and relatively new to his profession, was
assigned to lead the inquiry.

The expedition had been ready to depart Darthan when word
came that a team of natural philosophers would accompany them.
These thinkers were not interested in the destruction of a far-off
industrial facility. They were going to Eulysta to send a small
experimental ship into the heart of the supernova remnant.

Being of a more practical mind than the philosophers,
Periskay could not see what purpose their expedition served.
However, the Collection of Thinkers was providing half the fuel his
ship would be using during the voyage, giving him an incentive to
aid the philosophers in their study.

When he arrived at Corlis, Periskay offloaded the philosophers
in orbit and landed his ship near the destroyed mineral extraction
facility. He and his workers began probing the destruction, looking
for some evidence of the cause.

Despite their extensive excavation efforts, they found no
bodies. Presumably, the manager of the facility, one Varlan, and all
of her workers had perished in the flood. Yet, if this were so, where
were their corpses? When the upstream dam broke, the duty crew
must have been working in the tunnels. If so, they should still be
there, yet Periskay's workers found none of them.

Pondering the problem, he wondered if the missing workers
were associated with the missing ore carrier. Perhaps it had rescued
the survivors of the disaster and then been lost en route back to the
home stars.

While Periskay pondered his problem, the philosophers
studying the Evil Star finished their preliminaries and plunged
through the stargate into its heart. Periskay received their message

announcing their departure, and did not think of them again until he realized that they, like the ore carrier, were overdue.

#

# Chapter 3

The viewscreen aboard the Altan Space Navy Blastship *Conqueror II* was ablaze with ghostly fire. The fire was produced when energetic particles slammed into the ship's anti-radiation shielding. The anti-rad shield absorbed both charged particle and high-energy electromagnetic radiation – rays ranging from X- to gamma – as they streamed in lethal doses away from the madly spinning neutron star at the center of the nebula. Once absorbed, the energy was reradiated in the visible spectrum in scintillating sheets of multi-chromatic luminescence. Within the high-energy environment of the Antares Nebula, the human fleet glowed like a string of tiny iridescent soap bubbles adrift in a hellish sea.

It had been a tension-filled week since *Conqueror II* and her consorts had entered the maelstrom. One instant they had hovered amid the blackness of space with the yellow-white globe of Napier far below them. The next, they were deep in the electric glow of the nebula's gas and dust, with the tiny dynamo of the Antares neutron star a distant eye-searing speck. In the telescopes, the tiny star was wracked by a violent explosion every minute or so. White-hot plasma arced into the sky, only to be wrenched back to the glowing surface before the geysers of fire had a chance to properly form, pulled down by the star's rapidly rotating magnetic field.

The Antares/Napier foldpoint lay near its pre-nova position high above the neutron star. Their destination was the Antares/Eulysta foldpoint, only 200 million kilometers distant. In any normal system, they would have accelerated into a flat, hyperbolic orbit and made straight for it. Unfortunately, nothing was that simple in the hell of radiations that made up the interior of the nebula. With the neutron star pumping out multi-gigawatts of power each second, it was dangerous to approach to within even 700 million kilometers. Despite the fact that it was invisible, every ship's astrogator was wary of the imaginary curved surface that marked the outer boundary of the "death zone," the volume surrounding the neutron star within which their anti-radiation shielding would be of as little protection as a layer of tissue paper.

So *Conqueror* and the rest of the first wave performed a maneuver that was, in effect, a giant skidding turn around the nebula's periphery as they approached their jump-off point. Even so, they were lucky. The fleets coming through the Antares/Goddard foldpoint would have to circle nearly halfway around the star to reach the back door into Ryall space.

That the maneuver was necessary to stay alive did nothing to calm Richard's nerves. Drake was new to fleet command and as Admiral Belton had intimated, he was not sure that he liked it. *Conqueror II* was the invasion fleet's flagship. Like every flagship since the Greeks beat the Persians at Salamis, she housed two separate command entities. A senior grade captain named Pelham Carter commanded *Conqueror II*. He and Drake had served together twice previously – once aboard *Discovery*, where Carter had been Drake's second officer, and before that, in the Destroyer *Parthenon*, where both of them had been junior officers together.

It was Carter's job to fly and fight the big blastship, leaving strategy to the admiral and his staff. To help him keep watch over the invasion as a whole, Drake commanded nearly a hundred officers and ratings. These manned the Fleet Operations Center and fed the admiral the information he needed to see the overall shape of the battle. The FOC (spacers learned not to snicker at the acronym twice) might as easily have been aboard any of the invasion fleet's blastships; and, in fact, could be transferred in the event of an emergency. As far as Drake was concerned, *Conqueror* was just one more glowing icon on his situation display, to be ordered where it would do the most good in battle.

The problem with being an admiral, he had discovered, was that his subordinates were entirely too efficient. They did their jobs without direction and left very little for him to decide. He knew that would change come first contact with the Ryall, but for now, he was at loose ends. After 160 hours inside the maelstrom, he was ready to climb the bulkheads. Since that would have been unseemly for an admiral, he compromised by sitting in his acceleration chair and pretending to look bored.

"Anything yet, Mr. Carey?" he asked the communicator seated at the console to his right. One of the perquisites of command was an armor-glass aerie high above the Fleet Operations Center, a private perch from which he could command in quiet solitude. Drake shuddered at the thought, preferring the bustling main deck of the fleet center, surrounded by his staff. The battle console he occupied was normally his chief-of-staff's station, but Commander Parkinson was currently assigned to the mid-watch, giving his admiral the welcome opportunity to get down amid the action.

"No, sir. No contact with Guard Force Antares. The range is still a little long for our lasers to penetrate this soup. They are no doubt tracking us with their specialized detectors and will contact us as soon as they can."

"Very well," Drake replied. He wanted to say more, but refrained lest he betray his impatience. Instead, he let his eyes scan the FOC. The change in just eight weeks was striking. When they left Altan orbit, fully one-quarter of the consoles had been inoperative, many with wire bundles hanging out of maintenance panels, and others with nothing on their screens but multicolored static. The premature departure had meant a lot of work while underway, but they had finally gotten the big cylinder with its oversize outrigger pods ready for combat

*Conqueror II* and her brood, the century-old battle cruisers *Discovery, Dagger,* and *Dreadnought,* along with the dozens of newer ships that had come out of the orbital shipyards over the past three years, had departed Alta immediately following the report that the Ryall had penetrated the nebula.

Nor were they alone.

All over human space, the warning message that the Ryall were in the nebula had caused more than a thousand ships to hurriedly load personnel, ammunition, and consumables before shaping hyperbolic orbits for the nearest foldpoint. Blastships, cruisers, destroyers, frigates, speeders, high acceleration scouts, and dozens of more specialized craft streamed toward the systems around Antares. Ships from Sol and worlds on the eastern edge of human space gathered in the Goddard System, while the colony worlds of Alta and Sandar sent their fleets via Napier and New Providence. Other fleets rendezvoused in the Grundlestar, Faraway, Klamath and Braxton systems. Each would enter the nebula via one of the pre-nova foldpoints, all of which still existed inside the plasma maelstrom. There they would rendezvous at Antares' seventh foldpoint, the new one that led into Ryall space through the back door.

Nor had the fleets of warships been alone. Accompanying the combatants were their supporting auxiliaries: tankers, freighters, repair craft, and lighters. Had anyone been able to track the movement of so many ships, they would have discovered that the

Antares nebula was fast becoming the center of human naval power. Eight different task forces would take part in the invasion.

Nor were they the last vessels that would pass through the nebula en route to Spica.

Following the warships and their supply train were the largest mobile weapons ever constructed by men. In systems all over human space, heavy orbital fortresses abandoned their guard stations and began to follow their more maneuverable brethren. It would take months for the ponderous fortresses to reach Spica, but when they did, the balance of power within the Ryall Hegemony would shift in the direction of humanity. That, at least, was the plan. Reality might conspire to present humankind with an altogether different plan, of course, but that was the nature of war.

"Message coming through now, Admiral," Spacer-First Carey reported. "It's a data transmission, no voice. 'From: Captain Virgil Tennyson, Commander, Guard Force Antares. To: Admiral Richard Drake, Commander, Task Force Spica. Message Begins: Welcome to Hell, Admiral. Good to see you brought so many friends. Message Ends. Tennyson.'"

"Send this, Mr. Carey. 'Glad to be in Hell with you, Commander. You haven't, by any chance, seen a foldpoint around here?'"

#

"Good to speak face-to-face, Admiral," Captain Tennyson said from the depths of one of Drake's command screens two hours later. The picture was speckled with multicolored interference, and the sound had a tendency to fade out every few seconds, but the words carried with them an undertone of relief. The Terrestrial Space Navy commander was a young man of approximately 30 standard years. Only his eyes were old, a common malady among those who had seen too much of war.

"And you, Captain. What's the lizard situation?"

"Quiet, sir. Nothing has appeared in the foldpoint since we dispatched our intruder to the nether reaches. We think it may have been a research ship."

"Why do you think that?"

"It was small and unarmed, sir. We don't think they saw us, or our torpedo, before we dispatched them."

"Any idea of the Ryall presence on the other side of the foldpoint?"

"None, sir. We assumed they were observing the other side, either waiting for their missing ship to reappear, or else trying to determine what went wrong. If we had sent a scout through, I'm afraid we would have been spotted and lost the element of surprise."

"Glad you have a head on your shoulders, Captain."

On their first visit to the nebula, they had blundered into Eulysta while searching for an alternate route to human space. To keep their presence secret, they had first captured, and then destroyed, the mining facility on Corlis.

What preyed on Drake's mind was the possibility that they had missed something. One of the mine's workers could have gotten away. Their cleanup campaign might have missed a human boot print or a ration wrapper. All it would take was the discovery of one artifact of identifiably human origin on Corlis and the Ryall high command would fill the Eulysta System with warships. Even now, the Eulysta/Antares foldpoint could be the center of a fleet of blastships, each with weapons focused, ready to vaporize the first human ship to materialize within the interstellar portal.

If that were the case, the "surprise" they were counting on would be on them.

As Admiral Belton had remarked during one of their planning sessions, Task Force Spica's mission was an interstellar version of the ancient Triple Crown of horse racing. Eulysta was the first prize. Capturing it would not guarantee the success of the invasion, but failing to do so would doom their plans. True, Eulysta had strategic value in its own right. Possession of the system and its two foldpoints would push the Ryall back one more system from human space. It would also wreak havoc with the Ryall war effort for however long it took to fortify Carratyl, the next system in from Eulysta.

However, the capture of a single outlying star system would be a poor consolation prize if that were all they accomplished.

"Have your sensors detected any of our follow-on forces, Tennyson?"

"Yes, sir. In addition to your own group, sensors are tracking three-oh-seven other vessels within the nebula. Most are on the long orbit from the opposite side foldpoints, with more appearing every day. By the time you take control of Eulysta, we should have quite a traffic jam hereabouts."

"Glad to hear it. I am sure we will need the company about then. Astrogator, what is our ETA?"

The latter comment was addressed to Lieutenant Olivia Parker, at the navplot station slaved to the ship's official navplot on the bridge. Women aboard warships were an oddity in the Altan Space Navy, although becoming less so with each new graduating class from the space training academies. Like the rest of humanity's worlds, the war with the Ryall had forced Alta to commit its full resources to the battle, despite the colony world's long tradition against sending women into danger. Mostly, Drake thought that was a good thing, although he had a ways to go before he became as blasé as the terrestrial navy concerning women in battle.

"The fleet will cross the foldpoint boundary in 47 minutes, sir."

"Very well. We will establish Zero Hour for 13:00. Tennyson, pass the word. We go in..." Drake glanced a the chronometer display in the lower right corner of his screen, "... 218 minutes from now."

"Yes, sir! Wish I were going along with you."

"I'd be pleased to have you with us, Captain. However, your job is here. If anything goes wrong, we are going to need your guard force to stop any counterattack through the foldpoint."

"Understood, sir. They also serve who only sit and wait with their thumbs up their..."

Drake smiled. He understood the Guard Force officer's wistful tone. After more than a century of war, this was to be the last major offensive. Despite the danger, there had been fierce competition among officers to take part in the operation.

"That they do, Captain. Don't worry, there will be more than enough fighting for everyone before this is over."

"Too, true, Admiral. As I said, welcome to Hell. I will pass your orders to the rest of the fleet. They will be ready. Guard Force Antares, out."

"Task Force Spica, out."

#

"Attention All Hands. Stand by for foldspace transition. All departments report readiness to jump."

The echo of the jump announcement had barely died away when reports began flooding in from every compartment of the ship. Drake was unsurprised. Pelham Carter ran a taut ship. All his department heads had been reporting their readiness to jump for three days now.

Confident that *Conqueror* was ready, he listened over the fleetcom channels to the units of the Terrestrial Space Navy that had accompanied him from Napier. Admiral Belton's people prepared for jump with a professionalism that betrayed decades of experience at war. The communications traffic was gratifying in its brevity. Not that communications exchanges were not taking place. Multi-gigabytes per second of data passed between the shipboard computers that were themselves preparing for battle.

When *Conqueror II* engaged the Ryall, its computers would largely control the ship's offensive armament. Artificial brains would plot enemy courses, target weapons, fire at the optimum moment, and evade torpedo and missile fire inevitably sent their way. Computers would assess battle damage, control airtight doors and hatches, and direct damage control teams to the most critically wounded areas of the ship. They would communicate with the other ships of the fleet over secure comm links, coordinating *Conqueror's* actions with those of her sisters in the battle fleet.

Should a ship be holed and its crew killed, the computers would fight on as long as their power held out. That was what had happened to *Conqueror's* namesake at the Second Battle of Klamath. Even after multiple hits extinguished the lives of many of its crew and forced the survivors into life pods, TSNS *Conqueror I* fought on. The big blastship fought its way to the local foldpoint, jumped, and, finding itself in the heart of a supernova remnant, sought another foldpoint to escape the maelstrom. That second foldpoint had led to the Napier System, and a third to Valeria.

"Two minutes to initial jump and counting. All ships, report status."

The traditional command was unnecessary. Richard could see the status of the ten small vessels that would make up humanity's vanguard on his command screen. Surrounding the green blips were another 120 yellow blips that represented the ships that would cross over into Ryall space as soon as they received the All Clear. Surrounding everything were the dim red outlines of the foldpoint and the dozen magenta markers that showed the ships of Guard Force Antares.

The initial invasion force included the ten heavily armed, high-acceleration speeders of *Mercury Force's* Alpha Squadron. The squadron would jump as a group into the unknown on the other side of the foldpoint. If they found the foldpoint unguarded, nine of the ten would immediately began accelerating toward Eulysta's second foldpoint, the one leading to the agricultural system of Carratyl. The remaining speeder in the formation would jump back to the nebula to report to the fleet, before returning to Eulysta and beginning a long stern chase to catch its fellows.

If the speeders found enemy craft in the vicinity of the foldpoint, but not in overwhelming force, then Alpha Squadron would engage and hold the foldpoint long enough for Drake to bring up the rest of the Task Force Spica. If the Ryall blocking force proved overwhelming, then the speeders would return to the nebula as quickly as they could charge their jump engines. Seeing the survivors of Alpha Squadron suddenly reappear on his side of the foldpoint would be Drake's signal to deploy his fleet to repel a Ryall invasion of the nebula.

The ships of *Mercury Force* were specially built and crewed for this one purpose. Their crews were young, average age 22, and in superb physical condition. They had to be. Most of the journey would take place at up to ten gravities, and even submerged in liquid-filled acceleration tanks, the stress would take its toll on the human body. It would also be hard on the engines. Like cartridges in an old-fashioned chemical firearm, their cross-system dash would use up the speeders' propulsion systems. They would need overhauling before they could fight again.

Drake's biggest worry was that the ten small ships would be destroyed before they could report. He had nightmares of sending wave after wave of scouts through the foldpoint, and then waiting endlessly for their return.

"One minute to jump."

"Are your people ready, Captain Parsons?" he asked the too-young face on one of his screens.

Lieutenant (Acting Captain) Victor Parsons looked out at him and nodded eagerly. His lips did not move. With every cavity in his body filled with oxygenated fluid to allow him to withstand the coming acceleration, speech was impossible. Nevertheless, a computer generated voice replied, "Ready to stomp some Ryall tail, sir."

"Just make sure your designated scout jumps back here the nanosecond his engines are charged. I don't relish sitting here in the dark without knowing what faces me any longer than I have to."

"Understood, Admiral."

"Good luck, Captain. Give them hell!"

"Hell it is, sir. *Mercury Asgard*, out."

"Fleet Operations Center out."

*"Ten... nine... eight..."* The old chill raced up Richard's spine as the recorded countdown echoed through the compartment. He consciously controlled his breathing as the numbers wound down to the last few seconds. *"Three... two... one... jump!"*

On the screen, ten small green blips winked out as more than a hundred yellow ones changed to emerald."

"Start the two minute clock, Mr. Carey. Send orders to the fleet. All ships, prepare for foldspace transition."

#

# Chapter 4

Bethany Drake was worried. That was to be expected with her husband and half the male population of Alta off invading an alien empire. Even knowing that the battle would secure the future safety of the human race did not ease her fear. Nor did it help that she was pregnant.

Like most little girls, the subject of babies had always fascinated her. She and her friends had listened intently to the stories of older women as they spoke of the emotional storms brought on by the massive jolt of estrogen that accompanies the gravid state. The stories had not prepared her for the reality. It was disconcerting to be happy one moment, and then, for no apparent reason, to be overcome with sorrow. Knowing that the reaction was involuntary and unrelated to her true mental state did nothing to stop the tears as they streamed down her cheeks, sometimes for hours. Nor was the depression the worst of it. Her powers of concentration, always strong, were in tatters.

Even her normal, pre-blimp self, would have found the constant worry about her husband distracting. In her current condition, the natural concern was magnified until it shut out every other thought. She was lucky if she could focus on her work for ten minutes at a time before the cold fog of dread rolled out of the depths to grab hold of her consciousness like a clammy hand. When she was not worrying about Richard, she worried about what her mental state was doing to her baby.

"Nonsense," Dr. Fontain, the grandmotherly woman who watched over her pregnancy, said when Bethany mentioned her concern. "Do you think you are the first anxious mother in the history of the whole human race? Mostly what you are feeling is a byproduct of hormonal releases that are as natural as breathing. If babies were sensitive to mothers' mood swings, the species would have died out millennia ago. According to this morning's scans, your baby is developing optimally. If anything, he's farther along than most at this stage."

The doctor's words had reassured Bethany for about fifteen minutes before she fell to brooding again. Nor were her personal problems all she had to brood about.

The three years since she and Richard had returned from Earth had been hectic ones. She had expected her husband to be busy with his command, but she had not realized *how* busy. He often worked 40 hours straight at the Admiralty, coming home too tired to do anything but fall facedown on the bed while still in his uniform. Then there were the trips to orbit, sometimes lasting for weeks, and the journeys to other star systems through the nebula to coordinate details of the invasion. They had seen very little of one another, although their reunions had often been worth the separation. One such, in fact, was the reason why her back ached all of the time these days.

She had been busy herself, doing her part to aid humanity against the alien enemy. Except that she had trouble thinking of the Ryall as "the enemy." She thought of them as Varlan's cousins, and dreamed of the day when she would understand them well enough to end this stupid war.

Conventional wisdom among her colleagues held that the xenophobia of the Ryall was an evolutionary adaptation, something bred into their very genes. Most xenologists maintained that Ryall history taught them two species could never coexist peacefully. Indeed, it had taught them so well that they remembered the lesson in their very chromosomes.

The problem with that thinking was that it led inevitably to a conclusion Bethany refused to contemplate. What does one do if confronted by an entire race of mad dogs, all foaming at the mouth from rabies (a disease still very much a part of human folklore though it was 300 years extinct)? The only sensible answer was to exterminate them.

Before her current career as Ryall Scholar, Bethany had been a comparative historian. She had observed in her studies that extermination had seemed the answer far too often in history. "The only good Indian is a dead Indian," came immediately to mind. Despite hot rhetoric by one generation, subsequent generations always found a way to live together. Surely, a way could be found for Ryall and human to live in peace. The Ryall were intelligent beings, and intelligence trumps instincts.

Animals follow their genetic programming. Stimulate them the same way and you will always get the same response. Sapient beings, on the other hand, can choose their response. They have the power to short-circuit their natural inclinations — if only they choose to use it.

Could the Ryall control their instincts? That was what Bethany hoped to determine through her studies of Varlan. So far, her results had been mixed. Whenever she tried to get Varlan to thinking how their two species might cooperate, the Ryall had considered the concept for a day or two, then reverted to her doctrinaire position that all thinking beings were adversaries.

There had to be a better way, and Bethany Drake, aching back and all, was determined to find it.

If only the sobbing would go away and leave her with time to think…

#

"I suppose I never thought of your people living in cities," Consuela Aragon said to Varlan of the Scented Waters. The five of them, Varlan, Jorge Santiago, Olivia Southington, Consuela, and Bethany were all in the room where they had first met. Varlan was perched on the bed of rushes, and the four humans had pulled their chairs into a semicircle around her. Jorge Santiago had been quizzing Varlan about Ryall customs for two hours, and sensing that the alien was becoming irritable, Consuela had seized on one of Varlan's idle comments to divert the subject.

"Why not?" Varlan asked. "We build starships, why not cities?"

"Well, you are amphibians. What need have you for houses and communal structures when you have your lagoons in which to frolic? Surely you can't be trying to keep the rain off."

"How many lagoons do you suppose there are on any given world, Consuela?"

"I suppose not enough."

"Not nearly enough. True, we prefer to live near the water and our domiciles incorporate elements of water, unlike those you humans build – except for certain neighborhoods in the Homeport Hills," Varlan said with a touch of what she hoped was human humor. "If there is a nearby body of water, we use canals in place of streets. If not, we build roads the same as you. As for the need for roofs, they are more to keep the sun off than the rain. One of my species' greatest pleasures is to lie in the rain with our tongues out. The raindrops are aerated with oxygen, giving them an especially sweet taste."

Bethany, who had grown tired of Jorge Santiago's interminable droning, and even more tired of sitting on the hard chair, wobbled to her feet to allow blood to circulate once more in her lower extremities. As she did so, she felt a familiar pain in her abdomen. She gasped as she struggled to stand.

"Is something wrong, Señora Drake?" Consuela asked.

Teetering over her chair, Bethany grimaced. "Nothing wrong. It was just a minor contraction. I've been having them sporadically for the past few days."

"Perhaps you should sit down."

"I'm tired of sitting. I'll stand for awhile."

"Then hold onto the chair to steady yourself," Olivia Southington said. "You don't want to fall in your condition. Trust me, I know."

"Getting back on the subject at hand," Santiago interrupted, returning to the line of questioning that had previously elicited signs of agitation from Varlan. "I don't understand why you people believe the Tale of the Swift Eaters is anything more than a fable."

"The Swifts were real," Varlan replied. "We have their skeletons in our museums."

"I don't doubt it," Santiago agreed. "Still, the basic story does not make sense. There is the time factor, for instance."

"Explain," Varlan said sharply.

"Look, let me tell the story as your military caste usually relates it. Okay?"

Varlan bobbed her long neck, which produced a passable version of a human nod.

"The story told by females to their young is that once the Ryall were a race of happy fisher folk who lived in the estuaries and river mouths of Darthan, the home world. After many generations of idyllic existence, there appeared in the sky a new star. This star soon brightened to rival the three moons when they were full. It is said that one could go *dereln* hunting by the light because it drew the little beasts to the surface.

"Shortly after the Evil Star made its appearance, a great plague was visited upon The Race. Individuals began to grow sick and die. Their scales turned yellow, they vomited whatever they ate, and soon, they lay down and stopped breathing. That season's crop of hatchlings was not immune. Many of the eggs did not hatch, and those that did produced grotesquely misshapen young. This went on for many thousands of years, with each generation of Ryall plagued by mutations. Nor were the birth defects the only cost to The Race, for the Evil Star also brought the Swift Eaters.

"The Eaters were mindless predators that inhabited deeper waters of the World Sea. Shortly after the Evil Star appeared in the sky, the predators began raiding Ryall fishing villages and hatching grounds. They were fast and vicious, and over the generations, developed sufficient cunning that they drove the Ryall out of the sea. Your people retreated to the interiors of islands and the edges of continents, where you built villages on the land.

"As millennia passed, the Ryall became more intelligent. So, too, did the Swift Eaters. With your increase in intelligence, you began to hunt the Swifts just as they hunted you. At first, your hunters intended only to drive them from hatching grounds and away from the river mouths where you still harvested the *dereln*. You hunted them in the shallows, and slowly, because they were intelligent themselves, they learned to avoid the places where Ryall lived. Then, after a struggle that raged for generations, you began to hunt them in the deep.

"No longer were your ancestors content to drive off the occasional Swift marauder. Now the hunters went after *their* hatching grounds. You discovered the places where they lay their eggs and you methodically destroyed them. You sowed the waters with organic poisons to make the Swifts sicken and die. You learned about biology and cultivated a parasite that only lived on Swift Eaters.

"Eventually, your ancestors won their struggle with these monsters of the deep. One day they were no more. Despite a Darthan-wide search, the victorious hunters could find none. Your species, made vastly more intelligent by the rivalry, was the master of Darthan.

"Yet, in victory, you had been changed. No longer were you a simple fisher people. Now you were farmers, and smelters, and craftsmen — all trades of the land villages. You were fertile and multiplied, discovered agriculture, and built cities. Then, when the time came, you cast your eyes to the stars and left Darthan to seek other worlds to colonize.

"Yet, despite your new sophistication, you never forgot the lessons of the Swifts. What you had learned was that a single world was too small a place for two intelligent species. When two sentient races occupy the same territory, they must ultimately compete until one is dead. It is a lesson your race learned well, and one that you have exported to the stars. It is the lesson that caused you to react instinctively to destroy the first human starship you encountered, and the driving force behind this century-old war of ours.

"You Ryall believe that this war cannot end until one of our species is extinct. You believe it not because that is what you have been taught, but rather, because it is in the basic genetic coding with which you emerged from the egg."

"It is to be war to the death between your species and mine, because that is the way of the universe."

#

Jorge Santiago paused for breath and gazed at the obsidian eyes that were regarding him. "That is the Legend of the Swift Eaters, is it not?"

"It is," Varlan agreed. "You did a surprisingly good job of capturing the lyric poetry of the epic."

"For an alien, you mean."

"Yes, for an alien."

Santiago smiled, genuinely pleased. "Thank you for the compliment. I have studied this tale in your own language and although my species' poetic sense is not the same as yours, I believe that I am alert to many of the nuances imbedded in the words. It is this legend of yours that brought Olivia, Consuela, and me to see you, and it is this about which I would like to make some observations."

"Please do."

"Are you sure that I will not offend you? I assure you that is not my intent. However, among humans, questions about deeply held beliefs often trigger a violent reaction. I have no desire to do that to you."

Varlan thought about it for a long time, then 'nodded.' "I understand the concept. Since I have been among you humans, I have had to expand my own viewpoint about many things. Ask your questions. I will not take offense."

"Thank you. My first question, then, is how you maintain this story is true when it is rife with internal inconsistencies?"

"I do not understand."

"Just look at it logically. How can you believe what I have just recounted really happened?"

Varlan's tongue flicked into view in a display of some alien emotion, and then she turned her head sideways to fix the human male with one obsidian eye and asked, "Are you religious, Señor Santiago?"

"Certainly."

"Of the sect called 'Catholic?'"

"Yes."

"Then I must ask you how you can believe in your religion when it has so many obvious logical inconsistencies. Take the matter of the Virgin, for instance. Was the husband of this female so naïve that he believed that she was giving birth without first having been impregnated?"

Bethany, who had explained human religious beliefs to Varlan several months earlier, nearly choked as she suppressed a laugh. Apparently, the Ryall's jab had hit its mark, because Jorge Santiago was turning red. Finally, he got himself under control.

"Touché," he responded. "Perhaps we can discuss the Miracle of the Virgin Birth at some other time. However, the subject was the timeline of the Swift Eater legend."

"What of it?"

"Your story is that Ryall began to die of radiation poisoning and suffered a high rate of mutation over a period of thousands of years because of a nearby supernova, the so-called Evil Star."

"Yes."

"And that these same radiations caused your race to evolve at a furious pace, and also forced the evolution of a mindless predator called the Swift Eaters, until they too had evolved intelligence."

"Yes, Jorge. That is true."

"But the timescales, Varlan. How can you possibly explain the timescales?"

"I still do not understand."

"Supernovas last for a few months or years at most. After that, they may flood a nearby star system with radiation for a few centuries. It isn't enough time to generate the effects that the legend ascribe to it, and even if it were, how did the early Ryall correlate the new light in the sky with the radiation sickness and mutations? Those would have begun to appear years after the light in the sky had dimmed. Without a scientific understanding of the phenomenon, it is more likely that the early Ryall would have viewed the two events as unrelated."

Bethany, whose feet were now hurting, wondered if Jorge Santiago knew what he was talking about. She remembered the night back in Homeport when Antares dawnlight had first burst across the countryside. It had been the light of an electric spark, a searing blue-white point in the sky that illuminated forests and caused long, inky shadows to grow from the base of every tree. The scene had been surreal, so much so that she and her uncle had stayed up until Antares set just before dawn, marveling at the change in Alta's night sky.

She remembered thinking at the time that the light in the sky was an omen of things to come. Little had she known just how much of an omen. It was because of that electric spark in the firmament that she met her future husband, and the life of Alta was transformed from one of peace to the never-ending struggle of war.

"That is the way it happened, Jorge," Varlan responded, a bit stubbornly, Bethany thought.

"I am not doubting your sincerity, Varlan, merely the logic of your story. It takes time for a new species to come about, even with forced evolution caused by a high mutation rate. It must have taken a thousand generations at least before the intelligence quotient of your race began to increase.

"As for the Swifts, they were beasts of deep water, which meant that they were well shielded from the radiations in the sky. True, they laid their eggs in the shallows where they could get sunlight. Still, radiations from the sky could not possibly have been the initiating cause for their sudden increase in intelligence."

"What was, then?"

"Why, I believe it must have been their competition with you Ryall."

"You'd better explain, Jorge," Olivia Southington said. She had been watching Varlan intently the whole time the Ryall had been contending with Santiago.

"It's a fairly common pattern among species. Predator and prey are locked into a sort of an evolutionary race. It happened among the hunting cats and horses on Earth. As we study their histories, we find that both species initially started out small — the horse, for instance, was about the size of a medium dog. You understand these references, do you not?"

Varlan nodded. "I have had much time to study your people and culture, Jorge. I have seen pictures of all of the animals you are describing, and I have met several dogs. There is something about my smell that they do not like."

"Well, through the millennia, both cats and horses began to grow longer legs. One generation, the horses would have the advantage and the short-legged cats starved. The next generation, the cats were able to outrun the horses, and the slower horses with shorter legs were eaten.

"That is what I believe happened to you and the Swift Eaters. Their numbers grew to the point where population pressure forced them into your habitat. They found that your people were good to eat, and the competition between you caused both sides to grow bigger brains rather than longer legs."

"What of the tales of misshapen hatchlings?"

"Perhaps they are overblown. There will be some mutations and genetic defects in every generation. With their tale of the Evil Star, your chieftains became very sensitive to it and killed the hatchlings that appeared inferior. In this way, they bred your race for increased intelligence."

"What is your point?" Varlan asked after a pause to think.

"Only that your tale of a supernova-generated war of extinction with the Swifts may be an oversimplification of what really happened. If we can find the real truth, perhaps we can convince your people that war to the death is not always the answer when two intelligent species encounter one another."

Varlan was about to respond when Bethany held up her hand in a restraining gesture. "If you don't mind, I am very fatigued. Can we take this up tomorrow?"

"Of course, Señora. My apologies for taking so much time."

"Thank you, Señor Santiago."

At that moment, Bethany's phone rang on her hip. She slipped it from its belt case and pressed the activate key.

"Yes?"

The others watched her expression grow tense. She listened for a dozen seconds, and then replaced the phone in its carrier. The worry lines were evident in her face as she turned to face them.

"What is the matter, Bethany?" Varlan asked. She had gotten very good at reading her friend's moods in the last three years, and this mood was one of pain.

"That was my assistant. News just came in from the fleet."

Three human voices asked in unison, "What news?"

"Nothing definite. Richard's squadron jumped through to Eulysta two days ago and has not yet returned. Apparently, the battle is well underway."

Bethany turned to leave. Her bed, where she could lie down and put her feet up, had been much on her mind the past two hours.

She took a single step and then lurched to a halt. She felt for the back of Olivia Southington's chair, missed, and found her arm instantly steadied by Jorge Santiago.

"What is the matter?"

Bethany clutched at her belly and grimaced with the pain. After a dozen seconds in which she could not speak, she straightened up and sighed, "That was the worst contraction yet."

Olivia, who had been looking at the back of Bethany's skirt, said, "That was more than a contraction, Bethany. Your water just broke."

Varlan, who had also seen the stain, let her ears flatten against her head, a sign of distress in a Ryall. "Is something wrong?"

Olivia turned to the alien with a smile. "Nothing at all, Varlan. Bethany is about to have a baby!"

#

# Chapter 5

Periskay of the Distant Mountains in the Mist was frightened – not for himself – but for The Race. The mystery of the destruction of the Corlis mineral extraction facility was solved, and like many mysteries, the resolution had left him wishing that it had not been.

Five planetary revolutions earlier, his young assistant burst into his sleeping chamber and emitted the high-pitched danger signal. Periskay awakened to find himself on six legs, torso and head in the guard position, tail extended for use as a club, arms held high to ward off unseen blows. His ears were flattened against his skull and his teeth bared, ready to tear into whoever or whatever menaced him. Rather than the hated ancestral enemies, he found Dillatan of the Sleek Swimmers standing far enough from his bower to be out of reach.

"What is it?" he asked the youth whose scales were still developing their adult color. The irritation that accompanied waking to alarm was evident in his tone.

"The ship reports multiple contacts in the portal to the Evil Star."

"The expedition has returned?" Periskay asked.

"If they have, they are being chased by the entire Monster Navy. Spectrographic analysis has positively identified the craft as warships of the bipeds. A flotilla appears to be moving away from the portal at high speed."

"Coming here?"

Dillatan signaled a negative. "No, Storislan of *Star Wanderer* reports that they are headed for the portal to Carratyl at high acceleration. He asks your instructions."

"An invasion?" Periskay asked, incredulous.

"It would appear so."

Although an engineer-philosopher and not a warrior, Periskay hesitated not an instant. This situation threatened the very survival of The Race.

"Tell Storislan to run for Carratyl as fast as he can. He is authorized to burn out his ship's engines if need be. Just get through the stargate and spread the alarm that there are Monsters in our space!"

"Yes, Philosopher!"

Dillatan of the Swift Swimmers proved how his clan had received its name. He performed a maneuver that, had it been in the water, would have been called a "back flip" and he was gone. Periskay let the knotted muscles in his torso relax and followed at a more leisurely pace, as befitted his station. The order he had just given would likely end their lives. He required time to think through the implications.

Ordering the ship to break orbit and run for the home stars was the only decision possible with a hostile war fleet in Eulysta's sky. He did not need to see the velocity plots to know that the Monsters intended to englobe the gateway. Any logical mind planning an invasion would do the same. What he did not know was whether he had just ordered Storislan to his death. Whether *Star Wanderer* reached the portal before the bipeds would largely be determined by the relative positions of the two portals in the sky. Unfortunately, orbital mechanics was not one of his specialties, so he had no way to judge the probable outcome.

With a flash of insight, Periskay realized that something similar must have happened to the missing *Space Swimmer*. The Monsters had appeared from out of the Evil Star and caught the ore carrier before it could reach Carratyl. Captain Ossfil and his crew had undoubtedly died bravely when their ship was vaporized. *Star Wanderer* would likely suffer the same fate if it lost the race to the stargate.

Having taken the only action he could, Periskay turned to the problem of looking after the safety of his team. What could they do against a fleet of Monsters trapped on this alien world?

Again, he had an intuition that he was not the first of his caste to face this problem. The plant manager, Varlan, must have confronted the same quandary. She had obviously chosen to fortify the mine, and had made her stand in the deep tunnels. The condition of her facility showed that choice to have been the wrong one.

No, if the Monsters bothered to make a landing at all, safety lay in the trackless forests and marshes. The local flora and fauna was another subject that he had not bothered to study. What voracious appetites waited in those woods to devour the unwary? What plants were poisonous to The Race's metabolism and which were nutritious? What food supplements would they need to live off the land?

Periskay mulled over all that he did not know about Eulysta as he walked. His ignorance of local conditions was great, but ignorant or not, he had no choice. The previous tenants had demonstrated their fate should they choose to defend the mineral extraction facility. He had no desire to see history repeat itself; at least, not in that way.

No, their only choice was to scatter into the wilds, and they would not even be able to scatter very far. The only vehicles they possessed were heavy construction machines that would leave a trail through the trees that a blind *slongth* could follow. Their only hope of escape would be on foot, and while The Race was designed superbly for its aquatic home, their short legs were not designed for hiking.

When he reached the tent used for an eating facility, he found half his subordinates crowded around a communicator. Thossital, the senior worker, was speaking to the ship.

"That is Philosopher Periskay's command," Thossital was saying. "As fast as you can…"

Storislan was staring at them from the depths of the screen. He was too close to the visual pickup, which caused his snout to appear comically elongated. "I can get a lander to you in a tenth-rotation, and back here in two."

Periskay nudged his way into the crowd. By the time he reached the zone where Storislan could see him, his crew had parted like the waters of a home world lake before a *pezist* after its dinner.

The ship captain saw him. "Ah, Philosopher. I have been telling these workers of yours that I will send a boat down to evacuate you."

"No. Swim for the Carratyl portal. You must reach it before the Monsters."

"You don't understand. We have detected a second group of ships leaving the portal from the Evil Star. They appear to be coming here."

"We aren't important. You must get word of this invasion to Those Who Rule."

"I obey your orders, Philosopher," Storislan replied. "*Star Wanderer* will be under power within a dozen-squared heartbeats." With that, the ship captain signed off.

Periskay turned to look at his team. Two-dozen heads moved imperceptibly to focus on him.

"What are we to do, Philosopher?"

"Prepare our supplies for transport. We are going to scatter into the bush."

"On foot? What do we know of the dangers in the forest?"

"We know nothing of the dangers of this world," Periskay replied as he shifted his gaze to the blue cloth overhead. "We know what dangers lie in our sky, however. We will wait one planetary rotation to observe and make preparations. Then we disappear into the forests like beasts. Our task is to be well dispersed by the time the Monsters get here."

That is what they had done. Over the next rotation, they received transmissions from *Star Wanderer* advising of them of progress. As Periskay suspected, *Wanderer* was no match for the warships bearing down on the gateway to Carratyl. The situation put him in mind of a pack of Swift Eaters stalking a gravid mother en route to the marshes to lay her eggs. The outcome did not seem in doubt, and it was not good for The Race.

It had been the hardest thing Periskay had ever done to shut down the communicator and strike out into the wilderness with five of his subordinates. Two revolutions later, he was startled by the crash of a sonic boom. He looked up in time to see a small alien craft flying very fast just above the trees. The craft had been in view for a single heartbeat, but long enough for Periskay to observe that it had not been manufactured by The Race.

The sight of that single ship had driven a cold stake into Periskay's brain. If *Star Wanderer* had failed to escape and the Monsters were occupying Eulysta, The Race was truly in grave danger.

#

Sergeant Matt Cunningham, Royal Sandarian Marines, strode through the yellow-green vegetation and listened to the whir of insects at maximum gain via his helmet's sound pickup. With a portion of his brain, he matched his own position on the faceplate display with what his eyes were telling him, and compared that with the positions of the other members of his squad. The tactical situation was unchanged from what it had been for the past two days — frustrating!

The Marine assault on Eulysta from the troop carrier, *TSNS Mozart*, had begun at local dawn some forty hours earlier. The assault had been a textbook envelopment made after an approach at high gravs. Cunningham's company had entered atmosphere in their landing boats even before *Mozart* completed its first powered orbit of the planet. They swooped down on the river of mud where the Ryall mine had been, taking the place in a classic vertical envelopment. They found the place deserted save for several electric-blue tents that showed signs of recent occupation.

The signs were obvious. The lizards had excavated the muck, searching for a clue as to what had happened there. The extent of the digging suggested a large number of workers. Some of the men in his company speculated that they had evacuated to their ship as soon as the fleet appeared in the foldpoint. Cunningham doubted that. His intuition, backed by tactical analysis, was that there had not been time to flee. The Ryall vessel left orbit too quickly after breakout for the ground party to have been aboard.

If the Ryall had not escaped on the ship, and they were not hiding in the mine, then they must have taken to the bush. Cunningham and two companies of Marines began sweeping the area for refugees. Over the past to days, they had rounded up a dozen lizards.

None of the Ryall captured so far were warrior caste. That had not stopped them from putting up a fight. Luckily, battle armor is impervious to teeth, although one of the larger captives succeeded in breaking a Marine's arm during a scuffle.

It would have been easier to shoot them, of course; but orders were to get as many alive as possible for interrogation. Besides, even though slogging through this alien forest was hot, uncomfortable work, Cunningham still preferred it to the kidney jolting acceleration they had suffered during the approach to the planet.

"Sarge!" the familiar voice echoed in his earphones, momentarily cutting out the background noise of insects.

"Yes, Suharo."

"I think I see one of 'em."

"Where?"

"About fifty meters ahead of me. The analyzer just popped up a bogie on my screen."

"Shit, Private, you know how crappy the analyzers are on an alien world. They haven't had time to learn half of what they need to know."

"Want me to ignore it?"

"Negative. Approach with stealth and be careful. Just because the rest of them haven't been armed doesn't mean that this one isn't."

"Right, Sarge. I'm starting my approach now."

"Murphy and Gleason. Close Suharo's flanks and support."

"Will do. Right, Sarge."

Inside his battle armor, Sergeant Matt Cunningham began to whistle tonelessly. Things, it seemed, were looking up.

#

Lieutenant Mirabel Fortura lay strapped in her acceleration couch and let her gaze sweep across the screens. Save for her vessel's consorts and an expanding cloud of plasma fifty thousand kilometers distant, there was nothing in range. The golden symbol that represented *Mercury's Javelin,* her high-acceleration speeder, lay just beyond the pale red oval that represented the foldpoint to the next Ryall system. Around the oval, still moving into position, were the rest of the *Mercury-class* warcraft. Their engines were spent, and they would need to be towed to a shipyard in Eulysta orbit once one was set up, but their mission had been a success... so far.

The *Mercury* squadron had won the race to see who would reach the foldpoint first, if barely. Despite being outclassed, the lizard ship had kept coming on as they had all converged on the foldpoint. It had been an easy maneuver to missile the big Ryall freighter short of the goal. Now, all they had to do was hold on for the next four days while the rest of the fleet crossed from the Eulysta-Antares foldpoint. Military intelligence thought Mercury Squadron's patrol would likely be uneventful — a good possibility since the Ryall thought this system a cul-de-sac. Mirabel prayed they were right. Whether right or wrong, however, their mission was to hold the foldpoint and destroy anything that came through. Those orders were the same whether the intruder was the Ryall equivalent of a yacht, or the largest blastship in the lizard fleet. In the latter case, Mercury Squadron would be like a bunch of dogs nipping at the heels of a bear. No matter how many of her squadron died in the battle, no intruder must escape to carry word back to Carratyl.

In retrospect, Mirabel thought, as she still tasted the used-tennis-shoe flavor of acceleration fluid that had recently filled her lungs, the conquest of Eulysta had been a training text operation. If only the rest of the invasion went as well.

What was that they were always telling students at the academy? No plan ever survives contact with the enemy? So far, this plan had worked beautifully, which was, according to Murphy's Laws for Military Operations, when one was supposed to worry most...

#

Richard Drake sat at his console aboard *Conqueror II* and worried. That seemed to be his normal state of mind these days. Not only was there the invasion to execute, which was enough worry for any man, there was that other small matter. Bethany's due date had come and gone about the midway point in their mad dash across the Corlis System. Probably, he was the proud father of a bouncing baby boy. *Probably*, all had gone well for mother and child. *PROBABLY*, he should be overjoyed at his good fortune.

So, why didn't he feel overjoyed?

Despite a thousand years of obstetrical science, there were no guarantees where childbirth was concerned. Mothers still occasionally died during labor — from hemorrhage, stroke, or heart failure — despite everything 26$^{th}$ century medicine could do. One thing that men did not understand was that labor was just that, a strain on the mother's system equivalent to running up a hundred flights of stairs in a piggyback race. He remembered a female comedian on one of the entertainment channels at home. One of her biggest laugh lines had come when she compared childbirth to pulling a rag doll out of one's nasal cavities through a nostril. Drake suspected that the joke went back at least a few centuries.

Even if Bethany had come through the ordeal healthy, what of the child? True, the genetic tests had shown everything all right when he left Altan orbit, but what did the geneticists really know? Could they tell whether a child would be a holy terror by age two, or how he would do in school, or if he would be tongue-tied around young ladies as a teenager? When one considered the complexity of the human genome, it was a wonder that they could predict any of the unborn child's characteristics.

And what about disease...?

Drake made a conscious effort to suppress his nervousness at the imponderables of what was happening at home, and concentrated instead on the imponderables of what was happening around him.

Truth was, the invasion was going well, and that worried him. As expected, there had been a small Ryall presence on Eulysta when they had appeared from out of the nebula. The Ryall spotted them quickly enough, judging by the speed with which a ship had powered up in Eulysta orbit. The two hours that followed were the longest of Drake's life. He remembered the feeling of relief when Tactical finally reported the alien fugitive's vector. Unless the Ryall ship had more legs than they were showing, the speeders would overtake it just short of the foldpoint.

Assuming things went well, the leading units of the fleet would reach the gateway to the Carratyl system eight days after leaving the nebula. They would englobe the foldpoint for two more days while they allowed stragglers to catch up with them, and then they would begin the process all over again.

Carratyl was no mere outpost of the Ryall Hegemony. It was an agricultural world with a foldpoint leading directly to Spica. The lizards had a military base on one of the moons, with steady traffic between planet and foldpoint.

The next time a human fleet came boiling out of foldspace, they would find a Ryall force capable of blocking their advance. It would be necessary to fight their way through to the Carratyl-Spica foldpoint and englobe it. If they were lucky, they might get there before any Ryall craft could jump through to Spica. If not, then they would lose the element of surprise, and the invasion would turn into an interstellar meat grinder.

Drake grimaced as he visualized how his fleet would look after wresting Spica from a fully alerted Ryall Hegemony. Even if they maintained the element of surprise, casualties might be high when they reached the central system of Ryall Space. There was just no way to know. He had heard the expression, "fog of war," but had never really understood what it meant... until now. The only thing that seemed certain was that he was destined to live on coffee and stomach acid for the rest of the voyage.

As he pondered, he let his eyes scan the daily situation report. Eulysta was the one bright spot in his life. The planet was firmly in human hands and even now, Admiral Belton had begun construction of what would soon be the largest human base outside the Solar System. It was in the Corlis system that damaged ships were to be repaired, and where they would stockpile the consumables required by a fleet at war.

Of one thing, Drake was certain. Spica would not be a good place to run short of ammunition.

#

# Chapter 6

Varlan of the Scented Waters pondered life as she stood in front of the wide window and looked at the wiggling mass of pink protoplasm in the sterile room beyond. Richard Clarence Drake was a large baby (they told her), massing some 4 kilograms at birth. Bethany had allowed Varlan to observe the entire ten-hour process that had culminated in young Richard's entry into the world, and she could not decide whether she was more mystified or disgusted.

The humans called Varlan and her kin "lizards," after a class of beasts on their home world that bore a superficial resemblance to The Race. In reality, of course, that was all the resemblance was — superficial. For, as both human and Ryall exobiologists had discovered after finding the first world with life other than their own on it, different biospheres often lead to radically different solutions. As Varlan had learned in her studies of Earth, various species there were called "monkeys." These simian relatives of the humans had drawn her attention because their similar shape to the big bipeds made her think that she could learn about her captors by studying their close relatives.

It turned out that only *some* of the monkeys were closely related to humans. Those were the group dubbed the "old world monkeys." These monkeys shared a common ancestor with the humans, a small beast called a lemur. The other group, the "new world monkeys" — the distinction between "old" and "new" escaped Varlan completely — were descended from a different ancestor species, the tarsiers. The similarities between the two kinds of simians was coincidental, a result of similar environmental factors producing similar arrangements of shape and function.

So it was with Varlan and the lizards of Earth. Both possessed scales and similar coloration, but the differences between them far outweighed the similarities. For one thing, Varlan was warm blooded, and a hexapod. Her species had been semi-aquatic rather than land dwelling for much of its history — like the terrestrial crocodile, a beastie that reminded Varlan of her own distant, non-sentient ancestors.

The other similarity between The Race and lizards, of course, came from the fact that both laid eggs to reproduce, although a terrestrial lizard egg looked nothing like the thick-shelled iridescent equivalent of The Race. The humans had explained that mammals, a classification unknown on Darthan and most of the worlds of the hegemony, gave birth to live young and that the mother suckled the young (a disgusting concept) with the large glands that contributed so much to the basic female shape. However, hearing the process described and actually seeing it were two different things.

If repelled by the sight of that small head appearing at the exit of the birth canal, Varlan could at least intellectually understand the profound effect their reproduction process had on humans. Indeed, to understand mammalian live birth was to understand many of their basic attitudes.

First, there was their societal structure, which was formed by a breeding pair and their offspring. The human family was a smaller unit than clans of The Race. Among Varlan's people, clans were composed of several dozen individuals related by bloodline, but for whom relationships were much less clear than among humans. That was because females laid their eggs, and then left them alone to hatch. The offspring that resulted were raised communally since it was impossible to tell who was the child of which parents. True, some youngsters often had distinctive scale markings, or prominent snout or length of tail, distinguishing characteristics that were similar to those of one adult or another. However, to actually claim paternity/maternity, was something not often done by members of The Race. In fact, when a female became fixated on identifying which of the new crop of hatchlings were her own, the elders of the clan gave her a name... and the name was not a particularly polite one.

The human system of reproduction meant that mothers could not help but know who their offspring were. For one thing, they were always present when the offspring "hatched." Furthermore, the baby was utterly dependent on its mother for sustenance for a long period after entering the world, which meant that the bond between mother and child had to be a strong one.

The upshot of all of this mammalian biology was that human beings focused on smaller groups than did The Race. This "family" orientation led them to be more individualistic and less content with their chosen lot in life. Varlan was a member of the manager caste and would have it no other way. She was neither subject to feelings that her life was somehow unfulfilled, nor by longing to be that which she was not. Her observations of her captors had convinced her that both conditions were endemic in the human psyche.

"Beautiful, isn't he?" a voice asked from beside her.

Varlan had been so deep in introspection that she had not noticed the approach of Dr. Olivia Southington. She turned her head and replied, "I will take your word for it. This, after all, is the first human baby I have ever seen. He resembles some older males I have met."

Olivia Southington laughed. "I know what you mean. Without hair and with their faces all scrunched up like that, babies look like petulant old men. Still, we find them adorable. I suppose it is the same with your children."

"Yes. The hatchlings are much... I will use the human word 'loved' although the emotion is somewhat different."

"Perhaps 'cherished' is the word you are looking for."

"Yes, cherished, I believe is closer to the true feelings we have for them."

"It is a shame that the hatchlings have to be endangered by this war."

Varlan turned to stare at the female exobiologist. She had been among the humans long enough to recognize the transition from polite conversation to business, even when delivered in a light tone of voice.

"You wish to explore our attitude to this war, Dr. Southington?"

Olivia laughed. "Am I that transparent?"

"Your intention is not difficult to discern, even for an alien."

"Very well. If you cherish your hatchlings so, why do you risk their lives the way you do?"

"You miss the point. We fight this war because it is our experience that to do otherwise would risk them more."

Olivia nodded. "The Legend of the Swift Eaters."

"Despite what Jorge Santiago believes, the Swift Eaters are no legend. They existed and they nearly exterminated The Race. We fought them for a very long time. I am not sure you humans understand just how long our war with the Swifts lasted."

"For generations."

"For thousands of generations, Olivia. You humans have no comparable experience. I have been reading your scholarly literature on the subject and I am beginning to understand how you think. Your sociologists have this perennial argument over nature versus nurture, whether genetics or culture are more important in the development of your young. Trust me, Olivia. By the standards of The Race, you humans are *all* nurture. You are... blank slates? ..."

"Blank slate is the correct idiom."

"You are born blank slates and your parents and adults program everything you know into you at an early age. We, on the other hand, fought the Swifts for so long, and with such a high mutation rate, that we evolved an instinct to kill them. We do not need to learn to hate them. The coding is already within us. Surely you know individual humans who are frightened merely by the sight of some animal."

Olivia nodded. "I don't like rats, and a great many people have an aversion to snakes."

"I have an instinct to hate Swift Eaters and they have been dead for more than a dozen-squared generations. It is part of my psyche and there is nothing I can do about it."

"Must you take it out on us humans?"

"Our experience with the swifts taught us the danger of having two sentient species vie for the same territory. Conflict is inevitable. Unlike your species, The Race does not hypnotize itself in order to avoid unpleasant facts. Nor do we leave known problems for the next generation to solve."

"But you are putting this generation at actual risk to avoid a hypothetical risk in the future."

"We do not believe the risk in the future is hypothetical."

"For the sake of argument, let us say that your position has validity. Why attack us the moment you became aware of our existence? Why not wait until you had learned all you could about us, and then take the time to prepare for the battle?"

Varlan had pondered that very point many times since her capture. Would it not have been better to spy out the enemy's strengths before launching the battle against them?

"Perhaps it would have been better to pretend friendship until we knew enough about you human beings to safely defeat you. Unfortunately, you are the first sentient species we have encountered since we ended the threat of the Swifts, so we lack experience in these matters."

"Then you are saying that the original attack on the New Providence refugees was a mistake?"

"It was... an instinctive reaction. Whether it was a mistake will be determined by the fate of your invasion fleet."

"I appreciate you being so honest with me."

"My species does not see the need to hide from unpleasant truths, Olivia. We do not delude ourselves."

"Both of our species have flaws, Varlan. However, we also have intelligence. That intelligence gives us humans the ability to modify our responses to stimuli. Bethany thinks the same is true of Ryall."

"Yes, Bethany has talked to me of this concept many times."

"Do you possess the ability to have your intelligence override your instincts?"

"That is what you are here to determine, is it not, Olivia?"

"It is indeed."

#

Lieutenant Sean Parker floated in a pool of oxygenated fluid and stared at the instruments inside his tank. At his side, blue-tinged blood flowed through a clear umbilical cord away from his combat suit, while bright red blood flowed back through the return line. Both lines were attached to a socket just above his left hip, and from there to his circulatory system. Parker was not breathing. He could not. His lungs contained the same heavy fluid in which he was submerged. In fact, all of his body cavities were filled with oxygenated fluid.

"Mercury Squadron. Report status."

The words in his ears were delivered in the perfect contralto tones that marked the voice that produced them as computer synthesized. Like Parker, the speaker, his squadron commander, lay submerged in an acceleration tank, her lungs filled with oxygenated fluorocarbon, and unable to make a sound. Her words were produced by the small inductive pickup mounted behind her right ear. The pickup monitored the output of numerous electrodes that had been carefully implanted beneath her skull amid the valleys of her cerebral cortex

It was the surgically implanted enhancements, along with the long training to use them properly, that marked the elite flight crews of the Mercury Squadrons, the high acceleration craft whose mission it was to seize enemy foldpoints before the Ryall could spread the alarm.

"*Mercury Climber*, ready for jump," Parker replied, using his own implants to search among the prerecorded responses. He had adjusted his personal simulated voice to a deep baritone to distinguish it from those of his three crewmates.

He listened as the ten ships of his squadron reported their status, and then as the other two squadrons reported in. Following the jump from Antares to Eulysta, only a single squadron had been required to secure the enemy foldpoint. Eulysta was an outpost system and high command had wisely decided to conserve their resources. Alpha Squadron had spearheaded the invasion of Eulysta, but would not be going along this time. They had worn out their engines during the mad dash across the system, and until overhauled, were little more than intrasystem scooters.

This time, the duty and honor fell to the remaining three squadrons in the Mercury Force. Beta, Gamma, and Delta Squadrons would race across the Carratyl System to the Carratyl-Spica foldpoint. Nor was the force made up solely by armed speeders this time. Gamma Squadron including three destroyers modified for high acceleration attack. In addition to having engines and reaction tankage approximately quadruple the normal size, Mercury Force vessels mounted surprisingly heavy armament for ships of their class — proving that engineers can do wonders if their designs are not required to last beyond a single battle.

"Mercury Force, ready to jump, Fleet," came the report from Captain Danvers aboard *Mercury Rocket*."

"Very good, Mercury Force. Your advance scouts may start charging their generators."

"*Beta Squadron*. Begin charging your generators."

"*Climber*, acknowledges," Parker sent. Then on the ship's intercom, he said, "This is it. Strap down, it may be a bumpy ride from here on out."

The joke brought the requisite (and synthesized) chuckles. Floating as they were in their acceleration tanks, with their lungs and intestines filled with the vile tasting, worse smelling fluid, they had no need to strap down. In fact, *Mercury Climber* could run into a small planet at atmospheric aircraft speeds, and assuming his tank remained intact, Parker would survive the crash. The cushioning volume of acceleration fluid would protect his internal organs against accelerations fifty times standard gravity, and impacts even higher.

He just wished it weren't so uncomfortable. Worse than the surgeries and the endless hours training his body to control the implants, was the constant feeling that he was drowning. Nor did he look forward to the spate of coughing that would be required to empty his lungs of the fluid once they secured the foldpoint and were able to de-tank.

"Generators charged," Parker reported, followed in quick order by the other speeders.

"You are cleared for foldspace transition," Captain Danvers transmitted.

"Very well, foldspace transition in ten ... nine ... five ... four ... three ... two ... one ... transition!"

#

Drake watched the ten speeders disappear from his command screen and felt the same thrill that he had when they had departed the nebula.

"Two minutes, Admiral."

"Very well communicator. Get the fleet in position. The rest of Mercury Force will jump first, followed by the other squadrons in order. Everyone will begin accelerating immediately after breakout. They can sort out their formations en route. Send those orders and the general standby signal."

"Yes, sir."

The chronometer continued counting down the minimum time required before one of the speeders reappeared to give them the All Clear. As at Eulysta, Drake worried about what he would do if the two minutes elapsed and there was no word on conditions beyond the foldpoint. To occupy his mind, he counted his flock, which had swelled considerably since they had left the nebula.

More than a hundred ships made the initial jump from Antares to Eulysta. Of those, a dozen split off to capture the planet Corlis. Led by Admiral Belton's *Victory*, the raiding force including his old consorts *Dagger* and *Dreadnought*. They were still there, supporting operations to turn the uninhabited world into a forward base for the invasion. They were not scheduled to rejoin the fleet for nearly a month. Hopefully, *Victory*, minus its admiral, would rejoin sooner than that. The fleet needed the big blastship's firepower.

To replace them, the Terrestrial Third Starfleet, including four blastships larger than *Conqueror II*, had joined him. Indeed, in addition to Sergei Gower, Sandarian Navy, he now had three flag officers under his command, all senior to him in both experience and rank. Two of these – Kreuchner and Wu – would undoubtedly be happy to displace him if his leadership proved lacking. He did not much care for the stress that put him under, but it kept him on his toes. His life since leaving Alta had been one continuous mental game of wondering what it was that he had forgotten.

With the new replacements, Drake's fleet numbered nearly four hundred, counting combat vessels and armed auxiliaries. Three times that number of ships would eventually be required to secure Spica.

In addition to the combatants, some eighty of the big globular assault tankers were with the fleet. The tankers had been busy the past 24 hours as warship after warship moved in close to refill tanks depleted during the mad dash across the Eulysta System. Third Starfleet had arrived only six hours earlier; their tanks nearly dry from the speed run across the system.

Drake watched the screen counter wind down toward zero. Just as it touched that magic number, there was a report of a breakout.

"What ship?"

"*Mercury Climber*, Admiral."

"Patch me through."

"Aye aye, sir."

"Lieutenant Parker, *Mercury Climber*, Admiral," a synthesized voice said after a few seconds.

"Report, Mr. Parker."

"The foldpoint is clear of enemy forces, sir. The fleet can begin foldspace transition when you are ready."

"What of the enemy?"

"Sensors picked up a lot of space traffic in the short time we had to look. Most appears centered on the planet. There are some ships in transit between planet and the Carratyl-Spica foldpoint, sir. We couldn't tell whether they were coming or going, however."

"Understood," Drake said. It would probably take several hours of observations of their drive flares before they would be able to sort out those ships en route to the planet from those headed back toward Ryall space. They could safely ignore those moving away. Their velocity would make it difficult for them to turn around and retreat the way they had come. If some were en route toward the foldpoint, however, Mercury Force was going to have another race on its hands. "Any readings from the planet?"

"Nothing but general energy emanations, Admiral. The planet is on the opposite side of the system from where we broke out, so we could not get a very good look. It's for certain that they will have time to get ready for the ships assigned to neutralize that naval base."

Drake nodded. They had known that Carratyl's agricultural world would be on the opposite side of the system primary from the foldpoints when they planned the mission. In fact, they were counting on it to give them a chance to bottle up the system before the alarm could be spread. On the other hand, the ships assigned to pound the Ryall navy base into submission would be taking on an enemy who had plenty of time to prepare a defense.

"Anything else to report, Mr. Parker?"

"No sir."

"Are your generators charged?"

"They will be in 73 seconds, sir."

"Very well. That will be our mark then. Mr. Carey. Inform the fleet that the rest of Mercury Force, and Task Forces Darthan and Carratyl will jump with *Mercury Climber*..." Drake looked at the chronometer. "... at 10:27:16 hours precisely. The rest of the fleet will follow in their assigned order at one-minute intervals. All Ships, stand by for foldspace transition."

He listened as the order went out. All over the fleet, there were terse acknowledgements of the order and nothing else, yet he could almost feel the tension building with the foldspace jump fields. Whole squadrons of tightly bunched ships were preparing to jump into enemy space. Upon arrival, they would be jumbled randomly across the foldpoint, the victim of random quantum effects. It would take some time to sort things out.

"Ten seconds, Admiral."

Once again, the computer-generated countdown echoed throughout the ship. "Ten ... nine ... eight ... seven ... six ... five ... four ... three ... two ... one ... Jump!"

#

# Chapter 7

For an instant, nothing seemed to happen. The blackness on the main viewscreen appeared unchanged, as did the stars that dotted the firmament. Even the system primary looked the same, an especially bright star in a field of diamonds sprinkled across an ebon backdrop. For long seconds, the bridge was silent save for the susurration of ventilators and the background noise of powerful engines coming to life deep within the hull.

After a short pause, reports began flooding in from all over the ship. At first, departments reported that they had survived the transition with no ill effects. Then the sensor operators filled the comm channels with their observations. Wherever they were, *ASNS Conqueror II* was no longer high above a yellow-white star known to human beings as Eulysta.

"Admiral, we have located the planet. All seems normal... Admiral, ships are popping out of foldspace all around us. The nearest is the *ASNS Discovery...*" Drake smiled at the chance that would bring his old command out of foldspace so close to his new command. He considered sending a personal message to Rorqual Marchant, now commanding, but decided against it. Rorq had his own problems and so did he. "Mercury Force is departing the foldpoint at ten gravities. They are en route to the Carratyl-Spica foldpoint... Now we have Sandarian Tanker *Zanzibar* close to our zenith. She just popped out less than ten thousand kilometers from us ..."

No matter how precise a fleet's formation when it enters one end of a foldline, its individual components exit the foldpoint randomly dispersed. This phenomenon had cost attackers (both Ryall and human) more than one battle, since it is impossible to maintain a coherent formation following a jump. It is as though God throws the dice every time a ship's captain gives the jump order.

The jump to Carratyl was no exception. Ships that had been tens of thousands of kilometers apart at Eulysta could end up nearly scraping hulls when they emerged in the foldpoint high above Carratyl. Luckily, foldpoints contained millions of cubic kilometers of empty space, and there had never been a recorded case of two ships colliding at the end of a jump. Drake did not wish to be the first commander so blessed. Therefore, as soon as the spate of breakout reports subsided, he gave the order for the fleet to disperse beyond the foldpoint.

It took several seconds to synchronize computers and exchange data concerning the post-transition coordinates of the task force's more than 100 members. For if there is little chance of a mid-space collision coming out of foldspace, the chance of a mid-space accident increased dramatically once those ships began to move. In fact, having a hundred ships all leaving the confines of the foldpoint at the same time was like a traffic cop's worst nightmare, but in three dimensions. Added to that, of course, was the fact that 60 seconds after their initial arrival in the foldpoint, Task Force Avador's 88 members would be materializing at random among them. They would be followed sixty seconds later by Task Force Rylmar. Soon the foldpoint would be jammed with accelerating warships and tankers.

As he watched the colored icons begin to move purposely across the face of his command screen, Drake's practiced gaze began to pick out a pattern in the chaos. A minority of the blips were moving in the direction of Carratyl, while most others seemed to be powering into an orbit at right angles to the star. The first group was Task Force Carratyl, a heavy bombardment group centered on the Blastship *TSNS Archernar*, which would attack the Ryall's moon-based fortress and knock down the planetary defenses. The second group included *Conqueror II*, and comprised the main body of the fleet, which was moving out after the already distant Mercury Force.

"Admiral, all ships have finished their jumps. All accounted for and en route to their assigned targets. Orders, sir?"

"Tell the squadrons to form up on their leaders and execute the plan. No additional orders at this time."

"Aye aye, sir. Form up on leaders and execute the plan. Sending now."

His duties complete for the moment, Drake watched his screens for signs of Task Force Avador and indications that the enemy was aware of their presence. Of course, there was nothing yet to see on the last account. It would take light twenty minutes or so to reach the planet. Twenty minutes for the photons and gravity waves disturbed by their arrival to reach the planet, and twenty minutes before the photons carrying the Ryall response could return.

In forty minutes time, all hell would break loose in the Carratyl system. Drake decided to use the time productively. He considered for the thousandth time since entering the Antares nebula what it was that he had forgotten to do.

#

"We've got a problem, Lieutenant," the synthesized voice said in Sean Parker's earphones.

"What is it, Starky?"

"Bogie Seven Delta is going to beat us to the foldpoint."

"I thought we had that one licked."

"So did we, sir. However, he did not make turnover on schedule. He is still accelerating. That means that he has saved enough fuel for an emergency deceleration at the foldpoint. If he doesn't begin decelerating in seven minutes, he will get there first."

Sean Parker nodded inside his acceleration tank. It was about the only thing he could do with all of the tubes he was hooked into.

"What does Tactical say about the bogey's max accel performance?"

"They doubt he can do more than five gees. That is a guess, mind you, since we haven't been able to figure out what the damn thing is yet."

"Very well. We will assume a five gee decel. How long will they continue to accelerate?"

"The best guess is another couple of hours, Lieutenant. Then they will shut down and coast for six more hours, after which they will do a balls-to-the-wall deceleration. The projection is that they will reach the foldpoint a full hour before we do."

"Then we will have to prevent that, won't we?"

Most people think war in space is merely an extension of war as it was practiced by generations of fighter pilots. Nothing could be more wrong. War in the air is a matter of aerodynamics, of hypersonic wind rushing past sleek wing surfaces, and above all, of keeping the "pointy end into the wind." War in space is a matter of vectors. The acceleration vector is integrated over time to generate velocity, which in turn is integrated to develop position. The orientation of the craft is independent of its flight path. While under power, the warcraft of vacuum are aligned with the acceleration vector, often flying sideways or even backwards to gain advantage over an adversary. A chase in atmosphere is generally a matter of pursuer and pursued both flying at maximum speed and then seeing who is the faster. In space, things are more complicated.

Starships are able to leap across light-years in no time at all, but when in transit between foldpoints, are governed by the laws of motion first postulated by Sir Isaac Newton. A typical voyage has three parts: the accel, the coast, and the decel.

Bogey Seven Delta had departed the Ryall agricultural world (that humans were calling "Dogpatch") more than a week earlier. It accelerated to three times local escape velocity and then shut down its engines to save fuel. Presumably, in another week's time, it would again power its engines and decelerate at the same rate at which it first accelerated. The deceleration would bring the Ryall ship to a near halt within the foldpoint, after which it would jump from Carratyl to the big star that was the central hub of the Ryall Hegemony.

The arrival of human warships in the Carratyl-Eulysta foldpoint changed Bogey Seven Delta's plans as it had those of the dozens of ships en route to and from Spica. Within minutes of the invading fleet's appearance, each ship in transit reacted like a frightened chicken in the sights of a truehawk. Those ships inbound from the foldpoint ran for the planet as quickly as their fuel state allowed. Most ships leaving Dogpatch for Spica turned around and reversed course, a maneuver that would leave their tanks dry upon arrival. Only the few close enough to the foldpoint to have a chance of outrunning the invaders had headed for the system exit.

Unfortunately for the Ryall shipmasters, they had not accounted for the blazing speed of *Mercury Force*. Most would reach the foldpoint hours or days late. In fact, until Bogey Seven Delta failed to make turnover on time, it appeared that humanity would again win its gamble and prevent any escape from Carratyl.

Even if the Ryall craft entered the foldpoint with dry tanks, it would still be able to jump to Spica where it could begin broadcasting a general alarm. That is, unless Sean Parker did something to stop him."

"All right, put me on the force circuit."

"You are patched through to all ships, Lieutenant."

"This is Parker aboard *Climber*…" he began. He explained the dilemma. When he finished, he said, "Fuel state check. Who has the most in their tanks?"

When the tally was complete, he looked over the numbers and made a decision. "*Diablo*, you will be our hound. *Fox* and *Evelyn*, you will be the goats. Rendezvous with Elizabeth and transfer her a quarter of your remaining fuel. Keep just enough to get you there. Elizabeth, you will hold course after the rest of us make turnover, coast for three hours, and then do a maximum performance decel. Don't worry about stopping at the foldpoint. Take him out on the fly and we'll send a tanker to retrieve you if you run your tanks dry."

"Understood, Sean," Elizabeth Esperanza said from her cocoon aboard *Mercury Diablo*. Her simulated voice was almost as musical as her real voice. "All right, *Mercury Fox* and *Mercury Evelyn*. Close on me and coordinate engine cutoffs for minimum screwing around before the fuel transfer. I want all the time I have to nail that bogey at the foldpoint."

Parker watched the complex evolution and felt a surge of pride as the three ships formed up in close formation and then cut their engines in practically the same millisecond. All he could see was that three icons suddenly lost their violet acceleration vectors. The diagram on his helmet display did not show the frantic bursts of attitude control jets as each designated tanker moved in to dock in turn with Elizabeth Esperanza's ship, nor could he hear the frantic chugging of pumps as cryogenic hydrogen was transferred from one ship to another.

While the refueling continued, the rest of Mercury Force turned end for end and began decelerating. The three coasting ships immediately leaped ahead of their powered brethren. Then, the three icons separated and two of their number began to decelerate as well. Only *Mercury Diablo* continued on, velocity unabated.

"Good luck, Elizabeth."

"Thanks, Sean. We'll sweep the foldpoint clean for your arrival."

#

Lieutenant Elizabeth Esperanza was concerned, but not frightened. Whatever Bogey Seven Delta was, it maneuvered like a warship. That just made their task more interesting. She would be frightened later, after she had done her job.

*Diablo* was well ahead *Mercury Force*, the result of rushing headlong for hours while they decelerated for the foldpoint. The speeders and destroyers were a diminishing formation of glowing drive flares in the rear viewscreen as *Diablo* continued its breakneck race across the system. Ahead, and closing fast, was the blip that was their quarry. It had held its course far longer than originally projected, and had just begun decelerating for the foldpoint at six gravities.

Engines with that capability didn't usually power ore freighters or grain barges. Those kind of legs generally meant that the vessel possessing them was a warship.

"What do you suppose it is, Cas?"

She could almost hear her sensor operator shrugging inside his tank. "Could be anything from a message boat to a blastship, although from its flare spectrum, I would doubt we are up against anything larger than a destroyer."

"Great. They are only four times our size instead of forty! At least, we'll have a fighting chance when we get there."

"If we get there, Liz. Watch the time."

"You worry about your sensors and I'll handle the piloting, Stinky."

On her screen, a chronometer display was clicking off the seconds to the moment when it would be their turn to begin deceleration. She was not looking forward to that. In order to cut off the bogey, they would be going in at twenty gravities, and even then, would not slow down to system escape velocity before they reached the foldpoint. It was going to be one quick shot and then a long ride to infinity unless a tanker caught up with them.

The fluid in which she floated would theoretically protect her up to hundreds of gravities. Technology had not yet caught up with science. In truth, the twenty gravity capability of the engines was also the physiological limit of the crew, and possibly a little above the limit. Twenty gees would cause damage and would prematurely age her — how much, she couldn't guess. Elizabeth didn't fear dying. Her nightmares came when she saw herself as a broken down old lady of 28.

However, as an ancient philosopher once said, "No guts, no glory." So, Elizabeth willed the acceleration alarms to sound in each of the tanks and said, "Okay, pull up your socks, people. Here we go!"

With that, she ordered engines to full power. In seconds, her whole body was being squeezed as though in a vise. Her vision went gray and then cleared, as the pumps increased the internal pressure in her tank to compensate. However, there was blurriness to her peripheral vision that told her this condition was not good for her.

On the screen, the velocity display began to change with alarming rapidity and the range to target indicator slowed perceptibly. They were slowing at the last possible second. Already, the fuzzy red oval that marked the perimeter of the foldpoint was coming into view at the edge of the screen. On another edge was the icon that represented their enemy. It was closing on the foldpoint as well.

It was going to be close.

"Damn it, he just fired missiles!"

"Defensive weapons online and free," she responded instinctively. Their quarry had been identified. They were facing a warship. "Any guesses, Cas?"

"A destroyer for sure, Liz. Has to be. We have six vampires inbound. Anything smaller and they would have been hard pressed to fire half that at us in the first salvo."

"What about a cruiser that just decided to swat the gnat?"

"Don't think so. Not when you consider the stakes we are playing for here. Whoever he is, he just spit out a maximum salvo."

She considered it and had to agree with him. This was no time for half measures. The fate of two sentient species depended on the outcome of this particular space race.

"Return fire. Maximum salvo. Let's give him something to worry about."

*Diablo* bucked six times as long-range missiles spit forth from her magazines, demonstrating the truly awesome ratio of armament to size that was standard for the specially built ships of *Mercury Force*.

The symbols on the screen showed the two clusters of missiles as they raced between ships. At the current range, it would take a minute for them to cross the gulf between combatants. When half that time had passed, Elizabeth ordered another volley, and was not surprised when the Ryall returned the fire. The second group of missiles would significantly complicate the job of the defensive computers. They would learn lessons from the destruction of the first volley and would adjust defenses accordingly. Modern space war is primarily a battle between computers, and a race to see which learns the quickest.

*Mercury Diablo* began to accelerate erratically as the computer took over defense of the ship. Lasers flashed out invisibly in the vacuum, seeking out incoming missiles. Lasers are instantaneous weapons. If they can see a target, they can destroy it.

Unfortunately, their effective range against armored missiles is damnably short.

"Ready third volley," she ordered when the missiles of both sides disappeared before they could reach their targets. The distance between the two ships was now down to 45 seconds travel time.

"Liz! We've got a ship appearing in the foldpoint!"

"Belay that last order! Target the new arrival with the third volley. Fire."

Again, the ship bucked as the missile ejectors expelled heavy spheres into space where their matter converter engines could safely drive them toward the enemy. When the third volley was away, she ordered, "Ripple fire. Send everything we have at Bogey Seven Delta. Let's try to swamp him before he swamps us."

This time the speeder shuddered for a long time as they emptied their magazines. The Ryall ship also began continuous firing. It quickly became obvious that the destroyer's magazines were larger than *Diablo*'s.

"Evasive action. How long to the other target?"

"They should be getting there any sec…" On the screen, the newly arrived Ryall ship in the foldpoint exploded. Having jumped blind into a battle, they had not known what hit them.

Elizabeth turned her attention back to the problem at hand. The space between them and the bogey filled with ordnance and *Diablo*'s defensive computer fired lasers as quickly as they recharged. The target was jinking and firing lasers. The good news was that they were slower at it than *Diablo*. The bad news was that they had more lasers with which to work.

Suddenly, a million suns burst forth in the space between the two ships, effectively blinding them.

"Premature burst, probably intentional," Lubo Casimir reported. "They're trying to blind us."

"They're doing a damn good job," Elizabeth responded. "How much radiation exposure?"

"We'll live," Bill Ames, the engineer reported, "if we get help quickly enough."

"Ten seconds to regain sensors. All right, I can see through the fireball again. Enemy ship is destroyed. I repeat, enemy is destroyed!"

"What happened?"

"Apparently, one of our missiles got through. All I can see is an expanding cloud of plasma."

"Then let's get out of here! Engines to power. Run the tanks dry if you have ..."

Elizabeth Esperanza's order was cut off in mid-sentence when the nuclear-tipped Ryall missile that had been shielded by the mid-space detonation impacted *Diablo*'s engine module. In a dozen nanoseconds, far too quickly for human senses to detect, the speeder and four human souls ceased to exist. The Ryall had just drawn first blood.

However, by any measure, the battle had to be judged a decisive human victory.

#

# Chapter 8

Rear Admiral Achille Poledoris, Terrestrial Space Navy, gazed at the planet on the main viewscreen and felt a twinge of homesickness. White bands of cloud circled the girth of a blue sphere dotted with green-brown landmasses. The seas of Dogpatch were shallower than those of Earth, giving it a beautiful aquamarine color around the larger continent, which shaded abruptly to azure at the continental shelf. The sea was dotted with chains of islands that bespoke a volcanic heritage, including linear wisps of smoke that streamed downwind from several active island peaks. From space, the Ryall agricultural world was lovely, but then, so were most terrestrial worlds.

Poledoris's problem was that the view from space was not going to remain lovely for very long. Poor Dogpatch would likely suffer significant collateral damage in the next few hours, the result of the fleet action that was about to commence. The planet's big Luna-like moon would be the center of the action, but of course, any planetary defenses would also have to be neutralized.

Even now, he could see the Ryall defenses gearing up for action on his tactical screens. Megawatts of energy were streaming skyward from both planet and moon to paint the approaching human ships and determine their composition. Likewise, large light-amplified telescopes were undoubtedly tracking their progress from out of Carratyl, the system primary, attempting to analyze their propulsive efficiency by observing the spectra of the fleet's photon drives.

Poledoris's people were doing precisely the same thing to the Ryall defenders. Powerful telescopes scrutinized the Ryall moon, searching out the secrets of the naval base there. Intelligence classified the base as relatively weak, but with sufficient power to launch interdiction raids against supply convoys en route to Spica. That meant it would have to be, in the polite parlance of war, "neutralized." Whether the planet would also be occupied was one of the decisions for which Poledoris was responsible.

Around him were the twelve Terrestrial Space Navy ships of his command. In addition to the Blastship *Archernar*, he commanded the Cruisers *Saratoga* and *Brindisi*, the Destroyers *Achmed Khan*, *Irving Kirschner*, *General Murphy*, and *Tagaki*, and four tankers. The twelfth ship in his fleet was a converted freighter, the *Max Planck*, and the most dangerous craft in the formation. For aboard the *Planck* was a cargo of more than fifty thousand long-range missiles and other armament.

The *Planck* was a dual-purpose craft. Its primary function was to rearm the warships whenever they ran low on ammunition, but it was equipped with launchers of its own, and could act as an attack carrier. An attack carrier was the one ship that could overcome even the heaviest planetary defense. It did so by filling the enemy's sky with enough ordnance to swamp any defense.

The Ryall had used the tactic at the Battle of Sandar, where a mixed Sandarian-Altan force had beaten off the attack, barely. Poledoris had studied that campaign and knew how lucky the defenders were that day. They had managed to knock out the Ryall attack carriers before they could begin launching missiles. Had those ships filled space with their swarms of death, it is doubtful that the Sandarians would have made up a portion of Strike Force Spica today. It was as a defense against attack carriers that the two foldpoints in the Sol system were so heavily defended. Letting one of those monsters loose near Earth was a nightmare too horrible to contemplate.

"Admiral, *Khan* reports that the moon is launching more interceptors. These appear to be single-seat orbital fighters."

"How many, Tactical?"

"Two dozen, sir."

"Any action from the planet?"

"No, sir. All quiet there. They are scanning us, but are not taking offensive action."

"They will. Those sensor beams indicate an active planetary defense. Tell all captains to be on the watch for heavy lasers and other close-in defenses. Full countermeasures the moment they open up. Limit counter fire to laser-initiated fusion weapons. We don't want to 'dust' real estate we may be occupying."

"Yes, sir. I have a report coming in from Fleet Command, sir. It's an action report from the foldpoint."

"Read it to me."

"It says that Mercury Force has secured the foldpoint. One casualty. A speeder was destroyed in the action."

Poledoris clamped his teeth together in a movement that made his jaw muscles bulge. That the news had been inevitable did nothing to soften the impact.

#

*"Planet coming in range. All ships, cease acceleration. Cloud armor, now!"*

Achille Poledoris felt his body surge into its restraints as drive-gravity evaporated around him. The next moment, his screens were enveloped in a glittering fog that quickly dissipated, save for an occasional sparkle on the screen as sunlight reflected off a random particle. The fog-and-clear cycle repeated a dozen times, until the sparkles were like a flock of fireflies around the ship.

The phenomenon was caused by the release of tons of microscopic particles into the surrounding vacuum. The particles were micron-size crystal prisms, specially coated until they were nearly 100% reflective in wavelengths ranging from the infrared to ultraviolet. *Archernar* was the center of a rapidly expanding cloud of these tiny mirrors. Collectively, they formed the ship's "cloud armor." Virtually invisible, the reflective cloud was dense enough to effectively break up any laser beam that penetrated it, seriously degrading its power and coherence, hopefully to the point that the beam arrived little stronger than a bright searchlight. Failing that, the two-meter-thick ablative armor would explode outward and spew a much more dense cloud of particles from the point of impingement, scattering the beam before it could punch through to the hull below.

Like all defensive systems, cloud armor had its drawbacks. Since the ship's drive was photonic, the drive flare was reflected at random by the prism cloud. This had no effect on propulsion, but the reflected energy caused the hull temperature to increase. Then there was the problem of acceleration. A ship under acceleration tended to leave its protective cloud behind, negating its primary protection against heavy ground-based lasers. To remain within the cloud of mirrored particles, the ship had to shut down its main engines, which in turn caused other problems…

"Report," Poledoris ordered.

"All ships report clouds at effective density, Admiral," a defense systems operator responded. *"Khan* and *Kirschner* both report that they are under attack from the Planetary Defense Center on the main continent."

On the screen, a bright green star suddenly winked into existence on a peninsula jutting out into an azure sea at the edge of Dogpatch's largest continent. Poledoris did not need to see the sudden clouds of steam rising from the ocean to know that they were there. It required a lot of energy to deliver a beam powerful enough to damage a ship at the range of a million kilometers. That energy had to be dumped somewhere as waste heat. For the same reason, most human Planetary Defense Centers were also located near a coastline.

"Have them reply with missiles. One megaton warheads at one minute intervals until they knock that damn place out."

"*Khan* acknowledges and has the first missile away. *Kirschner* acknowledges and is firing now."

Poledoris heard the acknowledgement, but did not reply. Already, his mind had moved on to other problems. He would like to have stayed clear of Dogpatch's PDCs altogether, but orbital mechanics made that impossible. The fleet had materialized in the foldpoint from Eulysta, which was currently on the opposite side of Carratyl. His task force had executed a sun-grazing maneuver en route to the planet. The phase of their target moon was nearing full in Dogpatch's sky, which placed it beyond the planet. That required the fleet to sweep close by the planet to get to their objective. Any other approach would have added days to their maneuvering time.

"We've got ships coming up from the planet to meet us."

"Warships?"

"No, sir. Their drive flares and acceleration rates make them freighters."

"No doubt armed with every missile the Ryall can scrape up. Log them as attack carriers and assign *Saratoga* to take them out."

"*Saratoga*'s captain acknowledges, Admiral. He is moving into firing position. "Correction. *Saratoga* has been holed by a PDC laser. Two sections are open to space. No report on casualties."

Poledoris uttered a curse under his breath. *Sara* was his most powerful ship after *Archernar*. If she were badly damaged, it would cut his combat strength significantly.

"Ask *Khan* why they haven't taken care of that bastard, yet."

"*Khan* reports an explosion at the PDC's location. Spectrum indicates one of our torpedoes got through."

"Have *Kirschner* lob in a couple of more. Shake them up. Tell *Khan*, 'well done!'"

"*Kirschner* acknowledges the order."

"Send *Brindisi* after the attack carriers."

"*Brindisi* acknowledges and is preparing to attack."

The ensuing battle was mercifully short. The Battle Cruiser *Brindisi* emerged from its anti-laser cloud, moved into position, and then launched missiles against the two red pips moving away from the planet. First one blinked out of existence, then another. On the screen, another bright green point appeared. This was a secondary laser battery. A minute later, the green spark turned momentarily violet as a missile found its mark, and the laser shut off.

"Who was that?" Poledoris asked.

"*Kirschner*, Admiral."

"Good shooting. Pass it on."

"Damage report from *Saratoga*, sir. They have power restored. Offensive capability is 80 percent."

"Tell Captain Stewart to rejoin the formation. *Brindisi* will take over the lead."

"Acknowledged, Admiral."

On the screen, the fleet was a tight group of emerald icons that was approaching minimum distance from the planet. If the Ryall of Dogpatch were to give them trouble, this would be the moment."

Poledoris found himself holding his breath as they swept past perigee on their hyperbolic attack orbit and began drawing away from the planet. The "range to target" indicator ceased its mad downward cycle and began to climb once more. There was no further response from the planet.

"That seems to have been it," Tactical reported after the range had been opening for five minutes.

"What about the other PDC?"

"It is still below the horizon, Admiral."

"Surely they have battle mirrors in orbit."

"None obvious, sir."

The admiral nodded. A backwater planet, to be sure. It made little sense to build a ground-based defense center and then allow it to shoot only at things above its own horizon. An atmosphere-skimming attack would get a ship to within half a thousand kilometers of a ground target before it popped over that target's local horizon, by which time it would be far too late for them to do anything abut it. For full utility, a PDC needed to be paired with a constellation of orbiting battle mirrors.

Where Dogpatch's were, he did not know, but he was glad for their absence. Were he sure that they weren't playing possum, he could order the fleet to maneuver rather than sit inertly inside their anti-laser cloud until they were out of range of the planetary defenses.

"We have multiple missile launches from the planet, Admiral."

"Too little, too late," he replied. He could see the golden sparks rising into space. With the fleet on the outbound leg of its attack orbit, no ground-launched interceptor was going to catch them in a stern chase.

"We have missiles inbound from the moon," Sensor One reported.

"What class?"

"They look like Bravo-Sixes."

Admiral Poledoris nodded. "Second line stuff. Just what you would expect from a backwater military base."

"Interceptors are breaking lunar orbit and heading this way."

"Destroyers to interdict. Intercept Plan Alpha. Have *Max Planck* start its bombardment."

The admiral watched as his forces moved smoothly to carry out his orders and felt a slight lifting of the weight that had ridden on his shoulders since the start of the action. The Carratyl system was living up to the expectations of Naval Intelligence – a pleasant surprise in itself. Unless the lizards had something up their non-existent sleeves, the moon base was as good as neutralized. The only thing left to do was to tote up the butcher's bill.

\#

# Chapter 9

Richard Drake lay in his acceleration couch and listened to the labored pounding of his pulse in his temples, along with all of the other noises that are present aboard a ship at high boost. Somewhere deep within the cylindrical core of *Conqueror II*, massive pumps were delivering liquid hydrogen to the engines, where it was being converted into an intense beam of pure light which drove the blastship toward its destiny.

The photon drive is the most efficient means of propelling a ship through space ever devised. In fact, it is the most efficient drive that is even theoretically possible. The drive's efficiency, measured in terms of its specific impulse, derives from the fact that the "mass" of photon is a measure of its energy content and not its "rest mass," of which it has none. *Conqueror II* and her consorts propelled themselves with beams of light that were fifty thousand times more efficient than the engines of the first space shuttles. Despite their efficiency, however, photon drives were not without their problems.

The primary problem was thrust. The first truly efficient space drives had used beams of ions accelerated to near light speed by electric fields. And while these "ion drives" were hundreds of times more efficient than chemical rockets, their inherent thrust was never more than a few thousand dynes. Photon drives were even more efficient than ion thrusters, and with correspondingly low thrust. To overcome this deficiency, *Conqueror II*'s engines had to spew forth trillions of photons every nanosecond, and even then, the ship's maximum thrust was barely one standard gravity.

For high-speed runs like the one they were on, a stream of superheated hydrogen ions was introduced into the raging beam of light to augment the ship's thrust. As a result, the massive warhorse gulped hydrogen at a rate approaching that of the early chemical rockets that were her distant ancestors. Luckily, hydrogen is the one element the universe has in abundance, and Strike Force Spica was accompanied by dozens of cryogen tankers.

The hum of the pumps was more sensed than felt, a barely discernible vibration that suffused the ship. Other noises were louder. There was the soft hum of the ventilators as they strained to drive denser air than normal through the ship, and the various clicks, whistles, and buzzes that have accompanied electronic displays since the beginning of the computer age. Then there was the subdued buzz of voices as the various technicians manned their duty stations despite the three times normal gravity that tugged at them. The mood aboard *Conqueror II*, which had been tense in the minutes before and after the last foldspace transition, had settled down into one of dull routine, which was a source of never ending amazement to Drake. That the human animal can be bored and in mortal danger at the same time shows the resilience of the breed.

"I have a report from Admiral Poledoris, Task Force Carratyl, sir."

"Read it to me," he replied with difficulty beneath the weight of three men sitting on his chest.

"Mission accomplished. Dogpatch defenses neutralized, Lunar Base destroyed. One ship moderately damaged. Message ends."

"Does he say which ship?"

"No, sir."

"Very well. Keep me posted."

Drake settled into the soft cushions that had long since ceased to be comfortable and contemplated the news. One more worry eliminated. Intelligence had rated the Carratyl naval base as a minor one, with a limited defensive capability and virtually no offensive striking power. Of course, Intelligence had been wrong on occasion. Not that Drake had been worried that they would stumble across the Ryall equivalent of the Rock of Gibraltar in this backward agricultural system. Still, it was nice to have one's opinions validated. It was not beyond the realm of possibility that a massive Ryall war fleet might have been visiting Carratyl, perhaps on the Ryall equivalent of a war bond drive. Or possibly, the lizards took their rest and relaxation lying in fields of alien grain, and the whole of the Ryall fleet might have been taking a break here in this system when human ships appeared.

Even the limited action that Achille Poledoris had fought at Dogpatch was more than Drake liked. The plan was to get as many ships as possible through to Spica without alerting the lizards. If they could do that, they stood a good chance of capturing the central foldpoints of the Ryall Hegemony. If they could not, then they stood a good chance of losing the war.

Although having things go perfectly to plan was a bit disconcerting. To quote an ancient maxim of warfare, "When things are going precisely to plan, you are obviously walking into an ambush!"

He failed to see how the steady advance of Strike Force Spica could be anything but good news for humanity. However, every force commander in history believed that same thing right up to the moment the trap closed on him. They had been in the Carratyl system for more than a week, and under high acceleration between foldpoints for most of that time. There had been little for him to do but lie in his acceleration couch and let his imagination run wild.

Behind *Conqueror II*, the sky was alive with human ships and more arriving every hour. If this whole expedition proved to be a trap, humankind would pay dearly for falling into it. When it came time to jump to Spica, fully half the combined star fleet would be concentrated in this one out-of-the-way system. If the Ryall had laid an ambush, the situation could quickly turn desperate.

The destruction of much of humankind's star fleet here in Ryall space was not the worst thing that could happen, however. The nightmare scenario was that the Ryall, unaware of their own danger, would choose this particular time to launch a major thrust into human space. That both sides in a century-old war would attempt a *coup de main* at exactly the same moment was improbable, but not implausible. The history of warfare was replete with cases where victory had gone to the army that held a few hours' advantage over its opponent. The Battle of Gettysburg in the American Civil War was but one example.

If the unthinkable happened, both invading forces would overwhelm defenses stripped bare by the offensive operations in progress. Both spear thrusts would likely drive deeply into the enemy heartlands and would rain destruction down on civilian populations. Such mutually assured destruction would be horrifically costly in terms of casualties and resources destroyed, and it would pose a conundrum for both sides. What does one do when notified that their home world is under attack? Does the fleet pull back and rush to the defense, or press the attack in the hope that the other side will break off operations and run for home first? What if neither side blinked?

Then there was the possibility that a Ryall thrust at the weakened defenses of human space would move too quickly for them to react. Drake had visions of his ships returning home from a successful operation to find their homes blasted into radioactive ruin. He could not help thinking of Bethany and little Ritchie lying dead in the rubble of Homeport while he was away laying similar waste to the Ryall home worlds.

He had been a soldier all of his life, although in a Navy that had not had an enemy to fight until six years ago. Until becoming a father (probably), he had not appreciated how much parenthood changed one's outlook. Suddenly, he wished that foldpoint between Alta and the rest of human space had never reopened. If the foldpoint were still closed, his people would be ignorant of the carnage among the stars... ignorant, but safe.

He stretched to relieve the high-acceleration-induced depression that threatened to engulf him. It was a common psychological reaction that accompanied bone-weariness brought on by high gees. It was no less real for being artificially induced. It was a battle every man and woman in the fleet had to fight alone.

#

Bethany Drake awoke in the middle of the night. Her bedroom was dark and it took a moment for her to orient herself. Then the clamminess of her skin and the cold dampness of the sheets brought her back to reality. She lay there with racing heart and cold skin, and wondered what it was that had jolted her awake.

She listened for the cry of little Ritchie, who still faithfully announced the arrival of the 03:00 feeding each night. Instead of the quiet, stuttering sobs that presaged a steady, loud wail, there were only the night sounds of Homeport. She listened for a moment to the hoot-whistle of a *bilrobin*, a colorful double-winged flying thing that made its home in the boughs of the *tontin* trees out front. The trees had been planted by Clarence Whitlow, her uncle, to celebrate her marriage to Richard, and he had squandered innumerable hours keeping them alive over the past six years. The native plants of Alta generally fared poorly when mixed with the imported earth forms that the earliest colonists had brought with them.

Nor did Bethany hear any other noises in the house. Whatever it had been that awakened her, it had left her covered in perspiration and breathing hard. She wondered if she had suffered another one of her recurring nightmares, although usually the memory of those was sharp and clear after they jolted her awake.

The basic dream was always the same, with only the details of the horror changing from night to night. She saw her husband on the bridge of his ship as she had seen him so many times on their twin expeditions together, first to New Providence and then through the nebula to Earth. In her dream, he was the strong, commanding figure she had fallen in love with.

Then, without warning, a Ryall torpedo struck the ship, which seemed to be his old command, the Altan cruiser *Discovery*, rather than the new flagship. In her dream, she saw the nuclear tipped death plunge into tissue-thin hull plates and erupt in fire. The million-degree heat, which in reality would take only a microsecond, erupted in slow motion in her dream. She saw Richard frozen in time, his mouth open to issue a command, when the nuclear fire burst through the bulkhead and began its slow, inexorable way toward him. In her dream, he had time to turn and see the approach of death, and with it, the determination in his eyes turned to fear, then to anger, as though fate had robbed him of his destiny at the moment of his greatest success.

The dream always ended the same way, with Richard's mouth open to scream, "*Nooooooooooooooo!*" just as the fire reached him and his flesh began to melt. It was always at that point Bethany woke up.

The wifely premonition at the moment of her spouse's death was a staple for holovision and bad romance fiction. In a universe where information was limited to the speed of light save through the foldpoints, and where relativity had repealed the laws of simultaneity, such premonitions had no possible basis in reality. There was no way for her to know when her husband died, no matter how much they loved one another.

That she could not remember the horror this time caused her even more discomfort than usual. Could it be that her fright was so great that her conscious mind would not hold it any longer? Recognizing that sleep would not soon come to her, and that the baby would need feeding within the hour, she slid from bed and pulled a nightgown around herself before stepping through the door onto the raised patio that adjoined her bedroom.

The house she and Richard had built was perched on one of the hills above Homeport. From it, they could see the lights of the city bisected by the broad band of the Tigris River. Antares was in the sky, and while not the electric-blue spark that it had been in the early days following the coming of the nova, it was bright enough to give competition to the larger of Alta's moons. The double illumination caused the river to sparkle with a silver glow, much as it had that night so many years ago when she and Richard had taken a respite from their lovemaking to venture out into the night sky and talk about their future together. That had been the night she told him of her desire to be married on Earth, even though they had not known at the time that they would ever find it.

Find it they had, and rather than being the solution to all of their problems, it had only brought them years of hard work and danger. She wondered if she would ever feel safe again.

The problem was that two different instincts warred within her. One wanted the fighting to be over... not next year, or next month, or even next week. She wanted it to be over NOW! Nor was she alone. The entire human race was sick unto death of war. If a cessation of hostilities could be arranged on the strength of wishing alone, the war would be over in the next nanosecond.

The second instinct was based higher in her brain. The first impulse was that of a frightened four-year-old girl inside of her screaming, "Daddy, make it stop!" The adult Bethany Drake, new mother, loving wife, and comparative historian, knew something of her species' tendencies when its survival was threatened.

She feared not only for humanity, but also for their enemies.

#

Phillip Walkirk, heir-apparent to the Sandarian throne, lay in his acceleration couch and pondered his own problems. His people's long history with the Ryall had earned the Sandarians a place of honor in the line of battle. The Sandarian Blastship *Royal Avenger* would lead their task force through the Carratyl-Spica foldpoint in the first wave, and would strike out to capture the Spica-Darthan foldpoint, the gateway to the capital world of the Ryall Hegemony.

It fell to Phillip, as tactical officer, to ensure that whatever ships and weapons came boiling out of that foldpoint while they were in the Spica System, did not break free. Not only was it his duty to ensure that the blockade held, it was his destiny. It was also a matter of personal honor. To hold the foldpoint was what he and his shipmates had pledged, and that they would, even at the cost of their own lives.

"*Royal Avenger* to *Conqueror II*," Phillip said, "we are in position and ready to jump." His voice sounded curiously dead inside the helmet of his vacuum armor. He and every other member of the Sandarian flagship's crew were at battle stations, with suits sealed and weapons hot.

"Good to hear that, Commander," Richard replied from the Fleet Operations Center. "Stand by a few minutes while we finish refueling the second wave." Like Phillip, the fleet commander's image was that of a regulation vacsuit helmet with only the name emblazoned above his visor to identify him.

"Standing by, Admiral."

It was irregular to have the fleet commander and the heir apparent acting as fleet communicators, but the occasion was special. Around Phillip hovered much of the naval power of the human race. In a few minutes, they would enter the heart of enemy territory and the element of surprise, assuming they still had it, would be lost forever. Whatever happened after they disappeared from this spot and reappeared in another nearly 100 light-years distant, there would be no turning back. The Rubicon they were about to cross was as wide as the cosmos, in terms of both distance and repercussions.

As he lay in his couch and listened to the quiet preparations for battle, Phillip could not help think of all the friends he had lost over the years. There had been Bertie Simes, his roommate at the Royal Academy, killed in the abortive attack to break the Ryall blockade of the Aezer System ten years earlier. He could still hear Bertie's patient voice droning on as he helped the Phillip sweat his way through hyperdimensional physics. There had been Sir Roger Peterson, Phillip's first commanding officer, killed at the Battle of Sandar. There had been Niles Dracon, who had survived a dozen battles, only to fall victim to a training mission. These three and all the others who had died too young and too far away from their loved ones, all because two incompatible species had been thrown together by a cosmic catastrophe.

His reverie was interrupted by a gruff voice in the earphones of his vacuum armor. "Report, Mr. Walkirk."

"We've been asked to hold, Admiral. Refueling of the second wave is still underway."

"How long is this hold?"

"Just a few minutes, sir."

"Well they had better damned well hurry. If the Ryall know we're here, every second could be important."

"Yes, sir."

The commlink went dead as quickly as it had come alive. Admiral Sergei Fallon Gower, Seventh Viscount of Hallen Hall, commanded Task Force Darthan from his flagship, *RSNS Royal*

*Avenger.* Phillip was glad to serve under him. In his opinion, Gower was the best admiral in the Sandarian navy.

The seconds turned slowly into minutes, until Drake's voice echoed on the 'All Hands' circuit. *"Attention, All Ships. Refueling is complete. You may resume planned operations."*

Phillip chinned his command link and said, "We're clear to maneuver, Admiral."

"Very well. Resume the countdown."

"Task Force Darthan. All vessels, report status and readiness to jump."

In addition to *Royal Avenger* and another dozen Royal Sandarian Navy cruisers and destroyers, there were ships from four other systems in Task Force Darthan. Included were the Alphan battle cruiser *Discovery*, the Terrestrial Space Navy Blastship *Kong Christian* and her consorts, and a smattering of vessels from other worlds in human space. The fleet numbered some 60 fighting ships, with another 20 auxiliaries — freighters, cryogen tankers, and tenders — accompanying them. Even at that strength, they were merely the down payment on the defensive globe they would build around the Spica-Darthan foldpoint.

When all ships had checked in, Phillip ordered them to slave their jump computers to *Royal Avenger*'s own. He checked their deployment on his status screen. Eighty gold sparks hovered in an irregular splotch of red haze, surrounded by some three hundred additional sparks just beyond the foldpoint boundary.

"Task Force Darthan ready to jump, Admiral..." he said, then keyed for the command circuit and reported that same message to Richard Drake aboard *Conqueror II*.

Both orders came back simultaneously. "You may jump when ready."

Phillip sent the signal that would release the jump computers on all ships. Suddenly, his voice was replaced by a computer generated one.

*"All ships, prepare to jump. Two minute warning!"*

Phillip reached for his suit harness and pulled the straps tight. Around him, technicians and sensor operators did the same. The ride was about to get bumpy and no one wanted to be floating around loose should the ship suddenly switch from zero gravity to the varying accelerations of battle maneuvers.

*"One minute warning and counting. Attention All Ships, one minute to jump!"*

Suddenly, he felt globules of sweat begin to form on his forehead. In micro gravity, sweat has nowhere to go. It just clings to the skin and surface tension causes it to spread out until it is a thin sheen all over one's face. Then, when the ship resumed acceleration, the sheet of liquid had a nasty tendency to end up in the eyes, where it burned and blinded.

"Thirty seconds... twenty... ten..."

Admiral Gower's booming voice cut in on the automatic countdown. "Attention All Hands. His Majesty expects victory. Prepare for jump!"

"Five... four... three... two... one... jump!"

#

# Chapter 10

Galatan of *Far Seeker* lay at his control station and absorbed the sensations of the ship around him. The far-off hum of the engines vibrated his tympanic membrane, as did the quiet hiss of the ventilators and the subdued sibilants of the crew. The slowly moving air carried with it the familiar taste of river rushes and the pungent odor-smell of pigments that had still not fully dried on the control room bulkhead. His oculars swept across the impressionistic displays that told him the health of his ship, where bright yellows outnumbered the dimmer colors of the high infrared. Galatan watched, listened, and let the molecules of life tingle his combined sense of taste/smell. He observed and knew contentment for the first time in recent memory. It was good to be in space again after a seeming eternity, first in the medical bays, and then with his ship in the orbital dockyards of Paraster. Both he and *Far Seeker* were again whole and hale, and ready to rejoin the hunt for two-legged monsters.

Life could not have been better.

On its last patrol, *Far Seeker* had been ranging free through the System of the Red-Orange Sun when Guardians spread the alarm that Monsters were boiling through the stargate. Many a valiant warrior had returned to the Ancestral Egg that day, but their sacrifice was not in vain. Those ships of The Race not on guard duty had come to the aid of the hard-pressed defenders. The counterattack had been massive, and the Monsters, who had seemed on the verge of a breakout, were contained — barely. Toward the end, the two fleets had nearly been within ocular range as they poured destruction into each other. Slowly, the Monsters were thrown back. A rear guard of theirs had fought ruthlessly as ship after ship disappeared back through the stargate. It had been near the end of the fight, when victory seemed assured, that an enemy torpedo detonated near *Far Seeker*'s hull.

The nuclear blast had been close enough to crumple tough hull plates as though they were eggshells thinned by summer heat. Twelve-cubed tail-lengths closer and the weapon would have vaporized *Far Seeker*. As it was, fully two-thirds of the crew was either killed outright by the blast, or suffered injuries ranging from broken skeletal elements to radiation poisoning. Most of the latter victims had not survived their injuries.

Galatan himself had spent five cycles in a medical facility recovering from burns and loss of gray corpuscles in his blood. The enforced idleness as he lay on his stomach with legs, neck, and tail immobilized had given him time to think between bouts of nausea. Some of those thoughts had not been suitable to one of the warrior caste. Indeed, they had not been worthy of a member of The Race. That fact had not prevented them from floating freely from within that portion of his brain that predated intelligent thought.

These thoughts of mortality and what might have been were unworthy of a member of Galatan's profession. A warrior was supposed to look death straight in the snout, unwavering and coolly calculating. He should not lay rigid in fright, like a grub hiding from a Swift Eater. Yet, that is precisely how Galatan had lain with his injured scales submerged in a regeneration tank. The fear had beaten in upon him like layers of mud oozing up to smother him. The medical technicians had assured him that the reaction was normal, a response to having so much of his circulatory fluid damaged by radiation poisoning.

Galatan had known they spoke the truth, at least on the level where his consciousness lay. It was that part of him below the level of autonomous control that refused to listen to reason. A warrior, his inner self had proclaimed, must be fearless. After all, unlike the Monsters, among The Race, warriors were not trained. They were hatched.

Those Who Watched Over the Eggs had decided that he would be a warrior a few hundred heartbeats after the female whose egg he was had deposited him in the warm, wet sand. The demand for warriors had been insatiable since the first Monster starships appeared in their skies. Special hormones were injected into his egg sac, hormones that triggered certain physiological changes in the newly laid hatchling. They improved his senses, gave him faster reaction times, and heightened his natural aggression. As is the case in most of life, however, these improvements were purchased at a price. Warrior caste hatchlings matured thirty percent faster than their worker caste counterparts, with life spans shortened by a comparable factor. The speed of maturation also left most warriors less mentally capable than the manager caste.

Galatan was one of the few warriors whose cerebral development had been normal, a fact that Those Who Raise The Young identified shortly after his egg hatched. After his quickness of mind was confirmed by test, he was placed on an accelerated training schedule. While his egg-mates learned their place as part of a fighting unit, he learned the art of command. Often during that rigorous training program, he lay on his bed of rushes at night and wondered what it would feel like to be a simple warrior, with no responsibilities other than his duties, and no weight of command on his dorsal scales.

It was a dream that had returned to haunt him many times while he waited for his body to mend, and later, as he had supervised the repairs on his mangled ship. It was a dream that even now hovered just below the level of thinking.

"Shipmaster."

"Yes, Pelanau?"

"I have anomalous readings from the stargate."

"Which one?"

"The Carratyl Gate, Shipmaster."

"What do you see?"

"There are several ships in the gate and more appearing each heartbeat."

"How many ships?"

"Two twelves, and increasing as we speak."

Galatan pressed long digits to controls and brought up the display on his command screen. Pelanau was right. There were numerous ships arriving in the stargate. In fact, there seemed no end to them. Traffic ought not be so heavy from an agricultural world, unless this was a scheduled grain shipment. Why so many ships at once? It reminded him of the convoys they had devised in the System of the Red-Orange sun to keep the Monsters from raiding their supply vessels...

At the thought of Monsters, Galatan flicked his tail in a nervous twitch and began configuring his screen for spectral analysis. It took only a dozen heartbeats to confirm his horrid suspicion. Another digit reached out and, suddenly, the dying scream of a *zanfish* was echoing through the ship, catapulting every member of his crew automatically into hunting mode. Around him, tails stretched taut even as necks twisted to swivel snouts in his direction.

He keyed for the command circuit as soon as the alarm sound died away. "Warriors of *Space Eater*. To your posts. Prepare for the hunt."

"What is happening?" Essenau, egg-mate to Pelanau, and his second in command, demanded from a small screen in front of him.

"Monsters! We have Monsters in the Carratyl stargate. They are pouring out in more than fleet strength! The Race is in mortal danger! To your posts. We have a battle to fight!

#

"Breakout complete, Admiral."

"Very well, Miss Powell. Give me a status report on fleet disposition."

Lieutenant Enid Powell, one of the first Alphan women to graduate from the newly reconstituted Starfleet Academy at Homeport, was quiet for a moment while radar signals returned from their long journeys to probe surrounding space.

"We have two hundred and eight ships in the foldpoint, sir. The Sandarians appear to be forming up and moving off in the direction of the Darthan Foldpoint, accelerating at three standard gravities. Second Wave is still getting organized. No concerted movement yet."

"Send an order for them to get their asses in gear!"

"Yes, sir."

"What about the opposition?"

"No enemy craft within the foldpoint, sir. Computers have identified fifty-six Ryall ships in view. Most are aligned in what must be the regular shipping lanes. None are close to us."

"Right. Show me Spica!"

Spica, the central star of the Ryall Hegemony, was actually two stars. The larger was a B1 spectral-class blue-white sub-giant some seven times the diameter and 11 times more massive than Sol. Its companion, Alpha Virginis-B, was a B2 class dwarf with a mass of seven suns. The two stars were close enough that it took only four days for them to complete one complete circuit around their common center of gravity. Like long time lovers, the pair embraced one another with long spiral streamers of star stuff, turning two individual fusion furnaces into a complex couplet of glowing plasma. The smaller of the two was noticeably egg-shaped due to tidal stresses. Complicating the stellar dynamics further, Alpha Virginis-A was a short-period variable with an improbably short cycle of four hours.

The ultraviolet-laden sunlight, the solar flux variations due to the four-day orbital period of the star couplet, and the four-hour pulse rate of the system primary, all conspired to rob any planets in orbit of any hope of life. If that weren't sufficient, as a pair of profligate, blue-white stars, the Spica twins had lifetimes measured in millions of years rather than billions — insufficient time for life to develop in even the best of environments.

Spica's worth was not as a nursery for life. Whatever planets orbited the two stars had environments that were surely lethal to unprotected human and Ryall alike. However, the concentration of 18 solar masses, along with the twisting of the fabric of space-time caused by the pair's high rotation rate, was nearly ideal for the formation of foldpoints. Where Antares, a much more massive, but far more diffuse star, had possessed only half a dozen foldpoints before going supernova, Spica was parent to eight foldpoints. Not only were there more foldpoints, they were much closer to the central stars, which translated into inter-foldpoint transit times substantially shorter than was normal in human space.

This latter fact, namely that ships in transit spent only days moving from one foldpoint to another rather than the weeks required in most human-occupied systems, had long served the Ryall war effort. Assuming the invasion fleet could gain control of all eight foldpoints, the advantage would switch to humanity. Once they gained control of Spica, it would be the Ryall who would have to travel the "long way 'round" to launch their attacks. Humanity would be able to shift forces at will using interior lines of communication.

"Beautiful," someone said over the command circuit as the stellar couplet came up on the screen. The solar flares were massive and complex, visibly flowing along lines of magnetic force. Gigatons of plasma in turbulent motion also produced a continuous background roar of radio noise that made communications circuits useless over a wide range of frequencies. Luckily, fleet communications did not require those particular frequencies — just one of the millions of details that had gone into preparing for this, the ultimate battle.

Gazing at the massive stars locked in their eternal dance; Drake was reminded of the surprise he had felt when they initially discovered that Spica was the linchpin star of the enemy's home space. For, like all stars with ancient names, Spica was one of the brightest in the terrestrial sky — Number 17, in fact. For thousands of years, his ancestors had gazed up at Spica where it hovered low in the nighttime sky of summer, wondering what mysteries it hid. If only they had known, they would have been considerably less lyrical about it.

The ever-changing patterns of plasma around the star couplet were hypnotizing. Drake found himself staring at it as he would stare into the flickering flames of a campfire while holding his wife close. He made a conscious effort to return his attention to the job at hand.

"Report, Mr. Considine." Commander Jerome Considine was his tactical advisor.

"The second wave is beginning to move out of the foldpoint, Admiral. The third wave is arriving."

"Anything on enemy shipping, yet?"

"We have three bogeys that may be military. One of them a probable, two possible."

"What are they doing?"

"Nothing aggressive, sir. Perhaps they are trying to figure out who we are."

"They know who we are, Commander. Our drive flares began advertising our identity the moment they lit off."

"Yes, sir. Then I would say they are spreading the alarm."

"So would I. Let's see if we can do something about that. My compliments to the captain. Tell him to get this tub moving."

"Aye aye, sir."

A minute later, the deep throbbing of the engines began again in Drake's temples, as weight returned to the ship. It was a gentle hand that pushed him down into the soft embrace of his acceleration couch. He savored the moment. That gentle hand would soon turn into the jaws of a steel vise that would attempt to crush him.

#

"What ships do we have in the system, Falada?"

"We have three twelves of freighters, another twelve personnel transport, a few miscellaneous craft, and two other hunter craft, Shipmaster."

"What hunter craft?"

"*Far Reacher* and *Home Seas*."

"Both of the third rank. Not much to work with in the face of the Monsters' entire fleet. Show me the distribution of all of our ships."

The screen in front of Galatan's lounging pad came alight, showing a schematic diagram of the Twin Suns. Around the island-symbols that were stargates lay a sprinkling of ship icons.

"What ship is that?" he asked, indicating a small glowing dot near the Darthan stargate.

"That is *Keeper of the Kelp*, a machinery transport en route from Darthan to Cor. It came through the stargate half a demi-cycle ago."

"What is its velocity?"

The sensor operator read off the value.

"Too high. He will never turn around in time. What of this other?"

The second point of light was an ore carrier inbound toward the home system. It was twice as far from the gate as the machinery transport, but at least it was moving in the proper direction.

"Tell *Mist of the Morning* that he is to dump his cargo and make for the stargate at maximum speed. Make sure that he understands that is a warrior-command and the fate of The Race is at stake."

"Yes, shipmaster."

One by one, Galatan studied the tactical situation and picked a ship to carry the alarm through the stargates to the worlds beyond. In three cases, he picked two ships. As he worked, he was aware that the Monster fleet was breaking up. Not surprisingly, they seemed to be dividing into eight groups — seven to englobe the seven stargates other than the Carratyl gate and a large cluster of ships that seemed to have no particular destination. This, he knew, would be their reserve force. They would position themselves at a central point where they could support any of the englobed stargates when the inevitable counterattack began.

As he watched the alien drive flares, he realized that he had never really appreciated the importance of the Twin Suns to civilization. This one system was the crossroads through which virtually all trade between home worlds passed. Yet, here he was with the full might of the Monster fleet arrayed before him and only three fighting craft were available to defend the most important piece of vacuum in the universe. At the least, Those Who Rule should have ringed each stargate with a dozen heavy fortresses.

"Shipmaster. Malan of *Far Reacher* is signaling."

"Send his signal to my station."

A screen lit to show a familiar, grizzled muzzle. "Galatan, old friend. You have seen them, of course."

"I have, Malan." Galatan then went on to explain the messages he had sent ordering the nearest ships to the stargates to spread the alarm."

Malan spread his ears in the expression of unspoken assent. "I learned that when I got through to the shipmaster of *Mist of the Morning*. He was angry about the loss of his cargo."

"I presume you emphasized the importance."

His fellow shipmaster emitted a rumble of mirth. "When I finished with him, he was trying to crawl back into the egg."

"Good."

"How did the Monsters reach Carratyl?"

"I do not know," Galatan replied. "To my knowledge, there is no stargate between that system and Monster space."

"It must have been a new gate created by that cursed Evil Star in their region."

Galatan signaled his agreement. Even though the light from the supernova in Monster space had not yet reached any star system inhabited by The Race — there had not yet been time — Those Who Observe the Skies had long known of it. They had postulated that an exploding star was responsible when alien starships first appeared in Home Space. Captured bipeds had confirmed their guess. It was easy to think of the star's death as a long ago event. It was easy, but wrong. The expanding nova shockwave was still wreaking havoc across the entire region, and would do so long after Galatan had returned to the Great Egg, even if he did so at the end of a long life — which did not seem at all likely.

Yet, somehow, the Monsters had gained access to a world that Galatan and The Race had long considered beyond their reach. A new stargate must have formed somewhere beyond Carratyl.

"What are we going to do, Old Friend?" Malan asked.

"Do?"

"Where will our lives best be spent to blunt this invasion?"

It was a question that Galatan had been considering. As a warrior, he had sworn to defend The Race with his life. Indeed, that was the whole reason for his existence. As one descended from a million generations of hunters, and those who had tracked the Swift Eaters into their very lairs, he could do no less. Yet, his cycles in traction while his radiation burned body healed had made him introspective. Perhaps it was mere cowardice, but he did not see what benefit The Race would gain by his spending his own life and that of his ship in the current situation.

"What is your fuel state?" he asked.

Malan told him.

"Not very much."

"We are inbound for rest and refit. You?"

"Just out of dock, outbound."

"Then you should lead the attack on the nearest group. We will support. Perhaps we can get *Home Seas* to join us."

"I will not attack."

The shock in his old friend's eyes was obvious.

"We must!" Malan replied. "The Race is depending on us."

"To what purpose? Can we last even a heartbeat against any of the groups now moving to englobe the stargates?"

"Are you suggesting that we turn tail and swim for safety?"

"No, Old Friend. I suggest that we expend our fuel to gain velocity in the direction of the Sky Dragon," he said, naming the most prominent constellation in the Darthan sky, and one still recognizable here in the Twin Suns.

"That is away from the enemy."

"It is, and if we gain enough velocity, they will not likely expend the energy to follow us."

"You wish to run away?"

"I wish to remain alive to serve Those Who Rule when they smash their way through the stargates. They will be blind to what awaits them. By not throwing away our ships, we can give them vital tactical information when the time comes. It may be the difference between victory and defeat."

"I think you are rationalizing your cowardice, my friend."

"Use your brain, Malan. We can attack now and be destroyed, or we can retreat, bide our time, and be of use when Those Who Rule summon our fleet and break the blockade. At the least, we can save our ships for that fight. Do you want our fleet to attack blind?"

"It will attack blind whether we are here or not."

"But we will be able to signal them as soon as they materialize in the gate. We can alert them to the Monsters' disposition and their strength. That information alone would be worth the sacrifice of a sub-fleet."

"Your injuries have clouded your mind. I suggest that you turn over command of your ship to your Shipmaster-Second and return to your soaking pool."

Galatan ruthlessly suppressed the anger — and shame — that Malan's words produced. "Do as you will, my old friend. My ship will begin boosting in the direction of the Sky Dragon immediately."

"Goodbye, Shipmaster Galatan," Malan said formally, signifying his disapproval. "My ship and I go to meet the enemy."

The abruptness with which the signal ended was as much a reproof as if Malan had snarled at him. Galatan felt a deep sadness with the thought that his friend was going to his death thinking ill of him. Every instinct told him to join Malan in a death charge against the group headed for the Darthan gate. Only his intellect told him that it would be wrong. He considered one last time what he should do, and then touched the control that would send his voice to every member of his crew. He opened his mouth to speak and found no sound would come out. He tried again…

The order he gave was the most difficult of his entire life.

#

# Chapter 11

Blastship *Royal Avenger* hovered motionless in space with every sensor at maximum and all weapons hot and ready to fire. Nearby, dozens of other ships did likewise. The mad dash across the system had been over for more than three days. Since they had arrived at the Spica-Darthan Foldpoint, all they could do was watch and wait, straining eyes and sensors into the blackness, waiting for the first sign of an enemy that was sure to come.

Suddenly, a distant pinpoint of actinic light burst forth from the blackness. Sensors reacted and warnings sounded, only to be quickly silenced. The tension in the Combat Information Center was palpable until a voice quietly announced, *"Thruster!"* The big compartment was too large for the collective sighs of the duty crew to be audible, but there was no mistaking the sudden slumping of shoulders as a dozen crewmen resumed breathing.

Somewhere in front of them, another member of their flotilla had just fired a station-keeping thruster to kill the slow drift caused by the gravitational pull of the blue-white stellar couplet half a billion kilometers below. That the quick burst of white-hot plasma had been seen at all was an indication of the sensitivity to which the sensors were tuned. That it had caused such a reaction was an indication of how taut everyone's nerves were strung.

"Damn it, Your Highness. Why don't they come?"

"Patience," Phillip Walkirk counseled the jittery spacer at the next station. The pimple-faced boy was barely out of training camp and on his first combat cruise. "They'll be here soon enough."

"But what the hell is keeping them? ... Uh, sorry about the profanity, sir."

Phillip smiled inwardly. It was a reaction with which he was all too familiar. When crewmen discovered that their commander was also heir to the throne, they generally reacted as though they had been caught at a state dinner without their pants. It usually took a few weeks for them to settle down and treat him as they would any officer. He decided that it was time to alleviate the tension, not only of this Sandarian farm boy, but also of several others within earshot, some of whom were veterans who should have known better.

"They'll be here soon enough, Simon," he answered louder than necessary, using Spacer Cadwallader's first name to put him at ease — at least as at ease as it is possible to be while waiting to be killed. "Remember, that star system beyond the foldpoint is as large as our own Hellsgate, and it has an even larger collection of planets. First, they have to receive the warnings, then they have to decide what to do about them, then they have to assemble the ships, possibly calling in reinforcements from the other two systems on this particular foldspace string. That takes time. Even if they have the ships on hand, the Darthan-Spica foldpoint is a couple of billion kilometers above their star. It is not easy to get to. That will take time as well."

Phillip paused and noticed several faces turned in his direction from the surrounding computer stations. Good. Nothing calmed an enlisted man or woman's fears faster than listening to someone recount a list of the enemy's problems. "Frankly, I hope they take all of the time they need. I won't mind if they wait until the orbital fortresses come up to join us. They must have made it through the nebula and are halfway across the Eulysta System by now."

There was a general nodding of heads. The invasion fleet of which they were part was one of the most powerful humanity had ever assembled, but the full six hundred ships on station and the equal number making their way in this direction would have trouble forcing a foldpoint guarded by orbital fortresses. Some of those big metal planetoids carried weapons to rival those found in a Planetary Defense Center.

Every man and woman in the fleet would have liked to have the orbital fortresses in their vanguard when they attacked Spica. However, the mad dash across three Ryall star systems had made that impossible. Most fortresses were capable of accelerations ranging up to a quarter-gravity, and possessed an ability to maneuver that could be charitably described as "lumbering." Any fleet that waited on them would arrive to find the Ryall aware of their approach and in full strength.

The long days at high acceleration had ended when *Royal Avenger* and her charges decelerated to take up station around the egg-shaped foldpoint leading to the Ryall home world. They spent their first several hours on station seeding the foldpoint with antimatter mines — short range, high-acceleration torpedoes that would attack any Ryall vessel the moment it materialized. After that, they had begun their vigil.

So far, the invasion had actually gone better than planned. Only two Ryall ships had attacked the invasion fleet while it was en route to blockade stations, and neither closed to weapons range before being destroyed. A third ship, tentatively identified as military, had uncharacteristically turned tail and run. Even now, it was moving away at a velocity that would make it difficult to catch. Numerous other craft, tentatively identified as freighters, were also withdrawing from the scene of battle, although at a much slower pace. All of these would eventually need to be gathered in, but that task was low on the current list of priorities.

Six other task forces had reached the remaining Spican foldpoints and englobed them, the last only twelve hours previous. Task Force Ssoltas's deployment had been interrupted by the sudden arrival of three Ryall ships in the Spica-Ssoltas foldpoint. There had been no time to ascertain whether the three were warships or merely luckless travelers. All three flashed into plasma seconds after arrival.

In Phillip's opinion, it had all been too easy to this point. Although an adherent of the Sandarian state religion — as the next head of the Sandarian High Church, he had to be — like most spacers, he had his own set of superstitions. He firmly believed the gods of war eventually balanced accounts, and the ease with which they had captured Spica could only foreshadow a series of terrible battle to come.

Even as he attempted to calm Simon Cadwallader's fears, inside him, a small, frightened boy was asking, *"When will they come?"*

#

"I relieve you, Your Highness."

Phillip glanced up from the hourly report he was composing for fleet command, startled at the sudden voice in his ear. He noticed Commander Salton Connors, officer in command of *C.I.C* next watch, hovering over him. He glanced at his chronometer and discovered that Connors was fifteen minutes early.

"You're fifteen minutes early, Sal. What's the matter? Environmental system go haywire in your cabin and you couldn't sleep?"

"Admiral Gower wants to see you."

"Right now?"

"Right now."

"Did he say what it was about?"

"Well, Your Highness," Connors began in an exaggerated West Glacier drawl, "I don't really think its my place to quiz the admiral when he says that he wants me to relieve an officer and tell that same officer to get his butt to the admiral's cabin. I leave that privilege to you 'quality folk.'"

"Very well, *Commander* Connors," Phillip said with mock formality. "I stand relieved."

Connors watched as he touched the SEND icon. "Anything for me before you go?"

"Nothing. The Number Three antimatter projector was displaying a warning fault when I came on duty. The crew is checking it out. Otherwise, everything is hot and ready to fire."

"It had better be."

Phillip made his way down the same hatch through which Connors had entered and pulled himself along a series of "barber poles" to Admiral Gower's day cabin. The admiral's booming voice ordered him to enter almost as quickly as he signaled.

"Your Highness. Good of you to come. How is the crew?"

"Jittery, sir. They wish the action would start."

"Me, too. This sitting and waiting can get on a person's nerves. Still, when the action does begin, we will all wish that they'd waited another month or three."

"You wanted to see me, sir?"

"How would you like your own command, Your Highness?"

"Command, sir?"

"That's what I said."

"A combat vessel?"

"The Light Cruiser *Queen Julia*. Her captain came down with the galloping crud during the speed run and the bastard's just now reported himself on the sick list. Goddamned poor time to get sick, if you ask me. His exec is too inexperienced to fight the ship in case of battle."

"Do you think I'm ready for command, sir?"

"More ready than most men your age, Your Highness. Besides, you will command us all someday, if you live, and there is no time like the present to gain experience."

"Then I accept, sir. I'm flattered and grateful for your confidence in me."

"Just keep that ship in fighting trim and my confidence will prove well founded.

"How soon do I take command, sir?"

"How soon can you get to the Number Three Boat Bay?"

"Ten minutes. I'll stop by my cabin, stuff my extra uniforms and some underwear in a kit bag, and head straight there."

"No need. I have had all of your belongings packed. They are in the scout that is waiting to take you now. No telling when the Ryall will come pouring through the foldpoint. I want you onboard and in control of that ship when they do."

"Yes, sir. Thank you, sir." Walkirk steadied himself with one hand on an overhead pipe and executed a perfect groundside salute.

Admiral Gower, who was seat-belted into his workstation rack, returned one just as crisp. The old man's eyes gazed into those of his young protégé.

"Take care of yourself, Phillip. We are going to need a king after this war is over, and I don't want to be the one to tell your father that you won't be coming home."

"You, too, Admiral. We need men like you to keep the beasties at bay."

#

Richard Drake was also nervous, although on a grander scale. Like virtually every other officer in the fleet, he could not believe how well operation had gone to date. In fact, things had gone so well that he wondered if he had overlooked something.

The one thing that he feared most was becoming overconfident. In battle as in most life situations, circumstances can change at the speed of light — and in this case, faster. He was reminded of all the commanders who had seen their brilliant, flawlessly executed plans fall apart because the enemy refused to cooperate. He could still remember the reedy voice of Captain Stuart, his military history professor at the Altan Naval Academy, as he lectured about a battle that, in its day, had been as daring as the raid on Spica.

"... When the Japanese Imperial Fleet attacked the United States Pacific Fleet at Pearl Harbor, Hawaii, on December 7, 1941, Standard Calendar, they fully expected to lose half of their aircraft carriers — you young midshipmen can read that 'blastship' if it makes you more comfortable. They expected this because they were attacking an adversary with two orders of magnitude more resources than their small island nation.

"To the Japanese' surprise, they found the Americans asleep – literally. Most of their naval personnel were in bunks below decks on a Sunday morning following a hard night of drinking and whoring. Many sailors died in those bunks. The Japanese Naval Aviators sank virtually every capital ship then at anchor at a cost of 29 planes shot down, 55 pilots killed, and one midget submarine sunk.

"The Japanese fleet then made good their escape. Can anyone tell me what happened next...?"

Drake, who had seen an ancient movie about the event in his secondary school history class, had tentatively raised his hand.

"Yes, Midshipman Drake?"

"I believe the Japanese lost the ensuing war, sir."

"That they did. Can anyone tell me why?"

There had been general silence in the classroom.

"Because, my poor little midshipmen, *they attacked a nation with two orders of magnitude more natural resources!* In fact, many maintain that the attack on Pearl Harbor was the greatest tactical success and strategic disaster in the history of warfare. What the Japanese imperialists forgot was that wars are won on the factory floor, and in the fields, and in the bellies of fusion power reactors. Which brings me to my lesson for the day: 'Never irritate an enemy with the power to squash you like a bug!'"

"*... Never irritate an enemy with the power to squash you like a bug!*" Those words echoed in Drake's ears.

That he had irritated the Ryall was not in dispute. Now they were waiting to discover how much power they could bring to bear.

They had done all they could to strengthen the defense. They had seeded seven foldpoints with 70,000 antimatter mines. Seven task forces clustered around their seven foldpoints, ready to pour laser, antimatter projector, and missile fire into any force that materialized in their sights.

The strength of the task forces were allocated based on military intelligence's guess as to the strength of the star systems behind the foldpoints. The largest collection of ships was allotted to Sergei Gower and his Sandarians englobing the Spica-Darthan foldpoint. The second strongest force was assigned to the Spica-Talintan foldpoint, and so forth. *Conqueror II* had 80 ships around it, including the spare tankers and ammunition carriers. These were the reserve force, ready to support any Task Force as needed.

It should all work. In fact, the computers guaranteed that it would work — assuming the Ryall cooperated and played their part. As he sat and pondered his distribution of forces, Richard could hear the silent voice of a long-dead Japanese admiral saying, "It should work if the Americans play their part."

#

*"Ten-hut!"*

As Phillip rounded the last turn to the airlock leading to Boat Bay Three, an honor guard of Royal Sandarian Marines in battle armor sans helmets snapped to attention, their boots locked to the gridwork deck to keep them from floating away. He stopped and returned their salute, more awkwardly than in Admiral Gower's office. A dozen gauntleted hands snapped to rest position as the sergeant of Marines completed his salute.

"Thank you for the honor, Sergeant. Do you give all officers this sort of sendoff when they go to a new duty station?"

"No, sir. We heard you was coming and sort of organized this spontaneous-like."

"I thank you, but I don't think now is the best time for you to be away from your posts."

"No problem, sir. We are the damage control party for this section. Our post is right here. That's why we are all in armor."

"Very well. Have my pilots arrived?"

"Yes, sir. They are inboard the scout, checking it out. Your kit is onboard, too."

"Thank you. Carry on."

The curious Marines watched as he moved through the airlock and into the scout ship. Both his kit bag and his vacsuit were aboard. The suit was strapped into a seat as though it were a fellow passenger. He glanced at the helmet to make sure that it was indeed his — excited enlisted men had been known to make horrible mistakes when packing for others — and then proceeded forward to the pilot compartment. One of the pilots was a lieutenant – first grade. The other was a young blonde woman, an ensign. Both looked very young.

"Your passenger has arrived. You may launch when ready," he said as he strapped himself into the jump seat between the two.

"Wouldn't you be more comfortable in the cabin, Your Highness," the Lieutenant asked with proper decorum.

"I would be more comfortable where I can see out," Phillip replied.

"It's orders, sir. Passengers are to ride in the cabin."

"You can't make an exception for your future king?"

The two gave each other a look that Phillip recognized from long experience.

"Very well, Your Highness. Strap down and prepare for launch."

Two minutes later, the scout boat shot from the side of *Royal Avenger* into free space.

As they made a sweeping turn around the ship, Phillip looked over the old blastship with affection. She had been his home off and on for five years and it seemed strange to be leaving her on the eve of battle. On the other hand, he had dreamed since entering the Royal Navy of a ship of his own, and though the circumstances were not what he had dreamed, he would take one any way he could get it.

Being a future king was one thing, and being the commander of a ship in battle was another. A king could be good or bad at his job. There were functionaries, assistant functionaries, and assistant-assistant functionaries to isolate him from the consequences of his mistakes.

The commander of a ship in battle had no one. If he fought well and was lucky, he emerged victorious. Even if he were killed, those whose job it was to study battles would know whether he had done his duty. If he were foolish, or unskilled in the art of command, tactics, or ship handling, then they would know that, too.

As one groomed for command since infancy, Phillip relished the opportunity to test himself against a standard that could not be finessed to make the heir to the throne look good. The coming battle would prove him a man worthy to rule, or it would prove that he was not. Either way, the interests of Sandar would be served.

"Shall we take the direct route to *Queen Julia*, sir?" the blonde ensign asked. Her voice carried a twinkle in it that told him she was joking. His new command was on the other side of the foldpoint, and any attempt to cross directly to her would undoubtedly draw the attention of an antimatter mine.

"The roundabout orbit will be fine, Ensign."

"Yes, Your Highness."

The engines coughed to life for a dozen seconds and the scarred hull of *Royal Avenger* fell astern. Over the next half hour, the engines popped numerous times as they skirted the fleet, always being careful to stay outside the invisible surface along which the task force had deployed. All of the task force's weapons were pointed inward at the empty volume of space that defined the foldpoint. That would be no place for a scout boat if battle erupted during their crossing.

Despite his excitement, Phillip soon found the boat's journey monotonous and drifted off to sleep. Secured as he was in the jump seat, his arms floated free in the bent-up position a human arm assumes when relaxed in micro gravity. At a gesture from his copilot, the lieutenant swiveled his head to look at the lightly snoring future king, then exchanged knowing smiles with her. After that, they kept their conversation to a minimum.

Half an hour later, the female copilot softly called out, "Your Highness, wake up!"

Phillip emitted a short snorting sound, and then straightened.

"We're here, sir. There's *Queen Julia*," she said, pointing.

Through the armor glass was a toy ship, a cylindrical design with a series of cylindrical fuel tanks around her waist. Forward were multiple bumps and openings that were the working end of the space cruiser — the particle beams, lasers, and missile launchers. Two large parabolic antennas pointed into the center of the foldpoint, and other clusters of sensors focused there as well.

"She's beautiful..." Phillip began, and then stopped with his mouth open. Far off in the black, something had exploded in a point of violet-white radiance. A second, and then half a dozen more quickly followed the first explosion. Suddenly, the empty vacuum seemed as full of firebugs as a winter night in the Royal arboretum.

The two pilots sat transfixed as ever more explosions lit the black sky across nearly the full hemisphere in front of them. "What is it?" the female copilot asked.

"Antimatter mines! There are ships in the foldpoint. The Ryall attack has begun!"

He opened his mouth to order them to get him to his ship when the universe was blotted out by a blast of actinic light.

#

# Chapter 12

Richard Drake was in the shower when the alarms began aboard *Conqueror II*, having just come off duty. He swore as he slipped legs still soaking wet into a shipsuit and fumbled to close the seams. Then it was feet into ship boots, out the portal and hand over hand for the *F.O.C.*

"Status report!" he snapped as he belted himself into his acceleration chair in his personal duty station high above the operations deck. The Admiral's aerie was known colloquially as "The Tank", and from it, he could command every ship within communications range.

"The Ryall are probing the Darthan foldpoint," Lieutenant Commander Parkinson, his Chief of Staff, reported over the command circuit. "We had several dozen craft materialize simultaneously and they began spewing missiles in all directions. The mines whittled them down some and we returned fire. The survivors then disappeared again."

Drake nodded. "Reconnaissance probe, all right. Did they do any damage?"

"They got in a lucky shot. Sandarian Light Cruiser *Queen Julia* was hit. No report yet on casualties."

"Damn!"

"It's begun, Admiral."

"That it has. Alert all ships and all task forces to the action. Tell them to look for any signs of coordinated attacks. The Ryall may have a communications system we know nothing about. Get me Admiral Gower on the command line. What is the time delay between here and the Darthan foldpoint?"

"Twenty seconds each way, sir."

"Slow, but workable. Let me know when you have him. Make the response code, 'if tactical situation permits.' We don't want to jiggle his elbow at a critical moment."

"Yes, sir."

It took two minutes, but eventually, the Sandarian admiral's features were staring out of a command screen at Drake.

"Report, Sergei."

There was an interminable delay, following which Gower's immobile features came to life and said, "Forty-eight craft appeared in the foldpoint, Admiral. We destroyed thirty-seven before they recharged their jump fields and beat it the hell back home. They spewed missiles and laser fire in all directions while they had the chance. They hit one of our cruisers. The ship is off the air, so we have no information on damage. Radar and visual sensors indicate that *Queen Julia* is still there, but messed up pretty bad."

When Gower fell silent, Drake said, "Sorry to hear that, Sergei. Still, it was inevitable that we would take casualties. Why the long face?"

Again the wait. When the Sandarian admiral resumed his end of the conversation, it was with evident pain. "*Queen Julia's* captain came down sick. I gave the command to the Crown Prince. He left here an hour before the attack. He was scheduled to arrive aboard *Queen Julia* about the time she was hit."

It took a conscious effort for Drake to control his reaction. The thought of Phillip Walkirk dead left a cold chill on his skin. Still, he had no time to grieve. More pressing matters were at hand. "Do what you can for that ship, Sergei, but tighten up your defenses first. If they are probing you, they probably have a full scale attack laid on."

Long wait, followed by, "Aye aye, sir."

The screen went dark and Drake returned to his primary duty, which was worrying. Not for the first time he wished someone would invent a communication system not subject to speed-of-light delay. Coordinating a battle that covered an entire star system would be a lot easier if he and his commanders could talk to one another in real time. Since the most resistance was expected at the Darthan Foldpoint, he had positioned the reserve force closer to that one than the others. Even so, at a range of six million kilometers, it took too long to react to changes in the tactical situation. If he needed to reinforce Gower, the reserve force would take two days to get there, and it was just as likely that they would be required somewhere else.

Therefore, seventy ships would have to fend off whatever force the Ryall were about to throw at them. All Drake's force could do was mop up any Ryall ships that managed to break free of the foldpoint.

#

The scout boat bucked as though buffeted by strong winds and then began a slow yaw to port. Along with the sound of "hailstones", pounding their hull came the prolonged roar of attitude control thrusters as they fought the sudden rotation. In the control cabin, three sets of eyes struggled to see anything beyond the fuzzy green blob that danced in front of their retinas.

Whatever it had been, it had been close. Too damned close! Luckily, the optical coating on the outer surface of the armored windscreen had performed its function. Over the course of milliseconds, it had gone from perfectly clear to nearly opaque. Fast as it was, the sudden change had not been fast enough to prevent a sharp stabbing pain in their optic nerves.

"What the hell happened?" the male pilot asked.

"*Queen Julia* took a missile," Phillip replied as he blinked his eyes rapidly to clear them. Big globules of tears were forming in the corners, which did not help his ability to see. "Either that or they took a near miss. Get on the radio and see how bad it is."

The female copilot began punching controls, cycling through the fleet frequencies not drowned out by the twin suns half a billion kilometers below them.

"Nothing, Your Highness. Orders from fleet to tighten up the perimeter, but nothing from *Queen Julia* herself."

"All right ... what the hell are your names?"

"I'm Lieutenant Osmond Delson, sir. This is Ensign Tamara Mason."

"All right, Delson. Keep her steady. Mason and I will get into our suits. When we are ready, the ensign will relieve you so that you can get into yours. I want us buttoned up and vacuum tight in three minutes. After that, we will close with my ship and look for survivors. Questions?"

There were none. The tone of command in Phillip's voice ensured that there would not be. It was a tone he had learned from his father, and which had been reinforced by years of service in the Royal Navy. When everything is going to shit around you, he knew, it was important that the officer in charge sound like he knew what he was doing. If he also *knew* what he was doing, so much the better!

Phillip and Ensign Mason both arrowed through the rear hatch. Phillip moved to where his vacuum suit lounged like a paying passenger, unconcerned with the recent excitement. He unbuckled it, opened the clamshell hatch, and then pivoted in midair.

Donning a vacsuit in micro gravity is nearly impossible when the suit is not clamped down. He struggled with it anyway. He was still struggling when Ensign Mason, already in her own battle armor, came up behind him and held the suit steady while he slid his feet into the jointed metal legs. When he had the rear hatch closed and pressure integrity, he chinned the speaker control and said, "Thanks."

"Don't mention it, Your Highness." She continued forward, disappearing into the pilots' compartment. Lieutenant Delson appeared a few seconds later and arrowed toward the scout ship's suiting locker. He was back a minute later, encased in vacuum armor.

"What next, sir?"

"Let's approach dead slow, just in case the point defenses are still online. They've been shaken up and no telling what mode they're set in."

"Right."

Delson disappeared forward, leaving Phillip in the passenger compartment. He would like to have followed the pilot, but this was one time regulations had to be obeyed. The pilots' compartment was too small for three people in vacuum armor to fit comfortably, and it would not help his chauffeurs to be crowded during the approach.

Mostly he wanted to get to his ship, assuming that he still had one. In command for less than an hour, and already his ship had been shot out from under him. "Not a good omen," as his mother would say.

Mason's voice echoed in his earphones. "No sign that the point defense is active, Your Highness."

"Then bring us along side. How does it look?" he asked. The passenger compartment was windowless and the bulkhead viewscreen did not turn on when he activated it.

"Bad, sir. The bow is crumpled in. We can see big rips in the outer hull. There are a couple of bodies floating free in space."

"Suited bodies?"

"Negative."

He nodded. Not knowing how long they would have to wait for the Ryall to appear, the fleet had gone to Yellow Alert soon after englobing the foldpoint. That meant that they did not have to live in the uncomfortable, bulky suits. It also meant that they would take more casualties if the attack came without warning. In retrospect, Phillip thought, those spacers aboard *Queen Julia* now floating in vacuum would probably have preferred the discomfort.

One good thing about this situation — it was doubtful that anyone in the task force was currently lounging about in his or her shirtsleeves.

There were a series of thruster burps somewhere over his head and a tug of artificial gravity before Delson announced, "We're alongside, sir."

"Alongside, where?"

"Number Six Cargo Hatch. It looked to be the least damaged."

"Very well, secure us to *Queen Julia*, and then the two of you come back to give me a hand. Where are the medkits?"

"Second locker aft of the midships airlock, sir."

"Right. Let's get started."

#

The scout's airlock cycled open in silence as soon as they spilled the air inside to. The three of them were a tight fit, even more so when their suits puffed up around them as the air pressure dropped. As soon as the door opened, Phillip's faceplate automatically darkened.

Sunlight in the Spica system bore a striking resemblance to that put out by an arc welder. It hurt his abused eyes even with the aid of the polarizer. A meter in front of him was the cargo hatch surrounded by the yellow-and-black striping that identified its function. Aware of the taste of bile in his mouth and the stink of dirty socks in his nostrils, Phillip extended his armored arm and pressed the switch plate to the right of the door. To his surprise, the plate turned from green to amber, indicating that the lock was functioning.

"Good sign. It works."

A minute later, the outer door swung open to reveal the interior of the big cargo lock. Here, too, everything looked normal.

"Come on. Let's get inside," Phillip said. He and his two companions floated from the scout boat's lock into the airlock of the larger ship. Lieutenant Delson pressed the inner control and the door closed as silently as it had opened. Everything happened in silence until a sudden rush of air buffeted their suits and the indicator light turned from amber to green. The inner airlock door swung open of its own accord.

There was air inside. That was obvious from the thick haze of smoke that enveloped them. In micro gravity, smoke fills the whole volume available to it. There is no tendency to form a layer. Inside the airlock door floated two spacers whose necks were obviously broken, and a third writhing in pain. Just above the bloody knee of his shipsuit protruded the jagged white end of his thighbone.

"Mason, sedate him!"

"Yes, Your Highness."

"Delson, with me."

The two of them pulled themselves to the main fore-and-aft passageway. They did not move very far forward before they encountered a closed emergency door. A quick check of the telltales indicated that there was no air on the other side.

"What now, sir?"

"We work our way aft to see if we can hook up with the survivors. Then we see what we can do about pulling this ship out of the line. We'd be a sitting duck if the Ryall hit us again."

"What about Aft Control? They may be all right."

"Lead on."

Phillip followed the pilot as they made their way through corridors illuminated only by emergency lighting. Here and there, they saw figures moving through the haze or at the end of distant corridors. As they passed the big, vault-like door to the engineering spaces, Phillip poked his head inside. The engine room held small clusters of vacsuited men whose helmets dangled at the ends of lanyards. They were working on the massive engines, attempting to get them back online.

Finally, they reached the aft control room. There they found half a dozen spacers. A few monitored sensor arrays, while most worked feverishly to bring additional instruments online.

"Who's in charge here?" he demanded over his suit speaker.

A harried looking lieutenant straightened up from where he had been hunched over a display, and said, "I am. Who are you?"

"Commander Phillip Walkirk, newly assigned C.O."

"Oh, sorry, Your Highness. I didn't recognize you in the suit. I'm Harvey Weintraub, Executive Officer and temporarily in command until your arrival."

"What happened here, Mr. Weintraub?"

"We took one in the gullet, sir. One minute we were coolly picking off Ryall ships in our sector of responsibility, the next the deck comes up and smacks me in the face. I'm afraid things get a little hazy after that."

"What were you doing down here in Aft Control?"

"The captain abandoned sick bay as soon as the alarms sounded, sir. He sent me down here. He took charge of fighting the ship until... until..."

"Never mind." It was obvious the young man was on the verge of tears. Considering what he had been through and the number of friends he had just lost, Phillip didn't blame him. "How many survivors?"

"I don't rightly know, sir."

"Don't you think we need to find out?"

"Uh, yes sir. Just haven't had time. I thought it important that we get back on the air and contact fleet command. You understand, sir."

"I understand completely. Which of these men aren't doing something vital?"

"Spacers Garnet and Aviola, sir"

"Very well. Garnet, Aviola, you go with Lieutenant Delson and find Ensign Mason, who we left at Cargo Hatch Six, and the four of you sweep every part of this ship that holds air. Tell everyone you find to report to us here in Aft Control. Then one of you get a count in engineering. They seemed to be organized in there."

"Yes, sir."

"Now move. Lieutenant Weintraub, let's see if we can get that radio working again. Admiral Gower needs to know that we aren't all dead here."

#

"Commander Walkirk from *Queen Julia* for you, Admiral."

"Patch him through!"

Sergei Gower said a short prayer to whatever god ruled the battlefields of space. He understood the need for the heir to the Sandarian throne to risk his life like any other spacer in the Royal Navy, but he wasn't just another spacer. Gower dreaded having to compose a "message of regret" to His Majesty even more than he dreaded the Ryall fleet that would soon descend on them.

"Your Highness, you're alive!" he blurted out when Phillip's static-speckled features appeared on his screen.

"Yes, sir. We were approaching the ship when she was hit. Other than a few persistent spots dancing before my eyes, I suffered no injuries."

"Not even radiation exposure?"

"No sir. We have checked our personal readings. They are well within safety margins. I didn't even need to wear my lead underwear today."

"How is your ship?"

"A mess, sir. She is open to space everywhere forward of Bulkhead 50. The captain and the bridge crew are all dead. We have 65 survivors, of whom 40 can still function. The others are suffering a variety of contusions, burns, and broken bones. The doctor thinks that most of them will live. The exec is alive and now assisting me to get control of things."

"Can you fight?"

"No, sir. Fire control is gone. Most of our missile launchers are knocked out of alignment, and we only have two operational lasers. Engines are back online and we can maneuver at maybe a quarter-gee. Request permission to pull this hulk out of the line as a hazard to navigation."

"Permission granted, commander. Do you need any help from the rest of the fleet?"

"Not at this time, sir. We will make for the repair ship *Brandywine* to see if they can patch us together enough to get us operational again. Once we get the hull sealed, we ought to be able to do something useful, say like carry the mail... the lighter packages, anyway."

"All right, Commander. Pull well back from the foldpoint defense line. We don't want to mistakenly waste missiles on you. They cost money, you know. Good luck and report in periodically. Remember that I am still personally responsible to His Majesty for your safety."

"Aye aye, sir."

The screen went dark and Gower opened a commlink to his communications officer. "Send a flash message to the two ships flanking *Queen Julia*. She is pulling back, leaving a hole in the defenses. Have them close up and take over that quadrant."

"Close up and cover *Queen Julia*'s retreat. Aye aye, sir."

Gower sat back and breathed a sigh of relief. That was one less problem on his mind. Getting an injured cruiser back into service could take weeks, even with the services of a repair ship. It would be a good project for the young prince, teach him the value of hard work, and most importantly, keep him out of the line of fire for a while.

Feeling as though a weight had been lifted from his shoulders, Gower returned to reviewing the Ryall attack. He hoped that by analyzing the enemy's tactics, he might be able to predict what they would try next.

The first anyone had realized that the enemy was in their midst had been when an antimatter mine detonated in the center of the foldpoint. Apparently, one of the materializing Ryall craft had popped out almost on top of it and set off an explosion more quickly than the radar returns could bounce back from the targets that had not been there a millisecond earlier.

Four-dozen Ryall craft had appeared simultaneously in the foldpoint and immediately began spitting armament at the heavens. They had been dumping missiles so fast that he suspected they hadn't even preprogrammed them for a target. They just wanted to flood the volume of the foldpoint with ordnance before the carriers themselves were destroyed, and then rely on the missiles' own targeting capability to seek out and destroy human ships. In one case, that tactic had proven effective.

One thing that the playback of the short, one-sided battle demonstrated, the intruding Ryall had not been large craft. In fact, they had all been about the size of human destroyer, or smaller. As Gower had diagnosed at the time it was happening, this was not a serious attempt to break free of the foldpoint. No, this had been a reconnaissance in force, an attempt to gage the degree to which the human fleet had fortified Spica.

They got their answer at the cost of three-quarters of the attacking force, but had learned a great deal in the process. Presumably, the survivors were able to count the number of blockading ships and get some estimate of their type. They knew about the antimatter mines and might be able to devise a countermeasure. Most importantly, they knew the tales of human invasion of Spica were true and would just be waking to the mortal danger that fact presented their civilization. The knowledge that they had a limited time to retake Spica would cause them to redouble their attacks. They would need to dislodge Gower's ships before humankind had time to bring up reinforcements. That meant that the real attack would not be long in coming.

Nor was it. Even as he thought the words, his communicator sounded an urgent warning, "Something's happening in the foldpoint, Admiral."

"What?"

"We have a single bogey. Large. It just appeared. Two mines have attacked it and have been destroyed."

"Tell all ships to fill the foldpoint with missiles, random seekers. Stand by to open fire with beam weapons. Put the bogey on the screen."

The view that appeared on the main viewscreen was of blackness. Gower could see nothing. Then, a bright light appeared at the point where radar painted the bogey. The light expanded into a spherical shell of pure sunlight. It expanded and kept on expanding until it was impossibly large. Time slowed almost to a halt as Gower watched the shockwave race outward toward his ships. In the blink of an eye that seemed an eternity, the glowing ball of radiance dimmed and then dissipated well short of his command.

Gower had seen this tactic before. He knew what was coming next!

#

# Chapter 13

"Antimatter bomb!"

The Ryall had opened the Battle of Sandar with the same tactic. The bomb did not use the few milligrams of antimatter contained in the mines with which human forces had dotted the foldpoint. Within its magnetic containment field was stored a ton or more of the volatile substance.

The antimatter bomb that touched off the Battle of Sandar had been devastating. It destroyed several ships guarding the foldpoint and blinded every sensor pointed toward the detonation. That blindness allowed the invading Ryall fleet to fight their way free of the foldpoint defenses and had very nearly cost Sandar its existence.

The bomb in the center of the Spica-Darthan foldpoint was intended to blind Gower's ships just as the one at Sandar had done. However, human engineers had not been sleeping. One of the highest priority projects during preparation for the invasion had been the development of sensors that would withstand the radiance from a big antimatter bomb. Rather than being permanently disabled, the blockading fleet's sensors were back online the instant the blast dissipated.

The Ryall were more successful in their secondary purpose. Within an enormous volume of space, the ravening shockwave of high-energy gamma rays vaporized everything from the occasional dust particle, to the antimatter mines that defended the foldpoint. The result was a clear void into which arriving Ryall ships could jump in relative safety.

When humanity's sensors came back online following the blast, they discovered the foldpoint alive with Ryall ships. There were at least 200 of them!

"All Ships! Fire at will. Take the nearer ones first. The ones in the center will require a few minutes to clear the foldpoint."

Suddenly, black space was alive with Sandarian glow bugs. Five years in preparation had given the human fleet an offensive punch out of all proportion to its ships' size or numbers. Laser beams flashed invisibly through vacuum to focus on the hulls of opposing ships. Geysers of superheated plasma leaped skyward in the wide dispersion cones characteristic of explosions in vacuum. Most of these incandescent geysers were produced when ablative armor boiled furiously. Microscopic glass crystals in the armor dispersed the laser beams, momentarily reducing their punch. However, as soon as the lasers punched through to hull metal beneath the armor, spectral analyzers recorded the sudden appearance of iron in the incandescent plume, followed by oxygen and water vapor.

Nor were the Ryall ships passive targets in a cosmic shooting gallery. Lasers flashed outward as well as inward. Other holes were punched and other white-hot geysers erupted, this time from the outer shell of human ships. Sometimes there were other molecules in the superheated plasma, molecules that moments earlier had been living, breathing human beings.

On both sides, antimatter projectors sent their beams of particles forth at the speed of light. Electrically neutral atoms of antimatter hydrogen raced outward from the glowing mouths of projectors at nearly the speed of light. They drilled a hole in space until they encountered the hull of a ship. When they did, not even the anti-radiation shielding that had allowed the fleet to traverse the Antares Nebula was effective. Anti-proton encountered normal proton and powerful gamma rays sprayed forth to destroy whatever they encountered in their path. Any living being caught in that deadly zone of invisible radiance died. Computers fared little better. No matter how well shielded, the sleeting radiation ate away at delicate memory circuits, just as it did to their organic counterparts.

Then there were the weapons of brute force – the nuclear tipped missiles. Every ship in both fleets recoiled from the continuous launches as exhaust plumes impinged on their hulls and eye-searing points of light raced away on twisting, curving paths toward the enemy. Their kin from the opposing fleet intercepted most of these brutes in mid-flight. Still, some got through on both sides.

Although outnumbered, the human ships were able to hold their own against the invaders. In a foldpoint slugfest, the defender has certain inherent advantages. One of these is that they have time to prepare for battle and take up positions of mutual support.

The side that must arrive via foldspace jump is always at a severe disadvantage. No matter how carefully positioned a fleet is prior to a foldpoint transition, at the end of their jump, they find themselves scattered at random across the foldpoint. It takes precious seconds for the fleet commanders to comprehend where their ships are, and long minutes to flee the enemy's killing zone within the foldpoint, minutes in which much of the fleet can be smashed.

Nor was their formation humanity's only advantage in the fight. In addition to sowing the foldpoint with antimatter mines, Gower's ships had dispersed thousands of decoys throughout their formations to confuse enemy sensors. The Ryall had no such luxury. Being newly arrived, they had not the time to spoof the enemy sensors, nor would it have done any good if they had. Since their primary job was to exit the foldpoint as quickly as possible, spewing decoys out into space would have done nothing save leave a trail of decoys in their wake to mark their passage.

Nor had the initial bomb destroyed all of the antimatter mines. Beyond the effective radius of the blast, Ryall ships had as much as a one in ten chance of running into the small, high thrust weapons. More than once, Admiral Gower watched a Ryall ship, its lasers, projectors, and missile launchers blazing, suddenly disappear in a blast of atomic fire.

The carnage suffered by the invaders was lopsided for another reason, one that took Gower a moment to identify. Some of the Ryall craft were curiously quiescent. They accelerated for the foldpoint boundaries like their brethren, but they did not fire at the defenders. At first, he thought they were holding fire until they closed the range on the human fleet, but even those well within range seemed curiously pacific.

Understanding hit him like a bolt of lightning.

"Attention all Ships. We have Trojan horses here. I repeat. Some of the ships are decoys to draw our fire. Attack anything that shoots at you. Hold fire on the others until you have nothing of higher priority."

Two hundred ships are a lot for one star system to scrape together in less than a week. However, once control of a foldpoint has been lost, regaining its possession is the highest priority. For an enemy in control of one of these chokepoints in space can only get stronger. Whatever commander had sent this fleet to attack Sergei Gower's task force had cheated a bit. He had gathered every warship within range, and had supplemented their numbers with noncombatant craft, the better to diffuse human fire. While the task force was dealing with the decoys, the real warships could concentrate on killing human vessels and escaping out into open space where they could maneuver.

Nor was the battle going all humanity's way. Within seconds of the antimatter bomb blast, one of the defenders on the opposite side of the foldpoint exploded. Then another, and another, and then two more. Gower's force killed far more Ryall ships than it lost, but they were paying a price for their victories. That price was sufficiently high that a weak spot appeared in their defensive globe.

"We have breakout, Admiral!" the tactical officer declared.

"I see that. Tell the fleet to concentrate on the ships still in the foldpoint. We'll let the chasers take care of any ships outside our lines."

Suddenly, as quickly as it had begun, the battle was over. There were no Ryall craft left in the foldpoint, at least none that were alive. In the confusion, some twenty had broken through the quadrant where once had been the Terrestrial Navy Heavy Cruiser *Neverwhen* and the new Sandarian Cruiser *Duke Bardak*. Now those two ships were expanding clouds of plasma, and with them, a thousand brave men and women. According to sensors, some of the Ryall vessels had jumped back to their own system. These had mostly been the non-combatant decoys, the commanders of which had risked their ships to sow confusion, and were now attempting to save them.

As adrenaline continued to pump through his veins, Sergei Gower surveyed the carnage and decided that he could claim a victory... this time.

                                    #

Gower was not the only one who watched the battle with interest. Far above Spica, another pair of eyes noted the white flash of an antimatter bomb in the Darthan stargate and the subsequent lightning flashes of the deadly conflict that erupted in its wake. Galatan of *Far Seeker* felt a surge of excitement as the hoped-for counterattack of The Race began. Those few minutes of titanic violence in the stargate were the only moments of hope he had experienced for many cycles.

Galatan had not been sleeping well. Nor eating. Nor even existing. Every gland in his body had rebelled against the decision to avoid battle with the Monsters. It was not in the nature of a Ryall warrior to flee from battle. In fact, it was the worst obscenity he could imagine. Had Matanar fled when his clan was attacked by packs of Swift Eaters? Had Borada given ground when the voracious monsters invaded his Sept's breeding grounds? Neither of these legendary ancestors had turned away from battle. They had attacked without hesitation, and despite grievous wounds, had beaten back the ancestral foes of The Race.

What would future generations of hatchlings learn of Galatan? That when faced with an overwhelming force of the bipedal monsters, he had turned tail and swam away? The disgrace would be eternal. His name would be a cautionary tale for as long as The Race lived, just as Matanar and Borada were known to all even a thousand generations after their heroic deaths in battle.

Repulsed by what he had done, even his body had rebelled against him. Food would no longer stay put in his upper stomach sack, nor would his raging hormones allow him to sleep. As a result, his scales had taken on a deathly pallor and his eyes, once a healthy ebon, had turned gray. Even his joints ached, as though he were an elder who could do nothing but lie in the hot sand and dream of the conquests of youth.

The memory of what he had done seared his brain. At the sight of so many enemy craft in the central system of his race, he had wanted to send his ship hurtling into one of those tight little knots of vessels to wreak as much havoc as he could before being blasted from the sky. That is what Malan of *Far Reacher* had done. It had been glorious to watch. Heedless of his own safety or that of his ship, Malan had brought *Far Reacher* through a wide, sweeping turn and had taken aim at the group of Monster ships headed for the Darthan stargate.

Yet, glorious as the maneuver had been, it had also been for nothing. Before *Far Reacher* closed to weapons range, it had quietly disappeared in a flash of brilliance that emphasized the pointlessness of it all.

Despite his lack of appetite, his unhealthy complexion, and his insomnia, Galatan's brain continued to tell him that he had done the right thing. As *Far Seeker* continued to rise high above Spica's ecliptic, Galatan's sensors had been busy. His warriors charted what they could of Monster forces, noting with depression that they seemed to have control of seven of the eight system stargates – the eighth being the gate through which the Monsters had arrived. Presumably, the Carratyl gate did not require guarding since the Monsters occupied the system beyond. This presumption was confirmed every period as more and more enemy ships poured through to reinforce the Monster forces already here.

The Monsters' formations appeared to have three basic functions. The largest formations were those that englobed the stargates. These were largely invisible now, submerged in a sea of decoys that confused Galatan's sensors. They had been highly visible during their speed runs across the system. The strength of each group of blockading ships varied, and that fact depressed him as much as the shame at having avoided battle. It was to be expected that the strongest blockade group had headed directly for the Darthan gate, but the other groups had each seemed sized properly as well. That the Monsters knew the relative strength of The Race's forces behind each gate said that they possessed information to which they had no right.

A second formation of Monster ships hovered near each gate, but was separate from the ships on blockade duty. These seemed to be support craft - tankers, ammunition ships, foodstuffs and other consumables. However, a core of ships in these support groups were warcraft – judging from the spectra of their drive flares. These, Galatan realized, were the out swimmers. They would hunt down and attack any ship of The Race that managed to fight its way free of the ambuscades surrounding the gates.

Finally, there was a large formation on station far from any gate, but centrally located with respect to all of them. This was obviously the reserve force.

Having counted the Monster ships and cataloged them by type, he was now anxious to get this information to Those Who Rule. He did not know how he would accomplish this, and that, too, burdened his mind. He had information vital to the defense of The Race and he could not get it to those he served. Or was the information as important as he thought? Perhaps he was merely rationalizing his decision to run. Were his current thoughts the result of wisdom, or merely his own cowardice speaking to him?

His emotions had been at their lowest ebb when fighting broke out in the Darthan stargate. His cabin had echoed with the sound of a long hunting whoop when some of the attacking warcraft broke through the Monster blockade. It was difficult to tell with all of the distractions of battle, but it appeared that a twelve or more of The Race's ships made good their escape.

Happier than he had been in days, Galatan signaled for the warrior on duty in the control sphere.

"Yes, shipmaster?"

"Have you been watching the battle?"

"Yes, shipmaster."

"Begin plotting a course that will allow us to join our fleet with minimum fuel expenditure. We will send Those Who Command our information and then rejoin the battle."

"Yes, shipmaster. It shall be done!"

#

"Officer to see you, Admiral!"

Drake glanced up from the screen before him. Inset into the hatch to his space cabin was another screen. On it were the features of the Marine who guarded his door and kept unwelcome visitors from disturbing him. Something in the Marine's manner told him that he would not have done so now had this merely been a casual interruption.

"What officer, Yablonski?"

"Commander Walkirk, Royal Sandarian Navy, sir."

"Send him in!"

The hatch slid silently back into its recess, revealing the vacsuited figure of Corporal Lubo Yablonski, his helmet and riot gun both floating in front of him at the end of their short tethers, within easy reach. Behind him floated Phillip Walkirk, looking much less dapper than the last time Drake had seen him. The prince's uniform was rumpled, he was in need of a shave, and his eyes were sunken and had dark bags under them.

Despite his appearance, the heir to the Sandarian throne executed a flawless zero gravity entrance into the presence of a superior officer. He pulled himself along the handholds inset into the overhead and then used his arms to rotate his body into a semblance of an upright position. He even managed a salute while holding himself braced between overhead and deck.

Drake, who was seat belted to his desk, returned the salute even though that was not the custom in the Altan Navy.

"Your Highness, sit down and relax. You look like it's been awhile since you slept."

"Thank you, Sir. That it has."

"I hear you have your own ship now. Congratulations!"

"Thank you, Admiral. She's a fine ship, save for the fact that just about everything is gone forward of Bulkhead Fifty."

"And your crew?"

"Most are in shock at the loss of friends and messmates. The good news is that they aren't brooding. They haven't had the time. Everyone worked eighteen hours a day to patch things up on the orbit in. Now that we have the services of an orbital repair ship, we hope to get her spaceworthy enough that we can limp to a real orbital shipyard.

"Then you plan to take *Queen Julia* to Corlis?"

"About the only thing I can do, Admiral."

One of Admiral Belton's highest priorities was to move several of the big space docks from human space to Corlis orbit in order to repair battle damage and get vessels back into the fight. In his reply to Drake's last status report, the admiral had reported that the first dock was nearly ready to receive customers.

"It's not the only thing you can do. I'm sure Sergei Gower would assign another captain if you asked."

"Not on your life, Admiral. I have a ship of my own and I plan to keep it."

"Surely the heir to the throne can expect command of a Royal Navy vessel relatively early in his career."

"Of course. And you know just what sort of a ship it will be. Nothing too small or too large, a corvette or a destroyer, perhaps. The crew will be handpicked by the Admiralty, which means by my father. They will all be exceptionally competent fellows and every one of them will report directly back to my father's ministers. Hell, if I even fart on the bridge, the Council of Ministers will know what it smells like before the purifiers have a chance to scrub the air clean.

"No, I have a ship... a real ship with a real crew that needs me. Damaged though she may be, I would not trade her for the biggest blastship in the fleet. Even the crew is starting to forget that I am crown prince. Working alongside a man until you can barely stay awake will do that for you, you know."

"That it will," Drake agreed, nodding. He remembered a few cruises of his own that had been like that. "You gave both me and Admiral Gower a fright when the report came in that *Queen Julia* had been damaged. How close were you when the missile exploded?"

"Not close enough to worry the court physician about the future quality of the royal sperm, sir; but closer than I ever care to be to a nuclear explosion again. It's been nearly a week and I can still see the glowing green afterimage if I close my eyes."

"You'd better get your vision checked then."

"Already done, Admiral. I am a full 10-10. The afterimage is purely in my head. I suspect it will never go away."

"I suspect so." Drake let the smile slip from his lips, signaling that the business portion of their interview was at hand. In truth, he would have liked to spend an evening talking to the prince, say in a booth in the compartment that was, for no apparent reason, always dubbed "Ten Forward" aboard a human warship. However, everything aboard a ship in vacuum is rationed, even the time of the fleet commander.

"What can I do for you, Your Highness?"

"We've been pretty much out of touch en route here, Admiral. Among the things my ship is missing is most of its communications gear. I was wondering if you could tell me how bad it was at the foldpoint during the second attack."

Drake leaned back in his seat and steepled his fingers in front of him. It was an unconscious gesture of which he was completely unaware.

"In tactical terms, it was a smashing victory. Your task force took on an enemy nearly three times its size – well, twice, if you discount the Trojan horses mixed in with the actual warships – and defeated them decisively. About a dozen broke free of the foldpoint and Hunter Force Darthan is now pursuing them. They won't last long unless they hightail it for the system outskirts to join their fellow refugees.

"However," Drake said without pause, "our smashing victory means there will be 1200 families getting letters over the next few weeks, and 1200 good men and women who won't be seeing the stars of home. "

"Yes, sir," the prince replied somberly. "Have you a copy of the casualty list?"

Drake reached into his desk unit and popped out a reader crystal. "Here. I suspect you knew some of them."

"Yes, sir. I suspect that I did."

"You know," Drake said, "it's one hell of a way to run a universe."

"Yes, Admiral. That it is."

#

# Chapter 14

The Altan countryside was a'shimmer with a silvery glow as the groundcar came over a rise and out of the shadow of the escarpment known as the Homeport Hills. The forest around them turned instantly from dimly perceived tree trunks shrouded in the gloom of night, to black obelisks limned in silver surmounted by a glittering canopy of broad leaves. The reflective leaves were a twinkling lightshow as they fluttered in the gentle night breeze. Here and there through a break in the trees, a distant silver patch marked one of the ponds and small lakes that bordered the Tigris River down in the valley.

"I can never get over how bright it is," Olivia Southington remarked to Bethany Drake from the front passenger seat of the car that was quietly climbing the tortuous highway toward the summit where Homeport's elite made their homes. "What was it like in the days after the nova shockwave first passed Alta?"

"It looked like an electric arc welder had risen in the sky. We called it Antares dawnlight. We used to have a devil of a time getting the children to sleep while the nova was up. Luckily, children are very adaptable. After awhile, they took it as just another detail of daily life."

"Yes," Olivia replied. "Children make life worth living. What of little Ritchie? Is he sleeping all night now?"

"Yes, thank God! One of the things I miss with Richard being away is the ability to kick him out of a warm bed to go tend the baby at 03:00 hours."

"Just that one thing?" a male voice asked from the back seat in a tone that left no room to mistake his meaning.

Bethany felt her ears grow warm and was glad that the only illumination was from the car's instrument cluster. "There are other compensations to married life that I miss as well, Jorge."

Señor Santiago had hinted from time to time that if she were lonely at night, he was available to take her mind off her troubles. So far, she had managed to pretend that she didn't recognize the implications of his comments, although she knew that he knew that she knew... It was just one of the things that made being a member of a species with two sexes interesting. Besides, if rumor were to be believed, he had his hands full with Consuela Aragon, who was the fourth passenger in the car.

"So who is this woman whose party we attend this evening?" Santiago continued, oblivious to the sudden silence that had descended in the car.

"Evelyn Mortridge is one of the leading members of Homeport society. If someone is important on Alta, he or she usually ends up at one of Mrs. Mortridge's soirees. In fact, it was at one of her parties that I first met Richard."

"Who will be here tonight?" Olivia asked.

"The usual political crowd, of course. They will be talking about how high the war taxes are. Perhaps the captains of a few of the Terrestrial Space Navy ships in orbit will have been invited, along with their young officers to make the local maidens happy. A leavening of university professors and other professionals, some of Evelyn's upper crust friends for variety."

"All I am interested in is whether there will be booze," Santiago muttered in Bethany's ear. She could smell the *avarato* he'd had for lunch on his warm breath, which was wafting against her right ear.

"There will definitely be booze, Jorge."

The conversation was cut off as the big turbo climbed a final section of steeply rising road, and they found themselves atop the hill. Three hundred meters ahead on the left was a well-lighted house. Bethany slowed the ground car and turned into the curved driveway.

Two liveried attendants opened all four doors of the car almost before it stopped. Bethany swung her glimmersilk-clad legs out and pressed the control that would send the car to the parking area before climbing to her feet with the assistance of the attendant.

She stepped up on the curb and stopped to adjust her shawl. After a 125-year hiatus, Altan fashions were once again tracking those of Earth and she was not sure that she liked the current trend to bare shoulders, especially on a night that was signaling the imminent arrival of winter.

She started up the steps toward the lighted portico. Olivia followed close behind, while Jorge Santiago gave his arm to his assistant and followed at a more leisurely pace. Evelyn Mortridge was waiting at the top of the steps.

"Bethany, so good of you to come! How is the baby?"

"A little hellion, Evelyn."

"How old is he now?"

"He will be three months next week."

"I will have to see the little dear the next time I go down to the city."

"He's at the institute most days. Stop by sometime and I'll see you get the VIP tour."

"Is that wise, my dear?"

"Is what wise?"

"Exposing the child to that *thing*? God only knows what diseases it carries."

"Varlan isn't a thing, Beulah, nor is she an it. She is a Ryall and we know quite a lot about the diseases she carries. One thing we know is that none of her microorganisms will live on human biochemistry. If anything, Ritchie is safer around her than he is with the human staff."

"You let him in the same room with... her?"

"Sure. She even holds him and gives him his bottle sometimes, although she doesn't like it much when he spits up on her. The smell of used milk makes her nauseous, you know. Come to think of it, it makes me nauseous, too."

Her two decades of hostessing had taught Mrs. Mortridge how to change the subject. Instead of encouraging Bethany in her defense of that... that... *beast*... she turned instead to Bethany's companions.

"And who do we have here, my dear?"

"Mrs. Mortridge, I would like to introduce three colleagues of mine, all from the University of Buenos Aires, on Earth. Dr. Olivia Southington, Dr. Jorge Santiago, Señorita Consuela Aragon. They are a xenology team here to study Varlan."

"Buenas noches, my friends," she said, reaching out to take Olivia Southington's hand.

Olivia smiled. "I just work for the university, Mrs. Mortridge. I am not of Latino descent, myself."

"Buenas noches," Jorge said when it was his turn to greet their hostess. "Your welcome is most gracious." He took her hand and leaned over to kiss it, causing the matron to twitter.

"Do you still speak Spanish in your home country, Señor Santiago?"

He nodded. "In our homes. For business, of course, we speak Standard, just like everyone else."

"How charming. We have nothing like that on Alta. I have always wanted to visit Earth to experience the diverse cultures. It gets so boring having everyone just like oneself, don't you agree? Earth has long been a hobby of mine, reading about it that is. I never thought I would actually be able to go there.

"Well, enough of my monopolizing you charming visitors. My guests inside will not forgive me if I keep you any longer. Please make yourself at home. *Mi casa, es su casa*, I believe the expression goes."

"Thank you, good lady," Jorge purred. "I could not have said it better, and your accent is nearly perfect."

They passed inside just as another car pulled to the curb, impressing Bethany with the smoothness of the handoff.

"Quite knowledgeable," Consuela said, "even if she mangled the syllables. Why would someone on your planet learn Spanish if it is not spoken here?"

"I sent over your names this afternoon when I RSVPed. Obviously, Evelyn spent some time at the computer earlier today."

"Her skills as a hostess are well honed. She would fit in well at a faculty tea back home."

"Do they gossip at faculty teas?"

Olivia laughed. "Why, my dear, they do little else!"

There was a crowd inside the entrance hall and the strains of some tune Bethany did not recognize wafted from the back of the house. The music was emanating from a live band, Bethany knew. Evelyn Mortridge's parties never used recordings.

Jorge Santiago, with his arm wrapped around Consuela's waist, sauntered off in search of the bar. Bethany gestured for Olivia to follow her and led her into the main ballroom, where small clumps of people were standing around with drinks and talking to one another in that way that had been true of cocktail parties since time immemorial.

She spotted a familiar white-haired figure and gestured for Olivia to follow. "There's someone here I want you to meet."

Her target, who was half-facing in their direction, observed their approach and turned toward Bethany with open arms and a broad smile.

"My God, Child, you get more beautiful with every passing month. Motherhood becomes you."

"It has certainly filled me out in places, Uncle," she said as she embraced him and kissed him on the cheek. "There is someone I would like you to meet."

"Olivia, this is my Uncle Clarence. He was responsible for my upbringing after my parents were killed."

"Uncle Clarence," Olivia said, shaking hands.

"Oh, sorry," Bethany said hastily. "Olivia Southington, Clarence Whitlow, Hereditary Terrestrial Ambassador to Alta, and by the grace of God and his own good offices, the current Ambassador Emeritus."

"A truly important man," Olivia said.

"Hardly. They let me wear the sash on official occasions, but my First Secretary does all the real work."

"Come now, Uncle. You know that you are the best man for the job."

He nodded. "Considering that the job is coordinating our war effort with the Terrestrial Navy and the fact that I am a local who happens to know where all of the bodies are buried, I suppose so. If this were a normal diplomatic post, they would have put me out to pasture as soon as a real terrestrial diplomat got off the first ship from Earth. Still, the job has its perquisites, including invitations to Evelyn Mortridge's parties. She never invited me when I was just a pathetic old man who refused to believe that Alta was forever cut off from the Mother World."

"No one ever thought you were a pathetic old man, Uncle."

"Obviously, you don't travel in the same circles I do, young lady."

"What *are* you doing here tonight? I know you don't like these things."

"I'm doing my duty as usual. There is some skullduggery on Parliament Hill and I am here to ferret it out. In fact, you know the chief skullduggerer.

"Hello, Bethany," a familiar voice said from behind her. She turned to discover that same smirking smile that she had once found so attractive.

"Hello, Carl. It's been a long time."

#

Once upon a time, Bethany and Carl Aster had been engaged. That had been before a certain dashing starship captain had come into her life and had taken her away to far-off lands.

"How have you been?"

"Busy. The Prime Minister has been working my tail off up on the Hill. And you?"

"I work every day at the Institute."

"Still hope the little beasties will see reason?"

"They are a lot more intelligent than people give them credit for, Carl. It isn't all instinct. If it were, they would never build starships and they wouldn't have fought humankind to a standstill this past century."

"Still, you have to admit that their xenophobia is inherent!"

"That, it is. However, their tendency to attack anything that threatens them can be short-circuited. In fact, Varlan and Olivia were discussing just that subject yesterday."

"Really?" Carl asked, turning to Olivia. Bethany hurriedly introduced them before Olivia answered the question.

"While my colleague studies the Swift Eater legend, Mr. Aster, I am studying conflict resolution among the Ryall. They have quite a sophisticated system of obligations and duties among their clans, much the same as was developed on Earth during the Age of Chivalry. They even have a custom similar to the widespread belief among primitive humans that it isn't nice to kill someone after they have broken bread with you... at least, not until after they have left your camp. They call it 'Clan Honor.'"

"So the Ryall eat bread, do they?" he asked while lifting one eyebrow in an exaggerated questioning look.

Olivia laughed. "I can see why Bethany found you so charming. No, obviously, I was translating my findings a bit for my audience. The Ryall eat fish... squiggling, slimy, putrid-smelling aqua forms with tentacles, at any rate. Personally, I can't think of anything quite so disgusting."

"I think I agree with you," he said with a mock shudder before turning back to Bethany. "How go things at the front?"

"I don't know any more than you hear on the news broadcasts, Carl."

"What, they don't give the wife of the fleet commander special briefings?"

Bethany noted that Carl's emphasis on the word 'wife' was a little stronger than it should have been and wondered at his true feelings about losing her to Richard. "No, of course not. Loose lips sink ships, you know."

"Frankly, I don't know what all of the fuss is about. We're all humans here, aren't we?"

"Are we?" Olivia asked.

"What do you mean?"

"I mean, how do you know the Ryall aren't spying on us?"

"I don't see any six legged centaurs lurking around, unless you count Bethany's pet," he replied.

"Varlan is not a pet..." Bethany began before closing her mouth with a snap.

"They don't have to be here on the surface, watching us. It would be just as easy to sneak a ship through the foldpoint undetected and monitor our broadcasts."

"How could they slip a ship in undetected?"

"They've captured enough human ships to rig out a spy vessel. They could come through openly as a freighter or something, and then conveniently disappear en route to Alta. In fact, they may already have done something like that."

"Sounds farfetched to me."

"It probably is," Bethany answered, "but don't make the mistake of underestimating them."

"You're really into this shit, aren't you, Beth? How about my borrowing you for a minute to go talk to some people who are here this evening. That way, I can feast my eyes on your beauty just a while longer."

"Who are they?"

"Party people, mostly. They've an argument going about what we do after we conquer Spica. Some of the ideas being bandied about have spent less time in the oven than a loaf of barely browned dough. It will be good having an expert join the discussion."

"I'm hardly an expert and I really don't want to intrude in party business."

"Nonsense. You have logged more time with a Ryall than anyone else on the planet. There are serious decisions being made here tonight. It would be good for those making those decisions to hear another point of view."

"All right, Carl, but I'm leaving if any of them start to yell at me."

"They won't. I promise."

#

# Chapter 15

Evelyn Mortridge's home, like most of the mansions in the Homeport Hills, had been built in a style that had been popular three centuries earlier on Earth. Bethany had heard through the grapevine that a visiting terrestrial had called the house 'quaint' during one of Evelyn's weekly soirees and had nearly pierced the hostess's veil of hospitality. Having been born on Alta herself, Bethany could understand Evelyn's pique.

In the big room just beyond the library lay the main hall with its oversize fireplace and massive mantle. A fireplace was as much an extravagance on Alta as it was on most other worlds, and one that burned actual wood was even more so. That, of course, was why Evelyn Mortridge had one. How else to separate oneself from the common people except through the conspicuous display of wealth?

Gathered in front of the fireplace, but far enough from the roaring fire that they would not be toasted on one side, stood a familiar clump of partygoers. Bethany recognized most of them from the days when she accompanied Carl to Conservative Party functions.

The heated conversation halted when she, Carl, and Olivia Southington joined the group. Carl did the introductions all around, which took more than a minute. When it was over, Galston Highe, a member of parliament with a reedy voice, was the first to speak.

"Bethany Drake? Wife of Admiral Drake?"

"Yes, sir."

"Your husband made all of us proud when he was given operational command of the fleet."

"You can thank Grand Admiral Belton for that. I understand he thinks rather highly of Richard."

"We are indeed honored that you chose to join our little forum."

"Is that what this is?" she asked in her best imitation of a wide-eyed ingénue.

"Whenever two politicians get together to discuss the day's legislative agenda, it's a forum."

"Unless fists are thrown," a woman MP from the smaller continent replied, "in which case it's a brawl."

"... Or a riot," another member of the group interposed.

Highe ignored the banter. "Your husband and all the young boys and girls of our fleet have acquitted themselves quite well during these past few months."

Several of those around Bethany murmured their assent.

"Thank you for your support of my husband and those under his command. I will include your sentiments in my next letter."

"We would appreciate that, Mrs. Drake," Highe said smoothly. "Perhaps you can also relate to him our concern that this war be brought to a swift and successful conclusion."

"He needs no instruction on that point, sir," Bethany replied with a hint of frost in her voice.

"No offense was attended, I assure you," the MP went on smoothly. "It's just that we have been... discussing, shall we say... how best to conclude the hostilities. We have been wondering if there is an end game for this invasion of ours."

"The 'end game,' as you call it, has been clear from the first. We seize Spica, drive a stake in the heart of the Ryall economy, and wait for their civilization to fall apart."

"Don't get me wrong, Mrs. Drake. Your husband's plan has worked beautifully up until now. We have our foot on the necks of those scaly bastards and so long as we can keep it there, we will achieve our long-term objective. The question is whether we can afford to wait for nature to take its course. Perhaps we should take a more activist role in the process."

"Activist role?" Bethany asked. "We are destroying their ships as quickly as they pop out of the foldpoints. How much more 'activist' can one get?"

"The best defense would be a better offense. At least, that is what my side of the argument maintains."

Galston Highe's voice had been getting louder and his tone sharper as he warmed to the subject. It was thus a shock when a softer voice interposed itself into the momentary silence. "What are the current projections for economic collapse?"

Bethany turned to the gray-haired woman beside her. She had been introduced as Garnet Price, member from Nova Haven.

"Optimistic estimates are that it will take two years before they begin to run out of essentials to support their war machine.

Current pessimistic estimates are that they will be able to hold out for a dozen years, although with diminishing effectiveness."

"A dozen years," Price mused. "And we have been in control of Spica for what... eight weeks now? How many of our people have been killed in that time?"

"The latest casualty total is 8526. That includes all of the campaigns, not just the Spica operation."

"More than eight thousand killed in two months. We can't very well sustain that level of casualties for ten years, can we?"

"We cannot. Nor will we need to," Bethany replied. "Our strategists have mapped out the Ryall response to our invasion, and losses should decline as the Ryall weaken."

"A couple of their recent attacks nearly succeeded," Highe said. "According to the latest dispatches from Spica, the fight for the Cor foldpoint was a near thing last week."

"Oh, I hadn't heard about that one," Bethany said. "Casualty lists in yet?"

"No. They should be along with the next scheduled message sloop. I'm sure there will be more mothers, wives, and daughters weeping for their fallen loved ones this time tomorrow."

The MP's words sent a chill up Bethany's spine. The logical half of her brain told her that Richard's flagship had probably been millions of kilometers from the fighting. The unreasoning half, the part where the little girl terrified of the dark still dwelt, believed the worst, namely that the next time a message sloop materialized in the Val-Napier foldpoint, it would be carrying a message of condolence for her and Little Ritchie.

"If we have barely been able to stave off these desperation attacks, how can we hope to withstand a concerted assault?" a newcomer to the group asked. He had not been introduced and Bethany did not recognize him.

"Hopefully, we'll have the orbital fortresses in position by then," she replied. "When we have their firepower at our disposal, we should be able to beat back any force the Ryall throw at us."

"But we'll take casualties," Highe insisted.

"Of course. Casualties are an unavoidable part of war."

"What if they never stop attacking us? What if we have misconstrued their capabilities? What if they come up with the counter to our brilliant plan and attack us here at home while we have so much of our power tied up in the Spica operation?"

"I take it," Bethany said, "that you have a solution to that problem."

"We do, " the MP said. "We don't wait for the laws of economics to finish them. While we have them helpless, we go into their systems with overwhelming force, and wipe them out one at a time.

"Wipe them out how?"

"By doing to them what they have done and tried to do to too many human planets. We bombard them with every nuke we can scrape up, and then rain down antimatter bombs until their home worlds are nothing but vast fields of cooling lava."

"You're talking about exterminating them," Bethany replied as she tried to keep control of her temper.

"Damn right I am. Exterminate every one of the beasties, I say. Exterminate them before they exterminate us."

#

Engineer-Captain Mikhail Borisovich Andreev sat strapped behind his oversize desk and worked to peel off a few more items from his overflowing day list before his VIP visitor showed up. Extending beyond his office in every direction were the slate gray bulkheads and oversize machinery of Orbital Shipyard Delta Seven, recently departed from orbit around Halcyon IV, and now in orbit about Eulysta II, known to its former owners as Corlis. That, at least, was the human transliteration of the unpronounceable Ryall phonemes that made up the true name of the planet.

At its most basic, an orbital dockyard performed the same functions as its groundside counterparts. It just did so in micro gravity. Delta VII had the ability to build anything up to a light cruiser from scratch, and with some monkeying of the cradles with which it enveloped its wounded patients, could perform major surgery even on one of the big blastships.

At the moment, the big dock's restorative hangars were empty, and its first customer was to be a mere light cruiser, which didn't seem to justify the epic journey through the nebula that Andreev and his men had just completed.

A space dock is not quantitatively different in function from any other spaceship. To be effective, it had to have compartments conditioned to shirtsleeve environments in which its crew lived. Unlike a planet-based dock, one of the big spherical dockyards had to be mobile so that it could be moved to where it would be most useful, which meant it required power reactors and both normal space and jump engines.

In a war that extended across dozens of star systems and hundreds of light-years, it was unreasonable to expect a wounded ship to return to the place of its birth. It was more efficient for them to jump one or at most two systems back from the front lines and be repaired close to the scene of battle, the better to return as quickly as possible to the fray.

The fleet currently taking a pounding at Spica was merely the tip of humanity's lance. Behind that sharp tip extended a logistics chain that reached all the way back to Earth. So it was that Delta Seven had powered up engines for the first time in nearly a decade, turned on its newly installed suite of anti-radiation shields, and made its way through the heart of a century-old supernova to this alien star system that was fast being transformed into a powerful bastion for humanity.

Andreev's annunciator beeped and the female corporal who served as his receptionist announced the arrival of his scheduled visitor.

"Captain Walkirk of *Queen Julia* to see you, sir."

"Send him in," Andreev ordered.

The uniform of the officer who floated through the open hatch was unfamiliar to Captain Andreev, but that was hardly unusual in this combined human fleet. Most provincial navies guarded their home systems, leaving offensive operations largely to the Terrestrial Navy.

"Captain Walkirk, Royal Sandarian Navy, commanding *Queen Julia*, reporting to the Space Dock commander."

"At ease, Walkirk. Welcome aboard. What can we do for you? You are our first customer, you know."

"I won't be the last, sir, not from the casualties we're taking."

"That's what I hear. Any news from the front?"

"You probably know more than I do, sir. We have been a solid month nursing the *Queen* this far. We thought we would have to abandon her back at Carratyl."

"Well you made it and you're in good hands. What do you need?"

Phillip explained the damage that his ship had taken in a few carefully composed sentences. The repair officer listened, then nodded slowly."

"Standard *Illustrious*-class light cruiser, isn't she?"

"Yes, sir. Built last year at Sandar from Terrestrial Space Navy specifications."

"Good, then you use all standard modules. That means that we will be able to work quick and dirty. Rip out everything that doesn't work, weld on a new bow section, and then stuff the hull with new equipment still in the packing boxes from the factory. We won't even try to repair your old equipment, just ship what seems salvageable back to human space for a depot to handle. When we get through with *Queen Julia*, she'll be better than new."

"How long?" Phillip asked.

"A month, six weeks at the max. That assumes that something with higher priority doesn't materialize in the foldpoint and have you kicked out of the bay before we have time to finish the job."

"Can my crew help?"

"Sure. We can always use some trained hands and that way, they will be up to speed on the new stuff when we send you back to space with a shiny new coat of paint inside and out."

"Thank you, Captain. You don't know how frustrating it has been to turn our backs on the action and limp here when our mates are getting the hell kicked out of them."

"Captain Walkirk," Andreev replied with a wistful tone, "I have been a repair officer for sixteen years and seen ships and men head out into the deep black to fight the enemy, never to return. I know precisely how frustrating it is..."

#

# Chapter 16

*... Like many other aspects of their physiology, the Ryall reproductive cycle is tied to the march of seasons on the species' home world of Darthan. Ryall females enter estrus toward the end of winter in order that their fertilized eggs will be hatched early in the spring, thereby giving the hatchlings the maximum maturation period before they must survive the harsh weather of another winter on their own.*

*With the onset of cold weather here in Homeport, Varlan is showing the physiological and psychological changes that mark the onset of her fertile phase. Her body temperature is consistently 0.75 degrees above normal, her appetite has increased, and her weight has risen by nearly 10% during the buildup to mating season. She has become noticeably more irritable, especially at Jorge Santiago's incessant questions regarding the roots of Ryall myths. In this, I find I cannot blame her, as his personality has been getting on my own nerves of late.*

*She has entered mating season twice before during her captivity, but the changes this time are more pronounced than they were during the previous two cycles. Although reluctant to discuss her current condition and moods, Varlan has informed me that these changes are the result of an especially heavy release of hormones in her body, brought on by her lengthy period of enforced celibacy. She will lay infertile eggs in a few weeks, as she has on the two previous occasions, and will not suffer through one of these "hyper" mating periods for several years thereafter.*

*When I suggested that I would arrange to have one of the prisoners held by the Navy made available if that would relieve her suffering, she actually hissed at me, stating, "only a pervert would allow the young to be hatched into captivity."*

*The urge to reproduce is stronger in her than I have ever seen it, yet she refused my offer with an intensity that convinces me that the response was genuine. Since the urge to reproduce is as strong in the Ryall as it is in humans, this negative reaction is evidence that they are not chained to their instincts, and that, like humans, they use their intelligence to modify their biological impulses when the need arises. This observation has the most profound implications for human-Ryall relations and offers hope that perhaps they will be open to reason once they realize that we cannot be dislodged from the Spica system.*

#

Bethany paused in dictating her research diary and considered that last statement. Having found the clue for which she had been searching so long, she now faced the quandary of how to test her conclusion. How much of what she had just dictated was based on objective evidence, and how much was her wanting it to be so?

Of all the fields of science, exobiology was possibly the most fraught with instances of investigators being led astray by their own unconscious assumptions. The problem was inherent in the way the human brain works.

Show a human being a pattern of random dots and within seconds, they will begin to see forms in the patterns. That is why inhabitants of every world with a sizeable airless moon perceive an identifiable face in the craters that pockmark their satellite, and why cloud watching is a popular summer sport among those young enough to have the time for it. Likewise, the pattern recognition circuitry in the human brain causes images of Jesus Christ and the Virgin Mary to appear in water stains on ceilings and walls in Christian cultures. Presumably, other images dot the water stains of non-Christian cultures.

In scientific research, this innate urge to make sense out of chaos causes researchers to string together facts like pearls in a necklace. The problem is that sometimes those facts do not really belong together, except possibly in the researcher's own mind.

The most dangerous aspect of this phenomenon for an exobiologist was reasoning by analogy. Repeatedly, researchers found themselves expecting an alien organism to behave like the terrestrial organism it most resembled. This was the "if it looks like a dog, it must react like a dog" fallacy.

As professors of the various "exo" sciences were quick to point out to their students, the actions of an alien animal can be expected to be *alien*. Just because it resembles a fat old tabby cat you once owned does not mean that it will curl up in your lap and begin purring.

Bethany wondered if she were not subconsciously assigning human characteristics to Varlan and then making judgments on that basis. Was the Ryall's refusal to breed in captivity a case of

Varlan's intelligence overriding her instinct? Or was it another instinct interfering with the reproductive drive? Perhaps Varlan's refusal to mate was merely a rationalization for an instinct that told her to remain unencumbered by hatchlings so that she could better take advantage of any opportunity to escape. In such a case, the instinct to mate would be suppressed by that of self-preservation, and Bethany's whole thesis would be invalid.

Thus, the question remained what it had always been. Were the enemy slaves to their xenophobic instincts or could they override their natural desire to slaughter human beings if given proper motivation – say while negotiating under the weapons of a flotilla of human blastships?

The question had taken on a renewed urgency for Bethany in the month since that night at Beulah Mortridge's. She had been shocked to find members of the Altan parliament speaking so casually of the extermination of entire worlds. Even when aimed at humanity's mortal enemies, such callousness bothered her and had caused her a number of sleepless nights.

"A deci-credit for your thoughts," a voice said from behind her.

Bethany started, suddenly aware that she had been staring blankly at the work screen on which her research diary was displayed.

"Hello, Olivia. I didn't hear you come in."

"I'll say not. You seemed in a trance. I thought about tiptoeing my way out, but figured that might spook you even more than my interrupting. Problems?"

"No, just something that has been bothering me."

"Anything I can help you with?"

"I've been thinking about what Galston Highe said that night at Beulah Mortridge's soiree."

"Highe? The MP with the irritating whine?"

Bethany nodded.

"All I remember was a bunch of political blowhards trying to make themselves sound important. Surely you didn't take their arguments seriously."

"How can you not take someone seriously when they speak of sterilizing planets as casually as Highe did that night?"

"Don't let him bother you. He is frightened and frustrated. People inevitably talk like that when they are afraid of what the future holds. It is just so much hot air."

"The sentiment seems to be taking hold with the public, too. I hear commentators on the holo nets becoming more rabid with each casualty report that comes in."

"It's a common human reaction."

"But genocide! You hear about such things in history, but you don't expect to encounter them in real life."

Olivia sighed. "Your people were isolated a long time, Bethany. We terrestrials harbor no such illusions. Perhaps it comes from our much longer, not to mention bloodier, history."

"But extermination is so final."

"It is what the lizards mean to do to us if they win."

"That doesn't make it right."

Olivia Southington met Bethany's objection with a dismissive wave. "The next thing you will be telling me is that 'It isn't fair!' Personally, I just think people are blowing off steam. They would probably be shocked if the Navy actually carried out the bloody-minded campaign they are advocating. Still, you need to prepare yourself for the fact that we are not in control of events out there. You know what a tiger is, don't you?"

Bethany nodded.

"Well, we have one by the tail and we are riding it. If the battle goes against us, or the Ryall prove more resilient than our computer models allow for, we may find it necessary to go into their home systems one by one and spend the human lives needed to overwhelm their defenses."

"But the Ryall can be reasoned with, Olivia. I think my work with Varlan proves that they can overcome their instincts."

"That's news to me, and I have been following the literature on the subject very closely. Most experts seem to think that a Ryall is about as programmed as a computer, and its reactions are just as automatic."

"The experts are wrong."

"Then it is too bad that they have the ears of the powers-that-be and you do not."

Bethany fell silent. That was what had been bothering her ever since that night Galston Highe had made his dreadful suggestion. She had information vital to the prosecution of the war effort, but no one was listening to her.

There was one person who would *always* listen to her... She just did not know what he could do to help.

#

Clarence Whitlow was in his garden, tending his roses, when his niece arrived. His joy at seeing her was tempered by his first sight of her expression. Whatever had prompted this visit, it was not a social call. He had seen that look too often during her teenage years to mistake it for anything but trouble.

"Uncle," she said as he got stiffly to his feet from where he had been kneeling as he mulched one of his prize plants. She hugged him tight, eschewing the one-armed technique she had employed as a teenager. In those days, Bethany had been embarrassed by her burgeoning breasts, and had taken to avoiding bodily contact anywhere near her chest. However, as such things were wont to do, that phase had passed, as had so many others. Now she was a glowing young mother, and Whitlow took pleasure in the fact that he was the person primarily responsible for how well she had turned out.

The atmosphere in which they embraced was hot and humid, the natural condition of the greenhouse. Around them was the quiet buzzing of terrestrial bees, which he prized almost as much as his roses. The insects had never adapted well to Alta's native environment, and each bee was worth its weight in fissionables.

"What brings you here, Child?" he asked as they parted reluctantly (more so on his part than hers, he sensed).

"I have something I would like to discuss with you, Uncle. Have I come at a bad time?"

He smiled. "I see you too little as it is. My roses can wait. Come, let's go into the house and talk about it over hot chocolate. I seem to remember that is your favorite beverage."

Her laugh was forced and brittle when it came a few milliseconds too late. "It was, until I started to blow up like a walrus fish. Do you remember how I cried when I couldn't fit into that beautiful prom dress you bought me?"

"I remember a certain emergency tailoring job, although I thought it fit fine as it was."

As hereditary terrestrial ambassador to Alta, Whitlow had made it his life's work to study Earth history—not the history in history books, but actual contemporaneous records that revealed how the people of various cultures had viewed life and the world around them. Offhand, he could not think of a single culture, ancient or modern, where the teenage girls had not worried about being fat.

The two of them walked arm-in-arm across the small shrub-covered expanse of Whitlow's lawn, toward the low house built in a style now 200 years out of date on Earth. Heating the milk and preparing two steaming cups of brown liquid took another ten minutes. Only when they were comfortably seated in his breakfast nook, with its view of the nearby Colgate Range, did Whitlow broach the subject of Bethany's unexpected visit.

"What is it, Child? You know you were never very good at keeping things from me."

It was almost with a sob that Bethany poured out her frustrations of the previous month, beginning with the cocktail chatter of Galston Highe and ending with her conversation with Olivia Southington just that morning. Whitlow listened quietly, judging the degree of anguish behind her words. It was, he noted, considerable.

"So you believe you have discovered something important?"

She nodded with downcast gaze.

"So what do you plan to do about it?" he asked gently.

"I don't know what to do, Uncle. I suppose I should write up my findings and submit them to one of the xenology journals."

His sputtering brought her head up as anxious eyes surveyed his features. She wasn't sure whether he was choking or laughing. Finally, she decided that his sudden fit was the latter.

"What's so funny?" she asked in a hurt tone.

"Sorry," he said, wiping chocolate from his face with the grimy sleeve of his work shirt. "I thought I knew you well, Child, but that was the last thing I thought you would say."

"What else *can* I do, Uncle? No one in the government will listen to me. They all think I'm a crackpot who has fallen in love with her alien pet."

Whitlow considered his next words carefully. "So you truly think that the Ryall can be reasoned with, even if at the end of a gigawatt laser?"

"I do."

"Then you have to do something about it."

"I know that. But *what*?"

"I think you know the answer. Richard needs to be told of your theory and its ramifications."

"Richard? He already knows about my ideas."

"Does he know about your new finding?"

"No," she said slowly, as though contemplating a strange new idea. "I suppose I could write him a letter telling him what I've found."

"Do you think that will be sufficient?"

She paused and looked at the person she had come to for advice almost as long as she could remember – certainly since that terrible night when her parents were killed in the groundcar accident.

"What do you mean?"

"You know what I mean."

Bethany furrowed her brow, then gazed at him with steadily widening eyes as understanding began to seep into her brain. "You mean take the news to him, personally?"

He nodded gravely.

*"But I can't!* I have a newborn to look after."

"And you also have information vital to the war effort, information that can only be delivered in person... that is, if it is to be acted upon."

"Surely you aren't suggesting that I take Ritchie with me?"

"No, I'm not suggesting that." His eyes did not waver from hers, and his voice was soft enough to frighten her. Just as he knew all of her moods, Bethany had seen her uncle under every manner of stress. His earnestness was as strong as she had ever seen it.

"Abandon my baby?" she asked in a near shriek. "You ask too much!"

"I ask what is necessary. This information has to be delivered as quickly as possible and you are the only one who can deliver it."

"But I can't!"

"But you must."

"A... a mother doesn't abandon her baby!"

Clarence Whitlow, who had been gently massaging the back of his niece's hand, suddenly straightened and leaned back in his chair. There was a look of triumph in his eyes.

"There, you've said it! Good. Now we can get to the crux of the matter."

"What crux?" she asked petulantly.

"You say that you have discovered that the Ryall can overcome their instincts, yet you can't even overcome your own."

"It's not the same," she answered stubbornly.

"It is precisely the same. You have an overpowering urge to protect Little Ritchie. That is natural. After all, maternal instinct is the product of millions of years of human evolution. Throughout history, our species has had two automatic reactions to trouble. At the first clatter of weapons, women grab up the children and run in the opposite direction, while men grab their spears and head directly for the sound of battle.

"That instinct is as deeply imbedded in our genes as the Ryall xenophobia is imbedded in theirs. The question is whether you can overcome your instincts to do what is necessary. What does your heart tell you?"

"My heart tells me to grab Ritchie and run directly away from the sound of battle. I want to climb into bed, and pull the covers over us until we wake up in a sane world where there are no xenophobic lizards."

"Yes, that would be nice, wouldn't it? However, you don't mean that."

"Don't I?"

"No. What you have discovered is too important to hide from your duty."

"A mother's duty is to her baby."

"Yes, it is. Nevertheless, the expedient thing is not always the best for our children. If it was, I would have let you have that pony you wanted."

"But what do I do with little Ritchie if I go gallivanting off to war? Who will take care of him?"

"Who would take care of him if you were killed in a groundcar accident?" he asked softly.

"You, Uncle? But he's an infant. I was 12 when I came to live with you."

"Do you suppose an infant is more trouble than a teenager?"

Bethany blushed as her uncle's comment brought back memories she would just as soon stay buried.

"Most men your age don't become fathers, especially single fathers."

"I will manage. Don't worry, his physical needs will be taken care of. I will hire nurses and possibly a housekeeper to help me. As for love, I can give him all of that he can take."

Bethany blinked and noted that the wizened old man's image was becoming blurry.

"But what kind of a mother will people think I am, abandoning my baby for long months, maybe even a year or more?"

"It isn't the type of mother they think you are; it's the sort that *you* think you are. And if you can have any influence on shortening this war, you will do Ritchie far better service in leaving him than you will by staying."

The emotions raging within were too much for Bethany. The tears that had been welling in her eyes began to roll freely down her cheek. Within seconds, she was sobbing uncontrollably.

Whitlow, moved his chair across the decorative tile, and then folded the sobbing woman into his arms as he had done so many times in the past. The tears, he knew, meant that Bethany had made her decision. It was a choice that caused him no joy and certainly one that would bring her pain. It was, however, the right choice.

Under the circumstances, it was the *only* choice.

#

# Chapter 17

Commander Phillip Walkirk, Captain of His Majesty's Light Cruiser *Queen Julia*, used his arms to lever his body out of the access hatch in which he had been submerged the past four hours. Around him, the millions of scintillations that decorate the interior space of a photonic computer were like a particularly dense, microscopic star cluster. As he emerged into the light of the Number 4 axial passageway, the glare of the corridor overheads caused him to suddenly squint as he rotated his body parallel to the deck. He then hooked the toes of his ship boots into the deck grid and gently pushed with his hands to pivot himself into a "vertical" position. The whole maneuver was performed with the unconscious ease of one who has lived continuously in micro gravity for months.

Under the bright corridor lights, Phillip looked less like the heir to the throne than one of the unfortunates who congregated each night to sleep next to the warm air exhausts of the Royal Terrarium in Capital. His dungarees were not so much stained as they were decorated – in multiple strata of unidentified substances that constituted a record of his activities since last he'd had the opportunity to change his clothes.

Despite Phillip's impatience, repairs on *Queen Julia* had progressed with surprising speed after the tugs maneuvered the crippled cruiser into the all-encompassing embrace of the big space dock. As Captain Andreev, the dock commander, had pointed out, repairs were greatly facilitated by the cruiser's design, which was based on the Terrestrial Space Navy's *Illustrious III* class of warships. Like her *Illustrious* sisters, *Queen Julia* used standard modules throughout her hull.

The damage to *Julia* was sufficiently extensive that had the cruiser been one of the older ships of the Royal Sandarian Navy, or of the Altan Space Navy for that matter, she would probably have been scrapped. Repairing those 150-year-old designs would have taken too much time and too many scarce resources. For modern ships, with their interchangeable parts, repairs were the equivalent of a child's game of building sticks.

The space dock technicians had begun the repair by slicing away the cruiser's smashed-in bow with a laser as powerful as any carried by a blastship. It had been disconcerting to look at his ship and see it in cross-section, with compartments, passageways, and utility conduits all open to space. It had been even more disconcerting to watch the minor surgery that had followed the amputation of the bow. For more than a week, dockyard technicians had swarmed over the ship, cutting out partially melted sections of hull and interior structure, stripping away kilometers of optical cabling that had been clouded by radiation exposure, and emptying equipment racks of components that triggered fault messages when queried by diagnostic routines. At first, Phillip and his crew acted as unskilled helpers in this systematic vandalism, taking direction from the dock's skilled cadre of ship wreckers.

As 16- and 20-hour days began to blur together, however, the cruiser's crew began to take on more of the repair tasks themselves. Not only were they becoming more skilled, but also the dock's personnel were increasingly diverted to service other cripples.

Altogether, *Queen Julia* spent 22 days surrounded by space dock scaffolding and movable work centers. At the end of that time, when the ship was once again vacuum tight, Captain Andreev ordered his dock cleared so that he could begin repairs on another victim of the continuing contest over who would control Spica. Phillip had watched from an inter-orbit scooter as the dock's massive clamshell doors opened and his ship was again exposed to Eulysta's warming yellow rays.

Interior work on the ship proceeded apace even while tugs gently shifted the recuperating cruiser to a parking orbit aft of the repair dock. Repairs continued for four more weeks as *Julia*'s crew slowly put their ship back together. The list of things needing fixing seemed endless. There were networks to synchronize, interface nodes to reconnect, missile launchers to align. Most of these tasks required the attention of skilled technicians, all were time consuming, and Phillip never seemed to have enough labor of the right sort to satisfy even half of the demands for immediately attention.

Yet, despite workdays that were much too long and infrequent sleep periods, looking back on it, he could not remember a time when he had been happier.

As *Queen Julia* was slowly transformed from a collection of scrap metal to a functioning ship of war, Phillip felt something that had been too often missing from his role as heir to the throne. He felt the quiet satisfaction of having accomplished a difficult goal through his own efforts. On this job, there were no Sandarian court councilors to smooth the way, no deferential treatment accorded the King's son, no overeager functionaries to make good on his smallest whim. Most of those he dealt with daily knew nothing of his exalted status at home, or if they had heard rumors that he was some sort of a prince, they went out of their way to show him that he was not *their* prince.

He was especially proud of his crew. When he boarded the cruiser, they had been a dazed mob of survivors in a state of shock. Over the difficult weeks and months, first as they coaxed their damaged ship across two star systems, and subsequently through the long refit, Phillip had knit his band of survivors into a smoothly functioning starship crew.

The original crew had been supplemented with a pickup group of replacements, every one painfully acquired through cajolery (and some out-and-out bribery). It was in requisitioning manpower that Phillip's court training proved most valuable. The terrestrial forces resupply system had nothing on the Sandarian court when it came to intrigue, mutual back washing, and favors received for those given.

The new men and women, none of whom was Sandarian, were melding well with the remnants of the original crew.

On that wondrous day in the not-too-distant future when the final control-and-comm module was online, when the ship's last scar had been welded closed and painted over, when the engines were once again brought to power, on that day *Queen Julia's* young captain would not only report his ship ready for space. On that day, he would report her ready for battle!

"Captain," a voice called.

Phillip rotated in midair to see his executive officer pulling himself hand-over-hand along the corridor "barber pole."

"What is it, Mr. Weintraub?"

"Captain Andreev sends his compliments, sir, and requests that you report to his office at 16:00.

"Sixteen hundred?" Phillip asked, consulting his chronometer. "That's twenty minutes from now."

"Yes, sir. Your comm unit did not respond, so I came looking for you. You barely have time to change before you are due at the airlock. Kaminski has the gig standing by."

At the reminder, Phillip reached up and patted his dungaree pocket. There was the familiar answering beep. He had turned off his communicator because, while photonic circuitry was immune to electromagnetic interference, some of the diagnostic equipment on his cluttered tool belt was not.

"Did Captain Andreev say what he wanted?"

"No, sir. Just that you are to report at sixteen hundred."

"All right. Tell Kaminski that I will be there in seven minutes, and that I want to be underway in ten."

"Yes, sir."

With that, Phillip kicked off and arrowed forward to where Circumferential Corridor Beta intersected Axial Passageway Four. His cabin was a quarter turn around the ship, and two decks forward.

If he were going to run a razor over his stubble and splash cold water over his face, then he wouldn't have time to change his uniform. He would have to take his clean uniform from its storage compartment and change in the confines of the orbital gig.

He suspected that Corporal Kaminski, who was a woman, would regale her grandchildren with the story of the day she had been cooped up with the future king of Sandar in a bubble little bigger than a soundproof comm booth, and the heir had stripped to his skivvies. That assumed, of course, that Connie Kaminski lived long enough to have grandchildren and he lived long enough to become king.

#

The wall screen in Captain Andreev's outer office announced that it was 16:02:36 when Phillip floated through the hatch. The enlisted man strapped into the reception desk looked up from his work and said, "The Captain is expecting you, Commander. I'll announce you, and you can go right in."

Phillip pulled himself to the inner hatch, rapped once as protocol demanded, and then pulled himself through as soon as the hatch slid silently back into its recess.

"Commander Phillip Walkirk, commanding *Queen Julia*, reporting as ordered, sir." he said.

Andreev, who had been talking to a woman strapped into one of the "chairs" in front of his desk, said, "Thank you for coming, Commander. I believe you know my visitor."

Phillip twisted sideways to observe a familiar silhouette. "Bethany! What are you doing here?"

"Hello, Your Highness," she said, pivoting in her seat and extending a hand to shake the one he had free. "How have you been?"

"Busy," he replied. He pulled himself into the framework seat next to hers and strapped himself in. When he was secure, he rotated to face her and said, "That doesn't answer my question. How the hell did you get here?"

"Through the good auspices of Grand Admiral Belton," Andreev replied. "Mrs. Drake, it seems, is on a mission. Unfortunately, I don't see how it can be a successful one as she lacks authorization to continue her journey beyond Eulysta."

"Mission?" Phillip asked.

Bethany nodded. "I have been explaining my problem to Captain Andreev. Knowing that Sandar and Alta are sister colonies, he asked if I knew you."

"... And since you and Mrs. Drake are old friends, I thought I would pass her and her problem to you, Commander," Andreev replied. "You may be better positioned than I am to assist Mrs. Drake, or at the least, to explain to her why what she is asking is impossible."

"It sounds mysterious."

"Not at all," Bethany answered. "It just takes too long to explain it properly."

"Are you hungry?" he asked.

Bethany nodded.

"Good, then you can explain over dinner.... If that is all right with you, sir."

Andreev made a gesture like someone pushing away a particularly heavy cargo container that has somehow broken loose and is floating aimlessly around the cabin. "You are most welcome, Commander. I'm afraid that Mrs. Drake's needs are beyond both my purview and my pay grade."

"Very well, sir. We will leave you to your reports. Bethany, how about a short trip to the mess compartment?"

"Thank you, Your Highness."

"Please, my name is Phillip. I'm trying to get people used to thinking of me as just one more colonial naval officer."

"How is it going, Your High... uh, Phillip?"

"Surprisingly well," he replied. "Just ask Captain Andreev. The dock supply officer seems to take special delight in sending my requisitions back stamped "Denied.""

#

Orbital Shipyard Delta Seven was more than just an oversize body and fender shop. In addition to its primary function, it sported a completely equipped orbital hospital where doctors worked to heal injured crewmembers while the dock technicians attempted to repair their ships.

For those who had come through the stress of battle without physical injuries, there was a large rest and relaxation facility to administer to bruised psyches. Part of that facility was a first-rate restaurant that served delicacies to crewmembers mortally tired of space rations. In fact, the shipyard's chef could easily have cooked for the finest restaurants in Paris had it not been a robot.

Phillip sipped wine from a drinking bulb as he sat in a small booth across from Bethany. A steady cool breeze wafted past him, the air having been set in motion by the booth's built-in suction system that at least gave the illusion of gravity.

"You look more beautiful than ever, Bethany," he said as he returned the drinking bulb to its container. "Motherhood becomes you."

"She felt herself blushing, then thanked him for the compliment. "I take it that Richard has mentioned our son, then?"

Phillip laughed. "Mentioned him? Hell, he must have sent baby pictures to every rating in the fleet! I would venture to guess that your son is the most famous baby in the whole of the Spica System."

Bethany was momentarily horrified "You're joking, right?"

Phillip smiled. "Exaggerating, perhaps. He has Richard the Second's picture on the home screen of his command unit. I know. I have seen it there. Apparently, every attachment you have ever forwarded him is filed for easy access."

"I hope he isn't boring people with baby pictures."

Phillip laughed. "Admirals don't 'bore' lesser ranks. They 'instruct' them. You should know the Navy well enough by now to know that. How is your wine?"

Bethany glanced down at her own drinking bulb, which contained a pale pink liquid that was distinctly different from the frosty amber tinged concoction that Phillip was drinking.

"It's fine. What did you call it?"

"Sandarian Slowglo, made from a mixture of jaffa vine and terrestrial pomegranates."

"Sweet and tart at the same time. How do they get that effect?"

He shrugged. "You will have to consult a mixologist for the formula. I merely consume them. Come, drink up and we will order another round. You can tell me about this mysterious project of yours while we wait for the main course."

Bethany raised the drinking nipple to her lips and pressed the dispenser lever until the flow of the sweet-tingly liquid came to a sudden stop. She then watched Phillip key in an order for two more bulbs before she began to speak of her studies with Varlan.

Speaking to Phillip proved surprisingly easy, and before she realized it, they had consumed two more drinking bulbs of liquor and had worked their way halfway through two hydroponics salads. That his skills as a listener would serve him in good stead as a king, and had therefore been drilled into him from early childhood, did not occur to her.

When Bethany finally stopped talking, she was surprised to discover that she had nearly finished the covered tray of filet mignon in front of her.

"So," Phillip said, "having decided that the Ryall can be reasoned with – or, at least, Varlan can – you hopped a ship through the nebula to Eulysta to tell us about it."

Bethany nodded. "Something like that. I need to get to Richard and tell him what I have found. He is the only one I know who is likely to take me seriously."

The way she said it told him that she was leaving something out. From her wistfulness when he had joked with her about her son, he thought he knew what it was.

"And you felt so strongly about this that you left your infant son at home in the care of your uncle, and decided to risk your life by heading into a war zone?"

Bethany thought about it and then nodded. "Do you think I'm a horrible mother for abandoning him?"

"No. If you feel that strongly, and if there is even a tiny chance of ending this war, then you had to come. As for your theory..."

"You think it's crazy?"

"I won't lie to you. It seems completely alien to my experience and to the experience of just about everyone I have ever met, and my people have been fighting the Ryall from the very beginning. What proof have you?"

"Just the fact that she refused my offer of a prisoner with which to mate even though her instincts were screaming otherwise."

"Perhaps she has learned what it is that you want to hear," Phillip said, gently, trying to dissuade her.

To his surprise, Bethany nodded and said, "It's possible, I suppose. Still, I think I have gotten to know her better than that in our time together."

"Perhaps you have," he agreed. "Why has no one else gotten a prisoner to be reasonable on the subject of humanity's existence? If Varlan isn't lying to you, then this is the first conversion of a prisoner I have ever heard of."

"Maybe that is because all of our prisoners are from the military caste," Bethany replied. "We haven't captured very many of their administrative or scientific castes, have we?"

"Well, I can check I suppose." Phillip pulled his command unit from its holster at his belt and scrawled a request across its face. Its screen flickered and he studied the output, and then whistled softly.

"What is it?"

"Would you believe that there is at least one more administrator-caste Ryall in captivity, and he's here on Corlis?"

Bethany blinked, and then turned to stare at the blue-white world hanging above the nearby view port. "Corlis? You mean *our* Corlis?"

"The very same. I take it from your expression that this news has piqued your interest."

Bethany barely heard him. Her mind was racing too quickly. Finally, she looked at Phillip and said, "I would like your honest opinion. Please, don't spare my feelings. If you think I have cracked, please tell me."

"Of course."

"You are worried that Varlan might be playing me for a simpleton, correct?"

"I would have put it more diplomatically, but yes."

"You agree that the managerial and administrative caste thinks differently from the military caste?"

He nodded. "Granted."

"So, what if I add a second Ryall to my study? What if I can convince this other administrator that it is possible for our two species to co-exist in peace?"

"Then I would say that you have twice performed a miracle."

"Perhaps I can get Varlan to help me," Bethany mused.

"I beg your pardon."

"Oh, didn't I tell you? Varlan is accompanying me to Spica. That is one reason why I have been having so much trouble. No warship is going to let a Ryall onboard."

"Oh, I don't know about that. I can think of one that will, once we get her put back together, that is."

"What ship?"

"*Queen Julia*. We will be returning to the battle in another month and might have room for a small menagerie."

"Does that mean that you believe me?"

"It means that the stakes are high enough that we can't reject your wild-eyed scheme out of hand."

\#

# Chapter 18

Varlan of the Scented Waters lay draped over two human acceleration couches in as comfortable a position as she could manage, and watched the familiar landscape beyond the port of the ground-to-orbit ferry craft. In the next row behind her, Bethany did the same, as the aquamarine seas, forested mountains, and broad plains of Corlis grew larger by the moment to the accompaniment of the keening of the hypersonic wind beyond the hull.

"What a beautiful world!" Bethany said to no one in particular.

Varlan turned her head atop her long neck to point toward Bethany. "Yes, it is beautiful to Ryall eyes as well."

Bethany sighed. "That is really the problem between our two species, isn't it? We both covet the same sort of real estate. Perhaps it would have been better if one of our races had evolved on the frozen plains and liquid helium pools at the outer edges of our respective star systems."

"An interesting thought," Varlan agreed. One thing she had grown used to in Bethany's presence was the constant stream of "interesting" thoughts. This voyage they were on, for instance. It was predicated on one of Bethany's most enduring lunacies, namely that two sentient races could coexist peacefully in a universe where aggression is the only survival skill.

The problem for Varlan was that Bethany's lunacies were contagious. After so many cycles of her human captor/friend's constant cajolery, Varlan was no longer sure of her own beliefs. Over time, the idea of peaceful coexistence with humans had ceased to be ludicrous, and had come to seem, if not reasonable, then at least something that might be contemplated. Bethany thought Varlan's willingness to consider the idea was evidence that humans and The Race might one day live side-by-side in peace. Varlan knew that there was another, more likely explanation.

Her newfound mental flexibility might well be a sign that her long captivity had unbalanced her. Such things had happened from time to time in the long history of The Race.

The thought that she herself might be going insane did not particularly bother Varlan. She wondered if that, too, might be a symptom of insanity. On the other hand (her use of that human expression, she realized, was an indication of her mental state), perhaps there was a core of truth in Bethany's alien insights.

Varlan had never seen a Swift Eater, save in artists' renderings and skeletons in museums. That did not mean that Swifts were merely a long ago memory from prehistory. She merely had to slide the nictating membranes over her oculars and conjure up one of the beasts from her imagination in order to bring her body to combat readiness.

Since the Swifts had been voracious eating machines, there had never been any question of negotiating with them. The choice faced by Varlan's ancestors had been no choice at all: kill or be eaten. But what if it had been otherwise? Might there have come a time when it was possible to reason with them?

#

Periskay of the Distant Mountains in the Mist was bored. It had been $12^3$ heartbeats since First Meal, and would be three times that long until Second. He had already performed his waste expulsion activities for the day, and had nothing even remotely interesting in his future until Eulysta set behind the nearby hills, when it would be time again for slumber. In other words, this day was shaping into a day like every other since his capture by The Monsters.

It would have been different had he someone of his own caste to talk to, but of course, engineer-philosophers were not well represented in the population of the Corlis Prisoner Compound. In fact, he was the only one.

Dillatan of the Swift Swimmers, his assistant, did his best to converse with Periskay, but after so long in captivity, they had largely run out of things to talk about. Or rather, Periskay had learned the limitations of Dillatan's conversational skills, which were typical for one of his youth.

To keep his sanity, and out of necessity, Periskay had taken to studying their captors. Relatively early, he had learned to recognize the subtle differences between Monsters – or humans, as they styled themselves – and to identify them as individuals.

There was Privatesuharo, with his subtly different pigmentation and the elongated shape of his ocular coverings. It had been he who captured Periskay and half-a-twelve of his workers as they made their way through the bush. Then there was Sergeantcunning-something, with the unpronounceable name, whose status was higher than Privatesuharo's. Having noticed that many human names shared the first few syllables, Periskay had first thought they were egg-mates. Lately, however, he had noted a tendency for the humans to sometimes drop the redundant leading syllables. Privatesuharo was Suharo to his messmates, and Sergeantcunning-something was Cunning-something to those who shared his Sergeant pre-syllables, except when Suharo was Yoshi and Cunning-something was Matt, which completely confused Periskay.

He was beginning to suspect that *Private* and *Sergeant* were honorifics of some kind, or possible designations of status, a conclusion he had come to after Dillatan pointed out that all the "privates" seemed to defer to all "sergeants" and both groups tended to change their behavior in the presence of "lewtnants" and "keptens." Perhaps the human social structure was just too alien for even an engineer-philosopher of The Race to decipher. Or maybe they were just doing it to confuse him.

If human social structure was difficult to decipher, their language seemed to be equally obtuse. It was positional, with the meaning of syllables dependent on the order in which they were uttered, except sometimes, that order could be changed without altering the information content, and other times it could not. A few of the human utterances were clear from their context. The monosyllable "no" was a negative and denoted that the prisoners should cease whatever it was that they were doing. The strangely formed sibilant "yes" seemed to have the opposite meaning, but sometimes did not mean that the prisoners should continue to perform the task in which they were engaged. When uttered with a rising pitch at the end, "yes" seemed to be an interrogatory, with little correlation to the same sound when spoken in an even voice. Then there was a monosyllable that the guards emitted when they were exasperated, surprised, or angry. The precise meaning of "fuck" escaped Periskay, but from the number of times the humans emitted the sound, it must be a verbal formula with powerful connotations.

Periskay's musings as to the alien nature of aliens were interrupted by the appearance of Privatesuharo. Like Periskay, Suharo had learned to distinguish the individual members of The Race in his charge and he made directly for the spot where the engineer-philosopher lay sunning himself. His lips moved and rapid-fire Monster speech issued forth in a long string of gibberish that sounded like, *"Com'on-professor-the-big-brass-want-your-carcass-in-HQ-pronto."* A heartbeat afterward, the translator box on the warrior's belt said, "Philosopher, you are summoned immediately to the council chambers of those who command this facility."

*"Yessss,"* Periskay replied, practicing his command of the enemy speech.

Privatesuharo led the way. He moved among the captive workers and warriors without weapons and without fear. If the prisoners had any inclination to rebel, they were dissuaded by the fact that they were trapped on an alien planet with a Monster war fleet hovering over their heads, and home was at least three star portals distant through enemy held space. Besides, hanging on each guard's belt was an instrument called a *cattleprod*, capable of rendering any member of The Race senseless with a touch. The descriptions given by the few who had been touched dissuaded the others from chancing the experience.

The administration building of the prisoner compound was a typical design for a human portable structure, if the others of its kind Periskay had observed were any indication. It was dome-shaped, with the approach from the compound through a long tunnel. Inside, the temperature was too cold for Periskay's comfort and filled with the right-angled compartments so preferred by humans. Even those rooms that abutted the circular perimeter were box-shaped on the other three sides.

Privatesuharo led Periskay to one such room and motioned him inside. Within was a human – a female to judge by her physiological differences from the guards – and a single member of The Race.

"Greetings," the newcomer said in The One True Tongue. "You are Periskay of the Distant Mountains in the Mist?"

"This one is he. Who are you?"

"I am called Varlan of the Scented Waters."

Periskay's ears went vertical at that information. "The manager of the Corlis Mineral Extraction Facility?"

Varlan made the motion of assent. "I take it that you came looking for me when *Space Swimmer* went overdue."

"Yes. I was assigned to investigate the disaster that befell you. Unfortunately, I only realized what had happened when Monster war craft began exiting the portal from the Evil Star."

"And your own ship?"

"I sent it on a race for the portal to spread the alarm, but the Monsters were faster. It was destroyed."

"Good hunting to the souls who were aboard," Varlan said reverently.

Periskay made the requisite sign in response and barely waited the required two heartbeats before asking, "You are a prisoner of the Monsters... the humans?"

"Yes, I was taken shortly after they captured *Space Swimmer*. I have been their prisoner ever since. My guardian is Bethany, once of the Lindquists, now of the Drakes. That is she standing beside us."

"She seems interested in our conversation. Does she understand The One True Tongue?"

"Not as well as I would like," the female biped answered. Despite the strong accent forced on her by the inadequacies of her vocal equipment, Periskay had no trouble understanding her meaning. He was so surprised that his nictating membranes momentarily covered his oculars. When he finally overcame his reaction, he turned back to Varlan and acted as though the human were not present. "Why are you here? I detect that you are gravid. Am I to be your mate?"

"I am gravid," Varlan confirmed, "but there will be no mating. To bring a hatchling into captivity would be immoral."

"I agree. Why have I been summoned then?"

"Bethany has been my constant companion since I was taken. She is studying me, as I am studying her. She has some odd ideas that she wishes to explore with another of our kind."

"Why?"

"I believe that my long captivity may have caused me to lose grip of reality. She is seeking another of our species, one who retains all of his faculties."

"Why have I been chosen?" Periskay asked.

"Because you are the only philosopher currently in human hands, or at least, the only one within easy reach. The humans have concluded, or rather, Bethany has, that our race may be more diverse in its outlook than they are able to observe in the warriors who make up the large majority of their prisoners. You are to be the test of that hypothesis."

"Diverse? I do not understand."

"It is Bethany's belief that our two species may be able to treat one another as we treat others of our own kind with whom we have fallen into conflict. She would like you to listen to her proposal and give her your assessment."

Periskay signaled his irritation. He had been hoping for something to happen, anything to frighten away the boredom, but this seemed too outlandish to qualify for a proper diversion. "Why should I aid this human?"

"Because," Varlan said very slowly, "if she is satisfied with your response, there is a chance that both of us may see home again; and if she is not, it may well lead to the extermination of The Race."

#

Bethany listened to the quick interplay between the two Ryall and was aware that their quiet hisses carried a high emotional content. She understood a quarter of what was said, although the context in which the words were used often made no sense. After what seemed like an hour, but was probably less than three minutes, Varlan turned to her and said, "Periskay will listen to your proposal and will give you his honest opinion."

"Thank him for me," Bethany said, then held up a hand. "Never mind, I will do it myself."

She tilted her head and carefully pronounced the phrase-of-appreciation that Varlan had taught her, making sure to spread her fingers in a palm-down gesture at the end. She was rewarded by the answering gesture from the Ryall, an acknowledgement that while he might object to her personal habits and body odor, at least her status was somewhere above "potential dinner." It was an acknowledgement that she was his equal, at least for the duration of their conversation.

"Periskay," she began before remembering to turn on her translator. She pressed the control that activated the machine and began again: "Learned one! As Varlan has told you, we have studied one another for many cycles. Varlan has tried to understand how we humans view the universe while I have made a similar effort with regard to your species. We are products of different worlds, different biochemistries, and different evolutionary histories. Yet, as intelligent beings, we share a great deal. We both care for our offspring. Our sciences are more alike than they are different. Both of our species travel between stars and colonize the homelike planets we find.

"I submit to you that these similarities betray a certain likeness in our brain structures and in the way we think. Were we not so alike, there would be no reason to fight. I propose that we use our common intelligence to see if we cannot find some common ground – or as your race would say, calm water."

"To what purpose?" Periskay asked.

"To the purpose of stopping this endless killing."

"How is such a thing possible short of one race exterminating the other?"

"That is what we are here to explore. I believe our species' brains respond similarly to logic. That is why I have sought you out. I need one schooled in the laws of logic, not the laws of war, to whom I can explain my ideas. I need an engineer-philosopher rather than a warrior."

"It is true that members of my caste are problem solvers," Periskay replied. "However, it is difficult to solve a problem if one refuses to accept reality. We leave it to others to lower their nictating membranes in order to view the cosmos in a soft, white glow."

"Excellent. Then I would like to propose an hypothesis to be tested against reality."

"What hypothesis?"

"That intelligence overrides instinct in sentient beings."

"We of The Race believe that our brains give us the ability to modify our instincts. How else to explain our ancestors' destruction of the Swift Eaters? Those ancient hunters sought out the nesting places of the Swifts in deep water, yet their instinct was to cower behind thick stockades on land."

Bethany paused. It had never occurred to her to attribute the long hunt to the Ryall overcoming their fears. Still, Periskay had given her something with which to work. Seeing the opportunity, she took it.

"Yes, that is a case of intelligence overriding instinct. It must have been a difficult thing for your hunters to plunge into the ocean depths armed only with stone spears. I would ask that you consider that a similar level of courage is required of you now."

"Yes," Periskay agreed. "With your war fleet so deep in our space, our warriors will require courage to dislodge you from our realm."

"No, Periskay. The courage of a Ryall warrior is built in, as is his aggression. The courage of which I speak is of a different order. Your species faces destruction. Do you have the courage to go against your strongest instincts to save The Race?"

She could see from the way Periskay flattened his ears against his skull and dipped his muzzle that her last statement had sunk in. When he spoke, it was with a wary demeanor, or possibly, she just imagined it.

"You speak of destruction. Is this a boast on your part?"

"No boast. We are speaking reality. Surely, you know enough of your species' economics to understand the long-term effect of a human blockade of your most important star system. Eventually, the Hegemony will lose its ability to make war, and when it does, our fleets will turn your home worlds into glowing cinders. Your populations will be devastated one world at a time, until finally, the only hatchlings left alive will be in human zoos."

"If all of this is true, why are you speaking to me?"

"Because, I believe the destruction of the Ryall species can be avoided, if only your people can be made to understand. However, many of those humans in command of our war effort do not believe as I do. They think I have allowed my friendship with Varlan to lead me into delusion.

"Are my superiors correct? Am I deluded? Is there hope that we will be able to talk sense to Those Who Rule The Race, or must we destroy your people to make our people safe?"

Bethany paused and looked into the one jet black eye that fixed on her. "That is the pivotal question. I require your honest evaluation. Given the facts as I have described them, if we convince Those Who Rule that your species faces certain annihilation, will they surrender to spare The Race?"

As she finished speaking, Bethany was surprised at how tired she felt. She had not slept well the night before. Every time she closed her eyes, she had seen her son looking up at her, asking why she had abandoned him. It was a recurring dream, and had largely supplanted the one in which Richard was incinerated on the bridge of his ship. Having said all that there was to say, she waited in silence for Periskay's response.

The Ryall pondered for a long time. The silence stretched into minutes. Finally, the alien engineer extended his head to full elevation and looked at her intently. The long mouth came open to reveal double rows of razor-sharp teeth and Periskay answered her question.

It was not the answer she had expected.

#

# Chapter 19

"*Queen Julia* in position and ready to enter the foldpoint," the voice of the cruiser's communicator said over the command circuit.

Phillip Walkirk floated lightly in his command couch in the middle of the cruiser's bridge, restrained only by his lap belt. Micro gravity was a relief after days spent at double gravs en route to the Eulysta-Carratyl foldpoint. He watched his bridge crew go about their duties, struck by how well they worked together after so short a time underway. In the week since they had departed Orbital Shipyard Delta Seven, they had largely gotten through the inevitable shakedown period that any crew undergoes at the start of a voyage.

Of course, most crews did not have the dubious advantage of three months of working long hours in close proximity while they reassembled their ship. During the long refit, nearly everyone aboard had become intimately familiar with the idiosyncrasies and foibles of their shipmates and officers. As a result, they were able to communicate with a minimum of lost motion as they went about their duties. Long before *Queen Julia* approached the foldpoint, what had once been a collection of shell-shocked survivors and a pickup crew of replacements had transformed itself into the brain and central nervous system of an interstellar ship of war.

"Stand by, *Queen Julia*," the foldpoint controller answered in response to their request to enter the foldpoint. "We have priority traffic in front of you."

"Standing by," the communicator responded. He turned at his station and said, "Looks like it will be a few minutes, Captain."

"Right," Phillip replied, pointing to the bulkhead-mounted viewscreen at the front of the bridge. "Look at that."

The screen showed the usual black of space sprinkled with a scattering of individual stars. In addition to the dimensionless points of light, there was a small manmade sphere, half in light, half in shadow. The diminutive size was misleading. The object was actually a quarter-kilometer in diameter, and except for one of the cryogen tankers that kept the fleet fueled, was one of the largest objects ever constructed by man. Ahead of them, preparing to jump from Eulysta to Carratyl, was one of the orbital fortresses that, until recently, had guarded the approaches to Earth.

The communicator gave a low whistle as he read the telltales at the bottom of the viewscreen. "No wonder they want us to wait. We want to be well clear of that monster when she jumps. No telling how much it would mess up our jumpfield if we got too close."

"It wouldn't do to collide with them before we jump, either."

"Or after," Technician-Third Falcone replied.

The sight of the orbital fortress making its ponderous way toward Spica warmed Phillip's heart. Within its cavernous volume, the fortress packed the wallop of a planetary defense center. At the first sign of a breakout, it could fill a foldpoint with such a dense cloud of missiles, lasers, and antimatter beams that the attacking fleet would likely be decimated before the Ryall ships finished their first sensor sweep.

Phillip watched the fortress for long minutes. Then, suddenly, the edges of its image became indistinct, as though viewed through turbulent water, before the tiny half-moon shape blinked completely out of existence.

"You are cleared to enter the foldpoint, *Queen Julia*," the voice of the far-off controller said.

"Acknowledged," Communicator Falcone replied before turning to his captain. "We're free to maneuver, sir."

"Very well. Helmsman, take us in."

Phillip heard a sudden clearing of a throat immediately behind him. He glanced over his shoulder to see Bethany Drake braced between deck and overhead. She wore an unadorned azure shipsuit of the Royal Sandarian Navy. On her, it looked good.

"Bethany, when did you pop through the hatch?"

"A couple of minutes ago, Captain. I didn't want to disturb you. Permission to enter the bridge, if you aren't too busy preparing for the jump."

"The captain is never busy if he has a well-trained crew. Permission granted. Strap into the observer's couch and you can watch the transition."

She pulled herself into the couch next to his and strapped down. "How long until we jump?"

"Another ten minutes or so. Are your passengers prepared?"

She nodded. "Both are tucked into their fluid beds and strapped down."

"How are they holding up under high gravs?"

"They don't like it, but they are unharmed. Varlan complains of being tired all of the time and Periskay spends the whole day sleeping on a fluid bed with his neck stretched out and his legs tucked under his torso. He says that it is the only way he can breathe."

"I believe him. Two standard gravities for us is nearly two-and-a-half for the Ryall."

She nodded. "I know Varlan used to complain about the gravity on Alta. She said she couldn't understand how we could stand erect without the aid of six feet under us."

"Sometimes I have wondered the same thing after a night spent in certain spaceport drinking establishments," Phillip replied.

"What was that ship that went through just now?"

"That was no ship. That was Orbital Fortress Seven Two Nine, the *Bunker Hill*. They are headed the same place we are, but we'll get there weeks before they do."

"Do you think the orbital fortresses will make that big a difference?"

"A huge difference. That one fortress has more firepower than one of our big planetary defense centers back on Sandar."

"And the fortresses will free up the ships to raid into Ryall space, won't they?"

"Not for awhile. The Ryall have had time to bring up fortresses on their own side of the foldpoint. That means we can't force the chokepoint going in any better than they can force it coming out. It will be a stalemate, at least until their economy begins to fall apart."

"That is what I have been telling Varlan and Periskay."

"And what do they say?"

"They just look glum and let their necks droop."

"How successful have you been in getting Periskay to come around to your way of thinking?"

"Not very," she replied. "He listens to my arguments, but I'm not sure how much is getting through."

"Why did you bring him along then?"

"Because I need to determine whether my success with Varlan was a fluke. If I can convince Periskay to consider the possibility of peaceful coexistence, then I will have demonstrated that all Ryall have the capability to use their intelligence to override their instincts. If I can't, then I may have to admit that Varlan's fears are correct."

"What fears?" Phillip asked.

"She is worried that her long captivity has caused her to lose her mental moorings; that she has, in effect, gone insane."

"Do you think she has?"

"I think she is more sane now than when I first met her; but, of course, that is the human viewpoint. Periskay is my control subject. If he will listen, they all will."

"So long as we hold them prisoner and force them to listen. Have you considered how you are going to get word to their leaders that we want to parley?"

Bethany's brow furrowed in response. Finally, she said, "That is a problem. Any ship of ours that shows up on the other side of the foldpoint is likely to be vaporized before they can get two words out. I'm afraid that I don't know any way to short circuit their automatic attack reflex."

"I doubt anyone does," Phillip replied.

"There must be some way to make them listen long enough so that we can get our message through to their high command..."

"Captain," the helmsman said from his console. "Sorry to interrupt, but we are ready to jump."

Phillip let his gaze sweep across his various command screens. All was as it should be. "Very well, Mr. Ninkara. You may jump when ready."

Suddenly, the two-minute warning echoed through the ship. The usual pre-jump formalities were over quickly and the bridge grew quiet as *Queen Julia*'s generators charged.

Then after a short countdown, one set of stars disappeared while a different set took their place and they were one star system closer to the scene of the titanic struggle from which they had been so rudely ejected all those months ago.

                                    #

Richard Drake sat in his command cabin and read the latest casualty reports, a task he had come to dread. Back on Earth, when he had first thought up the invasion, it had seemed so neat and tidy. They would fight their way into Spica, block the enemies' interior lines of communications, and then hold on with the tenacity of a terrier until the Ryall economy collapsed.

It was the holding on that was proving to be the difficult part. No matter how many Ryall ships they destroyed in the foldpoints, there always seemed to be more in reserve. It was as though the enemy had unlimited forces to hurl against humanity's wall.

As in all things, the illusion of infinite military power was just that... an illusion. There is a limit to how many resources any society can divert to the art of war, and after a century and a quarter of conflict, both species were up against that limit. The two adversaries were evenly matched, having proved that by fighting to a stalemate for six generations.

No, the Ryall power behind the foldpoints, though massive, was finite. Even a society whose soldiers were grown in the egg must someday run out of them if they were expended too profligately. In fact, the furious attempts to break through the blockade were actually in humanity's interest. They would use up ships and warriors faster than more careful military strategies. This would hasten the inevitable collapse.

Of course, that was cold comfort to those who perished throwing back their onslaughts. It was even colder comfort to their loved ones. How does one tell a grieving mother that her son has given his life to "hold on?" What do you say to the widow of a man whose atoms are intimately mixed with those of his ship in interstellar space? Can a dead crewman's children take solace in the fact that the fleet has inflicted vastly more damage on the enemy than they have received, especially when their father is one of the unlucky few?

A military man all of his life, Drake had experience with death. Yet, he found this slow, steady drumbeat of casualties debilitating. It was not the constant sense of bereavement that was gnawing at his conscience. Rather, it was the feeling that casualties were becoming routine. He worried that those who died – vital, breathing, sweating, cursing, belching, living, loving human beings – would slowly, inexorably, be transformed into dry statistics, mere numbers in a database: *TSNS Tanganyika* lost with 724 officers and crew. *RSNS Excalibur* damaged, 316 dead and half a thousand injured, half critically. *ASNS Sunchaser* exploded, all hands lost...

It was the dehumanizing effect of the constant barrage of such numbers that threatened to numb everyone's conscience. It had happened before. There had been the first global conflict back on Earth, when a thousand men were lost in France on days when nothing particularly special was happening on the battlefield. No attacks, no retreats, just the desultory shelling of artillery. The generals of the time became so inured to the slaughter that they had taken to referring to this unremarkable carnage as "seepage."

*Will we, too, grow so tired of thinking about our dead colleagues that we will block them out of our memory?* he wondered.

In this contest of attrition, who would break first? The Ryall or the Humans: the former by losing their economy or the latter by losing their humanity?

Drake shivered and sat a little more erect in front of his work screen. This was not the proper mood for a conquering admiral, he thought. Better to concentrate on the present and leave the future take care of itself.

The present brought with it some disturbing signs that the enemy was getting smarter. They were still throwing all manner of attacks at the blockading forces, but the timing of the last few probes had indicated better coordination than the wild melees in the early days of the blockade.

The previous week, small Ryall forces had appeared simultaneously in three of the foldpoints. Luckily, the quick, sharp battles had lasted only long enough for them to scan circumambient space and jump back to their home systems. However, it had been the simultaneity of the attacks that was worrisome, and not their strength.

As the tactical computers predicted when he first analyzed the capture of Spica, the Ryall Hegemony had responded to a human invasion fleet in their skies precisely as humanity would have done if the situation were reversed. Each home world initially launched a furious attack through their local foldpoint with all the force they could quickly scrape together.

Their goal had been to punch through one of the foldpoints before humanity could erect proper defenses. However, with the human fleet astride their interior lines of communication, the Ryall ability to quickly communicate battle plans between star systems was disrupted. As a result, the quick response attacks were uncoordinated and relatively ineffective. In every case, the power of the defense had proven too great a handicap for the attackers to prevail.

That the last probe had been a simultaneous one against three separate foldpoints indicated that the Ryall were beginning to coordinate between cut off star systems. There were other, more circuitous routes between the home stars than the ones leading through Spica. They involved up to nine foldspace transitions and were slow to use, but they allowed the passing of messages between planets in different islands of foldspace.

With intersystem communication restored, they would begin developing a coherent breakout strategy, one that might be successful.

He suddenly became aware that he had been staring at the casualty list, unseeing for the past several minutes. Taking a deep breath, he scanned down the list of names one last time, not recognizing any of them on this iteration. He sighed loudly, and then was ashamed of himself. Were the lives of strangers less valuable than those of people he knew?

Slowly, he reached out and tapped the key that would attach his digital signature and send the list for coding in this week's message to Admiral Belton on Corlis. Almost at the same instant, the communicator on his desk beeped for attention.

He keyed for acceptance and said, "Yes?"

"Sir, I have an incoming message for you," Spacer Archon Carey, fleet battle staff communicator, reported. "It's from Captain Walkirk of the *RSNS Queen Julia*."

"Phillip is back?" he asked, feeling his spirits rise with his interest. "Read me the message."

"It reads as follows: *'From: Captain Phillip Walkirk, Commanding RSNS Queen Julia. To: Admiral Richard Drake, Commanding Task Force Spica. Message follows. Will arrive Conqueror, 16:22 Hours. If you are not too busy, request that you meet us at the airlock. Have VIPs on board and think it would make a good impression. Walkirk out.'* Message ends."

"VIPs? Does he say who?"

"Negative, sir. That is the whole message."

"What kind of a message is that, for God's sake?"

"Should I ask him to clarify, sir?"

"Negative. He must have his reasons for being close-lipped. I just hope he isn't signaling that his father is onboard."

"His father, sir?"

"That's right, Carey. You don't know Captain Walkirk, do you?"

"No, sir."

"His father is King of Sandar. Better roll out the Marine guard just in case."

"Aye aye, sir."

# Chapter 20

Like her dead namesake, *Conqueror II* was a giant cylinder of a ship, shaped more or less like the cans in which coffee is shipped. When under thrust, everyone and everything aboard was pulled toward the aft bulkhead, making "down" the direction opposite that in which the ship was accelerating. However, when the engines were shut off, as they had been ever since the fleet established itself athwart Spica's lanes of commerce, the ship was spun about its central axis to provide artificial gravity. In this configuration, "out" became "down," and everyone lived on the curved outer decks and studiously ignored the various furnishings and pieces of equipment retracted into the aft walls of compartments.

It was this need to generate "centrifugal force" – a mathematical fiction with no reality in the universe, but a concept that human beings stubbornly refuse to discard – that drove the design of virtually every system aboard the big blastship. The ambidextrous arrangement of the living quarters was only the most visible accommodation to the ship's need to fight and function whether thrusting or spinning. Both modes required a high degree of dynamic balance in three orthogonal axes, a balance continuously adjusted by transferring fluids between tanks via a complex network of valves, pumps, and pipes.

Farthest aft were the fuel tanks. They took up nearly thirty percent of *Conqueror*'s interior volume and consisted of six large cylinders wrapped in meter-thick layers of mirrored insulation that were arrayed in a Star-of-David pattern just outboard of the big photon resonator tube that drove the ship through vacuum. Forward of the fuel tanks were the other consumables. Mirrored spheres tinted green contained liquid oxygen. Most were paired with larger cryogenic tanks tinted blue that contained liquid nitrogen. White spheres contained potable water while slate-gray held wastewater waiting purification. All of these liquids were sufficiently dense that redistributing them among the various storage tanks had an effect on the ship's balance. The system was so precise that it even compensated for the perturbations caused when off-duty crewmen used one of the main circumferential passageways as a jogging track.

While spinning the ship to provide artificial gravity solved a variety of problems for the crew, it presented the original designers with any number of difficulties. Many of the weapons and sensors objected to being spun like a can at the end of a rope. For these, the ship had two large outrigger booms that extended the full length of the hull. The booms were mounted on bearings, and remained steady in space even when the central cylinder of the ship was rotating. Another problem had been where to locate the large open volume in which the blastship's auxiliary craft were stored. When the ship was spinning at nearly two revolutions per minute, the only safe place to take a smaller vessel aboard was along the spin axis, and because the engines monopolized all of the available real estate at the stern, Hobson's choice dictated the location of the hangar bay. It was forward, with the doors inset at the center of the concave bow.

Like the ship herself, *Conqueror II*'s hangar bay had been constructed oversize. It was a hollow cylindrical cavern stretching from the bow halfway back into the cylindrical hull. In fact, the six big thrust girders that were the blastship's backbone formed part of the hangar bay's structure, making it one of the strongest compartments in the ship. The main cylinder of the bay was intersected forward of its midpoint by three smaller circular openings. These were *Conqueror*'s "sally ports," unobstructed shafts leading to space doors in the outer hull and used to disgorge auxiliary craft quickly during battle.

Normally the bay was crowded with the various smaller ships necessary to keep a blastship operational in enemy space. There were the armed scouts, vessels with six-man crews that swept space in front of the fleet, engaged enemy scouts, and harassed the enemy out of all proportion to their size. There were inter-orbit ferries, the ugly collections of geometric shapes to whom fell the mundane tasks of transporting personnel and supplies between the larger ships. There were small repair craft with grappling arms and oversize thrusters, as well as other specialized craft.

Because the hangar bay was not airtight, operations inside the bay were overseen from one of the three observation galleries inset in the inner bay wall between the thrust girders. Roofed over with armor glass, these gave a panoramic view of everything going on in this miniature spaceport at the heart of the blastship.

Drake felt a spring in his step as he entered the Number 2 Gallery. This close to the axis, spin-gravity was only one-quarter what it was at the outer hull – just enough to keep everyone attached to the deck. He strode to the center of the gallery and tilted his head back to take in the panorama of the bay overhead.

With many of her auxiliaries away on missions, *Conqueror*'s bay was as empty as Richard had ever seen it. Forward, the big hangar doors were retracting slowly into their recesses, revealing the black of space beyond and a small scout boat waiting to enter. The boat was stationary with respect to the open doors, having matched its roll rate to that of the big blastship. The universe beyond cartwheeled. Although the stars were invisible, the angle of the sunlight streaming through the open doors changed continuously, making a complete circuit twice each minute.

As he watched, a long, multi-segmented arm came into view, reaching up toward the nose of the scout. The grapple mechanism on the end of the arm attached itself to the ship's bow, and several green lights blinked to life along the scout's hull. The lights signified that the small ship's controls and been locked and its engines disabled. Had they not, *Conqueror*'s traffic control officer would not have allowed it inside the bay, a paranoid attitude of which the commanding admiral heartily approved.

The arm pulled the small ship slowly inside. The hangar bay doors began to slide ponderously closed as the arm moved the scout ship to the docking port just forward of Gallery Two. The scout had appeared tiny compared to the scale of the bay, but now that it was docked just beyond the gallery's armor glass roof, it looked like the capable interplanetary craft that it was.

There were the usual noises as the docking fixture latches engaged and the disembarkation tube filled with air. Drake watched as the airlock telltales blinked from red, to yellow, and then to green. As the lock made the customary soft sighing sound, he signaled the Marine in charge of the band standing by opposite the airlock.

The leader, a Sergeant-Major whose primary duties involved ship security, repelling hostile boarders, or in rare cases, boarding enemy craft under fire, signaled his men, who launched into a passable rendition of the Sandarian national anthem.

The inner door swung open and there was no activity for long seconds until a familiar figure stepped out onto the landing stage. Phillip Walkirk looked around, saw Drake, and then with a military form that would have made his father proud, marched to where the admiral waited and saluted crisply.

"Captain Phillip Walkirk of the Light Cruiser *Queen Julia,* reporting for duty, sir!" he said, shouting over the echoing music.

"Welcome back to Spica, Captain. You have been missed. Now who is this VIP you have aboard? You didn't say in your message."

Phillip grinned. "No, sir. I didn't want to spoil the surprise."

"What surprise…?" Drake began, just as he caught sight of a second familiar figure exiting the airlock. His words did not so much chop off as gurgle to a halt. He was unaware of the spectacle he presented. It was not, after all, every day that those under his command were privileged to see the admiral with his mouth hanging open. Finally, after long seconds, he remembered to breathe and managed to squeak out, "Bethany!"

Bethany, who had spent the last several hours alternating between being sick with tension and making sure that her appearance was just right, smiled broadly and nodded, her rehearsed speech completely forgotten.

Drake was not sure which one of them moved first, or indeed, had any memory of either of them moving at all. Suddenly, the two of them were entangled in one another's arms and he was enveloped in the smell of her perfume, the taste of her lips, and the soft feel of her body against his. These were sensations he had longed for virtually every day of the current campaign. With his senses in overload, the cares of battle seemed, for the moment, far away. Long minutes passed before either of them was again aware of their surroundings.

#

What may well have been the longest kiss in the history of the Spica System slowly ended and Richard contented himself with the primal pleasure of holding his wife close with his nose nestled in her hair. They stood this way for more than a minute as he slowly returned to the present. The Marine band, which had ceased playing sometime while he had been elsewhere, were standing rigidly at attention, their eyes averted from their commander and his mate. He noted with interest that several of them were having trouble keeping their features immobile as they fought the smiles that were welling up inside. For some reason, this did not irritate him, as it normally would have.

No, not "for some reason." He held the reason in his arms.

Slowly, he disengaged from Bethany and thrust her out to arm's length to better look at her. His first impression had been correct. She was as beautiful as he remembered her. More beautiful, in fact. The last time he had seen her, she had looked like she swallowed a beach ball. Now she was as svelte as the day he had married her. She was not *more* beautiful; she was differently beautiful. Drake considered all of the things he wanted to tell her, to ask her, to confide in her, but found that no words issued forth. His emotions were too jumbled to gain control of his traitor tongue. As he struggled to control them, a new emotion bubbled to the surface in the boiling cauldron of his brain. The emotion was a mixture of irritation, pride, and an overwhelming curiosity.

"What the hell are you doing here, darling?" he demanded, "and where is the baby?"

"He's safe, Richard. I left him with my Uncle Clarence and hired a nanny. As for what I am doing here, it is much too long a story for the moment. Can't that wait ... just a little while?"

He pondered the question, sorted out the implications, and grinned. "I suppose so, now that you mention it!" He drew her close until someone cleared his throat nearby. With reluctance, he released his wife, straightened, and turned to Phillip, who was standing a meter away, studiously ignoring them.

"Thank you for your 'surprise,' Captain. Bethany was the last person in the universe I expected to pop out of that airlock."

"You are welcome, sir. I hope my little theatrical stunt won't hurt my chances for promotion."

Drake folded Bethany under one arm and made a show of pondering Phillip's future as a naval officer. "I don't know, Captain. Is there a rank higher than 'King' in the Sandarian Navy?"

Phillip grinned. "Come to think of it, Admiral, I don't believe there is. Now, sir, if I may be dismissed..."

"You are dismissed, Commander," he said, not really noticing the Sandarian prince as he swung Bethany around and headed for the hatch. They had gone half a dozen steps when she tugged at him and the two of them turned to face Walkirk once again.

"Phillip, will you take care of ..."

"Your cargo? Consider it done."

"Cargo?" Drake asked. "What cargo?"

"Later, darling," she responded. "Now, how far is it to your cabin?"

"It would be too far if it were just beyond this hatch!"

#

The cabin was dark save for the one small blue night-light required by regulations. Richard opened his eyes and for a moment could not remember where he was. The cabin was familiar, but there was someone in his bunk with him. Then he remembered and he smiled. Last night he had made love to his wife for the first time in more than a year, and it had been like the first time all over again ... actually, like the first *three* times.

The hurried stroll to his cabin had proved something that he had always suspected, namely that scuttlebutt aboard ship is transmitted at the speed of light. It seemed that every crewman they encountered knew that the admiral's wife had come aboard. A steady stream of grinning crewmen snapped to attention and executed a perfect military salute as they passed.

They had finally made the sanctuary of his cabin and had savored another long kiss before other needs intervened and their reunion dissolved into a laughing race to see who could get out of their clothes first. Bethany won and helped Richard, after which they fell onto the too-small bunk in a tangle of arms and legs. What followed had been an urgent striving together, an athletic contest where there were no winners or losers. There had been no time for subtlety or soft caresses; just a hard coming together that expunged the memory of lonely fearful nights spent on Alta and with the fleet.

Their second spate of lovemaking had been slower, but still the act of lovers rediscovering things once known, but temporarily forgotten. After a short period of slumber, they had come together a third time. This time their act of love had been slow and languorous, the unhurried coupling of married people. The last had been best and they had remained entwined as sleep overtook them yet again.

As Richard's memories of the previous night returned in a flood, he glanced at his sleeping wife. Her hair was a tangle over her face and she was emitting quiet snoring sounds. His left arm had gone to sleep where she was using it as a pillow. Her own left arm was thrown carelessly across his naked chest. One of her breasts was trapped between his torso and her arm, forcing it into an interesting shape – although, he reminded himself, he could think of no uninteresting shapes. He raised his head from the pillow and gazed down his own body to where her naked hip rose like a gently rounded hillock to one side while one of her legs was thrown across his.

He dropped his head back on the pillow and stared at the overhead that would become a bulkhead when next *Conqueror*'s engines came alive. He willed this moment to go on forever. Forever lasted two minutes until Bethany stirred, then stretched, then opened her eyes.

She looked around the cabin, then discovered him looking at her, and smiled.

"Good morning, husband."

"Good morning, wife."

"What time is it?"

"Coming up on 05:00 hours. Time for breakfast if you're hungry."

"Starving," she replied. "I don't normally get so much... exercise."

"Me neither. Shall we 'exercise' again before we head for the mess?"

She raised her head from his arm and glanced down his torso before looking down at him from above. "It would seem the gentlemen is more gallant than practical," she replied with a grin.

He sighed. "You may be right. Breakfast it is, then."

There had been a time when living space had been a privilege of rank aboard a ship of war. Richard had once read that Christopher Columbus's cabin consumed half the living space aboard the *Santa Maria*. No longer. His cabin was no larger than that of any other officer, and actually smaller than the cabins provided enlisted personnel – although, to be fair, enlisted ranks were bunked four to a compartment. There was just enough space in Drake's cabin for one person to dress comfortably. It took the two of them longer to wash, dress, and make themselves presentable than he would have thought possible. Of course, the process was interrupted frequently by kisses and gentle caresses.

Bethany bemoaned the fact that in their hurry the previous evening, she was separated from her kit bag, and as a result, had nothing new to wear.

"We'll find it," Richard said as he kissed her one more time. "It's probably out in the corridor right now, waiting for us to open the hatch."

"Do you think so? Let's look."

He moved to the hatch and opened it manually, cracking it open just enough to search the corridor beyond. There was no kit in evidence.

"Not to worry," he said when he reported failure. "We'll find it. It can't have gotten too lost aboard ship."

"But all of my baby recordings are in that bag. I wanted to show them to you while we eat."

"We'll have plenty of time to see them later. In the meantime, you can tell me why you left our son with your uncle, and came traipsing out here where you could get yourself killed."

"Are you going to be cross with me, Richard?"

"After last night? Never. However, it must have been a damned good reason"

"Believe me, it was."

#

# Chapter 21

The corridor between his cabin and the officers' mess was more crowded than usual for this early, Drake noted. Every officer and crewman they encountered seemed to have a barely suppressed grin on his or her face. The female crewmembers were the worst as they gazed at Bethany with looks bordering on envy.

After it had happened a half a dozen times, Bethany said, "Does every woman onboard have a crush on you, Richard?"

"I beg your pardon?" he asked. As they proceeded around the Alpha-Six circumferential corridor, his ears had been growing progressively redder. If this foolishness did not stop, he was going to have someone on report.

"The women. They all look at me as though I've stolen you from them."

"Not likely," he replied. "They are probably thinking that we just blew hell out of the non-fraternization regulations."

"A man can't even sleep with his wife aboard this ship?" she asked.

He laughed. "Frankly, I'm not sure the subject has ever arisen."

Like most interstellar colonies, Alta had always been protective of women. Sociologists noted that this parochial attitude was a nearly universal reaction of human societies when faced with populating a new planet. Females were too important to a society's future health to risk them needlessly. Thus, for much of Richard Drake's career, the Navy had been a males-only organization. In fact, Bethany herself had been the first woman with whom he had served aboard a starship. That was because her uncle, the hereditary terrestrial ambassador, had refused to give up control of *Discovery*'s jump codes for the first expedition following the restoration of Alta's foldpoint unless his niece went along as his representative.

Alta had only begun recruiting women into its navy after it became obvious that every available human resource would be needed to defeat the Ryall. Even then, there had been resistance to the idea. Unlike other space navies where mixed crews had been the norm for centuries, the Altan Navy was still not comfortable

with the idea of women aboard warships. As a result, most of the
regulations concerning social interaction between the genders could
be summed up in a single word: DON'T!

After what seemed to Drake to be an eternity, they reached the
officer's mess. Inside, they found Captain Carter and most of his
staff already seated at the various tables bolted to the gently curving
deck. Phillip Walkirk was also there. He occupied a table by
himself in the far corner of the compartment. As Bethany entered,
the officers quickly got to their feet.

"Captain Carter, I would like to introduce my wife, Bethany,"
Drake said to the blastship's commanding officer. "Bethany,
Captain Pelham Carter. He commands *Conqueror*. This is his ship.
He just lets me ride along if I keep out of trouble."

"Hello, Pel," she replied, shaking the captain's hand.

"You two know each other?"

"We met at one of Mrs. Mortridge's parties."

"You have an excellent memory, Mrs. Drake."

Slowly, Drake introduced her to each of *Conqueror*'s officers
and those of his battle staff. She had met a number of them at
parties they had thrown at their house while the fleet was preparing
for battle. Other officers were new to her, having joined the
blastship recently. She greeted each of them warmly.

The most junior of them, an ensign, making conversation,
asked Bethany if she had slept well.

"Quite well, Ensign Mabry," she replied, ignoring the sudden
reddening of his complexion as the implications of the question
seeped in.

"Mabry, make room for the admiral and his wife," Captain
Carter ordered.

"Please, keep your seat, Mr. Mabry. My husband and I will
join Commander Walkirk, if he doesn't mind. You don't, do you,
Phillip?"

"My honor, Bethany."

"Can we, Richard?" Bethany asked. "Or does protocol require
you to sit with the other officers?"

"One of the advantages of being the commanding admiral
aboard my flagship, I can sit wherever I damn well please. Besides,
we've caused Mr. Mabry enough inconvenience this morning."

That comment increased the blush on the ensign's cheeks.

They pulled out chairs tethered to the table with bungee cords
and sat down. Almost immediately, Richard found a white-coated

steward at his elbow. The steward, like the band members, was a combat Marine. He took their orders and then withdrew discreetly.

"I don't remember having such luxuries aboard *Discovery*," Bethany said. "The wardroom sported a century-old self-service dispenser. You actually had to get up to get your food."

"Service aboard the flagship has its advantages," Phillip agreed. "Our little cruiser doesn't even have a dispenser. You have to make the sandwiches yourself."

"Which brings up a question," Drake said, suddenly aware that the prince should have been back onboard his ship by now. "Why are you still here, Commander?"

"I asked him to stay, Richard," Bethany replied. "I wanted him here when I explained my reason for coming. I figured you wouldn't yell at me as loudly if there were witnesses."

Drake glanced around the crowded compartment. "Why do I think that I'm not going to like what's coming next?"

"We can wait, if you like, darling."

"Better to get it over with. What are you doing here, wife? What was important enough to leave the baby? And what is this cargo Phillip took care of last night?"

"The last question is the easiest. The cargo consisted of two Ryall."

"Two? You brought Varlan with you?"

She nodded.

"Who is the other one?"

"Periskay. We picked him up on Corlis."

"What are you doing, starting an interstellar zoo?"

"I'm continuing my studies," she replied with a sniff. Then, she leaned forward and she said her next sentence all in a rush. "Oh, Richard, I think I've discovered something."

"What?" he asked.

"I believe I know how to bring this war to an end short of exterminating the Ryall."

Drake sat back and regarded his wife with narrowed eyes. It was as though a switch closed in his brain. Gone was the loving husband, replaced by the cold, calculating, admiral with responsibility for the lives of the hundreds of thousands who served under him, and for the fate of the human race.

He did not speak for nearly a minute. When he did, it was to say, "Perhaps, darling, you were right. This is best discussed in my command center. I take it, Commander, that you are a party to my wife's discovery?"

"She has briefed me, Admiral."

"Then you had better come along. Steward! Put our breakfasts in a box. We'll eat them later."

#

If Richard's cabin was no different from that of any other officer, his command center left no doubt that an admiral worked there. His personal battle station was in the transparent bubble suspended above the Fleet Operations Center. At the touch of a control, he could opaque any section of the glass wall and replace it with a holographic display, even to the point where he was completely surrounded by information about the ongoing battle for the Spica System. There was a second set of bulkhead-sized displays in the operations center below, displays his staff used to plan battle strategy, deploy fleets, track the use of consumables, and make sure that the foldpoint blockades were as robust as resources allowed.

Like the Control Center from which Captain Carter maneuvered the ship, the Fleet Operations Center was located at the spin axis, sandwiched between the hangar bay and the engine spaces, which meant that spin gravity was essentially non-existent. Drake pulled himself hand over hand to the powered chair behind the semicircular desk and directed Bethany and Phillip to take the two seats in front. Below them, a dozen watch standers sat at consoles nearly as complex as Drake's own and monitored the fleet. Drake glanced at the big threat board that dominated the operations center. There, a tiny red star was surrounded by eight glowing foldpoint symbols. One of these he did not have to worry about. That was the Spica-Carratyl foldpoint, through which poured a steady stream of reinforcements. The plot board showed numerous dimly glowing lines that marked the orbits of newly arrived ships as they spread out to deploy to their assigned positions in one of the seven separate blockade forces. One glowing line marked the transit of the first of the big orbital fortresses, already halfway to the Spica-Darthan foldpoint.

The seven foldpoints leading to Ryall space glowed a satisfying emerald-green, indicating that things were quiet for the moment.

Drake slipped the meal packet onto the desk in front of him and keyed the magnetic field that would keep it from floating away.

Bethany and Phillip did the same. When all of them were secure, Richard said, "Let's have breakfast before it gets cold. In between bites, wife, you can tell me what you have discovered. Begin at the beginning. I don't want to miss anything."

While the impromptu picnic continued on his desktop, Bethany told him of her research since he had departed Alta to join the invasion, and of her growing empathy with Varlan, especially after little Ritchie's birth. She recounted how she had attended one of Mrs. Mortridge's parties, and had been shocked to hear members of parliament casually discussing the destruction of the Ryall home worlds. She spoke of the growing pessimism at home as the public absorbed each new casualty report and of the swelling desire to be done with the war.

Drake, who had listened quietly in between bites of food, commented on the latter point. "We feel it out here in the fleet as well. Frankly, I was primarily worried about the battle to take Spica away from the Ryall. I think I underestimated how difficult it would be to hold on after we established our blockade. Somehow, casualties sustained while advancing on an objective are easier to take than this continuous bleeding we have been doing while on blockade duty."

"Are you saying that the Ryall are winning?" Bethany asked, suddenly wondering if she were on a fool's errand herself. Showing the Ryall mercy was one thing if they were prostrate before the human fleet, and something else again if they were winning the battle. In fact, the difference was crucial to the success or failure of her plans.

"Not at all. We destroy fifty of their ships to every one we lose. The problem is, they have more than twenty worlds strung out behind those seven foldpoints. A world is an indescribably large resource for them, a reservoir of strength and supplies. We, on the other hand, are at the end of a supply line that stretches back a dozen foldpoints. We are woefully outmatched in the number of ships we can commit to battle, while they have to feed their forces through the foldpoints to get at us. That gives us the advantage so long as we have enough ships and ammunition to maintain the blockade. Currently, supplies are adequate. Patience is the commodity we seem to have in the shortest supply. I just hope we can stand the strain long enough for them to run out of resources."

Now it was Bethany's turn to nod agreement. "That is the problem at home. People are losing patience with the war. They think they perceive the end of the nightmare, and they are anxious to wake to a bright new day."

"Sorry I interrupted you, dear," Richard said around a piece of warm toast. "Continue with your story."

"The breakthrough came when Varlan was in another of her fertile phases. The physiological changes were especially severe this last time, so I offered to assist her..." She told Richard of her idea to obtain a Ryall prisoner to fertilize Varlan's eggs and, in effect, ease her misery. She then described her surprise, and then growing excitement, when Varlan adamantly refused. She then paused for effect and noticed the look of incomprehension in his eyes.

"Don't you see the significance, Richard? I offered her an option that would have satisfied one of her most basic instincts, yet she refused... violently. For a second, I thought she was going to bite me."

"Did she say why when she refused?"

"She told me that it would be immoral for a captive to bring hatchlings into the world."

He nodded. "That's certainly a reasonable point. We would probably have reacted the same."

"Of course we would have. The sublimation of the mating urge while held captive by our enemies is a perfectly reasonable act among humans. It is not reasonable for a Ryall. Why are we at war with these beasties?" she demanded, aware that her voice was becoming shrill, yet unable to control it. "They attacked us on first sight and without warning because that is the way Ryall are built. Xenophobia is not an attitude with them. It is in their very genes, a relic left over from their long war with the Swift Eaters. They attacked because that is what their instinct told them to do. Varlan's instinct told her that it was time to mate, yet her intelligence overrode the instinct."

"Your point?"

"Simply this. If the Ryall are intelligent enough to avoid having offspring in captivity, then surely they are intelligent enough to know that we will exterminate them if they leave us no other choice."

"So?"

"All we need do, my darling, is point this danger out to them with sufficient vigor that even the stupidest among them will understand it, then give them a more palatable option – surrender."

"Not once in more than a century of warfare has there ever been a case of a Ryall ship surrendering before we managed to pulverize it into scrap metal.  Then the survivors don't really surrender.  They merely allow us to collect them after their situation has become hopeless."

"They haven't surrendered because one Ryall warship is not significant in the grand scheme of things, at least, not the way they look at it.  Things have changed, Richard.  You and this fleet have changed them.  We are now in position to destroy their entire species.  While they were winning the war, their instincts and their intelligence were in harmony.  Both told them that the best way to keep the hatchlings safe was to destroy us.  Now that we sit astride their major lanes of commerce and are slowly throttling their economy, they know that we will soon be in position to rain atomic fire down on their heads one home world at a time."

"That is why they are working so hard to break through the blockade."

She nodded.  "Consider what it must be like on the other side of the foldpoint.  Suddenly, after more than a century of fighting, the dreaded bipedal monsters are preparing a knockout blow.  The Ryall instinct is to fight, but their intellect is telling them that the fight will likely be futile.  No longer are their brains in sync with their instincts.  A fight to the death is a lot more attractive when it is the other guy you expect to do the dying.

"The Spica invasion has shaken their confidence to its core, Richard, and as a result, if we give them the proper incentives, the lizards may be ready to listen to reason for the first time in more than a century."

Drake opened his mouth to reply, but no words issued forth.  At that moment, alarms began to sound all through the ship.

#

## Chapter 22

Admiral Sergei Gower was on duty in his Combat Center when the nearby Spica-Darthan foldpoint exploded in photonic fire. Six distinct points of light lit up the blackness of space before turning into boiling nebulae of radiance that expanded outward at nearly the speed of light.

"Report!" he ordered.

"They are tonne-yield antimatter bombs, Admiral. Six of them. Distribution across the foldpoint appears to be random, as you would expect at the end of a jump. They have added something new, however. Those clouds are a smorgasbord of ionized atoms, with high oxygen content. It seems to have been brewed up especially to make it difficult for our sensors to see through the clouds."

"Primarily ionized oxygen?" he asked.

"That's what the spectral analyzers say, Admiral."

"Damnit! Oxygen will corrode hell out of most of our sensor coatings."

"Yes, sir. I suspect they know that."

"How long until the first cloud engulfs our closest units?"

"Ninety seconds, sir."

Gower scowled and punched for the fleet-comm channel. "All ships. They are trying to mess with our sensors. That cloud contains highly energetic oxygen ions. Calculate when you will be engulfed and shut down all but essential sensors required for combat. You will secure no earlier than fifteen seconds before you are engulfed, and remain secure until concentrations again drop to safe levels. High Guard, shift to maximum sensitivity and relay to all ships. Keep sharp up there. You will be our eyes for this battle."

Gower watched as pinpoints on his battle display acknowledged his order. High Guard consisted of half a dozen sensor-laden craft stationed well back from the foldpoint. Their offensive power was nil, but they had the best eyes in the fleet, and more importantly at the moment, the best protected eyes. The problem was communications delay. There would be a nearly one-tenth second delay between observation and relay, and in a space battle, where milliseconds counted, one-tenth second was an eternity.

"Decoys are being destroyed in Quadrant Seven, Sub-Quadrant Beta, Admiral. They seem to be concentrating their fire there."

"What force have they sent through?"

"No identification yet. We should have them in another few seconds. The clouds are dissipating quickly. ... Coming through now. I make it two hundred ships, including three heavies. Shit! They are orbital fortresses, Admiral. They are pouring everything they have into Seven Beta!"

Gower again activated fleet-comm. "All ships. This is a major push. Their fleet has three orbital fortresses with them. All weapons, maximum rate of fire. Concentrate on the heavies. I repeat, major fire on the heavies."

He had no sooner finished his order than *Royal Avenger* began to buck as electromagnetic cannon accelerated missiles out of their launchers. At the rate they were firing, the blastship would run dry of ordnance in less than fifteen minutes. Hopefully, the Ryall would not stick around that long.

"Report from *Constantine*, Admiral. *Farragut* just exploded. Communications reports that *Constantine* ceased transmission in mid-sentence. *Rohatan* reports *Constantine* took a major hit, but is still on their screens. FleetPlot reports general movement by all Ryall craft in the direction of Seven-Beta. First contact, 35 seconds..."

Gower set his jaw and listened to the continuous drone of damage reports on the command circuit. In quick order, his fleet lost six ships, including two heavy cruisers, one vaporized with all hands.

The good news was that the lizards were paying dearly for their audacity. As quickly as blue icons representing human ships were blinking off the screens, red icons were disappearing faster. Almost as quickly as he gave the order to concentrate fire on the orbital fortresses, one of the big, lumbering brutes flashed into incandescence. Gower gave thanks to whoever or whatever had gotten it. Of course, any ordnance it had managed to launch between breakout and destruction was still en route and would remain dangerous until it either ran out of fuel or exploded against a human ship.

The expanding clouds of ionized plasma from the antimatter bombs produced an unexpected effect. The bombs had polluted space with several hundred ionized atoms per cubic centimeter. As a result, the powerful laser and particle beams no longer drilled their invisible holes in space. The passage of each energetic beam left a ghostly emerald trail of turbulent plasma in its wake.

The battle had turned into a surreal light show with thousands of glowing green threads weaving their deadly webs through the oxygen-rich plasma. The scene would have been beautiful had it not been so deadly. Sergei Gower's admiration for the sight soon turned to horror as he thought through the tactical implications of those straight lines of translucent radiance.

Since the start of the Ryall-human war, it had been a military fact that the force defending one end of a foldline had a nearly insurmountable tactical advantage over an attacker. Not only did the defender have time to sow his mines and deploy his ships to optimum advantage, but he could also hide them among millions of decoys. In effect, he could hide his fleet in plain sight.

The six expanding clouds of plasma from the antimatter bombs had largely enveloped the two warring fleets and were on the verge of merging into a single large cloud. The ghost-like tracks left by the passage of laser and particle beams had little effect on the Ryall tactical situation. Their ships were thrusting at maximum power for the developing hole in the human blockade and their drive flares ended any hope they might have had of camouflaging their position.

Sergei Gower's ships, on the other hand, had been deployed with the care of a geneticist combing over the genome of his first-born. The oxygen-rich plasma cloud effectively defeated all of his best-laid plans for defense of the foldpoint.

With plasma trails leading back to every ship that had fired either its lasers or particle beam cannon, it didn't take too many shots before each human ship was the focal point of dozens of threads of dim radiance of their own making. The Ryall ships noted where these threads crossed to pinpoint the positions of their adversaries. Sorting out the human defenders from among their decoys suddenly became easy. The decoys were the blips that were not shooting at them.

As ship after ship in the affected quadrant began to be hit by return laser fire, Gower considered ordering a halt to beam-fire altogether, but quickly discarded the idea. Lasers were primarily antimissile weapons, and while enemy long-range lasers might punch holes in hull armor, they were ultimately far less destructive than a nuclear warhead.

"All ships. They are tracking your beams through the soup. Take evasive action, Evasion Beta Three."

While he watched, other Ryall ships continued to wink out of existence. What had started as a fleet of two hundred was down to eighty and dropping.

The same display that showed him the growing Ryall losses also outlined the sudden gaping hole in the human blockade globe. The general movement of Ryall ships continued in that direction.

"We have breakout," a calm voice announced in Gower's ear.

"Seven Beta?"

"Yes, sir. At least a dozen enemy ships have cleared our formation and are accelerating away at high speed."

Gower nodded. That was to be expected. The first job of any breakout force would be to complicate his tactical situation. In this case, that would probably mean a high-speed run to Spica, a gravity well maneuver around it, and then a high speed dash back here, arriving just in time to help the next breakout wave as it materialized in the foldpoint.

"Tell Fleet about the breakout. We are going to need backup."

"Yes, sir."

Five minutes passed slowly. One of the surviving orbital fortresses exploded sometime in that period, but Gower was too drained to feel any triumph. With the second fortress gone, fire shifted to the third and Ryall ships began to disappear of their own volition as they began to jump back to their side of the foldpoint. With the breakout successful, the need for courage had evaporated and the Ryall commanders' duty shifted to saving what ships they could.

The first to go was the surviving fortress. It did not get away unscathed. Spectral analysis showed it leaking oxygen and water vapor before it disappeared back into the foldpoint. Still, whatever damage had been inflicted, the fortress still had use of its jump generators.

The smaller survivors quickly followed. Within seconds, the foldpoint was empty of everything but the dead and the dying.

#

The battle staff manning the Fleet Operations Center aboard *Conqueror II* had been enjoying a quiet morning. For once, there were no Ryall probes in any of the foldpoints, and humankind's possession of the Spica system was temporarily unchallenged.

Aboard the flagship, as aboard the rest of the ships in the fleet, exhausted crews used the weeklong respite to make repairs, replenish their stocks, and run diagnostics on their ships and armament.

In the Fleet Operations Center, that left time for catching up on overdue reports and speculating about the woman the Admiral had in his sanctum sanctorum. While it would not have been good form to stare, more than one officer – male and female – felt the need to turn around to check the secondary status displays on the aft bulkhead, and in the process, surreptitiously lift their gaze to check out the figures in the glass bubble suspended above and behind them.

The first alarm changed the easygoing character of the morning's activities. Suddenly, acceleration couches were raised to sitting position, and fingers began a staccato dance across keyboards to punch up status displays. Something bad was happening and it was their job to figure out what, and then coordinate the fleet's response.

Individual displays and their large bulkhead counterparts began to change as data flowed in from all over the system. The Spica-Darthan foldpoint switched from emerald to crimson, followed almost immediately by the Spica-Rylmar and the Spica-Tarnath foldpoints. In fact, when one considered the communication delay from each of the three zones of battle, whatever had set off the alarms had happened as close to simultaneously as Einstein's theory of relativity would allow.

"What is going on, Richard?" Bethany asked as hooting alarms filled the compartment.

"Something is happening in several of the foldpoints," he replied as he began rapidly punching up displays of his own. "It looks like the coordinated attack we have been worried about."

The transparent sphere that separated them from the operations center suddenly turned opaque as a holographic overview of the system formed in front of them.

"Dunbar!"

"Yes, Admiral," one of his staff officers answered over the command circuit.

"Get me a situation report from the affected foldpoints."

"Aye aye, sir."

"Toshida."

"Sir?"

"Any reports from the other four?"

"Negative, although two are still beyond our light horizon." Being 'beyond the light horizon' meant that the communications delay between the foldpoints and the fleet was longer than the time that had elapsed since initiation of hostilities. "We should know within ten seconds ..."

The seconds ticked down like minutes. At the end of that time, there were no more reports of fighting. Drake began to breathe again.

"We have Ryall activity in three foldpoints, Admiral," Commander Dunbar reported. "Looks like antimatter bombs with a new wrinkle. We have clouds of ionized gas racing outward from the site of the explosions. Our sensors can't penetrate it."

Over the next seven minutes, they watched the battle unfold, in not only the Spica-Darthan foldpoint, but all three of them. Drake's stomach turned to lead as he realized that the Ryall had achieved a breakthrough in the foldpoint from Darthan. Then in quick succession, reports from the other two foldpoints told of additional breakouts.

"How many ships total?" he demanded.

"We're getting the information in now, Admiral. A dozen at Spica-Darthan, eight at Spica-Rylma, and twenty at Spica-Tarnath."

"Where are they headed?"

"They all seem to be diving for the star, sir."

He nodded. "Gravity-well turn, of course. Tactical, any chance they might be trying to join up?"

"No indication one way or the other yet, Admiral. It would be the smart way to bet. A gravity-well turn around a star lends itself to a hyperbolic tactical rendezvous."

"That it does," Drake replied. Spaceships are not airplanes and have no need to 'keep the pointy end into the wind.' Usually when a ship wanted to reverse direction in vacuum, it flipped end-for-end and began thrusting in the direction from whence it came. While conventional, the maneuver was about as subtle as the kiss of a spaceport joy girl. In the current situation, it was also a good way to attract a missile, especially during that portion of the maneuver when the ship's velocity reversed. For an instant, the maneuvering vessel was hanging stationary in space and a prime target for any enemy within range.

The presence of Spica nearby offered the Ryall an alternative and significantly complicated Drake's job in the process. Instead of accelerating away from whatever foldpoint they had broken out of, then slowing and reversing course, the fugitive Ryall fleets were all accelerating directly for the system primary. By diving close to Spica, the escaped enemy ships could sweep by at high speed just beyond the star's chromosphere while thrusting directly toward the star. If done properly, their hyperbolic orbital velocity would sweep them safely past before they rammed the star. The result would be a tight orbit around Spica; followed by a fast climb along whatever orbital path they chose.

If the three breakout forces timed the maneuver properly, they would regularize their orbital planes during the gravity-well turn, link up, and come boiling out of the sun like a flock of mad hornet-birds, giving some blockade commander 40 additional enemy warships with which to contend during the next breakout attempt. It was the space version of the classic hammer-and-anvil maneuver that dated back to at least the Sumerians.

"Of course, we can't predict which foldpoint they will be aiming for until after they round the star," Drake said to his tactical officer via intercom.

"Unfortunately true, Admiral. When we do find out, it will be too late to get a true blocking force into place to stop them. A nice maneuver on the part of our Ryall friends."

"Any guesses?"

"Darthan, sir. They should have more resources behind that foldpoint than any of the others."

"So we send our reserves to back up Sergei Gower?"

"No, sir. Darthan is the best bet, but it could be any foldpoint on this side of the star. We'll have to wait to see their departure vector from Spica before we can move."

"By which time it will be too late to intercept from here."

"Yes, sir."

Drake furrowed his brow. Whoever had planned this particular attack had put as much thought into it as humanity had spent plotting the invasion of Spica. Until the errant Ryall ships committed themselves to a particular departure orbit following their gravity-well turn, there was no way to tell where they planned to strike. He thought Commander Dunbar's guess that the Darthan foldpoint was the logical target was a good one, but no matter how logical, he couldn't risk the future of the human race on a hunch, especially one that had only one chance in seven of being right.

It had cost the Ryall nearly five hundred ships in three foldpoints, but the cost may well have been worth it. In expending those ships, they had managed to temporarily turn the tables on his fleet. Following rendezvous, their breakout force would hold the advantage in both position and velocity, which in space war was the same as holding the high ground in an infantry battle. The only way he would be able to block their path was to get his relief force immediately underway. But underway for where? At the moment, he had nothing but conjecture to tell him where they were going. If he waited until the Ryall looped around Spica to get his ships underway, there would be no time to intercept the interlopers, let alone to destroy them.

He was in the sort of space-time box that every commander attempted to contrive for his opponent. The question was, how was he going to get out? If he did not know where they were going, how was he going to get ahead of them in time to do any good?

It was then that a stray thought materialized somewhere deep in his brain and floated tentatively to the surface. He mulled it over for long seconds, wondering if it were too obvious to be of any use, or just obvious enough to be brilliant.

The truth was that he could not predict which foldpoint the Ryall breakout force would hit, but where they were going was as plain as that glowing ball of hot gasses on the viewscreen. While the Ryall fleet could use a gravity-well turn to disguise their ultimate target, they could not disguise their destination. They were headed for the system primary. They would swoop low over the star, scrape the chromosphere nearly close enough to boil their hull plates, and then pop up on a beeline for one of his blockading fleets. While close to the star, however, they would have to follow a path preordained a thousand years ago by Sir Isaac Newton. Any deviation from their proper track and they would pop up out of the star and fly off in the wrong direction.

It would be during closest approach to Spica, when their sensors would be practically blind in the plasma soup and their environmental control systems running near overload, that they would be most vulnerable.

Richard considered his choices and risks. He felt his stomach turn to lead at what he was about to do, and then made his decision.

"Tactical, prepare the fleet for a speed run."

"Aye aye, sir. Where to?"

"Spica. We'll skim low on an opposing orbit and take them at their most vulnerable – while they have the star on one side and can't maneuver."

"Yes, sir."

Drake watched the blips showing the three separate breakout forces and tried to calculate when all three would pass behind the star. It was too much for one human mind, but no matter. The computers would tell them soon enough

He turned to Phillip, who had been standing by quietly, not wanting to disturb the admiral at his work. "Commander, you had best get back to your ship. We will be under high gravs within an hour. You will need the time to prepare."

"On my way, Admiral."

Phillip arrowed for the nearby hatch and was gone so quickly that Richard thought he could feel the breeze of the prince's passing. He turned to his wife and said, "We'd best get you to an acceleration couch."

"What is going on?" she asked. There was fear in her voice.

"We're going to slug it out with the Ryall as they make their gravity-well turn."

"What does that mean?"

"It means that we are going to fight a battle within the corona of a star."

#

# Chapter 23

Since the fleet's arrival in the Spica system, Richard Drake had spent many hours watching the ever-changing lightshow that were Spica A and B. Giant solar prominences would explode spaceward every few hours from each star, only to be wrenched into graceful spiral pinwheels by the combined gravitational and magnetic fields. The eternal pirouette was endlessly entertaining, and he had often wondered what the two stars would look like up close.

He wondered no longer.

His fleet of twenty-four ships was currently approaching the Spica twins close enough that their environmental controls were in danger of overloading. Fleet Force Spica Twelve was on a reciprocal heading to that of the Ryall breakout force. They, too, would whip around the star at high acceleration, to fly off into space more or less in the direction from whence they had come. The only difference was that they would round the binary stars at a slightly higher altitude than the Ryall were using, and would briefly have the enemy trapped between them and the twirling stars.

Spica-A was an angry blue-white football in the viewscreen, with its companion partially eclipsed behind it. Just looking at them made Richard feel hot. Even at minimum magnification and maximum filtration, the duet filled the screen and blasted the communications bands with static. Submerged as they were in electrically conductive plasma, nothing but comm-lasers could punch a message through to the rest of the fleet. The plasma and the heat also played havoc with the sensors. Many of the most sensitive instruments had been retracted into protective enclosures to keep them from burning up or shorting out, leaving the fleet half-blind as they groped for contact with the enemy.

Drake lay in his couch and watched his displays, ready to give the order that would send two-dozen warcraft into battle. He was not alone. Beside him was a second, newly installed acceleration couch. A familiar vacsuited figure lay strapped into its embrace. Just as she had done at the Battle of Sandar, Bethany was accompanying her man into harm's way. Just as he had then, Richard wished she were safe at home.

"Are you okay, darling?" he asked after making sure that his words would not go out over the command circuit.

"Fine," came the terse answer.

He didn't have to hear more. He had heard that tense monosyllabic response enough during their married life to know that she was frightened. Then, she had reason to be. Space battles tend to be quick and violent, and death often seeks out its victims too quickly for human senses to register.

Those were the lucky dead.

The unlucky dead were those trapped in helpless hulks on orbits to infinity, men and women whose blood cells had been destroyed by radiation blasts, or whose limited supplies of oxygen could be sensed by a popping of ears inside leaky vacuum suits. Then there were the really unlucky dead, spacers who found themselves unharmed and with plenty of breathing gas, but with neither food nor water to sustain them long enough for rescue.

Drake had done all he could to prepare for the coming battle, and when his preparations were complete, he put them out of his mind. He lay in his couch and watched his instruments in a stoic trance. It was as though his body knew instinctively to conserve its finite store of adrenaline, holding the vital drug in reserve for when it would truly be needed. As ten thousand generations of human warriors had done before him, Richard lay quiet and contemplative, waiting patiently to learn what his future would be this day.

As always, when battle was imminent, he was surprised to discover that he felt no fear. Or rather, the fear was there, but temporarily anesthetized. It was sleeping fitfully, just beneath the surface of his conscious mind.

In a space battle, things happen too quickly for the reaction times of mere synapses and chemical receptors. Thus, there is very little a human being can do to actually fight a starship in battle. Like lightning, many space weapons operate at the speed of light. By the time the human eye reacts to the flash, the actual event is long past. Only computers can keep up with the staccato pace of space battle in real time.

Human brains are superior when it comes to sensing nuances. Human eyes can detect patterns that are meaningless to cybernetic senses, even patterns that are not necessarily there. It is to gain these intangible skills that computers allow human beings to ride with them into battle. However, those same skills are the most vulnerable to fear or doubt. In order to maximize its effectiveness, the human brain performs an act of self-hypnosis before battle. Despite knowing better, it wraps itself in a cloak of calm invincibility.

The strange sense of calm that had descended on Drake would not last beyond initial contact with the enemy. Once the action began, he would experience excitement, concern, worry, tension, disappointment, and elation – often within the span of a few seconds.

Strangely, fear would not make its appearance until after the battle. Then it would be time for him to tally his losses and mourn his dead, assuming that he wasn't one of them. After the battle would be the time for his mind to race as it replayed every moment, wondering if there was some decision he could have made smarter, or action done or undone that would have been better otherwise.

"Where are they?" Bethany asked, her own eyes scanning the viewscreens just as every pair of eyes in the Fleet Operations Center below was doing.

"Patience. Unless they broke off the approach when they detected us closing on the star, we should see them in another two minutes."

The Ryall commander's tactical position in the coming battle would be one that Drake did not envy. In order to use the double star for a close-in gravity-well turn, the Ryall ships would have to maintain a very precise trajectory. There would be no room to maneuver or to dodge, as any deviation from nominal would skew the breakout force's departure course wildly wide of their target as they departed the twins.

From observations made before the Ryall ships disappeared behind the two stars, it appeared that their target would be the Spica-Darthan foldpoint. Orbital mechanics being what they are, that fact gave human strategists the exact time when they could expect the next Ryall force to appear in the foldpoint. Even now, ships were rushing to reinforce the Darthan blockade fleet. Some of them would actually arrive in time to do some good.

Of course, Drake considered; the whole thing might be a ruse. The breakout force could be heading for Darthan in order to take attention from one of the other foldpoints where the real breakthrough would take place. If that were the case, sending reinforcements to Darthan was merely cooperating with their plan.

Suddenly, alarms sounded and symbols flashed on the tactical screens. A telescope zoomed in on the disk of Spica-B and there, looking like a peculiarly linear array of miniature sunspots, was the Ryall breakout force.

"Attention, All Hands and All Ships," the voice of Commander Jerome Considine, his tactical officer, announced over the comm circuit. "Enemy in sight. Prepare to attack!"

#

Esssau of the Grassy Plain Below the Blue Mountains lay in his own acceleration couch, outwardly different from a human model, but performing the same function. The roar of his ship's engines was in his ears as he let his head scan side to side at the end of a long supple neck. Twin obsidian orbs scanned widely separated instrument readouts as an active brain searched for evidence of the enemy bipeds he knew to be somewhere among the solar prominences.

The close passage by the binary star had necessitated protecting many of the more sensitive instruments, leaving him feeling as though he were a half-blind balloon fish swimming in muddy water. Somewhere out there were the ships of the bipeds, and the fate of his species depended on him detecting them at maximum range.

The fact that they were probably outside his own close-in orbit did nothing to assist him in his task. His force would be silhouetted against the blue-white radiance that was threatening to melt hull plates, while the biped ships would be blackness against a black sky – at least, in the visible wavelengths. This close to the dual-star, they too would be glowing bright in the near infrared wavelengths, and that was where he had his sensor technicians searching.

"Monster fleet in sight. I make it two twelves, just as they were when we lost them behind the stars," his chief sensor technician reported.

"Where, Vistar of the Gorge Clan?" he demanded.

The coordinates he received translated to forward hemisphere, halfway to the zenith. The farseeing vision devices were already looking in that direction. They showed nothing yet.

"How long until we are in range?"

"A gross of heartbeats, Esssau."

"Signal the other ships. They are to begin firing at maximum range. I want space alive with our darters! Remember, our task is to get past them with as few losses as possible, not to engage in a fish fight."

While Vistar issued orders via comm-beam, Esssau made sure that everyone aboard *Swift Eater* knew their duty. They were a good crew. Their skill – and the Fates of Fortune – had brought them this far and would see them through the coming fight.

Esssau thought back to the terrible fight just finished. Two gross of The Race's finest ships had invaded the portal from Darthan. More than half of them had died before they could make good their escape. Esssau's eggmates numbering in the twelve-cubed had died with their ships, willingly sacrificing themselves so that a few of their number could break free of the bipeds' trap.

*Swift Eater* had been among the lucky survivors that had won free to the relative safety of open space, and since Esssau was the senior shipmaster among them, he had taken command. Later, as they had approached the dual stars that were this system's primary, two additional fleets of survivors had matched velocities with him, giving him just over three twelves combatants.

The combined fleets were numerically superior to the force the bipeds had sent out to intercept them, but this would be one battle where numbers did not count for much. It would do Esssau and The Race no good to slug it out with their enemies, trading them ship for ship. In this system, the bipeds had more ships than The Race, and if he were going to change that, he must keep an appointment back at the star portal.

No, he would have preferred to avoid a fight, but it was not to be. There they were, glowing bright in the infrared sensors, closing on his own ships with the combined velocity of converging orbits.

"Enemy in range. We are opening fire," came the hissing report from his tactical technician. *Swift Eater* recoiled as deadly fire-tailed orbs left their magazines to go in search of the enemy. Sudden expulsions of vapor told of ravening beams reaching out to intercept enemy ordnance.

"Enemy ship destroyed," the report came a dozen heartbeats later. "A seeker of the second order, it appears."

This battle was different from the one in the star portal. Then his ship had dodged and weaved, and varied its acceleration continuously in an attempt to confuse enemy computers. This time there was no acceleration other than the smooth, steady thrust that kept them on path around the star. Here, too, the Monsters had the advantage. Esssau could not change course if he was to complete his mission. His enemies were under no such constraints.

"*Etheldrel* just exploded. Also *Viran.*"

"Keep firing," Esssau ordered.

"Another enemy destroyed!"

For another dozen heartbeats, reports of dying ships flooded the communications bands. The two fleets had closed to their minimum approach distance and ordnance filled the gap between them. Just as at the star portal, the Monsters were taking a heavier toll of his ships than he was of theirs, but the kill ratio was nowhere near as lopsided as it had been.

"We are under attack," Vistar reported. "Multiple biped darters inbound. We are engaging with light beams. We are destroying them. It looks like we will be..."

Esssau, commander of the Ryall breakout force, did not have the opportunity to hear what his sensor operator had to tell him. He, his operator, and his ship became an expanding globe of plasma long before Vistar could complete his report.

#

"We got another one!" someone whooped on the command circuit.

Drake heard Pelham Carter order communications discipline, but paid it no attention. Carter would fight *Conqueror II.* Drake's job was the whole battle. So far they had been winning, but at a terrible cost.

Any hope he had that the Ryall would not spot them had evaporated when, upon closing to maximum range, the lizard fleet had begun spewing out missiles as if their magazines had infinite capacity.

Humanity's response had been to match them weapon for weapon, and then up the ante. Once again powerful lasers and particle beams had lashed out at the enemy, this time through the hydrogen-rich soup that enveloped the twin stars. Once again, the invisible beams were starkly highlighted by the plasma atmosphere.

*Conqueror II* resounded with a dull "thud" as missile exhausts washed across the hull. Ablative armor flashed momentarily bright as distant lasers found their mark, sending geysers of sparkling effluvium spaceward to disrupt the beams even as they struck home. Then the beam fire lessened as humanity's missiles drew near and the Ryall ships shifted their beams from offense to defense.

The space battle became a dogfight between ruthless automatons, as human computers matched wits with Ryall computers to see which technology held the edge in speed and programming. Missiles continued to pour forth into space; even as Drake began to worry that Captain Carter would shoot the blastship dry.

The Ryall had drawn first blood by vaporizing *ASNS Victrix*. Then it been a Ryall ship's turn to be blotted out of existence, followed by another human craft (he didn't have time to look to see who they had been), followed by three more Ryall. Then had come two minutes of steady, mutual slaughter. A dozen human craft were damaged or destroyed, while half again as many Ryall craft met the same fate. Then Drake ordered fire concentrated on the ship the computers had tentatively identified as the Ryall flagship.

Whether flagship or not, the Ryall craft was well defended. Missile after missile disappeared in a puff of vapor as defensive lasers reached out and swatted them like so many spring bugs. Then, when it seemed like their defenses were impregnable, the enemy flagship quietly blew up. One instant it was spraying missiles and laser beams in their direction, and the next, it was an expanding cloud of glowing gas ultimately destined to mix in with the plasma from the twin blue-white stars so close below.

"Keep firing," Drake ordered unnecessarily on his 'all fleet' circuit. The surviving human ships did just that, if anything, filling space with even more lethal hardware than at the beginning of the battle. In fact, it seemed that they were expending missiles faster than the theoretical maximum. At this rate, they would be out of ammunition in another two minutes. Of course, they would also be out of range.

A pea-size chunk of steel arced toward *Conqueror II*, impacting on the armor of the hangar bay hatch. One instant, the ship was hale and whole. The next, a plasma cloud flashed through the open bay, lighting it as though from a bolt of lightning, before slicing six decks deep to leave behind a cone-shaped zone of destruction.

The strike happened too quickly for anyone to be afraid. All Drake knew was that twin knives drove deep into his eyes as his inner sanctum flashed bright with violet light. Simultaneously, the armor-glass wall behind him blew out, sending sparkling shards spinning through the suddenly weightless ship. The throbbing in his eyes had barely begun when his body rebounded into the restraining straps and his vacsuit, which had been limp, went taut around his limbs.

"Bethany!" he yelled into his helmet microphone.

The silence sent a cold chill down his spine. Frantically, Richard clawed in the dark for the straps that held him to his acceleration couch. Whatever had happened to the ship was bad enough, but the only sound that answered him was that of his own ragged breathing. Suddenly, he found himself facing his worst fear.

#

# Chapter 24

"The flagship's been hit!"

Phillip Walkirk's gaze snapped from one screen to another at the report as a lead weight settled in his stomach. A quick glance at the tactical display showed that the Ryall breakout force, which had been closing ever since they had come into sight, was now receding. The two fleets had passed the point of closest approach, and the fury of their mutual slaughter should begin to quickly abate. The next few seconds would be dangerous, but after that, the two fleets would again be out of range.

"How bad?" he demanded of his tactical officer.

"Unknown, Captain. Their engines are down and they are on a natural hyperbolic orbit, although their hull appears intact."

"Match velocities, minimum time," he ordered. "Extend our defensive fire to cover them. Move!"

That last emphasis was unnecessary. As quickly as he gave the order, the steady one gravity of acceleration that *Queen Julia* had carried throughout the battle suddenly quadrupled as the engines roared. The steady stream of blue-white photons that drove the ship became a storm bright enough to overpower even the radiance of the nearby twins.

Phillip and the rest of the crew were flattened into their acceleration couches and his was not the only involuntary "oof" that issued over the command circuit. On Sandar they played the ancient game of football, suitably modified for the use of ice skates, as befitted a cold world. Phillip remembered being tackled once by a big bruising player whose respect for the Crown Prince was exceeded by his competitive drive. The weight on his chest as the bruiser had landed on him had been almost as great.

The vicious acceleration was mercifully short. As quickly as *Queen Julia* closed the distance between herself and *Conqueror II*, her engines shut down to share the flagship's trajectory. The sudden weight disappeared as quickly as it had come, and Phillip found himself rebounding into the straps, his arms and legs flying akimbo.

"Get me the admiral," he ordered.

"Sorry, sir. No response to our comm laser."

"Try radio."

"Too much interference from the stars, Captain."

"Damn it, Comm, we are practically hull to hull. We are close enough to exchange fiber optic cables. Surely you can punch a signal through the interference from this range."

"I'll try, Captain."

"Where is the rest of the fleet, Sensors?"

"Moving off fast, Captain. So are the Ryall."

Phillip began to relax. Whatever damage *Conqueror* had taken, with the two fleets on reciprocal headings, they were now passing out of range of one another. The mutual slaughter was at an end. It was time for both sides to count their dead and lick their wounds.

Stray missiles would remain a danger for another minute or so, but each second that elapsed reduced even that possibility. Deadly as they were, the nuclear-tipped missiles were optimized for high acceleration and relatively short range – at least on the scale of interplanetary distance.

Because the essence of a gravity-well turn is to get as close to a star as possible, and then attempt to dive directly into it while counting on your orbital velocity to swing you safely around, *Conqueror* and *Queen Julia* were also separating from the surviving human ships. When the flagship was hit, her powered orbit became an unpowered one. In matching velocities with the crippled behemoth, Phillip had placed his own ship in the same orbit.

If both ships remained in freefall, they would emerge from behind Spica on a vector thirty degrees different than the one they wanted. Their speed ensured that they would escape the gravitational embrace of the twin stars, and if unmodified, would turn into the classic voyage to infinity that is the terror of all spacers.

"No reply, Captain," he communications officer reported. "They are down across the board."

"Keep trying."

"Aye aye, sir."

"How long before we can send a rescue party?" he asked his executive officer.

"Not for another four hours, Captain. Our environmental controls are barely keeping up with the heat. Sending men in vacsuits out there now will only ensure that they are slowly broiled in their own juices."

Phillip uttered an oath ill suited for a future king. The truth was that now that they were out of danger from an enemy missile, there was nothing immediate he could do for Drake and his ship. Whether they lived or died would depend on how badly the flagship had been damaged. If *Conqueror*'s environmental controls were inoperative, for instance, they would be dead of heat prostration before anyone could get to them.

#

"Bethany!" Drake screamed as he clawed at the straps that held him captive. It wasn't a very military thing to shout, but he was past caring about his dignity as commanding admiral. All that mattered was the fate of his wife.

The screens were dark, as were the overhead lights. Only the emergency lights illuminated his command center, and beyond the shattered armor-glass wall, the Fleet Operations Center below. With both compartments devoid of air, whatever had hit the ship must have come in through the landing bay. That was about the only way for a weapon to reach the commanding admiral's private lair without first destroying *Conqueror*.

After a maddening fifteen seconds, Drake's gauntleted hands discovered the quick release for his straps. After an eternity as a captive flat on his back, suddenly he was floating. He carefully rotated his body until he faced Bethany's couch. With heart aflutter, he steeled his mind for what was to come next and pulled himself hand over hand to where she lay. He switched on his helmet light as he hovered over her. His heart stuttered as she squinted up at the bright light and raised one balloon-enclosed arm to shield her eyes.

"Are you all right?" he yelled at her.

Her lips moved, but no sound came out. He leaned over and pressed his helmet against hers and shouted the same question.

"Fine," came the muffled reply. "What happened?"

Rather than try to continue the conversation at full volume, he let his eyes scan her chest pack. The answer to their communications problem was there in the form of an amber light. Her comm unit was switched to operate via fiber optic cable to the nearby console. He reached out and switched the control to "auto."

"Can you hear me now?"

"Loud and clear," her frightened voice echoed in his helmet. There was also an undercurrent of relief in her voice.

"We were hit," he said, answering her first question.

"How bad is it?"

"I don't know. Everything seems to be out. That may be a ship-wide problem or just a local inconvenience. Let's get you free and see if we can figure out the extent of the damage."

"What about the Ryall?"

He glanced at the time display projected up into the corner of his faceplate.

"We're past minimum range and probably out of danger. In another minute, we'll be beyond the range of stray missiles."

In fact, by Drake's thinking, a stray missile was the least of their current problems. Being vaporized was a far cleaner death than some of the others they likely faced. He let his lamp play across the display on his wife's environmental pack, with special attention to the glowing red numbers that read out suit pressure. They seemed steady, but then, sensors could lie.

"How are your ears?"

"Too big for my own good my uncle told me when I was a little girl."

"No popping?"

"No, the pressure is holding steady. How about you?"

"The same," he reported.

Relieved, he swept his lamp around the compartment. The reason they were in vacuum was obvious. There was a meter-wide hole in the armor-glass bubble. A quick movement of his lamp showed a matching hole on the other side.

"It came in through the hangar bay, traveled across the sphere, and then out through the aft bulkhead. Wife, I would say that Rickie was damned lucky that he didn't become an orphan today."

She gurgled her agreement before gaining control of her vocal chords. "It looks like it passed no more than fifty centimeters above both of our heads."

"More like thirty," he replied.

Whatever the particle had been, it had been small and fast moving. In one respect, they had been lucky. With less energy, it would not have punched through the bulkheads cleanly. Instead, it would have penetrated and then bounced around inside until both of them were reduced to vacuum-wrapped hamburger.

"Look below, Richard!"

Drake turned and let his helmet light flash around the Fleet Operations Center. Many of his staff had not been as lucky. Red globules of freeze-dried blood floated everywhere, and at least two of the vacsuits strapped in front of sensor consoles were missing helmets... and heads.

Drake felt his stomach tighten at the sight. He warned Bethany to turn away lest she become nauseous. A helmet full of vomit would do nothing to help their situation. As his light penetrated the red haze, he was happy to note movement among the carnage.

"Who is that?" he demanded.

"Admiral Drake?" a frightened voice responded.

"Yes."

"Chief Swithens, sir."

"Anyone else alive down there, Swithens?"

"Commander Considine, sir."

"What about Lieutenant Commander Parkinson? Lieutenants Powell and Frank?"

"Dead, sir."

Drake felt his heart sink. To see the carnage was one thing. To have the death sentence pronounced on his staff was something else again. His first impulse was to clamber down the emergency ladder and assist Swithens, but his duty lay elsewhere. His next words were some of the hardest he had ever spoken.

"If you find anyone alive, get them to sickbay. My wife and I will see if we can find a damage control party to send to help you. I've got to find out what is going on in the rest of the ship."

"Yes, sir."

"We're heading aft. After you and Considine have helped anyone else alive, or if there are no other survivors, I want you to head forward to make contact with any survivors there. Understand?"

"Yes, Admiral."

"Good luck!"

"You, too, sir."

Drake turned to Bethany and said, "Come on."

"Aren't we going to try and aid them?"

He shook his head, forgetting that she could not see the gesture inside his helmet. "The most important thing is that we start making sense out of this mess. Every second we are in freefall, we are moving farther away from where we want to be. We have to get the engines back online. That takes priority."

He led her through a hatch and into one of the ship's main longitudinal corridors. They had gone only a dozen meters when they came to a closed pressure door illuminated by a blinking yellow lamp. The telltales inset just above a small armor-glass window told Drake that there was pressure on the other side.

Two meters beyond the closed pressure door was another, also with a blinking yellow light. He reached up for the manual valve set just below the window and warned Bethany to anchor herself. When he turned the spill valve, his suit was buffeted by an ethereal wind for a few seconds before it again grew quiet.

"What are you doing?" Bethany asked.

"Dumping the air between these two doors to make an airlock," he replied. With that, he unlocked the pressure door and pushed it back into its recess. As soon as it was clear, he gestured for his wife to cross into the small space beyond. He then followed her and reversed the process. When the door was again dogged tight, he rotated in midair and opened the spill valve on the other side. This time, the momentary storm ended when his suit deflated around him.

He opened the second door to discover that the corridor beyond filled with a thick haze of smoke. The blinking red alarm lights in the corridor gave the haze the look of a scene out of *Dante's Inferno*.

As Drake surveyed the damage, he thought the scene entirely appropriate.

#

Twelve hours later, the situation was improved, which is to say that the ship's condition had been upgraded from critical to merely desperate.

Whatever the particle had been, it impacted the hangar bay door about a dozen meters in from the edge of the dorsal quadrant. It had been a typical hypervelocity strike, which accounted for the neat round hole approximately ten centimeters in diameter in the armored door. Unfortunately, the physics of hypervelocity collisions dictated that the entry point was merely the apex of a long cone of destruction.

When the bullet from a high-powered rifle hits something solid, the force of impact flattens its round nose. When a bit of matter moving at dozens of kilometers per second does the same, the physics are entirely different. Matter moving that fast vaporizes in the same instant it hits a solid object. The phenomenon was first observed during anti-missile tests at the dawn of the Age of Space. When interceptor contacted warhead, both vaporized so quickly that their respective incandescent clouds interpenetrated and continued on their original orbits.

Being transformed into plasma did nothing to lessen the deadly energy of the hypervelocity particle. If anything, it increased the destruction. The ultraviolet-hot jet continued on its original course. In the flash of an eye, it traversed the length of the bay before slamming into the armored bulkhead behind which lay both the Fleet Operations and Combat Information Centers. Casualties in both compartments had been extreme as the plasma jet incinerated people and equipment in its path. The shrapnel that had nearly killed Drake and his wife had not been part of the plasma cone at all. Rather, it was a small chunk of secondary debris.

After decimating the blastship's battle staffs, the plasma jet had slammed into the engine spaces. There it had dissipated its energy among *Conqueror II*'s photon resonators, destroying two and damaging six. It had also killed half the ship's engineers when, in a final fit of fury, a small piece of the armored bulkhead had spalled off the inner control room wall and bounced around the enclosed compartment several hundred times before coming to rest in the main drive computer.

It had taken several hours to tally the butcher's bill. When they finished, the toll was one hundred twenty-seven dead, sixty wounded.

Phillip Walkirk boarded the blastship four hours after the particle strike, by which time the two ships were a quarter-million kilometers above Spica. They were still close enough to the intertwined stars to blister optical coatings, but distant enough that environmental systems no longer screamed in protest at the heat load. Drake was directing repairs on the engines when the Sandarian prince found him.

"How bad is it, Admiral?"

"Bad enough," Drake replied, happy to see Walkirk, but too tired to show much emotion. "Did you bring us any help?"

"*Queen Julia* is docked to your starboard airlock with a skeleton crew. Everyone else came aboard with me."

"Good. We can use everyone. We are hit hard. After rebuilding *Queen Julia*, your people have ten times the damage control experience that mine do."

Phillip looked around at the controlled chaos. "I can't say this is unfamiliar, Admiral. I just hoped I would never see it again."

"That makes two of us."

"How is Bethany?"

"Lucky to be alive. We both are. She is helping in sick bay."

That had been eight hours ago. Drake had lost track of Walkirk after that. His people seemed to be everywhere. Fully half the damage control parties Drake encountered were wearing the uniform of the Royal Sandarian Navy.

"Admiral, we're ready to try the engines," the Acting Chief Engineer, a squeaky-voiced youth who still showed evidence of acne, reported. He had been Third Engineer before the battle. Now he was head of the department, and one of the reasons Drake was giving his personal attention to the engine repairs. Mostly Drake just floated in midair and supervised, which gave him too much time to think. Despite his best efforts, his brain insisted on replaying those few furious minutes when he had lost more than half his force and nearly his flagship.

In the span of five short minutes, he counted fourteen human ships damaged or destroyed. As bad as that was, the lizards had fared far worse. They were down 30 vessels, including the group flagship, when the lights went out. Two more were destroyed as the fleets began to pull away from one another. That left eight survivors, and at least one of them had suffered significant damage. Long-range sensors were mostly out, but those still working showed a vacuum-thin cloud of oxygen and water vapor surrounding the fleeing Ryall craft. Oxygen and water vapor are sure signs of a hull breach, and probably more than one.

History, he imagined, would judge the latest Battle of Spica to be a tactical victory for humankind. After all, the Ryall had expended hundreds of ships and tens of thousands of warriors to achieve a breakout, and after their encounter with Drake's fleet, the breakout force was down to eight ships. They would not remain at that level for long. Already, Admiral Gower had dispatched six vessels to intercept and destroy the survivors.

The only problem was that the tactical victory had put the taste of ashes in his mouth. How could anything be a victory that had cost so many lives to achieve? His reverie was interrupted by the sudden return of weight beneath his boots. Slowly, gravity built up to what he judged to be half-a-standard-gravity.

"Engines are online, Admiral. We can maneuver again," the young engineer reported.

"Excellent, Mr. Ahmed. Tell Captain Carter that he can begin shaping our orbit back toward the fleet."

"Aye aye, sir. Where will you be, Admiral, in case he wants to know?"

Drake, who had turned to leave, turned back. "Tell the captain that I will be in my cabin. I suggest that you post your engineering watch and do the same. You look like you are going to collapse on your feet."

"I'm all right, sir."

"That is an order, Ensign. You are chief engineer now. Learn to delegate."

"Aye aye, sir."

Drake shuffled back to his own cabin. He thought about finding Bethany, but decided that he was too tired. Losing half his force had been worse than losing an arm or a leg. In fact, he would have gladly given both to save just a single ship. When he reached the cabin, he stripped off the vacsuit he had worn for the better part of a day, noting the smell as he did so. He hung it on its rack and then fell face down onto his bunk. He managed to activate the safety cocoon before he dropped into unconsciousness, barely.

#

Richard was shaken awake by his wife's hand on his shoulder. "Wake up, darling"

He opened his eyes. Sometime during the night, he had rolled onto his back. He blinked and a moment later, levered himself to a seated position. The noise of the engines permeated the bulkheads and he was pulled toward the bunk by a steady acceleration. It took him a moment to remember where he was. Phillip stood behind Bethany and looked down at Richard.

"How long have I been asleep?" he asked.

"Almost twenty hours."

"How is the ship?"

"Captain says that he has thrust up to one gravity and that we're on course for the Darthan foldpoint to reinforce the blockade."

"Can we get there before they try another breakout?"

"No, Richard," Bethany replied. "They made another attempt about an hour ago. Sergei Gower reports that it was a maximum effort and that we slaughtered them. Nearly two hundred Ryall ships destroyed to only ten of ours."

"What?" he asked. "They couldn't have."

"But they did," she insisted.

"They're early. The breakout force can't possibly get back to the foldpoint for another forty hours. They wouldn't try until that force is in position to support them."

"For some reason they decided to advance the schedule," Phillip replied. "They've had time to set up relay communications between their major home systems by now. Perhaps when they tallied up the number of ships that broke free on the last attempt, they realized that there were not enough of them. Maybe the breakout force was a ruse to confuse us. Or possibly, they just screwed up. Whatever the reason, they made a major attempt to break the Darthan blockade an hour ago and paid dearly for the effort."

Drake considered what he had been told, then got unsteadily to his feet and moved to the cabin's small wash basin. Cold water helped rinse the sleep from his eyes. He ran his hand over his chin and judged the length of the stubble. He had, indeed, slept most of a day. He wondered why he didn't feel rested, then remembered all of the people who had died under his command. He wondered if he would ever feel rested again.

Finally, steeling himself, he looked in the mirror. The face that stared back to him was that of a stranger, an old man with pronounced bags beneath bloodshot eyes.

"You know," he said to the other two people in the cabin, "back when I was planning the Spica Campaign, it seemed so straightforward. We would invade, catch them by surprise, and blockade their foldpoints until their economy collapsed, then go in and mop up whatever resistance remained one system at a time. So neat, so surgical, so clean. Yet, look at us now."

"We beat them back, Admiral. That's the important thing," Phillip said.

He looked at the Sandarian in the mirror. "Is it, Commander? Is it the important thing for all of those who died so far from home yesterday? It was easy enough seizing the prize. Why is it so damned difficult holding onto it?"

"Because we have a powerful enemy whose survival depends on them wresting the prize from our grasp, " Walkirk replied. "They have to defeat us. They have no choice. Likewise, we have to keep from being defeated. We have no choice either. If we have to sacrifice the lives of every human now in this system, Admiral, it will be worth it if we can just hang on."

"What if we run out of patience?" he asked in a tone that made it more a cry for help than a question.

"That is why I came out here, Richard," Bethany said. "I think I know how to end this damned war short of one side or the other being exterminated."

Drake shifted his gaze from Phillip to his wife, still looking at them in the reflection of the mirror. Despite her dirty face and tear-streaked cheeks, hair that had gone too long uncombed, and coveralls that bore stains best left unidentified, she was still the most beautiful woman he had ever seen.

"I think I am coming around to your point of view, Wife! If things continue like this much longer, half the parliaments and councils in human space will be screaming for a 'final solution' to the Ryall problem. They will order us to attack with planet busters. God knows how many good people we'll use up in a war of xenocide."

"Or if we could even do it," Phillip responded. "They are as strong on their side of the foldpoint as we are on ours."

"Let us at least *try* to end the bloodshed," Bethany pleaded. "If negotiations don't work, there is always the planet buster option. We go in, we talk to them, we tell them that we are prepared to destroy their worlds, and then we demand their surrender. Who knows, maybe their intelligence will be able to override their instincts just this once."

"How?" Phillip asked.

Bethany turned to him. "'How' what?"

"How do we talk with them? The first human ship that materializes on their side of the foldline will be vaporized before it can transmit a parlay message. That is one of the problems fighting aliens. We haven't been able to work out the conventions for arranging a truce."

"There must be a way," Bethany said stubbornly.

Drake, who had been watching the interplay in the mirror, suddenly turned. The movement made him dizzy. He regarded his

wife and the Sandarian prince, and for the first time since waking
him, Bethany saw something other than defeat in his eyes.

"I just may know a way," he said before he lapsed into a look
of sudden concentration.  Bethany knew the look well.  He had
worn it when he had first come up with the plan to invade Spica

#

# Chapter 25

Galatan of *Far Seeker* lay in a bed of rushes in his cabin and contemplated the horror that had recently occupied his screens. Twice in a two twelfth-cycles, he had watched ships of The Race pour out of the stargates and hurl themselves against the blockading forces. Both times furious battles had erupted and hundreds of ships and crews had perished in atomic fire. Yet, when the radiations of battle dissipated, the Monsters remained in firm control of the vital stargates. Despite the reckless courage and audacious tactics of his fellow warriors, the Monsters had triumphed again.

The first incursion gave Galatan his greatest hope. Ships of The Race actually broke free of the cursed englobements and dove for the entwined stars. From there, they would shape an attack orbit for one of the stargates. His hopes were tempered when he detected a large biped fleet in pursuit. A single watch was all it had taken his tactical crew to plot the Monsters' course as a reciprocal orbit that would bring both fleets to battle close to the twin suns.

The battle itself was hidden deep within the central radiance. All Galatan saw were flashes of actinic light as warheads exploded deep within the double corona. Only later had it been possible to determine the outcome. This he had done by counting the number of friendly and enemy drive flares that reappeared when the two fleets headed back into deep space. Both fleets were substantially smaller than they had been, but of the ships of The Race, he counted only eight.

Galatan's depression was briefly interrupted when his sensor technicians reported a new battle raging in the stargate from Darthan. Once again, entire fleets threw themselves against the bipeds' defenses, and once again, they winked out of existence as quickly as they appeared. The disaster was so complete that it had seemed anticlimactic when the refugees from the Battle of the Twin Suns were subsequently destroyed by a small force of biped starships.

The strain of watching the enemy everywhere victorious had been too much for some aboard *Far Seeker*. The morning after the second battle of the stargates, his sub-commanders reported three dead crewmembers in their resting racks, victims of depression and medical potions ingested in massive quantities. The trio brought to twelve the number of Galatan's crew who had expressed their lack of trust in him by voluntarily returning to the Great Egg. He knew that if he did not take action against the bipeds soon, others would join them, and he would not have sufficient crew left to fight the ship.

The problem was that the range of possible actions, never very large, had dwindled to a single choice, and one that was no more attractive now than it had been on the first day of the invasion.

Since escaping the initial Monster onslaught and provoking the scorn of his crew, he had nearly exhausted *Far Seeker*'s fuel and other consumables while waiting for his chance to strike a meaningful blow. Twice he had been forced to flee Monster patrols by moving ever higher above the twin suns, until the stars were merely the brightest light in the sky. He had sufficient fuel to launch one good attack, if only he could find a proper target. As for food, he and his crew had eaten their way down to the emergency rations, and those would not last much longer. The time was approaching when he would have to make his move, or else resign himself and his crew to starvation. He had been searching for some Monster fleet against which to hurl *Far Seeker*. So far, he had not found what he sought.

The comm signal echoed through his cabin, disturbing his thought. Irritated, he called out to the ship's computer to let whoever was calling through.

"Shipmaster."

It was the voice of Sseltadar, one of the warriors that had come aboard straight from the hatchery, currently on duty at the sensor station.

"I am here, hatchling. What do you want?"

"We have detected a ship of the Monsters, Galatan. It appears to be headed in our direction."

"It is moving up out of the trade lanes?"

"It is. The drive flare is barely visible, indicating that the ship is thrusting in this direction. The bearing is steady and the light frequency is blue shifted."

"There is only the one ship?" he asked.

"So far, Galatan."

"Are they so confident that they feel they can take a Ship of the Third Order with only one of their own?"

He considered the enemy's actions, and decided that it was an insult. Perhaps they did not know how powerful a warship *Far*

*Seeker* was, or possibly, their recent victories had left them overconfident. Whichever the case, when they arrived, he would show them the sort of warrior his sept produced.

"How long do we have before they reach us?"

"If they continue as they have been, we should see them within three twelfth-cycles."

"Alert the Shipmaster-Second and the sub-commanders that I want to see them in my living quarters. If the bipeds think they can take us without a fight, we will show them what sort of warriors they are dealing with."

#

Phillip Walkirk was irritated. His control room, which he had honed into a well-oiled machine, was being disrupted. In addition to his normal duty crew, four visitors were crowded into the cramped space filled with display screens. One of the visitors was Admiral Drake, and though a friend, his status as fleet commander made Phillip nervous. The young captain reflected on the incongruity of the situation. As the crown prince of Sandar, his social status far exceeded that of any mere admiral from a sister colony world. However, as a professional officer serving under Drake, he was anxious to make a good impression, and had a tendency to hesitate when giving even the simplest order while he considered what Drake would think of it ... and him.

The second visitor was easier to take. Bethany Drake occupied the same observer's couch she had on the voyage from Eulysta to Spica. She was a familiar figure who knew the routine, and therefore, was nearly a member of *Queen Julia*'s crew.

The third and fourth visitors were the most disconcerting. Never would Phillip have guessed that he would host a couple of Ryall in the control room of his ship, especially when decelerating toward what might well turn into a battle with a well-armed lizard cruiser. Varlan and Periskay were huddled together in front of the main viewscreen, both secured to the deck with cargo tie downs to keep from sliding around during periods of changing acceleration.

Like the invasion of Spica, the idea for the current voyage had been Drake's. His plan to contact the Ryall high command was little more than an idea at first, but he and Bethany refined it with the help of the ship's computers during *Conqueror II*'s long voyage to the Darthan foldpoint. By the time Captain Carter ordered the blastship's engines shut down, Drake had worked out the details to his own satisfaction. The few officers he briefed could think of nothing he had overlooked, although most thought him crazy for thinking up the fool stunt in the first place. None would say that to his face, of course.

Drake's idea for contacting the Ryall high command was to send a Ryall ship through to Darthan with the offer to parlay. With luck, the foldpoint defenses would hold their fire when they identified one of their own, giving the ship time to transmit its message. Then, if the high command agreed, a human embassy ship would follow.

"Where are you going to get a Ryall ship?" Bethany asked as soon as he explained his plan to her.

"I was thinking of recruiting 'Wrong Way Charlie,'" he replied to looks of consternation.

He had explained that when the human fleet first boiled out of the Carratyl foldpoint, the Ryall ships in transit across Spica had done one of three things. The commercial craft had run for the safety of the nearest stargate, or else scattered to the far corners of the Spica system. Of the three warcraft, two turned to intercept the invasion fleet, futile though that gesture had been. The third, a vessel the computer identified as a heavy cruiser, had avoided the kamikaze option. Its commander had played it smart and fled, thus earning the human nickname of "Wrong Way Charlie." He was still lurking high above the normal traffic lanes, close enough to observe everything, but distant enough to make it inconvenient to eliminate him.

After arriving at the Darthan foldpoint, Drake transferred operational command to Sergei Gower and called Phillip Walkirk.

"Yes, sir, Admiral," Phillip said when he saw Drake's image on his screen.

"What do you think of my plan?" He had sent a copy to the crown prince as soon as both ships secured engines.

"Might work. Dangerous though."

"Is *Queen Julia* up to the task of chasing Charlie?"

"Yes, sir."

"When can you be ready for space?"

"Two days to rearm and refuel, Admiral."

"Very well. I'll transfer my flag tomorrow."

"You are going along, sir?"

"Do you have a problem with that, Captain?" Drake asked, letting a tone of command creep into what had heretofore been a friendly conversation.

"Not at all. It is just that there is no need for you to go personally, sir. We can fetch them back to you. You are more needed here."

"Doing what? I suppose I could turn a wrench or wield a welder while they put *Conqueror* back together, but I would not be very good at it. No, the action will be elsewhere for at least a couple of months. Gower can fight off future attacks. I think the best use of my time is to try to bring this war to a halt. Besides," he continued with a laugh, "my wife's menagerie has to go, which means Bethany will insist on going, which means that you will have to put up with me, too, Captain."

"Yes, sir. We'll begin clearing a couple of compartments for you immediately."

As promised, the admiral, his wife, and their two charges had arrived via ship's boat the next day and *Queen Julia* powered her engines less than 24 hours later.

The climb toward the fugitive Ryall cruiser had been long and uneventful. Phillip spent the time getting his ship once again ready for battle. Usually, he took his dinner in his cabin. However, he attended one dinner in the wardroom when his executive officer reported that the Ryall would be eating with them that night.

*Queen Julia*'s eight ranking officers lined both sides of the wardroom table, with Phillip, Drake, and Bethany seated at each end. Varlan lay at Bethany's right hand, with Periskay beside her. The conversation had slowly gotten around to the mission and Phillip took the opportunity to ask a question that had been bothering him.

"Periskay, you are to be the intermediary, are you not?"

"I am," the male Ryall agreed in heavily accented Standard. Varlan, it seemed, had whiled away her hours in captivity teaching him the human tongue. "I will carry your message to Those Who Rule."

"Are you are in sympathy with our quest? Do you wish to see peace between our two species?"

The Ryall's body rippled like a dog shaking himself dry, if not as violently. "I confess that I do not understand why you humans believe that peace is possible. I defer to Varlan's greater knowledge of human psychology."

"If you don't believe in the mission, why are you willing to do it?"

"Because I have given my kin-oath to Varlan. I will carry your message and deliver it precisely. In addition, it is my opportunity to go home. If I am to die at the hands of your warriors, I will die with my clan."

Bethany explained the Ryall concept of Clan Honor. Periskay had pledged to do what Varlan asked on his clan's honor, which was as ironclad an oath as any Mafia don on old Earth had ever elicited from a consigliore.

The conversation then turned to the details of what everyone hoped would happen when they reached the Ryall ship. With luck, they would make contact, convince the Ryall captain that they did not mean to blow him out of the sky, escort him back to the Darthan foldpoint with Periskay aboard, and let him jump to the Darthan home system. Then, if the Ryall were amenable, a human embassy ship would jump to Darthan and begin negotiations for the Ryall surrender.

Despite his misgivings, Phillip had offered *Queen Julia* as the embassy craft that would enter the Darthan system. It would mean disabling and removing the ship's weaponry, but the cruiser would be much more comfortable for the negotiating team than any Ryall ship.

Of course, that was what *ought* to happen if everything went well when they encountered the fugitive heavy cruiser. If it did not, their current voyage would likely end in a quick space battle and an expanding globe of plasma. The only question was whether the source of the plasma would be Ryall or human.

#

"The enemy craft decelerates too quickly," Pelanau, *Space Eater*'s sensor operator reported.

"What?" Galatan asked.

"They made turnover too soon and are now decelerating at a rate that will bring them to a halt well beyond our missile range."

"Then we must prepare to move to them to engage."

"Is this not an odd tactic?"

"It is. Your point?"

"That it would seem wiser for the Monsters to hit us while moving at high differential velocity. That way they minimize the time we could damage them."

"True. Your conclusion?"

"Perhaps they have calculated our fuel state and are attempting to run our tanks dry."

"How could they know this?"

"I know not, Shipmaster. It is something we should ponder, is it not?"

Galatan pondered it as he watched the symbol on the screen come to a halt in space at twice the range he could reach with his missiles. As for lasers and particle beams, these were short-range weapons. They would not raise the temperature of the enemy's hull plates at this distance.

Galatan was attempting to divine the bipeds' tactics when his comm operator reported, "There is a message coming in from the Monsters, Shipmaster."

*Space Eater*'s commander let the nictating membranes slip over his eyes for an instant, a sign of surprise, before answering, "What sort of message?"

"From a member of The Race. He says that he is Periskay of the Distant Mountains in the Mist. He is Philosopher Caste. He wishes to talk to you."

"Send his image to my screen," Galatan replied brusquely. This encounter with the Monsters was turning out different than he had imagined.

A moment later, the image of the philosopher appeared on Galatan's screen.

"I am Periskay of the Distant Mountains of the Mist."

"I am Galatan of *Space Eater*. What do you want?"

"I am a prisoner of the Monsters. They have charged me with delivering a message."

"Why would a philosopher demean himself to speak for beasts?"

"I am speaking for a fellow captive, Varlan of the Scented Waters. It is she who vouches for the importance of the message."

"Then why does not this Varlan speak?"

"She has been too long a captive of theirs and fears that you will think her mad. I was captured when the Monsters first invaded our space. I do not doubt my own sanity."

"And if I doubt it, Periskay?"

"Then you will not agree to what my captors want and they will destroy you and seek out another Ship of The Race to do their bidding."

"Tell me the message."

"The Monsters who style themselves human wish to speak to Those Who Rule. They cannot send one of their own ships through the stargate. It would be destroyed too quickly to communicate."

"True."

"Knowing this, they would like *Space Eater* to take me through the stargate so that I may speak directly with Those Who Rule."

"Are they mad?"

"By the standards of our species, I believe they are. However, this is what they have bid me tell you."

"It's a trap! They want to draw my ship close enough to their fleet that they can destroy it."

"They claim to be prepared to destroy it now if you do not agree to their request."

"They will find *Space Eater* a difficult meal."

"Perhaps so," Periskay replied. "I am not a warrior to know of such things. I have seen what the vessel on which I am riding can do. I was present at the battle near the twin suns and saw ship after ship of The Race destroyed. I am told that this ship was responsible for some of that destruction."

Periskay refused to let his ears droop in dismay, although that was the way he felt. "What do they offer?"

"The humans call it 'safe passage.' They will escort us to the Darthan stargate and allow us jump to the home system. Afterwards, you are required to return to this system to report the response of Those Who Rule. They demand a kin-oath to either Varlan or me on this point. Whatever Those Who Rule answer, you will be free to return to Darthan unharmed after delivering their response to the humans."

"A strange message," Galatan replied.

"The strangest I have ever spoken," Periskay agreed.

After a long wait, Galatan said, "I will have to consider it. I will speak to you again within one thousand heartbeats."

"I will be waiting, as will my captors. They advise that any attempt to power your engines in that time will be judged an attack."

"I understand."

With that, the message screen went black and Galatan began thinking about his response to a request that was the obvious spawn of a lunatic. The only question was whether The Race would be better served by pretending to believe the bipeds, or by attacking them? Either way, it appeared that *Far Seeker* was about to fulfill its destiny.

#

# Chapter 26

*Queen Julia*'s combat center had the look of a jewelry store display window following one of the great urban riots that had swept Earth in the mid-twenty-first century – or so Richard Drake imagined. The big display screens were still there, as were acceleration couches for a dozen weapons operators. Everything else was gone, with only gaping holes and truncated cables to mark where sensor and weapons control stations once stood.

*Queen Julia* had returned to the vicinity of the Spica-Darthan foldpoint in the company of *Far Seeker* a week earlier. Both human and Ryall warcraft halted in space a million kilometers from the englobed foldpoint and began the transition from ships of war to instruments of diplomacy – as alien as that concept was to Galatan and his crew. What had followed seemed like little more than vandalism to many of the Sandarian cruiser's crew. It had seemed like vandalism to Drake, as well, and he was the one who issued the order.

The cruiser's transformation involved dismounting the ship's offensive weapons and the systems that controlled them. Luckily, its modular design made unplugging the various missile launchers, lasers, and antimatter projectors not much more difficult than changing out the memory crystal in a hand computer.

*Far Seeker* was a different matter. Galatan adamantly refused to allow humans aboard his ship. He was even reticent about letting Periskay aboard, fearing that the two-legged monsters might have infected him with a bio-weapon of some kind. The Ryall shipmaster finally relented only after the philosopher was examined in quarantine by the ship's autodoctor and given a clean bill of health.

Negotiations over how to ensure that *Far Seeker* had actually disarmed remained stalemated for most of a day until Galatan suggested a solution. Whatever the Ryall cruiser's internal configuration, lion or lamb, its weapons were of little use without the ability to track targets. With its battle sensors disabled, the Ryall ship would be as helpless as an Altan tree slug.

So, while vacsuited bipeds swarmed over *Queen Julia*'s hull, dismounting lethal appliances, similarly equipped hexapods moved with surprising grace across the smooth ebon hull of their ship, disconnecting various antennae and other devices that fed data to the fire control system. Their objections to allowing humans near their ship were relaxed for a close-up inspection by Ensign Harkness of their hull. He reported nothing but naked external fittings where sensitive instruments had once stared deep into circumambient space.

A week of hard work had transformed both vessels from warships to mere carriers of personnel. At the end of the week, Drake, Phillip and Galatan spoke via videoconference.

"Is your ship ready, Shipmaster?" Drake asked and Varlan translated.

There followed a short burst of hisses and whistles, after which Varlan reported the Ryall captain ready.

"Captain Walkirk, please brief our Ryall companion regarding the coming mission."

"Yes, Admiral. Galatan, you have received your safe passage data?"

The Ryall head on the viewscreen tilted in a gesture of assent as he made his response, which Varlan immediately rendered as "*Far Seeker* has been taught the route to swim."

"*Queen Julia* will lead *Far Seeker* through the blockade and into the foldpoint. Once we reach the jump point, you will be free to charge your generators. You may jump when you are ready. That will start the countdown clock. You have precisely eight hours to return... no more, no less. We will deactivate the foldpoint defenses for a period of one minute exactly eight hours after you leave us. Varlan, make sure that he has the proper conversion from human time units to Ryall."

"He understands," Varlan replied. "Bethany and I both did the translation before the data was transmitted."

"Galatan, do you understand that though the foldpoint defenses are disabled, they can be switched back on in an instant?"

"I understand."

"If more than one ship materializes while the defenses are down, or if that ship is not *Far Seeker,* we will reactivate the mines and start shooting. Is that clear?"

"Yes," came the emotionless reply.

"One last thing, Galatan. You understand that if you fail to return to tell us of the decision of Those Who Rule, that we will assume that the answer is negative"

"I believe that the answer will be negative in any event, Admiral of the Drakes."

"You are still honor bound to come back and tell us."

"I have given your prisoners my clan oath, human..." Drake suspected that he had been called something else and Varlan had cleaned it up in translation. "... and I will return to give you the decision of Those Who Rule. Whatever that decision, I will return immediately to Darthan and begin repairing the damage to my ship so that when we meet again, it will be in battle."

"And if the answer is not negative?"

"Then I will escort you to the home world, where you will be the concern of those more elevated, and I will still repair the damage to my ship in preparation for battle."

Drake nodded. "That is all you promised and that is all we ask. Captain Walkirk, you may power engines when ready."

"Aye aye, sir."

Passage through the blockade went smoothly. At no time did *Queen Julia* detect any emanations from the Ryall cruiser to indicate that Galatan might have kept one or two active sensors in reserve. Passive sensors, of course, were another matter. No doubt, Galatan had his crew furiously scanning space for some sight of the human blockade force. However, telescopes have their limitations, and save for the possibility that a human ship might occult a star, it was doubtful the Ryall spotted anything.

When they reached the preprogrammed spot within the foldpoint from where *Far Seeker* was to jump, Phillip ordered *Queen Julia* to a safe distance as a precaution. Galatan had so far scrupulously upheld his end of the bargain, but Phillip did not want to tempt him into firing a spread of missiles as he disappeared into foldspace. Guided or not, a salvo delivered from close enough would likely find its mark.

The precaution proved unnecessary. After a few seconds of inactivity, the Ryall cruiser blinked out of existence, returning home to an uncertain welcome.

#

The hours that followed were nerve-wracking for everyone aboard *Queen Julia*. Bethany spent the time forming fuzzy threads into a complex network using long needle-like instruments that clicked together in a way that was somehow hypnotic. She claimed that the ancient thread art soothed her nerves.

As for Drake, he wondered if the tension of the past several months might have adversely affected his judgment. How else to explain the situation? Here he was, anxiously counting down the minutes until his disarmed ship would jump into the very heart of the enemy realm.

Nor was he looking forward to negotiating with Those Who Rule. Like most professional military men, he had a disdain for politicians and diplomats that he occasionally found difficult to conceal — a legacy of his term of service as the naval liaison officer to the Altan parliament.

This impromptu diplomatic mission was necessary because there were no professional diplomats with the fleet. No one had thought to include them among the flotilla's complement. After all, the invasion fleet's mission was to conquer the Ryall, not negotiate with them. The flaw in that particular argument, of course, was that there was no way to conclude the war without talking to the enemy, if only to accept their surrender.

Therefore, instead of a trained ambassador, there was only a colonial naval officer to represent humanity on this most important mission. Luckily, the message he would deliver was one that even the alien Ryall would be able to understand. It would be short, sweet, and utterly without nuance:

Surrender or face the extermination of your entire species!

He only hoped that the Ryall were intelligent enough to face the choice squarely. More than once in human history, members of his own species faced with that stark choice had chosen extinction. The ancient fortress of Masada came immediately to mind. After a siege of three years, the Romans had broken into the fortress atop its impregnable mountain, only to find that the Jewish zealots had killed themselves rather than surrender. That choice was still celebrated by Jews throughout human space.

His dark reverie was interrupted by the beep of his communicator. Bethany, who lay strapped into the acceleration couch next to his, looked up from the floating mass of brightly colored threads. Drake reached up and switched on the instrument.

"Admiral Gower online, Admiral," the voice of young Hamoush said in his ear.

"Patch him through and then secure the beam."

"Yes, sir."

The screen cleared to show the features of the gruff old Sandarian admiral. As usual, Gower had a scowl on his face.

"Yes, Admiral?" Drake said when the screen had cleared.

"We're down to the thirty minute mark, sir," Gower said, maintaining the deference he had shown Drake as operational commander.

"I make it twenty-nine minutes and sixteen seconds," he replied, "and you can call me by my name. At the moment, I am merely a supernumerary on a light cruiser under your command."

"Very well, Richard."

"Are we ready in case they pull a fast one, Sergei?"

Gower chuckled, a sound that Drake could not remember hearing emerge from him before. "If anything other than *Far Seeker* pops out of foldspace, we will give them a full spread. In any event, the mines will be reactivated everywhere but *Far Seeker*'s vicinity the second he pops out."

"Let's just be sure we don't make a mistake in the reactivations," Drake replied.

"If someone makes that mistake, he'll find himself on perpetual patrol down in the coronal fire of this system's twin suns."

Drake laughed. "That's one way to make them 'burn in hell,' Sergei. Sounds like you are ready. I suppose you will be just as happy if they don't show."

The Sandarian admiral did something else that Richard had never seen before. He looked surprised.

"Why would you say that?"

"I know that you would have preferred that we use some ship other than *Queen Julia* for this mission. It will be hard to explain Phillip's loss to His Majesty if we don't come back."

"His Majesty will understand. Prince Phillip must take his chances in battle with every other able-bodied spacer in this fleet. It is my job to see that he does not risk his life unnecessarily. If your mission ends this eternal war, then I call it a necessary risk. After all, Richard, you are risking not only your own life, but that of your wife."

"Trust me. If I thought I could deal with Varlan, I would have Bethany's ass on the first boat back home."

"If I could think up a plausible excuse to order the crown prince off this mission, I would do so as well. However, the heir to the throne must never look the coward."

"Noblesse oblige, Sergei?"

"Practical court politics. If you pull this off, Phillip's rule will be a long and placid one. If I order him from the mission, there would always be doubts."

"And I thought dealing with Parliament was difficult."

"There are advantages and disadvantages to both systems, Richard. I will not keep you longer. I merely wanted to wish you luck and to assure you that if there is treachery, you will be avenged."

"Thank you, Sergei. I'm leaving the fleet in good hands."

"I appreciate the compliment. Gower out."

"Drake out."

The screen went black and Richard returned to his inner thoughts and the sound of Bethany's knitting.

#

Alarms began to sound around the ship just after the countdown chronometer reached 00:00 on the screen. Despite expecting them, Richard Drake gave a start that caused him to surge upward into his restraints. Beside him, Bethany dropped her tangle of yarn and stared at the main viewscreen.

"Unknown ship materializing in the foldpoint," came the report from an unseen sensor operator. "Computers say that the ship is *Far Seeker*. It seems to be alone."

"Establish a comm link," Drake ordered. He turned to his wife and said, "Get Varlan in here."

There was a pause of nearly a minute before the screen cleared, giving Varlan the opportunity to scramble through the open port and secure herself beside Richard's acceleration couch. When the screen cleared, it showed a trio of Ryall with *Far Seeker*'s bridge behind them. Galatan was not in the central position in the tableau, the position of honor for Ryall as it was for humans. The shipmaster sat to the left of an elderly Ryall who Drake did not recognize. His age was evident from the dull, grayish cast of his scales and the slightly milky sheen of his obsidian orbs. Periskay sat on that worthy's right, and behind the other two.

"Greetings, Galatan of *Far Seeker*," Drake said through Varlan as soon as the trio appeared on the screen.

"Greetings, Admiral of the Drakes," Varlan translated Galatan's whistled greeting.

"You are as good as your word."

"My clan debt to this one is fulfilled," Galatan replied, gesturing toward Periskay.

"It is," Drake agreed. "Who is it that I have the honor to meet?"

"I bring with me One Who Rules. He is Tarsanau of the Islands of the Lesser Sea, one who is empowered to speak for Those Who Rule The Race."

Varlan translated the introduction, and then continued with, "In human terms, you would call him Senior Councilor to the Rulers of the Hegemony."

"Greetings, Tarsanau of the Islands of the Lesser Sea," Drake replied. "I am pleased that you accepted our invitation."

"It seemed prudent to do so," the elder Ryall replied. Somehow, he was able to make the whistling Ryall speech sound perfunctory. "What is it that you want?"

"We would speak with Those Who Rule."

"Who speaks?"

"I am Admiral Richard Drake. I command the human fleet in this system."

"You are the biped who swims in the lead position of this evil swarm that has taken our stargates?"

"I am."

"Then you have sufficient status to speak for your species?"

"On the subject at hand, yes. There are humans more exalted than me, but none in this star system."

"I will speak with you, then. I am empowered to communicate for The Race in this matter. Of what shall we speak?"

"Surely Periskay has explained our purpose in asking for this meeting."

"He has passed on your words. The concepts, however, are alien. There was no time to consult Those Who Rule The Race, so I came with Galatan to hear your words for myself."

"Very well. We wish to put a stop to this endless war before more of our two species' warriors are killed."

"Among The Race, war is a contest between clans or alliances. When there is a dispute, the contest continues until one side or the other admits defeat. When this occurs, the conceding clan vacates the disputed fishing grounds, or cedes the principle in question, or swears fealty to the superior clan," Tarsanau replied. "However, none of these outcomes are possible when the contest is between competing species. We occupy land you will one day need to raise your hatchlings. Likewise, you are in possession of planets that will someday harbor our expanding population of swimmers. How can two such species make peace with one another?"

"We do not want your planets. We have more than enough of our own."

"You must inevitably expand into our realm, or we into yours. That is the way of living things."

"We disagree. Space is wide and the number of suitable planets nearly infinite. If we are at peace, we can turn all of the effort we currently expend making war into exploration."

"Population must inevitably expand to occupy the available living space," Tarsanau replied. "That is the rule of life."

"That is the rule for dumb beasts. It is not the rule for intelligent beings. We can use our intelligence to limit our growth. So can you if you wish to."

There was a long silence, as though Drake was speaking a particularly convoluted language and the Ryall was having difficulty sorting through the words. Finally, he said, "An alien concept, and an interesting one. How do you propose that we end this contest in which we have been engaged for so long?"

"I propose that you surrender to us."

This time the response came close on the heels of Varlan's translation. "Surrender? Do you mean place ourselves at the mercy of monsters?"

"I mean precisely that, Tarsanau. If you surrender to us, we will spare your species. If you do not, we will destroy your worlds."

"If you had that power, you would have done so already."

"Without the Swift Eaters in our past to shape our evolution, we do not look at war that way. We fight only for our own survival, not for your destruction. Once our survival is assured, we have no desire to sterilize your planets. Indeed, in time, we hope to exchange goods and ideas with you. You have undoubtedly found some insights into the nature of the universe that we have missed. We have philosophies that you will find useful. It is our way to exchange goods and ideas, and thereby make our two species depend on one another."

"Then you are insane."

Drake nodded. "By your way of looking at the universe, you may well be correct. However, do you not agree that having the fate of the hatchlings in the power of insane monsters is a bad thing?"

"It is," Tarsanau hissed.

"Then let us speak of this difference in outlook. Perhaps we can come to a mutual arrangement that will forestall the massive bombardment of your home worlds."

"You will destroy them anyway."

"Perhaps," Drake agreed. "But isn't it worth discussing, if for no other reason than, while we are talking, we won't be bombing?"

The Ryall gave the gesture of assent. "There is advantage to us in prolonging the moment when your ships come through the star portals."

Drake nodded as well. "And for us."

"How do you propose to accomplish this insane arrangement?"

"We are prepared to follow you back to Darthan, where we will explain our thoughts to Those Who Rule. We promise that there will be no attempts to force our way through your defenses while we are speaking."

"What is the worth of an animal's promise?"

"Perhaps my word is worth nothing. However, Galatan has seen me keep my promises. Besides, how will speaking with us make your situation any worse than it already is?"

Again, there was a long pause. Finally, Tarsanau said, "I do not see how speaking with you will affect the Great Hunt in either direction of desirability. We will speak with you."

"And you will take a clan-oath to guarantee our safety? You will give us safe passage back here to our side of the stargate when we have finished our talks, regardless of the outcome?"

There followed a long exchange of Ryall speech, following which Varlan said, "He Who Rules has given me his clan-oath. You will not be harmed."

"Is Tarsanau able to make such a promise?"

"He speaks for Those Who Rule. His clan-oath is binding on them."

"Very well. Tell him that *Far Seeker* may lead us through the stargate."

Tarsanau signaled his agreement and Galatan said, "We will swim through the gate one human minute prior to your arrival, Admiral of the Drakes. The restrictions are the same for you as they were for us on our return. The gate defenses will be expecting one ship, no more."

"I understand."

"Once you are in our pond, we will send warriors to board your vessel. There will be an expert on Monster technology with them. You will show him everything, hiding nothing."

"Agreed."

Tarsanau said, "Once we know that your ship is not capable of attacking us, as Periskay assures us, then you will be convoyed to the home world where you will explain your heresies to Those Who Rule The Race. Is it agreed?"

"It is."

"Prepare your ship to dive deeply into the great invisible sea between the stars. Alert Galatan when you are ready."

"We are ready now."

"Very well. Follow us in one of your lesser time periods," Varlan translated literally.

"One minute."

A moment later, the Ryall cruiser was gone. Richard Drake gave the order to begin the countdown clock and transferred control back to Phillip Walkirk.

"I have the conn, sir," the Sandarian prince said over the intercom. For most of the next minute, swift orders flowed through *Queen Julia*'s electronic circuits. Finally, it was time.

"Standby for foldspace transition," Phillip announced. "Transition in fifteen seconds ... "

"Tied down tight, Varlan?"

"Yes, Richard."

"What about you, my love?"

"So tight I think I'm cutting off my circulation."

"Scared?"

"More scared than any time in my life," she replied. "I love you."

"I love you, too."

"*... Three ... Two ... One ... Transition!*"

#

## Chapter 27

*"Foldspace transition complete!"* came the announcement over the ship's command circuit.

Varlan of the Scented Waters heard the announcement dimly, as though through a vast expanse of water. She barely noticed it. She was too enthralled with the viewscreen at the front of *Queen Julia*'s stripped combat center to pay attention to her surroundings. It was as though the two humans strapped into their acceleration couches on either side of her had disappeared into a sound-deadening mist as Varlan strained every sense toward the screen.

That the viewscreen showed a starfield not outwardly different from the one they had just left was unimportant. Space is monotonous. It looks essentially the same no matter where one is in the galaxy. Unless the system primary is in view, all there is to see is an ebon expanse dotted with a random sprinkling of radiant points. What made this ebon expanse different was that these were not just any stars. They were the stars of home, stars that had decorated the night skies of Darthan since the days of the Great Hunt. As such, they infused Varlan with longing more intense than any she had experienced in her lengthy captivity. For the first time since the two-legged monsters overran Corlis, she was home!

"Varlan...!"

"Yes, Richard?"

"I need a translation."

"Sorry, Richard. I was overcome by the impact of being once again among the home stars."

Drake moved to replay the whistling-hissing speech that had been received seconds earlier.

"The warriors have requested that you join *Far Seeker* and follow him out of the foldpoint. You will follow to a rendezvous with a ship of the first class, where you will be boarded and searched. They want you to acknowledge that you understand."

"Tell them that we understand."

While Varlan relayed the message, she heard Richard on the comm to the bridge. She had barely finished speaking when there was sudden weight beneath her feet and she settled gently to the steel deck. It was good to have gravity again. It was even better to be home.

#

*Queen Julia* had emerged on the opposite side of the foldpoint from *Far Seeker* and moved to rendezvous with the alien cruiser. Then both ships moved slowly out of the foldpoint, penetrating defenses that were every bit as strong as those they had just left. It took nearly an hour to reach the point in space where a large Ryall ship awaited them. This was the "ship of the first class" to which Varlan had referred. The designation denoted a blastship-size warcraft, roughly equivalent to Drake's own *Conqueror II*.

"What now?" Phillip wondered when *Far Seeker* rendezvoused with the larger ship. The two Ryall craft joined airlocks. Soon after, a hangar bay opened on the larger ship and three small boats emerged and began thrusting for *Queen Julia*.

The three scouts had barely gotten underway when Phillip's comm unit came to life with Richard Drake's voice. "Captain, please join us at the hangar deck airlock."

"On my way, Admiral," Phillip replied. He did not want to leave the bridge with his ship in enemy space, but in truth, there was little he could do if the Ryall attacked.

Richard and Bethany, plus Varlan, awaited him at the inner airlock door leading into the hangar deck. The hangar doors were open, illuminating the interior in natural sunlight Varlan, Phillip noticed, had moved to where the rays of her native sun bathed across her body. He did not remember ever seeing the Ryall as relaxed as she seemed to be at this moment.

He pulled himself hand-over-hand to where the admiral and his lady waited.

"Good of you to come, Phillip," Richard said. "Where is the Marine welcoming party?"

"On their way, sir."

"No side arms or weapons, correct?"

"Yes, sir. Those are the orders I issued."

"Good." He turned to look through the view window and discovered that one of the Ryall scout boats was descending into the cruiser's small hangar bay. With incompatible airlock equipment, about the only way to transfer between Ryall and human ships was inside a pressurized hanger. Yet, in more than a century and a quarter of warfare, Phillip could not think of another instance of a Ryall ship voluntarily boarding a human craft, or vice versa.

He turned at the sound of movement behind him and discovered Sergeant Singh and half- a-dozen Royal Sandarian Marines behind him. He acknowledged the welcoming party's presence before turning back to the view window. The Ryall scout boat had grounded next to *Queen Julia*'s own boats. There was little room to spare, but following the grounding, the rear of the ebon egg cleared the hatch, which began to swing ponderously closed.

Overhead flood lamps sprang to life as the natural sunlight disappeared behind the closing hatch. A minute later, there were some muffled clanging noises and the compartment beyond the glass suddenly filled with expansion fog. The fog was momentary, and disappeared as quickly as it had come, signifying that the air pressure in the hangar bay was approaching equalization with the rest of the ship. A moment later, the airlock light turned from red to green and the double doors swung automatically open.

"Showtime, Sergeant," he muttered to the detachment commander.

"Yes, sir," Singh replied before ordering his men to pull themselves hand-over-hand into the hangar bay. When they had gone through, Phillip gestured to Richard and Bethany to follow, then Varlan. He brought up the end of the small parade. Then it took a few seconds to leverage his body to a standing position and insert his boot locks into the hexagonal grid inset into the deck.

When Phillip straightened up, he found himself at the end of one of two parallel rows of figures – seven Marines on one side and three humans and a Ryall on the other. Beside him, Varlan used four of her six legs to anchor herself to the grid, giving at least the illusion of gravity.

The black hull of the scout boat suddenly developed a lighted curved line in its surface, which quickly became a lighted arc as a hatch swung open wide. Inside, Phillip could see the silhouettes of six-legged, long necked beings whose ears were all spread to maximum sensitivity. The snouts of the owners probed the air like hound dogs seeking a scent. Perhaps, he thought, they were breathing in the cold metallic smell of air long in high-pressure storage. Or maybe they were sampling the smell of too many humans packed into too close proximity. The Ryall milled about for a moment in the open airlock, then the silhouettes parted and a single figure moved out of the ship and began to pull along the guide wire toward the human greeting party.

As the figure came closer, Phillip saw that it was a Ryall of advanced age. He recognized the Ryall as Tarsanau, who he had watched speak to Drake on a repeater screen. Suddenly, the purpose of *Far Seeker* docking with the Ryall blastship was clear. They had transferred the Ryall chief negotiator to the scout boat for transport to *Queen Julia* with the inspection team.

"Tarsanau of the Islands of the Lesser Sea," Drake called out when the oldster was five meters distant. "Good to see you in the flesh."

Varlan translated and was replied to in the Ryall tongue.

"I come aboard your vessel to speak with you," Varlan relayed, and then continued in her own voice, "It is a formal greeting. The councilor will be accompanying us to Darthan."

"Please express my appreciation to Tarsanau that he was agreed to speak with us, and tell him we are honored to have him on our ship."

Varlan twittered for a few seconds. Tarsanau's speech was short, and seemingly to the point.

"It is time for inspection," Varlan said. She let her hand sweep toward those still waiting aboard the scout boat. "These are warrior-specialists in alien technology. You will show them everything. If you cannot satisfy them that this ship is harmless, there will be no further discussions."

"Understood. Phillip, get your escorts down here ASAP so that we can begin the guided tour."

Phillip held his wrist communicator to his lips and gave an order. He then listened for a moment and replied, "They're on their way, Admiral."

"Good." Drake turned to Tarsanau. "If you will call your warriors forward, we will provide them with guides. I'm afraid we are short on those who speak Ryall, so Varlan will handle translation via wrist communicator."

"These are the guides?" Tarsanau asked, turning to indicate the Marines.

"No," Richard replied. "Those are our ship's Marines, ground warriors lined up to honor our visitors."

"They appear ready to capture your visitors," the elderly Ryall said.

Phillip suppressed a smile and wondered if the custom of lining up the ship's company to receive important visitors just might have its roots in a show of strength to awe visiting enemies.

Out of the mouths of aliens…

#

It took the Ryall some twenty hours to conclude that *Queen Julia* was nothing more than an unarmed embassy ship. Even after they finished their work and *Queen Julia* had powered up her engines to follow the alien blastship to the Ryall home world, they were constantly on the lookout for treachery. During the inspection, every human onboard had ample opportunity to observe members of the warrior-caste at close quarters, and most came away from the experience with strong impressions of their enemies.

Their hard obsidian eyes darted everywhere, and their rigid postures made them appear ready to attack at any provocation. They flowed through the ship, poking their snouts into everything, interested in the humans' every activity, including what they were doing in the small compartments where plumbing predominated. To assure the Ryall inspectors that nothing was happening out of their sight, Drake had ordered all hatch defaults reset to "open." Barring a depressurization accident, every compartment aboard *Queen Julia* would remain open for the length of the journey.

After giving the cruiser a going over that would have done the Altan Space Navy's Inspector General proud, the twenty Ryall warriors split into two groups. One group had specific duty stations where they planted themselves and pretended to be statues while they observed the activity around them. Duty stations included the bridge, the engine spaces, and for some unknown reason, the lifeboat bay. Each guard was on duty for fourteen hours, demonstrating a stamina that impressed more than one human spacer.

The second group of Ryall guards set up a roving patrol throughout the ship. On average, one could expect a Ryall to poke his head through a hatch every twenty minutes or so. The patrols appeared to be random. Thus, the minimum time between inspections was just under ninety seconds, while the maximum was 43 minutes.

Life aboard *Queen Julia* fell into a routine of sorts following their departure from the foldpoint. Ryall inspectors kept sticking their snouts through open stateroom doors, while humans studiously avoided glancing inside someone's living quarters as they passed in the corridor en route to their duties. Human and Ryall acknowledged each other's presence when they passed in the corridor, but there was no interaction. They each kept to their own parts of the ship when off duty – the Ryalls' part being the Number Two Cargo Bay, which they had converted to living quarters.

After a one-week dive toward the system primary, a half-sunlit globe appeared on *Queen Julia*'s viewscreens. Like all terrestrial worlds, Darthan was a blue marble of a planet, where oceans and continents were swaddled in swirling cloud formations. There was a marked increase in excitement among the human crew, and not a little apprehension, when their destination came into view. The biggest change, however, was in Varlan. She took to sitting in front of the viewscreen in the gutted Combat Control Center for hours; her tail twitching as she watched the intermixed bands of white and blue grow ever larger.

"That is your home world," Bethany said after finding her mesmerized the day after Darthan appeared on the screen. It was not a question. She and Varlan had talked about growing up on Darthan extensively.

"Yes," Varlan replied. She extended a long arm and finger in a gesture she had learned from humans. "There on the larger continent, where the great bay cuts into the coast to the south. Do you see it?"

Bethany stared, aware of the general area at which Varlan was pointing, but not sure that she could make out the quoted landmarks.

"That is the territory of the Scented Waters clan, my home."

Darthan was indeed a beautiful world. Like all terrestrial-class planets, it bore a striking resemblance to both Alta and Earth. In many places, the seas were more aquamarine than blue, indicating shallower depths than the seas of Alta. The planet also had three moons. The largest was bigger than Luna, and orbited slightly closer to its primary. That indicated that Darthan's tides were much larger than Earth's. The two smaller moons were little more than large asteroids. They orbited a few diameters above the planet and reminded Bethany of a poem she had once read, "... *the hurtling moons of Red Mars, racing across the firmament like twin Valkyries flying on the day of Ragnorak...*" Having had a chance to see pictures of Red Mars on her one trip to the Solar System, and not having been impressed, she wondered if the poet might have had some other planet in mind.

"It is very beautiful," Bethany agreed. "It will be even more beautiful when we make orbit tomorrow."

"Yes," Varlan agreed. "And the day after, when we go down to the surface!"

The ambassadorial party would be small, consisting of Richard, Bethany, and Phillip, plus the pilot and copilot of the shuttle that delivered them. Tarsanau would accompany them, of course, as would a few of their current crop of "bodyguards."

Choosing the makeup of the ambassadorial party had been a "no-brainer" — an ancient colloquialism that Bethany was fond of quoting. The members of the team were chosen for their perceived status in the eyes of the Ryall. Richard would lead, of course. Bethany was going because she was Richard's mate and a student of Ryall culture and psychology. Phillip was going along because he was heir to the throne of Sandar.

Varlan was to be their translator, although Bethany had the impression that Tarsanau would have preferred that she stay behind. From his reaction upon first meeting Varlan, she suspected that he found a "humanized" Ryall disturbing. Still, Varlan was the one essential member of the landing party. She would be their voice.

Periskay would also be joining them on the surface, although the philosopher's command of Standard was insufficient for serious negotiating. He would be available to take the load off Varlan during periods of "social interaction." What Tarsanau meant when he spoke of "social interaction" was not clear. Bethany just hoped the Ryall did not lie around a cold mud bog with their friends as a substitute for the cocktail party.

Over the years, Bethany had spent hundreds of hours learning about Ryall society from Varlan. She thought she had learned a great deal, but now that she was interacting with the Ryall in their home system, she was not nearly as sure of what she knew. For one thing, there were subtleties involved that an alien could never understand. The same was true when Bethany tried to explain human customs to Varlan. She remembered the fiasco that had resulted when she tried to explain why women talk to one another in public restrooms, but men do not. No matter how she approached the subject, Varlan had gazed at her with her unblinking ocular.

Ryall society, she knew, was organized around the clan – with the closest human analogy being the medieval Scottish highlands – and devoted to the welfare of the species. That was about the extent of what she *knew* she knew. If there were loyalties between these two extremes, Bethany could not identify them. What human beings called the Ryall Hegemony was actually a series of interlocking alliances between extended families, all of it held together by the concept of clan-honor.

Clan-honor dictated the makeup of the ambassadorial party. Tarsanau emphasized that Those Who Rule would not treat with "lesser beings," and Varlan explained that the councilor was not being snobbish.     Rather, the perceived status of humanity's emissaries was an integral part of the clan-honor oath under which they were awarded safe passage.     To send a party of lower perceived status to negotiate for humanity would have been deemed an insult, and could well invalidate their only protection in this enemy star system.

Not that it was difficult to understand the Ryall reason for minimizing the number of humans on their planet.     The fewer "ambassadors", the fewer sets of eyes to see things that might have military significance.

Richard had his own reasons for keeping the party small.  This was no trade negotiation, where compromises were arrived at after a decade or more of hard bargaining.  Their mission was simple – to stand nose to snout with those who ruled the Ryall and to issue their "surrender or die" ultimatum.

Seeing her friend was not in the mood to talk, Bethany left Combat Control.  She had to pack.  She also had to select the record cubes she would carry for reference.  Then there was the question of the weather.  Just what should she wear?

#

# Chapter 28

The landing boat keened through the upper reaches of Darthan's atmosphere, its wings at right angle to the hypersonic air molecules as they generated the fiery sheath that had characterized reentries for half-a-thousand years. Inside the boat, Drake sat strapped into the forward couch on the starboard side, while across the narrow aisle; his wife occupied the portside couch. Phillip was strapped in behind him. Varlan and Tarsanau, along with six Ryall warriors, filled the aft end of the boat where human couches had been removed and replaced with padding interspersed with hold down straps of the kind normally used for cargo.

Drake had to admire Tarsanau. The Ryall negotiator allowed them to strap him into the human landing craft without twitching an ear, which was how Ryall showed their nervousness. Drake wasn't sure that he would have been as blasé had they used a Ryall boat for the journey down to the surface.

That the Ryall were allowing them to use one of *Queen Julia*'s boats was due to one of those mundane problems that writers of escapist fiction seldom consider when they plot their adventures. If a human delegation was to meet with Those Who Rule, where would they live for the duration of the conferences? With their xenophobic instincts, it was certain that the Ryall did not possess anything akin to a Hotel Universal.

"We have no facilities for your kind," Tarsanau had told Drake when they discussed the details of the coming visit to the Ryall home world. "What prisoners we have taken have been housed... elsewhere."

The way he had said it sent chills down Drake's spine. The Ryall had been taking human beings off wrecked starships for more than a century, but there was little intelligence as to how they were treated. Most specialists felt that those taken prisoner were used for research to discover what it was that made human beings tick. The human approach to alien prisoners had been similar for most of the war, at least until Bethany decided to study Varlan intensively.

"We have survival shelters, rations, and other equipment for temporary housing. We will stock one of our own landing boats and use that as living quarters while we are on the surface."

"I will check with Those Who Rule."

Drake had heard nothing for two days while Darthan grew larger in the viewscreens. In quiet discussion with Bethany that night as they lay in their bed with the door open for inspection, they had decided that this was another aspect of the Ryall xenophobic instinct.

To Drake's surprise, Tarsanau agreed to allow a human boat on Darthan. Shortly after *Queen Julia* took up a high parking orbit around the Ryall home world, instructions arrived giving them the precise times and vectors for their landing approach. Their boat would make the approach without escort, something that caused a short spate of speculation until Drake pointed out that every ground and space-based defensive system on the planet would be aimed at them. The Ryall had no need for an escort. One computer command and they would be instantly vaporized.

The long drop from parking orbit was uneventful, and Drake made sure that the boat's pilot did not use his radar. Even so, they caught glimpses of a number of ships and orbital installations as they made their approach. For an object to be visible to the naked eye in orbit, it must be either very close or very large. Since the ultra-suspicious Ryall had kept them as far away from their orbital installations as possible, it quickly became obvious that there were hundreds of gigantic structures in orbit.

Which was understandable, Drake decided as he watched one particularly large space station disappear astern. After all, Darthan was the capital of an interstellar civilization, one that relied on trade between its various systems even more than did humans. Starships require infrastructure to keep them operational, and many of the activities that support the ships of space are best done in space.

Nor was infrastructure the only thing in orbit. The planet's parking orbits were probably crammed with starships trapped in the system by the blockade. Not only must there be commercial craft – bulk carriers, freighters, ore ships – but somewhere nearby, there was probably a fleet assembling to take another run at breaking through the foldpoint. Little wonder the approach instructions had been so meticulous. If they veered even a little off course, they could well run into something.

"Do you see what I see?" he asked Phillip behind him.

"Looks like an orbital shipyard," the prince said as a tiny spherical structure came into view silhouetted against the planet.

"How big?" Drake asked.

"No way to tell. Probably a kilometer in diameter, maybe larger."

"I have something big on my side as well," Bethany reported. "It looks like the framework of a large kite with the plastic covering peeled away."

"Probably a power station," Richard replied before going back to his own spotting.

Then had come a short period in which only the planet filled their ports, followed by the high pitched keening of air beyond the fuselage, and a return to weight as the landing boat began to decelerate.

Their path took them halfway around the planet, in which time they swept progressively lower over shallow seas, deep oceans, and land green enough to cause them a momentary pang of homesickness. The surface of this world was dotted with massive vessels plying the seas, while in the shallows they watched large fish herded by smaller figures. Toward the end of their approach, the landing boat swept low over a wide bay. Drake caught sight of hectic activity on the surface of the water, as well as beneath it. The Ryall were amphibians, and the city they swept over was less tall and vastly better integrated with the water than any human city would have been. In the few seconds he had to survey the aquamarine fingers of canals that jutted between large, domed structures, he was put in mind of pictures he had seen of Venice, Italy. The Ryall city beneath them was Venice writ large, with wide canals instead of streets, and both surface and submarine traffic.

Suddenly the water city was gone and a patch of soggy land appeared beneath them. The landing boat's underjets came alive to kick up spray rather than dust. The boat came to a halt in midair before settling onto a landing spot on a small hill covered with common concrete. The jets died away and silence permeated the boat for a dozen seconds. The pull of gravity, the gray-green land beyond the windows, even the several Ryall hurrying toward them, all said that they had arrived.

A low-pitched keening from behind Drake suddenly interrupted the silence in the boat. He, Bethany, and Phillip all turned in their seats to discover the source.

What they discovered was Varlan, standing in a tangle of straps, her tail and neck extended, and her snout tilted upward toward the sky. The noise grew louder as she slowly swung her head side to side.

Drake looked at Bethany.

"A howl of delight," his wife replied to his unspoken question, a broad smile on her face. "She's happy to be home."

#

# Chapter 29

The air of Darthan was heavy with moisture and thick with alien smells as Richard Drake stepped off the boarding ladder onto the half-cured concrete landing pad. The landing boat had grounded on a small island in the middle of a blue lagoon at the center of a large city. Overhead, the atmosphere was a paler blue than even the atmosphere on Earth. A bright yellow sphere hung halfway up the sky, bathing his skin in balmy warmth.

"It's beautiful!" Bethany said from behind him as she too descended the ladder to the surface of the alien world.

"It is, isn't it?" he answered, feeling a bit like one of the ancient explorers. If he ignored Varlan and Tarsanau, their six guards, and fifty or sixty other Ryall, he could easily imagine himself as Patrick O'Malley setting foot the first time on Alta. The caste of the numerous Ryall who surrounded their was obvious. Not only did each carry a weapon, they ringed the landing boat in a perfect circle.

"Sentries?" Bethany asked.

Richard nodded. "A living 'No Trespassing' sign, I would say. They're there to make sure we don't wander off, and possibly to keep the curious at a distance."

"Do you suppose the average Ryall is as curious about us as we would be about them were the situation reversed?"

"Why wouldn't they be? Curiosity is one of the necessary aspects of intelligence, or at least, that was the way they taught exobiology at the Academy."

"I was thinking about their innate xenophobia."

"These Ryall don't appear to be particularly frightened of us," he replied, pointing to the circle of guards. "At least, they aren't baring their teeth."

"A good point," she answered. "Besides, even if we evoke feelings of revulsion among their people, would that necessarily keep them away?"

They were interrupted by the arrival of Tarsanau and Varlan. The negotiator said something in the whistling Ryall language, and Varlan translated.

"I trust this dry land is suitable for you to set up your habitat, Admiral of the Drakes."

"Very suitable, Tarsanau. You have a lovely city here. Will we have a chance to see more of it?"

"Is that of interest to you?"

"Very much so."

"Why?"

"Just as we showed Varlan how we live, it would help us understand your species better to see how you live."

"Why do you want to understand us? Are you not here to demand our capitulation? If you believe yourselves to be in the position to demand that, what else matters?"

"Among our people, we believe that increased understanding between cultures promotes peace."

"Another strange alien idea," Tarsanau replied. "Those Who Rule are not yet ready to receive you. It will likely be several days. In the meantime, I can arrange to show you something of our city... so that you can better understand us."

"We would like that."

"You humans do not appear to be very efficient swimmers. Am I mistaken in this observation?"

"Compared to you Ryall, we can barely swim at all," Richard answered. "We are land animals, not amphibians. Our specialties are running, jumping, and climbing."

"Then I will make preparations. I will obtain a watercraft. We will embark in the morning. Now I must report your arrival to Those Who Rule. You may begin your work on your habitat if you like. You will not be molested so long as you stay within the ring of warriors."

With that, Tarsanau hurried away, moving quickly on his six stubby legs. When he reached the edge of the island, he did not hesitate before plunging into the water and disappearing beneath the crystal blue surface of the lagoon.

The small clump of humans watched his departure before Richard turned to them and said, "All right, people, let's get the camp set up!"

Five hours later, the yellow sun was low in the sky, casting long azure shadows across their new island home. Next to the boat were two igloo-shaped environmental enclosures covered with tough orange plastic. Designed as emergency shelters for all sorts of environments, they were airtight, with inflatable sidewalls and integral airlocks. Each shelter had its own atmosphere-recycling unit, humidity distillation still, and packing crates filled with emergency rations. The two shelters would support the five of them for thirty days without need for supplementing their diets from the local biosphere. In addition to their walk-in airlock entrances, the two hemispherical tents were connected via a tubular crawlway and powered through a heavy electrical cable from the landing boat's fusion generator.

In addition to food supplies, waste reclamation, and atmospheric regeneration units, the shelters had compact analyzers that gave them readings on the composition of the outside air. Darthan's atmosphere was a good five percent richer in oxygen and ten percent higher pressure than the atmospheres of either Alta or Earth. That extra oxygen explained the euphoric feeling they had been experiencing all afternoon as the five of them worked to set up the enclosures. Offsetting the oxygen-rich mixture was the fact that the air was saturated with humidity, making it difficult to get rid of body heat in the balmy sea-tinged breeze that blew across the lagoon.

"It reminds me of Paris Island in the Lesser Sea," Bethany remarked to Richard as they sweated to transfer the ration cases to their new home.

"It does, doesn't it?" he replied with a smile. He remembered their last trip to Paris Island with considerable fondness. For two weeks, they had done nothing but lie on the beach, soaking up Valeria's rays during the day, and making love at night. In fact, Ritchie was conceived on one particularly wild night during that vacation. At the thought of their son, Richard felt a pang of guilt that both his parents were so far from him. Still, if this worked out, their son would grow up in a galaxy at peace. And if it didn't...

"Well, it doesn't remind me of anything," Phillip said as he finished anchoring the last of the tent guy wires to the damp concrete and wiped sweat from his eyes. "I come from an arctic world."

Bethany laughed and pretended to shiver. "I remember."

One advantage of the high humidity of Darthan was that their distillation stills had topped off the emergency tanks with water before they finished their encampment. Richard did not particularly care for the flat taste of distilled water, but he wasn't about to risk ingesting any of the local microorganisms by drinking the local product. From what he could see, Darthan was close enough to

Earth and Alta that there might well be some degree of cross-susceptibility in their biospheres.

As he stood on this alien world and watched a star very much like the one under which he had been born, Drake felt a sense of belonging that was as out of place as it was real. No doubt, a Ryall standing on the sands of Paris Island in the Lesser Sea would have felt the same.

#

It was after dark when Tarsanau returned. The humans were seated around a cooking fire in front of their tents, just finishing dinners labeled "Emergency Ration Alpha-Four", when the negotiator popped from the lagoon like a seal hopping onto a rock, and then moved toward the yellow firelight. Overhead, the larger moon was nearly full and sprayed its blue-white radiance over the island and the surrounding lagoon and city. The moon was bright enough to remind Drake of Antares in those first days after the supernova wavefront swept through the Val System.

Rivaling the radiance of the larger moon was the soft, bluish light that emanated from somewhere underwater, lighting up the lagoon and the city's canals as though they were giant glow-tubes. This blue-white radiance lit the city from beneath, while light in various colors cascaded down from globes attached high up the domelike buildings. The glows from the larger moon, the underwater lighting, and the globes combined to give the city a surreal aspect, like something one would see in a dream or in an artist's fantasy painting.

As Tarsanau came into the warm light of the fire, all five humans rose from their campstools and faced him.

"Those Who Rule will meet with you in three days," he said without preamble.

"Is there a problem?" Bethany asked.

Tarsanau waited for the translation and then replied, "We have a delegation of Two Legged Monsters camped in the center of our city. They are asking for an audience with Those Who Rule so that they can threaten to destroy every living male, female, and hatchling of The Race. Under the circumstances, there are many problems."

Richard wondered if he should cut off his wife's questions, then decided against it. Evidently, Tarsanau's meeting with the Ryall rulers had not gone smoothly. Better to find out all they could.

"Is there something we can do to help with the problems?"

"There are clan leaders who wish to see you before the meeting. Will that be acceptable?"

"Certainly," Bethany replied. "What can you tell us about these clan leaders?"

"Tomorrow," the elderly Ryall replied. "We will discuss these matters during your tour. The watercraft will be here..." There was an exchange of Ryall speech between Tarsanau and Varlan "... two hours after sunrise. Is that acceptable?"

"More than acceptable."

"Very well. I will leave you to go to my lodging for the night. If you wish something, signal the sentries. They will see that your needs are provided for, so long as they are within reason.

"Farewell until the morning."

With that, he turned, scurried to the water's edge, and then disappeared into a pool of blue-white radiance.

Drake watched him go, and then turned to the others. "Well, 'early to bed and early to rise' appears to be the routine, people. Turn off the fire and into the tents. Try to get some sleep. It's going to be a busy day tomorrow."

#

"Richard, are you awake?"

Drake woke to the nudge in his ribs and the whispered question close by his ear. It took him a moment to remember where he was and to take in the familiar, soft touch of the warm feminine body beside him.

"What's the matter? Can't sleep?" he asked his wife, keeping his own voice to a whisper. The two of them shared a sleeping bag in one of the shelters. Their only companion was Varlan, who lay sprawled atop another sleeping bag on the opposite side of the shelter. Phillip and the two scout boat pilots were sleeping in the second orange igloo.

"Not very well," Bethany replied.

"What's wrong?"

"I don't know. The excitement, perhaps. Or maybe the strange night sounds."

"Or the fear...?" he asked.

"Or the fear," Bethany agreed, her hot breath wafting over his ear. "Do you think they could have bugged us this afternoon?"

"Listening devices? Sure. It would have been easy enough for one of them to insert all sorts of things into the shelter floor while we were around the fire. Then, of course, there are only about a thousand technologies for picking up our speech at a distance."

"How would they understand what they heard?" she asked.

"After a century of war, some of them must understand Standard. Don't worry about it. What's bothering you?"

"This city bothers me. It is so beautiful with its canals and lagoons. Every time I close my eyes, I see it destroyed by our bombs. Could we really destroy this planet and its billions of sapient creatures if it came to that?"

He paused long enough that she wondered if he had heard her. When he answered, there was pain in his quiet voice. "I don't see any alternative if they refuse to surrender. Our cities are equally beautiful and the Ryall would destroy them if they could."

"It just seems such a waste," she whispered. He thought he heard tears in her words and leaned in close to kiss each eye in turn. Sure enough, his lips encountered wetness.

"That is why we cannot fail in our mission. If they will admit that they have lost this war, we will have at least a generation to teach them the error of their instincts. At least we can teach them that attacking human beings is the fast way to Darwin's scrap yard. Now go to sleep. Dawn can't be that far off."

She snuggled close to him, entwining her arms and legs with his. "I'll try, Richard."

He held her until her breathing became regular and steady. Then as he closed his eyes, he began to notice the night sounds, which were different from those at home. Ten minutes later, Richard decided that he was wide-awake and would likely stay that way.

#

# Chapter 30

A fleet of watercraft arrived after breakfast, just as Tarsanau had promised. The small fleet moved out of one of the nearby canals and headed across the lagoon toward the island. At their appearance, there was a sudden general motion from the sentries. The encircling perimeter opened up and reformed into a horseshoe shape that allowed the humans access to the nearby beach.

Richard Drake studied the boats as they neared shore and was surprised at how conventional they looked. Their prows were pointed and their sterns squared-off. The helmsman sat in back with his right arm controlling a sticklike rudder control. *Form follows function even in the Ryall Hegemony*, he thought as he watched the small flotilla run their bows up on shore. There was a single large and five smaller boats. The former was covered with a flat deck that looked to be a quick addition to the design, giving the boat the appearance of one of the ancient aircraft carriers of Earth. Railings surrounded the deck and three uncomfortable looking tubular chairs designed for the human form dominated the deck.

Tarsanau lay on the front part of the flat deck with his forward legs shoved over the edge and both hands grasping the railing. Beside him was a second Ryall, who Richard recognized. The five humans and Varlan strolled down to the beach as the two Ryall clambered over the forward railing. As Richard had noted the previous day, they were better swimmers than climbers.

"Periskay!" Bethany shouted as the two Ryall clumsily dropped to the small beach at the edge of the island.

"Bethany of the Drakes!"

"I wasn't sure that we would be seeing you again."

"I have been kept busy by Those Who Rule," the Ryall engineer-philosopher said.

"Doing what?"

"I suspect telling them all about us," Richard replied. "Correct, Periskay?"

"They are naturally curious about the beings who have dared enter our realm and dictate terms to us."

"What did you tell them about us?" Bethany asked.

"I told them of my capture and detainment, and of how you found me on Corlis and brought me to Spica. I told them of how I learned the human speech from Varlan, and of your idea that our two species can live together in peace."

"Did any of them accept...?" Bethany let her question die in her throat as she caught her husband's warning look about being too nosey regarding delicate subjects. She continued with, "Sorry, just the old monkey-curiosity coming to the fore. I forgot where I was."

That required Varlan to explain about monkeys to Tarsanau, which consumed several minutes. When she finished, Varlan turned to Richard and said, "I will not be accompanying you on your tour of the city today. I have been summoned to meet the elder of my own clan. He wishes to discuss the coming meeting with Those Who Rule and to welcome me home."

"Then Periskay will be our guide?"

"I will be your translator," the philosopher replied. "Tarsanau will guide. This is not my city. I am as much a... tourist here as you are."

"Well then, let's get started." Drake replied. Everyone make sure you have your canteen and some energy bars. Otherwise it's going to be a dry and hungry day." He turned to the scout boat's pilot and said, "Sorry you have the duty, Nina. If any Ryall want access to the boat, do not stand in their way. Remember, they've got us outnumbered about a billion to one."

"Yes, sir," the statuesque Sandarian pilot said. "I'll try to make sure that they don't blow themselves up. Otherwise, I'll be the perfect hostess."

"Do that. Just keep an eye on them and let us know what interested them. If they haven't planted listening devices yet, today is the perfect time to do so."

"Jonas and I will keep alert, sir."

"I know you will. We should be back before nightfall."

"And if you are late?" Nina Hensley asked. A slight tremor in her voice betrayed the fear that she and Lieutenant Bartle might find themselves alone on a hostile alien world."

"Then we'll be late. There isn't much you can do about it, so don't fret."

"Yes, sir."

With that, he turned to Tarsanau and said, "We're ready."

They all climbed atop the large, flattop boat and took their places as the helmsman maneuvered it away from the shore. Drake sat in the foremost chair, with Bethany to his right and slightly behind, and Phillip in the same position to his left. Tarsanau and Periskay were perched on the decking in front of the humans, facing aft so that they could see the humans. Drake wondered if Ryall were subject to seasickness. He knew that he tended to become ill when forced to ride backward in a boat.

The small flotilla formed up in the middle of the lagoon. Surrounding their boat were the five smaller ones, each with a complement of three warriors from the perimeter guard in addition to its helmsman. The guard boats spread out, with three leading the fleet and two bringing up the rear. When everyone was seated and the guard boats in formation, Tarsanau signaled the helmsman. A deep vibration radiated from the hull as the boat picked up speed. The power source, whatever its nature, was utterly silent, leaving only the noise of gurgling water and waves pounding against the hull. As they angled toward a large canal on the far side of the lagoon, the boat climbed up out of the water and began to plane, sending white spray out to each side and leaving a deep, v-shaped wake in the clear water behind. Beneath the surface, the distorted shapes of individual Ryall swimmers could be seen to twist around to follow their progress. The guard boats maintained formation and were soon sending out white spray themselves. Soon, the only sound was the balmy wind whistling past their ears and the quiet hiss of the hull cutting water.

#

Twenty minutes later they were moving at high speed down a wide canal with round buildings crammed base-to-base on either side. On the banks of the canal, individual Ryall stopped to look at the two-legged beings before scurrying on their way. Suddenly, the canal ended and the small flotilla moved out onto a lake. The new body of water was wider than the lagoon and much longer, with treelike vegetation reaching down the slopes of low, rolling hills to the shore. At the other end of the lake was some sort of structure that showed as a black line, with periodic columns reaching toward the sky along its length. The flotilla increased its speed to 40 KPH or so and headed for the structure. After five minutes of leaping over the tops of light swells, Richard recognized the structure as a dam.

"Where are we going?" Bethany shouted at Periskay, her words punctuated by the thud-thud-thud of their motion across the wave tops.

"To the water control structure," the Ryall replied, moving his snout to point in the direction of the dam. His ears were plastered flat to his head and his words were barely understandable over the whistling wind that enveloped them all.

It took ten more minutes to reach the dam. When they were close enough, they could see the other side. Richard had expected to discover the river whose taming had formed the lake and a broad river valley beyond. Instead, beyond the dam lay a broad body of water that stretched out to the horizon.

The helmsman turned parallel to the structure and cut power, causing the boat to decelerate quickly as it sank once again into the water. The water on the other side of the dam was aquamarine rather than the clear blue of the water on this side, and it was a good two meters lower in elevation.

Tarsanau spoke rapidly in the Ryall tongue, and Periskay translated. "Beyond you see the Eastern Sea. At this time, the water is low because of … I do not know the Standard word for the phenomenon. It has to do with the pull of the Greater Moon."

"Tide," Bethany said. "The raising and lowering of water due to the gravitational pull of the satellite. What Tarsanau is saying is that the tide is out."

"Yes, the moon is in a position where the inner sea is lower than the city canals. These gates keep the water from running out too quickly. Later today, the inner sea will be higher than the water of the city. At that time, these gates will be raised to make sure that the water does not run in too quickly and cause a flood. If the water were allowed to rise and fall naturally, there would now be no water in the canals, and later today, your ship and tents would be drowned. So would many of the buildings of the city.

"Is that why you build domes?" Bethany asked. "In case of tidal flooding, the entrances can be sealed and the contents kept dry inside?"

"If I understand your meaning, yes, that is the reason for the round shapes of the buildings. Not so much to keep our possessions dry. As amphibians, there are very few parts of our lives that are completely free of water. However, the floods, when they occur, bring dirt and other contaminants into our dwellings, and require a great deal of effort to clean. Other clans, of course, do not have the problem of tidal flooding, and therefore, they build their dwellings in different shapes that are better for their habitat, be it coastal marsh or dry land. Some clans even build up in the mountains where the rain sometimes turns white."

"Ryall live in the snow?"

"If that is the name for it. Do not human beings live in all of the climates of your home world?"

"Yes, but..."

"Then why would it be any different for us? Life expands to fill the available space, does it not?"

"Non-sentient life, certainly," Richard interjected, detecting a potential problem with the way the conversation was going. "Sentient beings have a choice whether they will live somewhere or not."

Phillip had been following the interplay and decided that a change of subject was needed. "You speak of 'other clans building other shapes.' Does that mean this entire city belongs to a single clan?"

"This is a major center for trade on Darthan and many clans have interests here. However, of the city's inhabitants, eleven-twelfths belong to the Clan of the Windward Coast."

"They must be a power among your people to have built such a fine city," Bethany said.

"They are the most powerful of all the clans. They have two individuals numbered among Those Who Rule."

"Two? Is that unusual?"

"Very unusual for single clan. Their most exalted is Sandok. He is First Among Equals among Those Who Rule."

"And the other representative?"

"Tarsanau, of course."

Bethany turned to the other Ryall, who had been observing the interchange of human speech without understanding. "This is the city of your own clan, Tarsanau?"

After Periskay translated, she received an answer in the affirmative.

"Does your city have a name?"

There was a quick Ryall conference, following which Periskay replied, "The name in our speech cannot be translated well. It refers to the place where The Race first defeated the Swift Eaters. Tarsanau and I agree that you may call it, "Capital."

"The place from which this planet is ruled?"

"Oh, no," Periskay replied. "Not just Darthan. This is the city of Those Who Rule The Race. All of our worlds receive direction from here."

"Then 'Capital' sounds like a good name for it," she replied.

As Drake listened to the interchange, he studied the water control dam. He was intrigued that all of the floodgates were retracted until their lips were a centimeter beneath the surface of the lake. All along the length of the dam, small waterfalls cascaded down two meters to the aquamarine sea below, ending in a froth of foam. Water was leaking from the city's canals and lagoons at a controlled rate. When the tides turned, they would reset the gates' height to reverse the waterfalls. The daily flushing and refilling of the lakes and lagoons renewed the city's water supply, sweeping corruption and pollution out to sea and bringing in fresh water each day.

Somewhere he had once read that the city of Amsterdam, on the continent of Europe, on Earth, used much the same system to keep their canals free of pollution for century after century.

#

The tour continued. After the flood control dam, Tarsanau took them on an exploration of the waterways of Capital. Along one canal, they passed through a kilometer-long section where various species of climbing plants grew up trellises and across bridges until they formed one long, green-walled tunnel. The foliage was so thick that the sun barely penetrated, and the cacophony of alien smells assaulted human noses meter by meter. Some of the smells were quite pleasant. Others were far less so, and at least two threatened to trigger bouts of nausea. There was also the constant buzz of small flying creatures, one of which attempted to nest in Bethany's hair. The local Ryall were treated to the sight of one of the two-legged monsters suddenly bolting out of her chair and then dancing around the flat deck while flailing at the strange moss-like structure that exuded from her cranium. Eventually, with the help of her husband, Bethany assured herself that whatever it had been had flown off, and she resumed her seat with wounded dignity while Tarsanau and Periskay stared at her with expressionless obsidian eyes.

The next thing they saw was an open-air market. Here individual Ryall on each side of the canal bargained with one another with the enthusiasm of sellers and buyers in an ancient Baghdad bazaar. The medium of exchange they were using was not obvious. One thing that was noticeable, however, was the studious intensity with which they ignored the boats. That they had forewarning of a visit by the two-legged monsters was obvious. How much of their other behavior was staged was difficult to decipher. The small flotilla motored around a corner and entered a side canal fronted by swampy parks among which there were several life size statues of various Ryall.

"Who are these people?" Richard asked, pointing to the statues.

He received a lengthy explanation that left him none the wiser. Perhaps Varlan could have gotten the meaning across, but the task was beyond Periskay.

Twenty minutes after leaving the open-air market, Tarsanau signaled the helmsman to sidle up to a stone quay. As soon as the boat bumped against the shore, the two Ryall guides and their three human guests stepped onto dry land. There was a rush on either side of the quay as warriors scrambled from their guard boats to take up position in front and behind them.

Tarsanau led them to a series of oversize domes and through a large entryway, stopping long enough to show them the giant watertight door that would swing into position to seal the entrance in the event of a flood. The dome's interior was cavernous and decorated as a forest. Lighting was primarily through a single opening at the apex, with a number of glow globes supplementing the illumination around the periphery. Except where natural sunlight intruded, the lighting was blue, as though the Ryall were simulating night. Scattered through the forest were various holographic scenes of Ryall engaged in activities ranging from fishing to weaving. Visible in the background of several scenes were houses constructed of reeds and built on stilts. The ambience of the building was unmistakable.

"A museum?" Bethany asked.

"Yes, it is a place where we remember our past. If you wish to "understand" us as you claim, this is a good place to see," Periskay said.

"Where should we start?" Phillip asked.

"Follow me," Tarsanau answered, his short legs propelling him quickly across the main open space and down a side corridor. The three humans followed and Periskay brought up the rear. The warrior-guards contented themselves with forming a line across the entrance to make sure no one could enter or leave.

The corridor was actually a gallery with exhibits on either side. Bethany would like to have stopped, but Tarsanau led them forward without slowing. Many of the scenes were underwater. At the end of the gallery, the ambience changed abruptly. Hidden holographic projectors filled the air with wisps of color and light, generating the illusion that they were looking through meters of water. What they were looking at dominated the center of another cavernous domed expanse. Hovering over them as they entered the open space was a creature that hung suspended in mid air, its flanks illuminated by clear white light.

The being was fishlike, with twin horizontal flukes at the end of a powerful tail. The body was streamlined; with large fins set vertically midway along the body. The nose was sharp and streamlined, and flattened, with a pair of malevolent eyes balanced atop the snout on stalks. The nose, tail, and eyes were mere details, however, details to be noticed in passing. For the thing that grabbed their attention, as the museum's creators had intended, was the open mouth. The creature was posed with its back arched, its tail high in the air, and its mouth filled with razor sharp teeth reaching forward as though to snap up spectators as they entered the gallery.

"That is a Swift Eater?" Richard asked as he gazed upward at the apparition. If this is what their hereditary enemies had looked like, no wonder that the Ryall were still frightened of them.

"Yes," Periskay replied. "These are the creatures The Race fought for so long. Many millions of our people disappeared down that gullet before we exterminated them."

Tarsanau spoke for a few seconds and Periskay continued. "Do you understand now why we do not believe that our two species can live in peace?"

"It is completely understandable," Richard replied. "If we humans had such creatures in our past, we would probably believe the same. However, we believe it is dangerous to reason by analogy."

Periskay began to translate, then halted. "I do not understand what you are saying."

"We believe that nothing that happens in life is exactly the same as that which happened before. Two events may appear similar, but they are not the same. Therefore, one must be careful applying the lessons of the past. It is easy to be misled by unimportant similarities."

"And the point of this observation to our coming discussions?"

"Only that we are not the Swift Eaters. Lessons that led to your survival then, if improperly applied, may lead to your destruction now."

"An interesting, if alien, thought," Tarsanau replied. "I will have to consider its meaning. Would you like to see more of my species' history?"

"Very much, so. Please, lead the way."

As Tarsanau led them out of the Gallery of the Swift Eaters, all three humans cast nervous glances over their shoulders. The eyes of the creature seemed to follow them as they walked.

#

## Chapter 31

The tour returned to the island just before dark. By the end, Richard, Bethany, and Phillip had sunk into thoughtful silence. They had seen a great deal of the Ryall city of Capital, and their overall impression had been one of recognition. The arrangement of the buildings, the canals of clean water that were the city's streets, the open air markets and the arboretum, all of these could easily have been transplanted to almost any human world. Even the museum had been familiar. Of all the ways there are to display a species' past, apparently both human and Ryall had stumbled over the same template.

Form followed function in Ryall space as it did in human space.

For Richard Drake, that observation struck a chord, one that was more intuition than thought. A mood had been growing in him all afternoon, one that began during their tour of the flood control dam. By definition, an alien race ought to come up with alien solutions for their everyday problems. Yet, the city architect had not employed force fields to keep the Inner Sea at bay, nor a wall of living plants, nor even a bucket brigade of exotic beasts of burden. He had built a mundane, everyday, concrete dam to hold back the floods. There had been a few alien features to the structure, to be sure. Yet, the shape was that of an arch, just as a human dam would be. It was not because that shape is artistically appealing, but rather, because it is the best shape to hold back the force of the water. The floodgates were sections of large cylinders pivoted on each end and anchored into vertical columns so that they could be rotated to raise and lower the level of the water. The spillways had been barely visible under the cascading torrent, yet they were there, lined with concrete to prevent erosion. How was it, he wondered, that two species which built museums and dams so alike were such implacable enemies?

It would have been understandable if human and Ryall thought processes were so alien to that neither could make sense of their adversaries' way of thinking. Implacable hostility made sense if two species came from environments so radically different that they had no common points of reference. Ryall and humans, having evolved on worlds that were near twins of one another, had more things in common than not.

The air of Darthan smelled as sweet as that of Alta, or Sandar, or especially, Earth. The sky was a different shade of blue than the sky of Drake's home, but it was still a shade of *blue* and not green, or gray, or black. The gravity that pulled on his body was a little weaker than at home, and the star in the sky emitted its warming rays at a slightly different frequency and greater intensity than at home. Still, the gravity was not onerous, nor the rays harmful.

Darthan was so like Alta that, if he wished, he could strip off his clothes and dive naked into the lagoon without fear of being frozen, roasted, broiled, or vacuum dried. Save for the danger posed by microorganisms, there was nothing to stop him from cavorting with amphibian passers-by, or just floating with his body relaxed, with only his face exposed, luxuriating in the feel of warm water against bare skin. Each planet that puny humans could face without environment suits was a miracle in the universe, and to date, humans and Ryall had found dozens of such worlds.

Yet, despite their common heritage of sunny skies, and sea-covered worlds, the children of Earth and the children of Darthan strove mightily to kill one another. For despite evolutionary parallels without equal, they had developed along separate paths because of a single difference in environment. That had been the ravening appetite of a semi-sentient species of alien sharks; beasties that had gone extinct about the time human beings discovered agriculture. If the problem was that the Ryall saw human beings as Swift Eaters, then the solution must be to... what? That quandary had plagued Drake all day, and he could not shake the feeling that the answer was swimming just beyond the range of his outstretched mental fingers.

#

"Look, there's Varlan," Bethany said, interrupting Richard's reverie. "She's back from wherever she went and Nina Hensley is with her."

The small fleet was once again in the central lagoon, moving slowly toward the beach from which they had embarked that morning. He glanced up and saw the scout boat pilot waving to them. It wasn't the open palm "welcome home" wave, but rather the reversed cupped-hand, "hurry and come here" wave.

"What do you suppose she wants?" Richard asked.

significance of which he hoped the Ryall would not recognize, he continued: "We have come to demand your surrender."

There was a long pause, after which Sandok responded, "It is our observation that humans are bold in battle. Your request validates that observation. Tell me why we should place the future of our species in alien hands."

"Your future is already in our hands. It has been since we captured the System of the Twin Suns. With our blockade in place, your economy will soon collapse, and with it will go your ability to defend the stargates. Your defenses will grow weaker each day, and someday soon, you will weaken to the point where we will breach your defenses and send a fleet to destroy this planet."

"Our defenses remain strong. You should have noted that during our last attack."

"We did. Those warriors maneuvered their ships with great skill. They died bravely, and as a result, they are no longer available to you. The more ships and warriors you send against us, the more quickly you hasten your own collapse."

"Yet you fear us enough to demand peace," Sandok said.

"We respect you, and yes, to tell the truth, we also fear you. Your ships have brought death to a great many of our young men and women. Most families in human space have lost someone. However, fear of your warriors is not what motivates us. No, we have come to ask for your surrender because of something we fear more than you, our enemies."

"What do you fear more than the warriors of The Race?"

"We fear ourselves."

There was a burst of Ryall speech and Varlan translated, "We do not understand. You appear to be speaking in riddles."

"It would be better if my wife explained," he said, turning to Bethany. "Tell them why you decided to come on this mission, especially the part about how we humans lack patience."

She looked confused for a second, and then brightened, as she understood what he was asking.

Three Ryall heads swiveled at the end of long necks, to fix her with one steady, black ocular. "What my husband is saying is that we are here largely due to me. Through my studies of Varlan, I became convinced that The Race is more than the sum of its genetic coding. However, at the same time, I began to wonder if we humans could make the same claim. Let me explain ..."

Bethany recounted her long studies with Varlan and her many failures to make her captive (and friend) understand the human idea that sentient species need not be enemies. No matter how she came at the problem, Varlan's xenophobia thwarted her. Then Bethany recounted the breakthrough. Varlan's refusal to breed had been the first instance where she could identify behavior from Varlan that was unambiguously at odds with her natural instincts.

The third Ryall, Pasadon, said, "Her instincts were correct. It would have been to her disadvantage to allow hatchlings to become your prisoners."

"No, Pasadon, I disagree. Her *instinct* was to breed. Her intelligence told her it was wrong to do so. She followed her intelligence, not her instinct."

"You see a difference in meaning where none exists."

"We would say that I was 'arguing over semantics.' I do not believe that is the case, however. It is very important that we distinguish between what Varlan 'wanted' and what she 'decided.'"

"That seems an obvious statement to us," Valascar replied.

"Perhaps so," Bethany responded. "It did not seem obvious to us. Nor would I have considered it sufficient to talk my husband into launching this peace mission had something else not happened at the same time. To understand what I am about to tell you, I must first explain the human institution of the 'cocktail party'…"

Bethany went on to explain how Those Who Rule among humans had an instinct to gather at the end of the day, imbibe alcohol, and socialize with one another. It took quite a while to make them understand that these gatherings were where much of the real business of government was conducted. Finally, when the Ryall seemed to have a rudimentary understanding, she told them of the gathering at Evelyn Mortridge's house.

She then recounted, nearly verbatim, the conversation of the members of parliament who had grown impatient with the war and the mounting casualties, and how they had slipped effortlessly into talk of exterminating the Ryall.

"Their callousness frightened me," she concluded. "And so I gathered up Varlan, picked up Periskay en route, and went in search of my husband to convince him to come here to Darthan to plead with you."

"I am afraid that we do not understand the allegory you have just told us," Valascar replied, moving his head so that he could stare at Bethany with the opposite eye.

Bethany opened her mouth to answer, but closed it again when Richard signaled her to silence. He turned to the Ryall and said, "Our original was to blockade the System of the Twin Stars until your economy collapsed, and then to take control of your worlds. We thought that we would then be able to train you in our ways and transform you so that you would no longer threaten us. It has been our experience that enemies can be made into friends, and even better, trading partners. So, in our ignorance, we set out to tame you."

"We are not easily tamed."

"We can be persuasive, especially when our war fleet controls your skies. However, Bethany found the flaw in our plan. We overlooked the fact that we humans are also limited by our genetics. Your species is aggressive to all competitors. Our species lacks patience, a trait we inherit from our non-sentient ancestors. The truth is that we lack the patience to take the casualties required to bring about the collapse of your civilization. Long before our blockade destroys your economy, we will tire of our losses and will take more direct action against you. When that time comes, as it soon must, then we will forget about making you our friends, and switch to a strategy of extermination."

"Then you see this as a battle to the death, as do we," Valascar observed. "Humans, it would seem, are more like The Race than you claim."

He nodded. "We are both warrior species and if this war continues much longer, we may not be able to help ourselves… just as you could not help killing a Swift Eater if one were to appear in your seas. However, we, too, can control our instincts to an extent, just as you can. It is not yet too late. If you surrender now, before we run out of patience, then neither of our species need die. Who knows, over time we just might become friends. The choice is yours. Quit now, and your worlds will live; fight on, and you will most certainly die."

#

It was a confused group of Ryall who departed the island two hours after sunset. Afterward, the five humans and Varlan sat around a gas-fed fire, ate a hearty supper, and admired the greater moon, which seemed less full this night than the previous one. The lesser moons skimmed across the sky, as did other points of light representing various orbital installations.

"Did you understand what I was getting at?" Bethany asked Varlan.

"I followed your logic.  So did Those Who Rule.  You shocked them."

"Shocked them?  How?"

"By displaying how truly alien are the workings of your mind."

"How so?"

"You told us that you had no desire to exterminate us, but because of a weakness in yourselves, you will inevitably exterminate us anyway."

"That's right."

"If you had told us that your ships will rain down radioactive fire because we represent a threat to your species, then we would have understood, and even accepted that you think that way. However, to tell us that you will destroy us because you cannot restrain yourselves is truly alien."

"But it's the way we think.  It's logical."

"Is it?"

"Of course it is.  Richard, you agree, don't you?"

"Huh?" he asked.

"Weren't you listening to me?"

"Beg you pardon, my love.  I was looking into the fire.  What was your question?"

"Varlan thinks I'm crazy.  You don't, do you?"

He smiled.  "Sorry, I'll need more information to answer the question…"  Suddenly, the ache in his ribs was joined by a sudden pain in his left shoulder as her fist landed.

"Ouch, you shouldn't beat your husband in front of company."

"Say something like that again and I'll hit you again," she replied, laughing.  "Where was your mind just now?"

"Oh, I was thinking about the big audience day after tomorrow.  I was wondering what other arguments we can use to convince them to surrender."

"Any ideas?"

"One only," he said.

"Well, what is it?"

"First thing I'll need is a holo projector.  Think we can tear the one out of the landing boat and rig it with a portable power supply?"

"I'm sure the expertise exists among our little band," she replied.  "What do you need it for?"

"Maybe I don't. Still, it might come in handy if we can just find a picture in the computer's database."

"What sort of picture?"

"A terrestrial shark. A big one..."

# Chapter 32

The Ryall left them alone the next day, which everyone appreciated, as they needed the time to get ready for their audience with Those Who Rule. Richard, Bethany, and Phillip spent most of the morning in conference, fleshing out Richard's strategy for catching the attention of the Ryall leaders and holding it long enough to get their point across. Whether they would be successful in convincing the assembled worthies that their species' fate depended on their decision was anyone's guess. Drake suspected that not even the Ryall could predict what they would do. Come sundown tomorrow, no one would be able to say that they had not tried.

Phillip and the two scout boat pilots spent the afternoon disconnecting the boat's holo projector. A few adjustments and the projector's viewing sphere was expanded to nearly two meters, and to everyone's surprise, the database contained pictures of sharks, quite a lot of them.

Richard and Bethany spent the afternoon rehearsing their presentations. They decided that Bethany would explain the situation to the assembled leaders and that Richard would then drive the point home. Their presentation would be a variation of the 'good cop, bad cop' routine; except it might be better called 'bad cop, worse cop,' the way they were going to play it. The 64-billion-credit question, of course, was whether the Ryall leaders would react to the pressure the same way humans did. Bethany thought so, but she could not be sure – not based on studies of a single member of the species.

"What do you think, darling?" she asked toward the end of their rehearsal.

"About what, my dear?"

"If we were in their position and they presented us with the same ultimatum, what would we do?"

He looked up from his notes and, not for the first time this trip, saw his wife anew. She was perched on her campstool, her lithe body clad in shorts and halter-top as defense against the heat. Even so, a thin layer of perspiration glistened on her forehead, her upper lip, and most deliciously, in the valley between her breasts. Her earnest expression belied the casual look of her clothing and the windblown tangle of auburn hair.

"What would we do? I suppose that we would just go right on fighting until they overwhelmed us. I'm afraid we humans aren't very logical about this sort of thing."

"So what if the Ryall are as stubborn as we are?"

He shrugged. "Then we will have done our best. If they surrender, fine. If they don't, then our consciences are clear."

"Is that why we are risking our lives, Richard, so that we can destroy this beautiful city with a clear conscience?"

The pain in her voice drove him to lean forward and brush away a tear. "It's not the only reason, but it's one of them. We are not responsible for the phobia they picked up in their prehistory. We are only responsible for what we can do to assist them in overcoming the handicap. If they choose not to accept our help, then the consequences are on their heads."

"What a cruel thought," Bethany replied sadly.

"Realistic," he concluded. "Now, my dear, instead of fretting about the far future, let's just concentrate on the small slice of it that will take place tomorrow. Let's go over the points you will be making one more time..."

                                        #

The rain began just before dawn, a cold, drizzle that belied the tropical paradise they had made of Capital in their minds. Bethany woke, still entwined with Richard, to the steady hammering of droplets against the shelter roof and sidewalls. It took her a moment to realize what was making the sound. When reality came flooding back to her, she rolled over and groaned.

"What's the matter?" Richard asked, his voice still muzzy. He had lain awake until well past midnight, unable to sleep because his mind refused to shut down, and as a result, his body clung to slumber more than usual this morning.

"It's raining," she said, exasperation evident in her voice.

"Well, on a planet with this much water, you know it has to rain sometime."

"But why today?"

"Maybe our hosts scheduled it that way."

They lay in their sleeping bag until gray light became perceptible beyond the shelter windows. Another problem with their sleeping was that Darthan's rotation period was only about twenty-two-and-a-half hours, which disrupted the human body's circadian rhythm. As soon as it became apparent that the sun had definitely arrived above a thick layer of clouds, first Bethany and then Richard crawled out of their sleeping bag.

Half an hour later, both were dressed and feeling a little better after gulping down two steaming cups of *jazzra* juice. Both would have preferred real terrestrial coffee, but *Queen Julia* was a Sandarian ship, and so were her landing boats.

Phillip would accompany them to the audience, while they once again left Nina Hensley and Vincente Bartle to watch the ship. Richard made sure that Phillip was up.

After a breakfast prepared in the shelter, one in which Varlan quietly slipped away to eat far from the human cooking odors, Bethany slipped into a hooded raincoat and went in search of her Ryall friend. She found Varlan sprawled on a patch of what passed for grass on Darthan, luxuriating in the rain. Her scales glistened from the wetness as she stretched full-length along the ground. At Bethany's approach, she lifted her head.

"There you are! Don't tell me that you like this rain?"

"If feels wonderful on my body," Varlan replied. "I have never understood you humans' aversion to one of life's simple pleasures, especially when you insist on immersing yourself in water every night before going to sleep."

"Showers are hot. Rainstorms are cold. That's the difference."

"And I was under the impression that humans were warm blooded," the Ryall chided.

"Only to a limited extent," Bethany replied. She fell silent for a long minute, causing Varlan to regard her with the near eye.

"Is there something wrong?"

"No, I was just thinking. We don't have much longer together, you and I."

"That is true," her friend replied matter-of-factly. "After the meeting with Those Who Rule, you will be going back to the stargate and I will be staying here."

"Regardless of the outcome?"

"You have the oath of my clan to protect you, Bethany, once of the Lindquists, now of the Drakes. Valascar has promised me that he will see you safely out of this system whatever Those Who

Rule decide. Coupled with the assurances of Tarsanau's clan, that should be sufficient."

"I'll miss you, you strange-thinking lizard."

"And I will miss your monkey optimism. You have taught me many things. However long my life from this moment, I will think always of your teachings and how they might be applied to the benefit of my own species."

Bethany blinked tears away. "Come, breakfast is over and they've ventilated the shelter. It's safe to come back inside, and we need to get ready for the boats."

#

An hour later, the same flotilla that had taken them on their tour of the city arrived at the beach. The big flattop boat grounded as it had two days earlier, but this time there was an improvement. No sooner had it touched shore than a long ramp telescoped from under the deck and Tarsanau flowed down it on all six legs as though he had been doing it all his life.

"I see you've improved our transportation," Drake said as he climbed the ramp. Even slick from the rain, there was no tendency to slip.

"The better to maintain my own dignity," Tarsanau replied through Varlan.

When the three humans secured their equipment and took their places, Varlan and Tarsanau crouched beside them. The helmsmen stowed the ramp, then applied power to pull the boat away from the beach.

Richard watched the two pilots wave at them before turning back to the shelters. Their orders were to get everything but essential items packed up, stowed, and ready for a quick departure. This, he reminded them, would be one performance where the theatrical troupe might well need to beat a hasty retreat to escape the angry mob of theatergoers.

The boat transported them down the nearby canal, but in the opposite direction. They glided between warehouse-size domes painted white and smaller domes painted brown and yellow. As they rode in silence, the wind-driven rain began to slacken, allowing them to open their rain hoods and take more interest in their surroundings.

The canal left the crowded cityscape behind and passed beneath a pedestrian bridge into a large open park. The green space held winding slideways – sidewalks whose surfaces were maintained in a perpetual state of wetness to allow the Ryall to slither on their bellies while propelling themselves with their after pair of legs. There were large growths of the rush-like plants the Ryall scattered across the floor of their resting chambers, along with tree-like plants that drooped like terrestrial weeping willows or Altan vine trees.

The canal bent left through the park and after passing beneath another pedestrian bridge, straightened to point toward the largest building they had yet seen in the city. On the opposite edge of the park lay several domes painted in patterns of light and dark blue. The central dome was enormous, dwarfing the six smaller domes around it.

"Do you think that is where we are going?" Bethany asked Richard.

He nodded. "It's either the government center or a cathedral of some kind."

The buildings grew larger as they approached a section of the canal bank into which stone ramps led down into the water for the convenience of submerged swimmers. There was also an area where boats could tie up to disgorge passengers. As they had at the museum, the moment the boat nudged into the quay, Ryall and humans disembarked and stood for a moment until Tarsanau signaled them to follow.

They moved off down a gravel-covered pathway that paralleled one of the slideways. It had the appearance of being new. It led them to an opening in a nearby dome. Passing through the door, they found themselves in a short hallway lit only by the gray sunlight behind them. As they walked, it became dimmer in the hallway until they could barely make out their surroundings. Then Tarsanau turned a corner and they emerged into a brightly lit open space that, judging by its enormous size, must be the interior of the central dome.

The closest human analog was one of the colossal sports stadiums modeled on the Roman Coliseum. Circling a shallow pit were shelf after shelf of resting areas where thousands of Ryall, all crouched on all six with their forelimbs hanging over the edge, could observe the proceedings at the center of the hall. Bethany counted 23 levels of these shelves, each with an intricate system of ramps to facilitate the flow of spectators. Banks of glow tubes mounted high up the dome illuminated the viewing shelves. The tubes also illuminated the central pit and the artwork that decorated the single, circular wall.

The humans scanned the artwork, which consisted of larger-than-life pictures of Ryall triumphs. Some of these were underwater scenes depicting Ryall hunters skewering Swift Eaters on the sharp points of their spears. Yet, there were other scenes, many of which held no significance for the humans. The scenes appeared to be in chronological order moving clockwise around the stadium... arena... parliament... church? On their right, the scenes transformed from planetary views to scenes in space. The last few were of ships in battle, Ryall craft that slashed and thrust at other spaceships. If the ships were impossible to identify, there was no doubt about the bodies floating out of the rip in the side of one enemy craft. They were vaguely star-shaped, with four long points flung wide and a smaller point emanating from their spherical helmets and reflective faceplates.

The vast spectator shelves were largely empty, save for the two or three lowest levels. Here, small clumps of spectators had gathered close to the pit and lounged patiently as they waited for the action to begin.

Tarsanau led them to a footbridge that arced over the spectators and delivered them directly to the floor of the pit. There were lounging shelves here, as well. These, too, were arrayed in a circle that faced the pit, and unlike the shelves above, these were filled nearly to capacity. Here lay Those Who Rule, the powers-that-be in the Ryall Hegemony.

Inside the ring of ledges on the pit floor was a raised dais and an empty space where a table and three human-style chairs had been set up. Tarsanau ushered them to the table. Richard, who had been carrying the holo-projector, set it down and then took the chair to the right. Bethany took the one in the center, and Phillip sat down on her left.

Richard glanced around at the surrounding Ryall faces. Most had their heads turned right or left so that they could stare at him with one eye or the other. He glanced at the nearest Ryall. They were of several different body types and mixed sexes. Some in the spectator gallery were young enough that they had not yet grown their adult scales. Others in the pit showed the discoloration of extreme age. All had their ear spikes raised and their tympanic membranes stretched taut to catch every sound.

Like most domes, the building possessed exceptional acoustics. Finding himself awash in the chirping-hissing Ryall tongue, Drake let his eyes sweep the gallery until he discovered a group of spectators seated at least fifty meters distant whose body movements seemed to match the cadence of the sounds. When he casually said "Hello," the entire group fell silent and turned their heads in his direction.

There was a general movement of Ryall around the pit until a nearly hypersonic whistle pierced the cavernous space. Drake turned to see a Ryall had mounted the speaking platform at the center of the pit. After a moment, he realized that it was Sandok. In the time it had taken to turn his head, all noise had ceased. It was quiet enough that he imagined he could hear the individual molecules colliding with his eardrums.

Sandok began to speak.

Whatever he said took more than ten minutes. Early in the oration, Drake looked at Varlan, who said, "Sandok is greeting Those Who Rule and expressing his appreciation that they are attending this full meeting of ... you would call it a council. Shall I translate?"

"Not if he is just going through the formalities. Please translate when he gets to something important."

A few minutes later, Varlan said, "He is now explaining how your fleet invaded and captured the System of the Twin Suns. He is telling them how you, Richard of the Drakes, vanquished our ships in the system even though they fought valiantly, and how your alien hosts now sit astride our stargates, and how our great civilization has been sundered by your fleet. He is explaining in great detail how Richard of the Drakes is a warrior without equal among the humans, and that you have honored them by coming here in person to speak to them.

"Now, Bethany, he is describing you as mate to Richard, and a great philosopher in your own right. He tells how you saved me from the slave camps after your people captured me, and gave me a home where I might learn your ways. He is quite complimentary in his description...

"Phillip, he describes you as the future Leader of Those Who Rule among your people. He tells how it was your world that first took the brunt of our attacks. He tells them that you were able to repel our forces even while you evacuated your home world to escape the new Evil Star in human space. He says it with high poetry and an eloquence that will not translate.

"Now, Bethany, he is telling them that you would speak to them of the Great Hunt. He reminds them that you are of an alien species and that some of your ideas will be alien as well. He asks them to listen carefully and to consider well what you have to say, for the fate of the hatchlings will hang on the decisions made here today.

"He is now introducing you, Bethany, formerly of the Lindquists, and now of the Drakes. It is your turn to speak."

Bethany pushed back her chair and began to stand, when Richard leaned over and planted a kiss on her cheek. "Don't let them intimidate you. Remember, we're here to save their sorry asses, not vice versa."

"I'll remember, Richard. Just remember your own lines when the time comes," she whispered.

With that, she strode to the speakers' platform and ascended the steps placed there for human benefit. At the table, Richard warmed up the holo-projector.

A performance worthy of the Bard of Avon himself was about to begin.

#

# Chapter 33

Bethany stood and gazed at the audience that surrounded her. Except for their alien form, they might well have been a group of medical students watching an operation, or law students waiting to be enlightened as to the principles of civilization. Beside her stood Varlan, waiting to translate. There was a long pause in which Richard wondered if she had frozen from stage fright. Then her voice rang out in a loud, clear contralto.

"Members of the clans of The Race, thank you for coming here today to listen to what I have to say. As Sandok of the Windward Coast has told you, I am an alien and much of what I say will seem alien to you. I urge you to listen even though you may find my words at first difficult to reconcile, for I assure you that what I say is important for the future of both of our species."

Bethany paused to allow Varlan to translate, giving her time to consider her next statement. There were advantages to speaking in translation, she decided. It gave one time to think.

"My name is Bethany Drake. I am an historian by profession. That means that I evaluate modern events and try to find a time in human history when my people faced a similar situation. I then evaluate how our ancestors handled the problem and advise our own version of Those Who Rule how they may proceed."

(Pause)

"In a way, my husband and I are unique among human beings. We come from a colony world whose access to the stars was severed when Antares, which you call the Evil Star, exploded in human space. For six human generations, we had no knowledge of the existence of The Race, nor of the war you were fighting with humanity. Only after the nova wave front passed our star were we able to regain our stargate and to go in search of our fellow humans."

(Pause)

"What we found was a world made sterile by the radiation of the supernova. This we had expected, for no world could have survived being as close to Antares as New Providence was. What surprised us was the discovery that many of New Providence's cities were destroyed by war before the nova sterilized the planet. Much confused, we went on to our sister colony of Sandar, and there we were told of the aliens who had burst upon New Providence and had done great damage before being beaten back."

(Pause)

"That, members of The Race, was my first introduction to you. I was told that you were a pack of cowards, evil monsters who attacked our people while we were trying to evacuate a doomed world. I was told there was no reasoning with you, that the only possible outcome was your total destruction, or ours. We were shown prisoners, members of the warrior caste, who indeed seemed to be fearsome fighters. Then, while we were on Sandar, your ships savagely attacked that system. The Sandarians enlisted us in the defense and we threw back your ships at great cost."

(Long pause)

While Varlan translated, Bethany reached for the canteen at her belt and took a long drink of water. Orating, she discovered, left one's mouth dry. When Varlan signaled that she could continue, she replaced the canteen and then slowly swiveled to face each member of her audience in turn.

"We then discovered that the path to humanity's home world was blocked by your ships, and that even though we were once more free to leave our own system, we were still trapped in a region of space with no exit. Having no other way to reach Earth, we searched for stargates inside the Evil Star. We armored our ships and shielded them against radiation, and took a fleet into the heart of the nebula. After much work, we found a stargate, and sent ships through to investigate. That is how we first discovered the Eulysta System.

(Pause)

"To our surprise, the Eulysta System was inhabited and we captured the miners we found there, including Varlan. Not wishing our raid reported back to Those Who Rule, we hid the evidence of our presence in the system, and then returned with our prisoners to the Antares nebula. During our absence, our scientists had plotted another stargate and this one led to a system in human space, and eventually, to Earth."

This time when she paused for translation, Bethany looked down at Richard and mouthed "ready?" He nodded.

"Varlan was the first member of The Race that I ever met and she made me curious. Were you really as my people said you were? How did you think? What was it that motivated you?

"Therefore, I decided to study Varlan as I had long studied history. What I discovered was that you are not the monsters our people believe you are. Nor is your outlook so alien that we humans cannot understand you. In fact, your thought processes and our own parallel one another, with a single difference. Your evolution included the Swift Eaters and they left a mark in your very heredity."

She nodded to Richard, who turned on the holo projector. A brilliant blue globe materialized above the table. In it was a long, streamlined shape, with a vertical fin at the back, a dorsal fin in the middle, and a gaping mouth filled with razor-sharp teeth at the front. Atop the flattened head lay two beady eyes that gazed up at the spectators. It bore a striking resemblance to what they had seen in the museum.

"This is my species' equivalent of a Swift Eater. We call it a Great White Shark. In size, it is longer than a Swift, and I believe that it is at least as fast. It is less intelligent than they were, but it is the same sort of eating machine. That is all it does. It swims in the oceans of the human home world, and it eats..."

(Pause)

While Varlan spoke, Bethany watched the audience. Most of them had transferred their attention to the hologram. She wondered if the flattening of ears was an indication that the shark provoked the same visceral reaction as a Swift. She hoped so. In fact, she was counting on it.

"There are two differences between the Great White Shark and the Swift Eater. The first is that my species does not fear the shark. We do not have to. We are land animals, and as such, do not share its habitat. Save for the occasional unlucky swimmer, the shark is no danger to us. Furthermore, because we are only occasionally its prey, the shark never evolved a taste for human flesh. When sharks attack humans, it is most often a case of mistaken identity. Thus, we never evolved an aversion to sharks the way The Race evolved an aversion to Swift Eaters."

(Pause)

"Our lack of fear of the shark brings us to the second difference between them and Swift Eaters. Sharks inhabit the oceans of Earth to this very day. Even after we humans developed the capability to exterminate them, we did not. That is because they are no danger to us and they do some good in keeping other species in check.

"So you see, exalted members of The Race, our two species encountered nearly the same creature in our past. Because you shared your environment with the Swifts, and over the eons, had become part of their food chain, you exterminated them because they were an ongoing danger to you. Whereas we of Earth, because sharks posed no danger to our species, let them live and they swim our oceans even now."

(Pause)

"Both of our species have developed instincts that are completely rational when you consider our histories. Yet, we are both intelligent, another aspect of our evolution. In fact, our two intelligences are the result of similar histories. My species developed intelligence because the predators on our home world drove us out of the trees. Your species developed intelligence because the Swift Eaters drove you from the sea to the land."

(Pause)

"Which brings us to the most important difference between us. This war we are fighting is fueled by your instinct to destroy all potential competitors. Although my species lacks a similar instinct, we have a very strong drive for self-preservation. We fight because we have been attacked. Just as you had no choice when you found yourselves the victims of the Swift Eaters, we have no choice in resisting your attempts to kill us."

(Pause)

When the translation was complete, Bethany glared at the assembled representatives of the Ryall clans, and said, "In other words, exalted members of The Race, from the human point of view, *you are the Swift Eaters! You are the mindless killing machines who are after us, and so long as you maintain this attitude, we have no choice but to destroy you."*

#

Had the crowd been human, Bethany would have expected angry mutters, jeers, perhaps a few overripe *gange globes* thrown from the audience. She had just called them the worst thing she could think of, yet they sat there quietly with their snouts turned to one side, and their ear spikes lifted high over their heads, the translucent flap of skin between each spike pulled taut. Here and there, a tri-forked tongue appeared from within their mouths, to disappear as quickly.

Without another word, she walked to the edge of the dais and climbed down, passing Richard on the way. "They're all yours, Tiger. I hope I stirred them up for you," she whispered as they passed.

"Me, too, darling. Good job."

Drake ascended the dais and took his place beside Varlan. He stood for a moment and slowly pivoted until he had made eye contact with the entire encircling audience.

"Those Who Rule and Others. My name is Admiral Richard Drake, and I am the human who has defeated you in this war. I command the fleet that occupies the System of the Twin Suns. I have the power to deny your ships access to that system, and in a short time, I will have the power to rain fire down on this city and this world. Therefore, I call on you to listen to me and to heed my words.

"As my wife has told you, we have no instinct to exterminate you. Let me repeat that. *Human beings have no instinct to exterminate The Race.* We lack it because, unlike you, we have never had another species seriously challenge us for dominance of our home planet. We did not engage in The Long Hunt for generation after generation, until the instinct to hunt was part of our very chromosomes. We fight because we were attacked, and will continue to fight so long as you are a danger to us.

"This war between The Race and humanity has at its root two competing visions. You believe that to preserve your species, you must destroy us, else we will grow strong in the future and overwhelm you. This is the lesson you learned from the Swift Eaters. You see us as a new type of ravenous beast that will eventually devour you if you do not stop us. We, on the other hand, see you as a new breed of shark. You are dangerous, but you are not our hereditary enemy. You are merely the latest in a long series of survival problems to be overcome. We fight now because you threaten us. Yet, if we can ever figure out how to ensure our safety, we will be happy to let you live and swim freely in your native ocean, which we hardly ever visit.

"For much of this war, it did not appear that there was any possible outcome other than the one that you were seeking – namely the extermination of one of our two species. For a long time it appeared that you would win and we humans would be the ones driven to destruction. With our capture of the System of the Twin Suns, however, it now seems more likely that you will lose the battle. With our capture of your most important star system, we have struck you a mighty blow. Having done so, we have a short period in which we can change the outcome of this war. There is a solution that will leave both of our species intact, safe, and free to pursue our own interests. It is a solution, however, that requires both of us to rely on our intelligence and not our instincts. So, let me address your fears directly.

"You are worried that one day human beings will invade your home systems and displace you. This is false thinking. It is true that our two species inhabit worlds that are near twins. My companions and I have commented many times on how beautiful Darthan is to human eyes. However, in acknowledging your world's beauty, we do not desire to make it our own.

"The truth is that we will shortly be in position to command this world and many others. Yet, command does not equal possession. To take this world from you, we would have to bombard it into radioactive dust. In the process, we would render it useless for our own needs. Nor is Darthan a special case. It is a truism that an intelligent, hostile population can always deny a planet's resources to an invader. We have proven this many times in wars between humans. Knowing this, and having discovered that worlds like Darthan are common in the universe, we see no need to go to the trouble of displacing the intelligent species from any planet. We prefer exploration to conquest to obtain new real estate.

"So how do we bring about an end to this war that allows both humankind and The Race to survive and prosper? What is needed is a simple act on your part, but also one of the hardest acts those in this building will ever be called upon to perform. For we ask that you ignore your instincts, and use your intelligence to view the situation objectively. Rather than wait for us to smash our way into this system, we ask that you surrender your forces now and let us through the stargate without a fight."

#

Varlan finished her translation and for the first time, one of Those Who Rule stood up from his crouching position. "You speak with great confidence of the future, Two-Legged Monster."

"I am a professional warrior and one who understands the logistics of war. We have captured the central system of your stargate network. If we can hold it, your civilization will collapse.

It is inevitable, as I am sure your own warriors and economic philosophers have told you."

"You speak of surrender. What are the practical consequences if we heed your words, Monster?"

"Once you surrender, we will send ships through to your side of the stargates and set up fortifications there. We will oversee the destruction of your military fleets. Whether you choose to melt them down to recycle them into your economy or merely fly them into your system's star, we do not care. Once you lack the means to attack us, we will reopen commerce through the System of the Twin Suns. Your ships will be inspected leaving this system and upon arrival at their destination. So long as they are not carrying anything of military value, then they will not be molested.

"Eventually, we will send some of our ships to your home world with our goods and we will allow some of your ships to travel to human space with things you have produced. Over time, we will build trade between our realms. As we become more dependent on each other's goods, we will become less fearful of one another. We may even become friends. Even if we do not, eventually, neither of our species will be able to remember what the argument was about."

"And that is the reason you have come here?"

"It is. As I have told you, we have no inherent desire to destroy you. So long as we occupy the System of the Twin Suns, you have only two choices: surrender or die. Since we hope to one day add The Race to our list of trading partners, we would consider your destruction a waste of valuable resources. However, whether you take our offer is your decision. If you reject it, we will return to the ways of war and The Race will be one with the Swift Eaters — merely a tale that human mothers tell their hatchlings to frighten them into proper behavior."

With that, Drake strode down the too-steep steps of the dais, gathered Bethany and Phillip to his side, and then strode back the way they had entered. As they crossed the pedestrian bridge that lofted them over the resting shelves, a hundred necks turned to follow their progress.

"Well," Bethany whispered, "how do you think we did?"

"I don't know," he replied with a sharp exhalation of breath. "They'll probably be arguing for days. All we can do now is go back to the shelter and wait."

#

# Chapter 34

"Richard, wake up."

Drake became slowly aware of fingers on his face as he opened his eyes to darkness. The fingers were not human.

"Richard, wake up."

"I'm awake," he whispered. "Varlan?"

"Yes."

"What's up?"

"You need to wake up. It is time to leave."

He sat upright in bed and waved the light on. They had been delivered back to the camp on the island just before sundown, and after a quick meal of emergency rations, had gone to bed, tired from the tension of the day. He glanced at the chronometer and saw that it was near local midnight. "Leave? Have they made their decision already? Do we need to go back to the meeting hall?"

"They have made their decision. It is time for you to leave this world and this system."

"Are you saying the decision went against us?"

"I cannot say more. Those Who Rule have decided and it is very important that you leave this world immediately! Get up. Tarsanau has arranged for your boat to rejoin your ship and for *Far Seeker* to accompany you back to the stargate. We must hurry. There are many among Those Who Rule who would withdraw the oath of clan honor that protects you here."

"Richard, what's the matter?" Bethany asked, having been awakened from a sound sleep by their talking.

Varlan quickly told her that it was time to go and that *Queen Julia* would be escorted back to the stargate. "Go? Are they kicking us out?"

"As I have explained to Richard, you are still under protection. Tarsanau insisted that clan honor not be breached, and Valascar supported him. However, there are limits to our protection and those limits include time. That is why you must hurry."

"Are you coming with us?"

"I will accompany you to the stargate. That is for your safety and to translate if need be. At the gate, I will transfer to *Far Seeker* and return here."

"And you can't tell us what the decision was?"

"Not if you wish to leave this planet," she replied.

"All right. That seems clear enough. Bethany, go roust the others. How long have we to get airborne, Varlan?"

"Your clearance is good for..." she did a quick calculation and then said, "forty minutes from now. You must be on your way to orbit by then."

"Right, then there's no time to waste. Let's move."

Half an hour later, the scout boat's underjets came alive, tearing at the two orange igloos still anchored to their island home. The boat lifted into the dark, and soon left the lights of Capital beneath a thick layer of cloud. As they broke through the clouds, they found themselves climbing directly into the bright rays of the Greater Moon. Strapped into their acceleration couches and cargo netting were five humans and one Ryall, with only the clothes on their back and the instruments with which they had recorded their visit to the enemy home world.

As they climbed, five brains mulled over a single question: What had gone wrong?

#

To everyone's relief *Queen Julia* swelled in the viewports right on schedule. The three passengers floated on the starboard side of the cabin and stared out at the lovely sight. Then there were a series of quick hissing sounds as the landing boat made its way toward the cruiser's open hangar bay, followed by gentle accelerations as they were winched aboard.

Phillip was the first through the airlock into his command. He was met by his executive officer. After a cursory look around, he asked, "Where are all of your guardians?"

"They left, Captain."

"Left?"

"About an hour ago a Ryall boat came aboard and they all piled into it. That was when we heard that you were returning to the ship. What happened down there?"

"I'm not sure, but I think we got them stirred up. All the Ryall are gone?"

"Every one, sir. Can't say I am sad to see them go. Once the translators left, there wasn't much to talk about, and what there was, we had to use sign language."

"If you couldn't talk, how did you know we were coming back?

"We received a message in Standard on the comm circuit we had been told to monitor."

"Voice or data?"

"Data. It told us that you were headed back to the ship and gave us clearance for a departure orbit and orbital parameters."

"How long until our time slot?"

"About twenty minutes, sir."

Phillip whistled. "They aren't dawdling, are they?"

"No, sir. What's up?"

"Apparently the powers-that-be reacted strongly to our suggestion that they surrender. Everyone aboard okay?"

"No problems. If they didn't like what you told them, why are they letting us leave?"

"A good question, Lieutenant. I wish I knew. Perhaps they are going to wait until we get clear of all of this expensive orbital hardware they've set up so that they can missile us without worrying about collateral damage."

"Sorry I asked."

#

Back in Combat Central, Richard and Bethany were having essentially the same conversation. Their hurried departure had left them feeling disoriented. In the buildup to their audience, they had considered any number of Ryall responses to their ultimatum. Perhaps their hosts would tell them that they were not interested in the ravings of a couple of lunatic bipeds and then send them on their way. Or maybe they would have them killed, or locked away in the Ryall equivalent of a zoo. Then again, there was the very remote possibility that they might actually have surrendered.

What they had not expected was to be rousted out of bed in the middle of the night and kicked off the planet with no explanation at all.

As they strapped into couches in preparation for leaving orbit, Bethany turned to Varlan and asked, "Do you know what decision Those Who Rule came to?"

"I do."

"Can you tell us?"

"No. It would be a violation of my oath to my clan."

"If we knew what they had decided, we might be able to argue them to a different decision."

"No argument is possible."

"Can't you give us a hint?"

"No. All I can do is ensure that you return home before those who would deny you protection have their way with Those Who Rule. If that happens before we reach the stargate, you will be trapped here. I can say no more."

"You've said enough," Richard replied. He keyed his console for the bridge.

"Walkirk here, Admiral," came Phillip's reply.

"How long until we leave orbit, Captain?"

"Ten minutes, sir."

"Same sort of orbit as we had on arrival?"

"Pretty much. It is calculated to keep us from ramming the local space junk, I'm sure. We will link up with *Far Seeker* once we clear the planet and line up on the stargate."

"What's the acceleration rate they've figured?" Drake asked.

"Let's see, sir. I haven't checked that part of the flight plan yet..." Phillip whistled. "They have us headed back at two gravities, sir. They must want us out of here in a hurry."

"How long to the stargate at two gravs, Phillip?"

"I make it sixty hours, sir."

"Good. The longer we are in Ryall space, the more danger that they will change their minds and keep us here. We'll follow the flight plan as written."

"Aye aye, Admiral. Power in eight minutes and 20 seconds. Better get yourself secure back there."

"We'll be ready."

                                    #

Two-and-a-half days later, Richard Drake felt as if he had been on a ten-day bender. His eyes burned, his mouth tasted like the inside of an old shoe, and every muscle in his body ached to be in some position other than what it was.

*"I must be getting old,"* he thought. *"Sixty hours at two gees is a picnic compared to that acceleration run we made to catch* Conqueror I.*"*

"Acceleration will cease in ten minutes. Make sure that you are strapped down and prepared for micro gravity. I repeat, acceleration will come to an end in ten minutes."

The announcement echoed through the ship and brought sighs of relief in every compartment. Not only would the end of acceleration mean a respite from their toils, it signaled that they would soon be through the foldpoint and out of Ryall space.

Drake, Phillip, and the members of *Queen Julia*'s sensor crew had not been idle on the long climb back to the foldpoint. While their few active sensors remained de-energized, they made full use of their passive sensors, especially the ship's telescopes.

The Darthan system was awash in sights of interest to humans. Within six hours of their departure from the planet, they spotted a distant drive flare light off against the blackness of space. Within seconds, dozens, and then hundreds joined that first flare.

Drake's initial reaction was that the flares were from warships coming in pursuit of *Queen Julia*. He immediately put that thought out of mind. For one thing, there were enough Ryall ships around the foldpoint to stop a battle fleet from jumping to Spica, let alone one unarmed embassy craft. For another, there were far too many of them to be anything other than the mobilization of an entire fleet and three hundred warcraft after one unarmed light cruiser was overkill in anyone's book.

"What do you think?" Drake had asked the ship's command staff via comm circuit. In addition to gleaning much needed intelligence about the enemy, work on the drive flare sightings took everyone's minds off the drag of too much acceleration.

"We don't know what to think, Admiral. They appear to be assembling for another try at breaking the blockade, but if so, why would they allow us to watch them get ready?"

"A good question," he agreed. "Anyone have any answers?"

Answers, it turned out, had been in short supply that day and remained so.

"Thirty seconds to zero gee. All hands, secure for micro gravity. Grab hold and hang on. Ten seconds. Five ... four ... three ... two ... one ... engines off!"

As it had numerous times in his career in space, Drake's stomach did a quick flip-flop, and then stabilized as he floated upward into his restraining straps. As soon as he stabilized, he began clawing at the releases. When he was free, he glanced at Bethany, who was fighting her way out of her restraints as enthusiastically as he had. Varlan, between them, was unhooking much more slowly. She, too, had suffered from the high acceleration.

Richard keyed his comm screen for the bridge.  A gaunt Phillip Walkirk answered.

"Captain Walkirk, you look like hell! I thought future kings were supposed to keep themselves presentable at all times."

"May I suggest that the admiral look in the mirror before he comment on others?"

"No need," Drake replied. "I feel as worn out as I look. Too bad there is no time to go lie down in a nice micro gravity bunk for a few hours. How long to the foldpoint?"

"We'll cross the boundary in twenty minutes. So far no one seems to object to our going home, but I'm keeping my fingers crossed."

"What about that Ryall cruiser?"

Phillip looked away from the pickup, then back. "*Far Seeker* is moving to a position close aboard.  Their hangar hatch just opened and I would say that they are about to launch a boat. Better get Varlan down to the bay."

#

Ten minutes later, a somber party gathered in the compartment overlooking the hangar deck. Once again, a Ryall landing craft was slowly making its way to touch down between Queen Julia's own boats.  Richard, Bethany, and Varlan all watched the maneuver through the bay windows.

"I'm going too miss you," Bethany told her alien friend.

Varlan turned her head such that her right eye stared directly into Bethany's eyes.

"I will miss you also.  As I told you before, you have taught me many new and wondrous things. I hope that I can make better sense of them as I study them in the future."

"And you still can't tell us what Those Who Rule decided?" Drake asked.

"No, Richard.  To do so would break an oath to my species and my clan. All will become clear in time."

"Good clear or bad clear?"

"That depends on your point of view, does it not?"

He nodded. "Suitably ambiguous answer.  Well, I will stop pestering you. I will miss you as well."

"Thank you, Richard."

Bethany moved to hug Varlan, which considering the difference in their physiques, was not easy to do. Richard noticed that Varlan hugged her back. Learned response or true emotion? It was impossible to say what thoughts were going on behind those obsidian eyes.

Their farewell was interrupted by the sound of air flooding into the hangar bay. Bethany helped Varlan to the airlock door and waited for the overhead light to switch from amber to green.

"One last question," she asked her friend.

"What is it?"

"Did you personally believe what we were telling Those Who Rule, namely that we would like to be your friends, if only you would stop trying to kill us?"

"I believe, Bethany. Perhaps some of them did as well."

With that, Varlan turned to enter the lock as it cycled open, and pulled herself to the waiting landing boat. Fifteen minutes later, both Richard and Bethany were back in Combat Central and strapped down.

"We just crossed the foldpoint boundary," the astrogator on the bridge reported. "We can jump at any time."

"Very well," Phillip's voice said over the command circuit. "Charge the generators." His voice continued over a different circuit, one that connected the captain with the commanding admiral. "We're ready to go, sir. We jump on your command."

"Very well, Captain. You may jump when ready."

"I did just have a negative thought though."

"What?"

"We will be jumping premature. Our daily safe window won't open for another five hours and 12 minutes."

"We'll just have to risk it. If we don't run into a mine on breakout, presumably the fleet will have enough sense to deactivate them before one can home on us."

"I feel safer with the Ryall than trusting to the good sense of someone in fleet command."

"Life is a compromise, Captain. Jump when ready."

"Aye, sir. Starting the jump countdown now."

The ship's speakers came alive and said, "Foldspace transition in thirty seconds... twenty... ten... five... four... three... two... one. Transition!"

\#

# Chapter 35

Admiral Sergei Gower sat in his cabin, finished off his second piece of buttered toast for breakfast, and took one final sip of tea while he read the fleet morning report. The fleet's current condition was good; too good in the opinion of its commander.

Beneath two pages of boilerplate verbiage that said "we're one hundred percent ready for anything" came a listing of every ship in the fleet. Beside the vessels' names was each captain's estimate of his ship's combat readiness. The report made for boring reading. "*TSNS Atalan* ...100%, "*RSNS Arabesque* ... 100%, *ASNS Beauregard*...100%." Scanning down the column of green, glowing numbers, he occasionally found a vessel in the high nineties, but these were exceptions to the rule. Virtually every ship and fortress under his command reported itself in tiptop shape, with nary a computer glitch or missile malfunction to mar their numbers. Even those undergoing routine maintenance were doing so only on backup systems, with their primary systems on hot standby, fully ready for battle at an instant's notice.

In Sergei Gower's opinion, one could never be fully ready for battle.

The problem was that it had been more than two weeks since *Queen Julia* had disappeared through the foldpoint on that damnfool peace mission and the Spica-Darthan foldpoint had been as quiet as a tomb since. That was more than he could say about some of the other foldpoints in the cluster. A week earlier, a moderate-size Ryall force had attempted to break out of the Spica-Haeselyn foldpoint. The human blockade had held, but the fleet commander had screamed for reinforcements to replace his casualties as soon as the shooting stopped. Gower spent a hard morning combing his fleet lists to find a dozen replacements. All had come from other foldpoints, or from reinforcements that continued to pour into the system from human space.

In his opinion, whatever the Ryall were planning, their main blow would likely come from Darthan. At least, he was betting that way. Which was why the absolute calm in the Spica-Darthan foldpoint over the last two weeks had begun to wear on his nerves.

He was like a poker player who had signed over the mortgage on his house to cover another player's raise, sweating blood to see if he was about to lose everything.

He grumpily approved the morning report and made a mental note to see what he could do to get his forces 110-percent battle ready. He did not have time to complete the thought as alarms began to ring throughout his flagship.

"What is it, Rossforth?" he snapped at the duty officer as soon that worthy's features appeared on his work screen.

"A single ship has appeared in the foldpoint, Admiral. We're trying to get an identification now." There was a second's pause when Commander Rossforth continued excitedly. "It's *Queen Julia*, Admiral. She's returned from Darthan."

"Any problems."

"A mine seems to have locked onto them and is preparing to attack."

"Well stop the damned thing!"

"We have, sir. All the mines in that section have been de-energized."

"Have them take the quickest possible course out of the foldpoint. We don't want to take any chances on our simple-minded automatons getting them."

"Yes, sir. The order is going out now. The Crown Prince is in command and reports that everyone is safe onboard."

Gower glanced at the overhead and gave a small prayer of thankfulness.

"Sir, Admiral Drake requests a personal conference. He says that it is urgent."

"Vector *Queen Julia* around the fleet and then here to the flagship. Tell him that I look forward to his report."

"Aye aye, sir."

#

Richard Drake was the first to enter *Royal Avenger*, followed by Bethany and then Phillip. As the three of them exited the airlock at the far end of the embarkation tube, a full company of Sandarian Marines snapped to attention and a band struck up *God Save the King*. The three paused for the playing of the anthem, and then pulled themselves hand over hand to where Sergei Gower waited. A broad smile split the craggy features of the gruff old admiral.

"Welcome home, Admiral Drake," Gower said, snapping him a salute.

"Glad to be home, Sergei," he replied, mirroring the salute.

Gower greeted Bethany next. "My lady, it is good to see you again. I see you are missing your pets."

"Good to see you, Admiral. Yes, Varlan and Periskay stayed behind this trip."

Richard and Bethany moved out of the way for the arrival both knew Gower was really glad to see.

"Your Highness, welcome back!"

"It's good to be back, sir," Phillip said. This time it was Phillip who saluted first, but Gower's response was no less enthusiastic than had been his salute to Drake.

With the formalities complete, Gower said, "I understand you are in a hurry to give me your report, sir. Shall we adjourn to my conference room?"

"That will be fine, Sergei. We've a lot to tell you."

Five minutes later, the four of them had transitioned to the spin-gravity section of the big blastship and were striding along one of the axial corridors. Gower ushered them through an airtight hatch flanked by two Sandarian Marines. Five minutes later, each of them was seated around a large briefing table anchored in front of a viewport. Beyond the port, the universe performed a pirouette every minute or so.

Gower activated the table's built-in recording gear and in a clear voice, announced the date and time and then turned to Drake, "If you please, sir, you may begin your report."

Richard began to speak. He began with their arrival in the Darthan system and their rendezvous with the Ryall blastship, and then went on to describe their visit to Darthan itself. He turned the narration over to Phillip and Bethany from time to time, and then spoke of their meeting with Those Who Rule. Finally, he told Gower of the hurried departure in the middle of the night and of the high speed run back to the foldpoint, while all around them, the drive flares from Ryall ships came alive and seemed to be chasing them.

The debriefing took more than an hour. Gower did not speak the whole time, preferring to listen and not upset the trio's chain of narration. Only at the end, when Drake mentioned the drive flares, did he ask a question.

"How many flares in all, sir?"

"Phillip, what was the total your sensor team picked up?"

"We did a quick count while you were getting Varlan off the ship, sir. We counted 312 drive flares spread all over the ecliptic. From Doppler measurements, they all looked to be converging on the foldpoint."

"What do you conclude from the fact they let you see that, Admiral?" Gower asked.

Richard rubbed three-day-old stubble and said, "Either the whole thing is a ruse to disguise the fact that they are consolidating forces somewhere other than Darthan; or else we really pissed them off, and this is their way of telling us what we can do with our ultimatum. I think we had better play safe and assume they will hit us here with everything they've got."

"When?"

"It will take another two to three days for those ships we monitored to actually make the foldpoint," Drake mused. After some thought, he said, "I would say a week at the outside. How ready are we to repel such an attack?"

"Better than before you left, Admiral. We've had two orbital fortresses join us in the last two weeks, both transferred from the Earth foldpoint defenses."

Richard whistled, remembering the behemoth fortresses they had encountered when they finally entered the Solar System.

"And what if it was a ruse?" Phillip wondered. "What if all of those drive flares were freighters pretending to be warships, and their fleet is massing against one of our other foldpoints?"

"Then we may have a problem, Your Highness. I have been operating under the assumption that the blow will fall here."

"And if it falls somewhere else?"

Gower shrugged. "We have six other possibilities. Shall I get out my dice? We can't be strong everywhere."

"Well, there is one way to discover if they were spoofing us," Drake said

"What is that?"

"If a week goes by and there's no attack here, we may need to contemplate other deployments. Any indication of the Ryall forces opposite the other foldpoints?"

"Only negative data," Gower responded. "No matter how cleverly we try to get a look at the other side, our instrumented probes never come back to us. They are being destroyed as they materialize at the other end of the foldline."

"Well, all we can do is be prepared to repel them everywhere. That is the end of our initial report. Get that off to Grand Admiral Belton, and we will work at getting a full report as quickly as we can. At the least, we have a lot of recordings of the enemy homeland."

"Excellent, sir. When shall I arrange the Change of Command ceremony to relinquish the fleet back to you?"

Drake shook his head. "The situation is too critical to disrupt the fleet just now. I'll serve under you until such time as we are past whatever pending crisis the Ryall are planning for us."

"Yes, sir. Where would you like to serve?"

"I assume *Conqueror II* has been sent back to Corlis to be patched together?"

"No, sir. We repaired her here. The patches aren't pretty and she's missing some weapons mounts, but she can still fight and I have assigned her to Sector Six of the blockade."

"Very well. I will transfer to my old ship. I hope Captain Carter won't mind having me underfoot again. I will split my time between helping Bethany with the report and getting myself up to speed on fleet operations. If the Ryall haven't done something in two weeks, we'll have that Change of Command ceremony."

"Very good, sir."

"What about my ship, sir?" Phillip asked.

"*Queen Julia*? With her offensive weapons stripped out of her, Your Highness, about all she is suited for is courier duty."

"We can get her offensive armament put back in faster than you can blink."

"That will be difficult. Most everything you stripped out has already gone into repairing other ships of the fleet. Much of your equipment was used to put *Conqueror II* back into fighting trim. I'm afraid there is very little left for you to replace."

"Courier duty, sir?"

"Don't care for that, Your Highness?"

"Not when we face a major Ryall attack."

Gower frowned. "I suppose I could find something for you aboard *Royal Avenger*. It would mean temporarily giving up command of your ship."

"So long as it is temporary, sir."

"You've done well enough that perhaps we can get you a larger ship."

"I accept, sir."

"Very well. Admiral Drake, you will want transport for yourself and your wife to *Conqueror II*."

"Yes, thank you, Sergei."

Gower switched off the recording equipment and opened up small black box to retrieve the record cube. He handed it to Richard. "Here's your copy, sir. I'll get the original to our strategists and on the way back to human space as quickly as possible."

They all rose from their chairs. Gower beamed. "It is truly good to see the three of you home. When you disappeared through that foldpoint, I frankly didn't think I would be seeing you again..."

"We had our own doubts a time or two, Admiral," Bethany replied.

Gower nodded, his features pensive. "... I am happy to see you back, My Lady, but I would be happier if I understood why they let you go. It just doesn't make sense."

#

As Sergei Gower had said, *Conqueror II* had been patched together and assigned to the Spica-Darthan blockade, a less lofty position than Flagship of the Combined Fleet, but honorable employment. After nearly a week aboard, Richard was still getting used to the contrasts.

Much of the ship looked as new as the day she had come out of Alta's Orbital Shipyard Number Two. Yet, it was possible to step through a pressure-tight bulkhead to discover oneself in a fire-blackened hell. His old quarters, along with the Fleet Operations Center, were burned out hulks of their former glittering glory. Captain Pelham found them another cabin and a small cubicle to use in preparing the formal report on their adventures on Darthan.

For the next seven days, Bethany spent every waking hour putting her impressions of their trip into the report to fleet intelligence and the psychologists back home. In fact, the demand for the report was so great that she was working on the fourth edition of what was quickly becoming a monster document. It might not have made the bestseller lists back in Homeport, but she could rightly claim to be the author of the most read work in the Spica System.

Once having gotten most of what she wanted to say down in glowing phosphors, she began cataloging the recordings they had made. Richard's harness camera, in particular, retrieved some spectacular views of the council chamber and Those Who Ruled. If that were not enough, she started a monologue on the interlocking rights and obligations of the Ryall clan system.

"That's an awful lot of words to hang on the impressions from a three day tour, don't you think?" Richard asked from their bunk one night as he watched her compose at the drop-down desk in their compartment.

She turned to him and smiled, "You military men just don't understand the scholarly mind."

For his part, Richard contributed as much as he could to the final report, including a long section on the meaning of the confusing events of that last night on Darthan. His conclusion: It did not make a damned lick of sense for the Ryall to throw them off the planet in the middle of the night.

"... Now if they had marched us into the Council Chamber, told us to go to hell, and then thrown us in the deepest dungeon on Darthan, that would have made sense," he muttered after reading his own conclusion for the tenth time. Despite his misgivings, he transmitted the report the next morning.

In between helping prepare the report, he spent the rest of his time cramming to get his old job back. He did this by poring over communications logs and reading the deadly dull prose of status reports. It was surprising how much could happen in a fleet the size of Task Force Spica in the short time they had been gone.

The previous week, the Ryall had tried to force the Spica-Haeselyn foldpoint, but the attack was beaten back with minor losses among the defenders. The other foldpoints remained quiet, which led him to wonder what the Ryall were waiting for. Each day that went by without action saw the blockade fleet strengthened with reinforcements. That fact was as obvious to Those Who Rule as it was to him, so why hadn't they attacked?

His worries about when and where the Ryall would attack were resolved on the seventh day following their return. He and Bethany were having breakfast in their compartment when the shriek of the 'battle stations' alarm echoed throughout the ship. Simultaneously, their cabin intercom began buzzing.

"Speak!" he ordered the young officer on the other end of the circuit as soon as he stabbed the accept key.

"Sir, you'd better get up here. The foldpoint just exploded!"

#

# Chapter 36

Dasanu of *Star Hunter* reviled the two-legged monsters with a hatred that was deep and unreasoning. The very idea of sharing the universe with them filled him with rage. On those occasions when he was in the presence of biped prisoners, he had to suppress the desire to reach out, place their ridiculously designed necks between his jaws, and clamp down hard until their red circulatory fluid stopped jetting from torn arteries.

Moreover, he had a better reason to hate humans than most. For Dasanu was First Commander of the Warriors of The Race. It was his task to drive the two-legged monsters back into their lair, and then destroy the lair. Through a dozen generations of hatchlings, his predecessors had driven the bipeds from four of their own star systems. Ever since taking command, he had continued the attack. Sometimes he won, sometimes he lost, but each time, the enemy was weaker and less able to swim against the torrent of his wrath.

All that changed abruptly with the first reports of biped starships pouring through the Carratyl stargate into the System of the Twin Stars. Those reports, which he had initially disbelieved, forced Dasanu to give up all thought of taking the fight to the bipeds. They, instead, had brought the fight to The Race. Between two flicks of a nictating membrane, the very nature of the hunt changed. The hunters had suddenly become the prey.

Of necessity, his first efforts to dislodge the invaders were hasty, ad hoc attacks mounted by ships that happened to be nearby. In those early days of the invasion, speed was paramount. He hoped to drive the invaders away from the Darthan stargate before they fully took possession of the space around it. Had he been able to do so, he could have outflanked the various blockading forces one at a time. First he would have driven them from the Twin Suns, then from Carratyl, and finally, from Eulysta. He would have driven them back through whatever damned hole they had used to sneak through in the first place, and then use that hole as yet another portal to attack their home worlds.

The warriors who mounted that first, hasty attack had shown the courage of their ancestors. They hurled themselves bravely at the surrounding enemy without hesitation, and when the battle was over, fully eleven-twelfths of those who bravely swam through the stargate failed to return home.

Having lost the opportunity for a quick victory, Dasanu limited his operations to probing attacks long enough to strengthen his own defenses, lest the bipeds attempt to strike one or more of the home stars. He had also moved aggressively to reestablish communications with the systems that had been cut off from Darthan. It had been frustrating to wait for the courier boats to navigate the long series of stargates between the suddenly far-flung systems. Despite sluggish communications, he had finally arranged a second attack. This one was scrupulously prepared and launched simultaneously against four blockaded stargates.

Initial reports were encouraging. Despite murderous fighting, a number of ships broke free of the biped blockade. In accordance with orders, each ship accelerated directly for the Twin Suns. The plan had been for the survivors to link up, swing around the system primary in a gravity-well turn, and then hurl themselves against the rear of the force blockading Darthan. They were to time their attack to coincide with the second phase of Dasanu's attempt to break the blockade.

The plan had been as good as he could make it, yet when the second wave of starships swam through the stargate, they had fought alone. Of the breakout force, there had been no sign. Despite great courage under fire, the battle went against them and the warriors of The Race had again retreated.

As one trained in war from the egg, Dasanu had to grudgingly admire the bipeds' strategy in capturing the Twin Suns. Stocks of replacement parts and weapons were already in short supply, and other shortages were beginning to be noticed. Between the loss of ships and warriors, and the degradation of the resupply effort, he calculated that The Race had perhaps one more chance to break out of the cage into which the two-legged monsters had placed them.

To get ready for what would likely be the final assault, he had stripped twelve star systems, unconcerned with the impact from what amounted to sanctioned looting. Slowly, he built a force of overwhelming power, one that ought to break the blockade by the simple expedient of exhausting the enemy's ammunition supply. Nor would there be any retreat this time. To enhance the fighting spirit of his warriors, Dasanu decreed that ships sent through the stargate would have their star drives disabled. Once engaged in battle, they would be unable to jump to safety even if they wished to. This fight would be to victory, or to death.

Consumed as he was by his preparations, the last thing Dasanu expected was that the bipeds would invade The Race's ancestral star system. After all, time was on their side. All they had to do was wait, and eventually, The Race would be unable to mount a defense. Thus, it was a surprise when he received the report that *Far Seeker* was in the stargate with a message from the two-legged monsters. He was even more surprised when Those Who Rule agreed to speak with them. He watched in helpless rage as a biped ship swam through the stargate and was escorted to Darthan. Later, even as his preparations for the attack entered their final phase, the bipeds' pirate craft was escorted back to the stargate, and in contravention of all military logic, allowed to leave.

Then came the final insult. With the fate of The Race in the balance, with ships and warriors and the massed weapons of interstellar war assembled to do his bidding, Dasanu received his final instructions from Those Who Rule. They were the greatest surprise of all. He stared at the symbols on his work screen and wondered what sort of lunatic would issue such orders.

More importantly, what sort of lunatic would follow them?

Still only half believing what it was they directed him to do, he keyed for his master command circuit and quietly said, "Move the bombs into position. Ready the first wave. *Death to the Swift Eaters!*"

#

Since joining the blockade, Captain Carter had ordered spin taken off *Conqueror*. Thus, as Drake swam onto the blastship's bridge towing his vacuum suit, he found everyone else in the compartment suited up, with their helmets clamped within easy reach. This was not unusual. The battle crews had been standing watch in their suits for weeks, expecting an attack.

"What happened?" he asked as he floated to one of the observer couches behind the captain's station. As he did so, he hung his suit in midair, lifted his feet, and shoved them into the legs in the awkward motion of someone who, having been caught *en flagrante delicto*, is now trying to put his pants on while running from a jealous husband. Once his legs were ensconced in the slick fabric, he bent double, lifted his arms over his head, and slipped into the torso section, then sealed the waist joint.

Captain Carter turned around, noticed his presence, and said, "There you are, sir! We just had twelve anti-matter bombs go off in the foldpoint. Big, dirty ones. They must have massed a million kilos each from all the crap they vaporized when they exploded. We read oxygen, iron, manganese, uranium, fluorine, iodine, several rare earths, and practically everything else in the periodic table. It looks like they're trying to clear out our mine fields, and doing a damned good job of it."

Drake nodded. They were trying the same trick as when they had made their breakout, except this time they would get no points for subtlety. By filling the foldpoint with charged particles, they not only screwed up the fleet's sensors, they were disabling the nasty ordnance so lovingly sown throughout the foldpoint over the past several weeks.

"What sort of dispersal did they get on the bombs?"

"Completely random so far as we can tell."

"Any Ryall ships come through?"

Carter shook his head. "Density is still too high. We should be seeing them in approximately two minutes."

Polluting the foldpoint with energetic plasma was effective at disabling the automated weapons. However, the tactic had its drawbacks. Any Ryall starship materializing in the middle of that witch's brew would be blind and helpless until the plasma dissipated to below critical density. By exploding the bombs, the Ryall were telegraphing their intention to attack, giving the blockading fleet time to prepare. Giving up the advantage of surprise was not as great a handicap as it might have been, however. With the human fleet at full alert round-the-clock, there was a limit to how much surprise an attack would generate.

Having gotten into his suit, Drake buckled himself to the acceleration couch and activated the small banks of screens around him. By rights, he should be down in the Fleet Command Center, concerned about the entire action and not merely this one ship. However, his old battle station remained a burned-out hulk, and with Sergei Gower still in operational command, there was little for an unemployed fleet admiral to do.

Not wanting to bother Captain Carter further, Drake thought of the one person he could talk to without degrading the quality of the defense. As soon as he plugged into the comm system, he called Bethany.

"I'm here, Richard," she said immediately. Somehow, it seemed longer than five minutes since they had been having breakfast together. Her voice had the anechoic quality of someone sealed into a vacsuit.

"Is your helmet on?" he asked over the audio-only circuit. With ship bandwidth currently being used by the computers, there were no resources left for full vision comm calls by the crew.

"It's on. All lights are green and I'm strapped in."

"Stay that way."

"What's happening?"

"They've sent anti-matter bombs through to clear the foldpoint of our mines and sensors. We're waiting on their main attack any minute now."

"So Those Who Rule rejected our offer?" she asked, her voice plaintive despite her attempt to keep it light.

"I'm afraid so, love. Well, it was worth the try. Whatever happens now is on their heads."

"We should have argued when they kicked us off Darthan. Maybe if we'd just…"

"Don't beat yourself up over what-ifs," he said. "Just keep buttoned up, and if the alarms sound, get to a lifeboat."

"What about you?"

"I'll get to one near the bridge." There was a long pause, after which he said, "I love you."

"I love you, too, darling. Do you think there will be many of them when they come?"

"As many as they can manage," he replied, "and they're here!"

#

While talking to his wife, Drake had let his eyes sweep the large tactical screen at the front of the bridge. The twelve antimatter bombs with their heavy loads of contaminants had transformed space. Gone was the black velvet of pure vacuum. In its place grew a dozen incandescent flowers, their blooms visibly expanding in deadly symmetry. They had not yet filled the foldpoint with energetic particles – it was too large for that – but they filled enough to take out more than ninety percent of the high-acceleration mines and to blind the forest of sensors that controlled many of the foldpoint's countermeasures.

Nor were the clouds the green, glowing things they had been before. This time they were multi-hued, evidence of the rich mixture of elements with which the Ryall had clad their antimatter toroids. The glowing clouds were becoming perceptibly more diffuse as he watched. It was once again possible to see stars through the clouds. Suddenly, the empty vapors were filled with enemy ships and alarms blared all through *Conqueror*, signaling that the battle was joined.

Space being as vast as it is; only the nearest Ryall warcraft were visible in the magnified view. The remainder were invisibly small, hidden in the blackness and among the still energetic plasma clouds. Yet, numerous devices vastly more sensitive than human eyes detected the invisible enemy and plotted their positions on the tactical screens as glowing red icons. One moment, space had been free of Ryall ships. The next, a thousand of them filled the foldpoint.

Most humans would have hesitated a moment as the full import of the menace on their screens sank in. *Conqueror's* computer was not human. Within milliseconds, the ship resounded with the first *thump* of a missile launch. It was the first of many. With so many targets, the tactical computer had given up on point-and-shoot. It immediately switched to maximum-launch-rate mode and began to fill space with deadly nuclear-tipped darts, confident that it would be able to find targets for all of them.

Nor was *Conqueror's* computer alone in its evaluation of the tactical situation. All around the foldpoint, other ships and fortresses poured weapons into space as quickly as their reloading mechanisms would cycle. Within the ships, a steady stream of missiles moved from magazine to launcher to space. Lasers opened up to rake across the hull plates of the enemy and antimatter projectors vomited their ravening beams of neutral antiparticles at the nearer enemy ships.

In the maelstrom of danger, Ryall ships began to disappear in actinic flashes of radiance. All over the multihued sky, the deadly firefly pulses of warheads exploding punctuated the blackness. The foldpoint burned with eye-searing explosions and bursts of gamma rays. Richard Drake watched as a Ryall ship twice the size of *Conqueror* exploded and was gone, replaced by a glowing cloud of iron-rich plasma.

All of the destruction was not in humanity's favor, however. Here and there in the blockade force, similar bursts of radiance brightened and then dimmed, each marking the deaths of hundreds of human beings.

In the gap between the two forces, laser beams stabbed out and killed incoming missiles before they could reach their targets. Where the lasers were slow to tunnel through the missile bodies, warheads exploded in an attempt to damage their targets. Given enough sensor damage, a ship would either have to retreat or face imminent destruction.

The contest of slash and parry continued for a full minute that seemed an eternity. As quickly as they had appeared in the foldpoint, the Ryall ships noted the shortest path to freedom, and began accelerating in that direction. As they closed with the blockading force, they were sprayed with every weapon in the human arsenal.

After a full sixty seconds of hell, Drake frowned. During previous attacks, Ryall ships that emptied their magazines always jumped back through the foldpoint to safety. This time, none of the enemy craft was leaving the carnage of their own accord. True, the count of enemy ships in the foldpoint was falling steadily, but only because of the wholesale destruction there.

He activated the comm circuit to Captain Carter. "They aren't retreating, even when disabled. They just fight on until we explode them."

The captain agreed. "Looks like they aren't even trying to recharge their jump generators. This must be a do or die effort. ... What the hell?"

Drake looked at his tactical displays just as another alarm sounded through the ship. The Ryall fleet, thinned considerably by the slugfest, had suddenly been reinforced, and not merely by another wave of ordinary marauders.

"Those aren't starships," he exclaimed. "They're orbital fortresses!"

#

Dasanu of *Star Hunter* watched the last of the stargate's massive forts disappear into nothingness and wondered how his warriors were faring a hundred light years distant. For just a moment, he wondered if it had been smart to disable *all* of his ships' star drives after they swam through the gate. Perhaps he could have left some active in order to receive reports of the battle. But no, authorizing some ships to depart the carnage would have been bad for warrior morale.

Unbidden, he was reminded of a story related by a biped prisoner to one of Dasanu's interrogators. The beast, it seemed, had been of a clan called "the Greeks." He recounted a story of his ancestors, of a sept called "the Spartans." It seemed that these Spartans were trained as fighters from the egg. When female Spartans sent their hatchlings into battle, they did so with the admonition to "Come back with your shield, or on it." Dasanu had required considerable explanation before he grasped the meaning of the sentiment, which was that Spartan warriors were expected to achieve victory or death. It was a sentiment that seemed particularly apropos for a Warrior of The Race, especially in the battle now raging beyond the stargate.

With the stargate's fortresses gone to battle, there was only one force left to commit to the struggle.

"Move the ship into position," he ordered *Star Hunter*'s astrogator. "Prepare to swim through the gate."

#

Ponderous, slow, and packed to the hull plates with heavy missiles and fusion generators, orbital fortresses were the guardians of the foldpoints on both sides of the battle lines. Human fortresses guarded every important foldpoint in human space, or had before several were moved to Spica to support the blockade. A quarter-kilometer in diameter, they were the most powerful mobile constructs ever built. Their Ryall counterparts were even larger.

"They must have stripped the defenses," Drake said as soon as eighteen of the big, ponderous spheres materialized in the foldpoint. "They're sending everything through, not holding back so much as a scout boat."

"Concentrate fire on the fortresses," a disembodied voice announced over the comm circuit as though it were ordering dinner. Of course, the owner of the voice could afford to be calm in the face of the enemy. It was a computer.

The fleet of which *Conqueror II* was a part shifted its steady stream of missiles and beams. Instead of picking off the smaller Ryall craft, most ordnance now concentrated on the sluggish behemoths. Adding to the firepower were the half-dozen human fortresses that had once guarded foldpoints throughout human space. In quick succession, two of the eighteen new arrivals exploded silently into expanding clouds of plasma. Not, however, before they killed a double handful of human ships.

"We may have a problem," Carter said over their private comm link to Drake.

"What?"

"Look at your consumables display."

Drake's eyes shifted to one of his small screens. There was displayed a list of everything the blastship consumed in combat – from missiles to the ablative coolant used to cool the lasers. Beside each consumable was a color-coded bar, and everywhere, especially the missile magazines, the bars were shifting from yellow to red. *Conqueror* was running low on ammunition.

"They're trying to swamp the defense!"

"And doing a good job of it," the captain said. "Here comes a new batch. It's going to be close."

#

"Engage the nearest biped warcraft!" Dasanu ordered. *Star Hunter* had materialized near the edge of the stargate and found numerous enemies within range of its weapons. While *Star Hunter*'s crew took care of the local enemies, Dasanu worked his screens, attempting to make sense of the carnage around him.

Throughout the stargate, ships were accelerating directly for their enemies and spewing out the deadly tools of war. Beams flashed, leaving freshly ionized trails through the roiling plasma. Other beams traced back along those bright, glowing paths, carving hull plates and searing the living flesh inside. Everywhere his sensors looked, they found the remains of his ships spewing oxygen and water vapor to vacuum, or seeding the vacuum with expanding clouds rich in vaporized iron.

The enemy globe appeared to be holding, although there were several gaps that ships of The Race were attempting to exploit. Yet, holding or not, the bipeds had been hurt. Even as he watched, the density of missiles entering the stargate declined perceptibly. He queried his computer. Sure enough, some of the smaller biped warcraft had stopped firing missiles, their magazines having been exhausted. They were now firing only their beams in defense of themselves and their brethren.

Dasanu's forces, too, were slackening their rate of fire. However, in their case, the loss was due to the destruction of so many ships. The fortresses seemed to be the focus of enemy fire, which was good news for the battered starships. As he watched, a fortress took a near miss from a missile and a great gout of flame erupted from its side. Moments later, another missile entered the gaping hole and exploded at the fortress's center. Dasanu watched as it flashed out of existence.

On the other side of the line, a biped ship exploded and tumbled away into blackness with half its length gone and the hulk spraying bodies and droplets of molten metal into space.

"First Warrior, we are coming under attack," his tactical specialist reported.

"Begin defense. Return fire against the ships that are firing on us. Engines to full. Aim for that hole in their globe directly in front of us."

Dasanu felt the shudder of missiles leaving his flagship as their white-hot exhausts washed over hull plates. He sank deeper into his acceleration frame as the engines began driving *Star Hunter* toward the spot where moments earlier, a biped cruiser had guarded space.

On his screen, small representations of missiles neared his ship as beams winked out and destroyed them. Yet, the points of destruction seemed to be floating closer with each one destroyed.

"Begin evasive maneuvers," he ordered.

It was the last order he ever gave.

A quartet of pinpoints did not stop. They hurtled toward *Star Hunter*. Lasers reached out and destroyed two missiles cleanly, while detonating a third. Unfortunately, the flash of nuclear fire blinded the ship's sensors for nearly three heartbeats. That was sufficient for the surviving missile to seek out its prey.

There was a spherical flash of light, and suddenly, *Star Hunter* was no more.

#

Sergei Gower frowned as he watched a duel between two orbital fortresses. His bridge screen displayed the tactical situation throughout the foldpoint. The slaughter of Ryall ships had been horrific. Of the more than one thousand ships with which the enemy began the battle, they had fewer than four hundred left. Of the eighteen fortresses that had made the jump into the Darthan-Spica foldpoint, only six remained and they were taking damage at a prodigious rate.

He, in turn, had lost some thirty ships destroyed and another fourteen damaged sufficiently to put them out of action. Yet, the lopsided score was deceptive. For despite their losses, the Ryall fleet still far outnumbered his own and the human ships were beginning to run out of ordnance.

"Give me a display of all ships and their remaining ammunition stocks," he snapped at his tactical officer.

The needed schematic appeared on his local situation screen. Fully half of the cruisers had already shot themselves dry and even the blastships were beginning to move over into the red.

Gower swore under his breath and wondered if they were going to be overwhelmed after all.

Suddenly, the Ryall fortress he had been watching exploded in silence and the human fortress shifted its fire to the smaller ships desperately attempting to flee the foldpoint. The fortresses, at least, had the magazine capacity to keep firing long after the other ships of the fleet exhausted their missiles. As he watched, dozens of Ryall craft near the fortress began to explode.

Smiling grimly, he keyed his command circuit and sent a message out along the spider web of laser beams that knitted his ships into a single command.

"All fortresses, concentrate on the smaller ships. Their defensive fire appears to be diminishing. Repeat, all fortresses, fire on blastships and smaller."

The human fortresses shifted fire and slowly, over long seconds, the number of explosions within the foldpoint multiplied. Even the enemy fortresses seemed to be affected. Six Ryall fortresses became four within the span of two seconds, then four became three.

Gower watched as the count of enemy ships began decrementing downward. The process seemed to grow on itself. The smaller the number, the faster the total decreased. As he held his breath, the Sandarian admiral watched as the number of enemy ships dropped into double digits. Just as it did, the last of the Ryall orbital fortresses exploded.

"Keep pouring it on, people," he muttered to no one in particular as it became clear that humanity was gaining the upper hand. Now if only the Ryall didn't have another couple of thousand ships to throw against them…

#

"Damn, I think we're going to make it!" Drake said to himself as he watched the last Ryall orbital fortress explode. *Conqueror II* was one of the ships that had been spewing missiles at it after Admiral Gower ordered the human fortresses to begin whittling down the Ryall ships.

In space warfare, obtaining a kill was mostly a matter of saturating an enemy's defenses. This was done by a combination of knocking out their sensors and presenting them with too many offensive missiles to handle. Given a sustained rate of fire against a ship, eventually, it will miss an incoming warhead.

That was what happened to the fortress. A couple of near misses took out a large portion of sensors on one side, and then the defending computers proved unable to keep up with the hailstorm of ordnance thrown at them by three human blastships and two cruisers. They had been picking off the missiles regularly, but suddenly, one struck home and detonated.

There is a natural human reaction in battle to concentrate all of one's attention on whoever is trying to kill you. Thus, when Drake glanced at the tactical screen and took in the big picture for the first time since *Conqueror* began its duel with the orbital fortress, he was surprised to discover fewer than eighty Ryall ships were left.

He blinked and discovered that there were 78, and then within the space of two breaths, there were 60. As the number of enemy craft decreased, more human ships shifted their fire to the survivors. The process became a death spiral. Suddenly, almost without his being aware of it, the number of Ryall craft fell to one, and then to zero as a lizard cruiser exploded.

Richard could hear his heart pounding in his ears as a deathly silence fell over *Conqueror*'s bridge. For a long minute, there was nothing but silence as anxious eyes scanned the screen for new enemies. Then, someone cheered. Richard was not sure whether the cheer came over the comm circuit or from someone in the compartment with him. Whoever had initiated it, suddenly hundreds of voices were screaming in excitement and the ship filled with pandemonium. From the open command circuits all over the blockading fleet, other voices screamed their joy.

After half a minute, Captain Carter ordered, "Pipe down, people. Tactical, what's our missile state?"

"We have 28 left, sir."

"Lasers?"

"Down to twenty percent on coolant."

Drake whistled. They had just barely made it. Looking at the screen with its still glowing plasma, he visualized all of the wreckage that filled it, the remnants of ships and lizard warriors. Contemplating the disaster that had befallen humanity's enemies, he suddenly had a horrid thought.

"What if they aren't through?"

Pelham Carter did not turn around. He did not have to. Richard noted the sudden reddening of his neck where it cleared the helmet seal of his vacsuit. It was obvious that the thought had just occurred to him as well.

With dozens of worlds to draw from, who said the Ryall had only gathered up a thousand ships to send against them? In fact, given sufficient resources, Drake would have struck his enemies in two waves. First, he would send through half his force, exhaust the defenders' magazines, and then while they were congratulating themselves on their victory, surprise them with the other half of his fleet.

He did not have the opportunity to voice his suspicions. Suddenly, alarms rang on the bridge and throughout the ship. As they did, his heart leaped into his throat and his stomach, which had been slowly relaxing, was once again a hard lump in his abdomen.

"Enemy breakout in the foldpoint!" the computer voice announced in its too calm soprano.

"How many?" Carter demanded.

There was a pause until the tactical officer said, "Just one, sir. We have an identity on it. It's *Far Seeker* and they are asking to talk to Admiral Drake."

One of his local screens flashed and he found himself looking at the head and snout of a Ryall he recognized. It was Varlan.

"What is it?" he asked as soon as the familiar features appeared.

There was a pause far longer than any communication delay. Then Varlan opened her mouth, showed the tip of her tri-forked tongue, and said, "We surrender, Richard. Those Who Rule accept your conditions."

\#

## Chapter 37

*Royal Avenger*'s hangar bay was a beehive as Richard Drake departed his landing boat and made his way to the airlock where Phillip awaited him. The Sandarian flagship was still in zero gravity to facilitate the comings and goings of the repair boats and medical craft rendering aid to those ships hit in the recent battle. As he pulled himself along the guide rope, he halted to allow two medics to pass. They were towing a pressurized stretcher from which a low groan emanated. Drake set his jaw and cursed under his breath as he resisted the reflex to avert his eyes from the contorted features of the injured crewman visible through the transparent bubble. His wife was fond of quoting someone called the Duke of Wellington, who had once stated, "The only thing worse than a battle won is a battle lost." Since beginning this campaign, Drake had developed a new appreciation for the sentiment.

"Good afternoon, sir," Phillip said when Drake finally made it to the airlock.

"Your highness. Any damage to *Royal Avenger*?"

"No, sir. We came through the storm without a scratch. Unfortunately, we lost a lot of friends on *Wanderer* and *Amethyst*. I suspect you met some of them when you were at court."

"Yeah, I heard. We lost *Dagger* with all hands, too. There are going to be tears in Homeport when the news gets there." *ASNS Dagger* was one of the old terrestrial cruisers that had been trapped in the Alta system when the Antares supernova had isolated the colony. She was the sister ship to *Discovery*, which had been Drake's command during the expeditions to New Providence and Earth. "I'm afraid that everyone has someone to grieve this time."

"It's a damned waste, sir," Phillip replied.

"It sure the hell is," Drake agreed. "Lead off, Captain. We'd best not keep Admiral Gower waiting."

Phillip led him through the familiar corridors until they reached the admiral's command center just aft of *Royal Avenger*'s bridge. A dozen ship captains were arrayed around the conference table, each strapped into a tubular frame bolted to the deck. As

Drake and Phillip entered the compartment, the prince moved to an empty place halfway down one side of the table while Drake moved to the foot. A ship in micro gravity is no place for the snapping to attention nonsense practiced by wet navies and ground armies, so Drake strapped himself in without ceremony.

When he was secure, Sergei Gower intoned, "Admiral Drake, I relinquish command of the fleet to you."

"Thank you, Admiral Gower. I receive the command from you." Drake replied formally. He then paused and looked around the table at the assembled captains. "Ladies and Gentlemen, I trust your ships are operational."

There was a general nodding of heads. That was no surprise, as this council of war had been assembled only from the starships that came through the battle intact. That single criterion left several familiar faces absent, and unfortunately, some of them were dead.

"Each of your ships is being resupplied as we speak, or will be shortly. As soon as your magazines are topped off, you will form Fleet Force Darthan Prime and proceed through the foldpoint to determine if the Ryall surrender offer is genuine. If you are fired upon, you will defend yourself and jump back here as quickly as your generators can recharge. If there is no resistance, you will secure the foldpoint and send a ship back here to report. We will then dispatch orbital fortresses to strengthen your force. Under no circumstances, are you to make any moves that might be construed as a threat to the planet. Any questions?"

"Yes, sir," replied Vice Admiral Aguerre. His force of Terrestrial Space Navy ships had reinforced the Darthan blockade the previous month. His flagship was the Blastship TSNS *Michigan* and he would command the expedition into Ryall space. "What makes us think that this surrender offer is legitimate?"

"We don't know what to think, Admiral. We believe they stripped their foldpoint defenses to build the force they hurled against us here. The presence of 18 orbital fortresses in the attack makes it probable that we just saw their maximum effort. However, you may also be jumping into a trap, which is why we want you strong enough to hold your own until you can get back here."

"Where is the Ryall representative now, sir?" Captain Anderson, a blonde terrestrial with a scar on her cheek asked.

"Varlan has been taken aboard *Conqueror*, where she is being interrogated by my wife. We should have a reading on her story before you jump."

He let his eyes sweep the faces of the assembled commanders. "I want it understood that there are to be no heroics. Your job is to go in, look, and run like hell if you encounter resistance. Given the depleted state of our foe, there is a good chance we can assemble enough ships here to take whatever they have left. However, before we can commit to an attack, we need tactical intelligence. That is your one and only job, Ladies and Gentlemen. Assess the situation and report.

"Now, is there are no further questions, you may return to your ships. Good luck to you all."

#

Bethany Drake sat on the edge of the cramped bunk she shared with her husband next to a small pile of possessions. At her feet was an open kit bag. She ignored both the pile and the bag, and concentrated her attention instead on the small, glittering rectangle held gently between thumb and forefinger. A full color, three-dimensional mirage hovered a few centimeters above the glasslike polymer, an image of her son. It was the picture she had taken just before abandoning little Ritchie to her uncle. It was the image she kept always near her heart, and the one she looked at every evening before going to bed.

As she gazed at her infant son's upturned pink face, his twinkling blue eyes, and his impish smile, she remembered how much trouble it had been for the baby holographer to coax that expression out of him. All he had wanted to do was crawl under the chair occupied by his anxious mother. Ritchie had his father's stubborn streak and she suspected that he would be a handful in ten or twelve years because of it. Still, she would not trade him for any other baby in the universe.

Unbidden, tears welled up in the corners of her eyes. They became a flood as she thought of how much he must have grown since she had kissed him goodbye in Homeport. As her vision blurred, she reached up to wipe the tears away, only to have the storm turn into a flood.

She had always resented her tendency to cry at inopportune moments. It was one thing she envied in men — their ability to fake impassivity in moments of great emotion. She wished she were better at it. Yet, the watery veil through which she viewed her surroundings was not the result of sorrow. The tears that filled her eyes were tears of joy.

In less than 24 hours, she would begin the long journey home. In another two months, less if she were lucky with her connections, she would once again bounce her son on her lap and coo baby talk into his ear. On that day, she would begin to forget. Slowly, she would put out of mind the hardship and fear, the death and suffering, the tension and danger of these past few months. Someday, she knew, the war would recede to nothing more than a bad memory. Eventually, if she lived long enough, she might even look back on it, if not with fondness, then possibly with the warm glow of nostalgia. For all of the rest of her life, she would have the satisfaction of knowing that she had played an important part in concluding the century-old horror.

She had come to Spica to convince her husband and everyone else that, despite their alien thought processes, the Ryall would always act in their own best interest – that being the classic definition of "intelligence." In retrospect, Bethany realized, her long association with Varlan caused her to fall into the most basic trap of xenology – anthropomorphism.

There is something in the human mind that ascribes human characteristics to animals and inanimate objects. The tendency to anthropomorphize has its uses. For one thing, it is responsible for mankind's first great partnership with another species — the ancient alliance between man and dog.

The identity of the first human being to realize that the wild wolves of the forest could be tamed is lost in the mists of prehistory. Even so, the bond that formed in that long ago time has survived undiminished through the millennia.

It helps that both humans and dogs are pack animals, and therefore, possess similar cultures. To humans, dogs become part of the family, surrogate children that are subject to children's rules. In most families, Fido is treated as a smaller, furrier version of little Johnnie. To dogs, humans are the leaders of their adoptive pack, the alpha animals of the relationship, the source of a steady supply of food and affection.

To live together, humans and canines each imagine the other one of their own kind, and modify their actions accordingly. The dogs can be forgiven the error since they do not know any better. However, humans, who intellectually recognize the inherent differences, nevertheless insist on telling themselves that dogs are just little people.

It had been that way with Bethany and Varlan, although she never thought of the Ryall as a pet. As she came to like the Ryall prisoner, her attitude toward Varlan changed subtly. Where before she had only seen the long snout, rounded head, mobile ears, and obsidian eyes as alien, with familiarity, she had developed the empathy required to see past the alien physique to the soul of a friend.

It had therefore come as a shock when, following the Ryall surrender, Varlan demonstrated how utterly alien were the thought processes of her species.

The most inviolable law of life is that every species, whether intelligent or not, must conform to the universe as it is. That the capture of Spica would eventually cause the Ryall economy to collapse was a given. What no one had known was how effective the tactic would prove, especially when aided by the massive expenditure of ships and warriors in attempts to break through the human blockade.

By the time *Queen Julia* materialized in the Darthan foldpoint, Those Who Rule had begun to see real disruptions in their war effort. They could project when those disruptions would cause their defenses to collapse and had come up with a far shorter span of time than had human planners.

Apparently (she made a mental note that she might again be humanizing Varlan's version of events), the presentation she and Richard made to the Ryall rulers left a deep impression, although not the one intended. Faced with the collapse of their industrial capability, Those Who Rule faced squarely the unpalatable choice between surrender and extinction. In this, at least, Richard's plan had worked flawlessly.

What had not gone as planned was the Ryall response to their surrender demand. When forced to confront their predicament, it had taken Those Who Rule only about four hours to decide that they had to either break the blockade, and soon; or else, surrender. Having come to that conclusion, they lost no time in taking action to resolve their dilemma.

Long before *Queen Julia* entered Darthan, Those Who Rule began assembling a massive force of ships and warriors. After hearing humanity's ultimatum, they merely accelerated their plan for one last, desperate attempt to break the blockade. After all, they reasoned, surrender would cost them their warriors anyway, so why not expend them in a last attempt to break out of the trap?

As Varlan explained, her assignment had been one of last resort. *Far Seeker* was to be the final ship sent to Spica. If on her arrival, she found her species victorious, *Galatan* would add his weapons to the battle. If, however, they found the Ryall fleet broken and the foldpoint defenses intact, her orders were to transmit their surrender.

During her debriefing, Varlan had cleared up another mystery. The reason *Queen Julia* had been allowed to leave Darthan was to carry word of the surrender negotiations. Had the diplomatic ship not returned, it was likely that any Ryall ship materializing in the foldpoint would be instantly destroyed, making it impossible for humanity to learn of The Race's capitulation. By allowing the peace party to return to the fleet, Those Who Rule had kept their options open.

It was the cold-bloodedness of the calculation that finally convinced Bethany of the alien nature of the Ryall mind. She doubted her own species could have made such a decision, and never as quickly as had Those Who Rule. Human beings do not surrender meekly when faced with overpowering odds. Rather, they fight on long after fighting makes no logical sense.

Bethany wondered if the Ryall knew the risk they had been taking when they decided to launch a ferocious attack, *then* surrender. The temptation to put a missile into *Far Seeker* might have been overwhelming to spacers who had just seen thousands of their friends killed.

Still, everything had worked out in the end.

The war was far from over, of course. For one thing, only Darthan had so far surrendered. There were dozens of other Ryall worlds. Each would need to see reason before missiles and laser beams ceased arcing through the black sky. A thousand things could still go wrong – everything from bad faith by one side or the other, to interspecies misunderstandings, to bad luck. Still, the end was finally in view.

Despite the aching emptiness Bethany felt each time she thought about her infant son on far-off Alta, she knew that her decision to abandon him had been the proper one. It meant that she would miss his first birthday party, and that he would probably be walking before she saw him again. Those treasured moments would be lost forever, never to be retrieved. However, there would be other moments. She would be present for his first day of school.

She would attend his college graduation. She would weep from the front row when he said his marriage vows.

One thing she would never do, however, was wave to him from a spaceport gallery as his shuttle blasted skyward to take him ultimately to his death among the stars. True, she had abandoned her baby, but in the process, she had secured her son's future.

Peace was not yet at hand, but it was in sight. After more than a century, the bloodshed would end and mothers everywhere could once more plan their children's future without fear. Yet again, a naked ape from a small planet orbiting a nondescript yellow dwarf star had persevered.

Humanity would live, as would a race of intelligent lizards that had once fought a voracious fishlike killer.

That was an accomplishment of note, and certainly one worth a good cry.

#

The End

# Author's Biography

Michael McCollum was born in Phoenix, Arizona, in 1946, and is a graduate of Arizona State University, where he majored in aerospace propulsion and minored in nuclear engineering. He is employed at Honeywell in Tempe, Arizona, where he is Chief Engineer in the valve product line. In his career, Mr. McCollum has worked on the precursor to the Space Shuttle Main Engine, a nuclear valve to replace the one that failed at Three Mile Island, several guided missiles, Space Station Freedom, and virtually every aircraft in production today. He is currently involved in an effort to create a joint venture company with a major Russian aerospace engine manufacturer and has traveled extensively to Russia in the last several years.

In addition to his engineering, Mr. McCollum is a successful professional writer in the field of science fiction. He is the author of a dozen pieces of short fiction and has appeared in magazines such as Analog Science Fiction/Science Fact, Amazing, and Isaac Asimov's Science Fiction Magazine. His novels (originally published by Ballantine-Del Rey) include *A Greater Infinity*, , *Procyon's Promise*, *Antares Dawn*, *Antares Passage*, *The Clouds of Saturn*, and *The Sails of Tau Ceti*, His novel, *Thunderstrike!*, was optioned by a Hollywood production company for a possible movie. Several of these books have subsequently been translated into Japanese and German.

Mr. McCollum is the proprietor of Sci Fi - Arizona, one of the first author-owned-and-operated virtual bookstores on the INTERNET. *Gibraltar Earth*, the first book in the *Gibraltar Stars Trilogy*, was the first original novel published on Sci Fi –Arizona. *Antares Victory* is the second.

Mr. McCollum is married to a lovely lady named Catherine, and has three children: Robert, Michael, and Elizabeth. Robert is recently married and a financial analyst for a computer company in

Massachusetts. Michael is a Military Police Specialist with the Arizona National Guard. He has found the promise of "one weekend a month and two weeks a year" to have been optimistic in the post-September 11th world. Elizabeth is a student at Northern Arizona University, where she is studying to become a lawyer. She will be good at it. She inherited her father's personality.

# Sci Fi - Arizona

## A Virtual Science Fiction Bookstore and Writer's Workshop
### Michael McCollum, Proprietor
### *WWW.SCIFI-AZ.COM*

If you enjoy technologically sophisticated science fiction or have an interest in writing, you will probably find something to interest you at Sci Fi - Arizona. We have short stories and articles on writing– all for free! If you like what you find, we have full length, professionally written science fiction novels in both electronic form and as hard copy books, and at prices lower than you will find in your local bookstore.

Moreover, if you like space art, you can visit our Art Gallery, where we feature the works of Don Dixon, one of the best astronomical and science fiction artists at work today. Don is the Art Director of the Griffith Observatory. Pick up one or more of his spacescapes for computer wallpaper, or order a high quality print direct from the artist.

We have book length versions of both Writers' Workshop series, "The Art of Writing, Volumes I and II" and "The Art of Science Fiction, Volumes I and II" in both electronic and hard copy formats.

So if you are looking for a fondly remembered novel, or facing six hours strapped into an airplane seat with nothing to read, check out our offerings. We think you will like what you find.

## NOVELS

### 1. Life Probe - US$4.50

The Makers searched for the secret to faster-than-light travel for 100,000 years. Their chosen instruments were the Life Probes, which they launched in every direction to seek out advanced civilizations among the stars. One such machine searching for intelligent life encounters 21st century Earth. It isn't sure that it has found any...

### 2. Procyon's Promise - US$4.50

Three hundred years after humanity made its deal with the Life Probe to search out the secret of faster-than-light travel, the descendants of the original expedition return to Earth in a starship. They find a world that has forgotten the ancient contract. No matter. The colonists have overcome far greater obstacles in their single-minded drive to redeem a promise made before any of them were born...

### 3. Antares Dawn - US$4.50

When the super giant star Antares exploded in 2512, the human colony on Alta found their pathway to the stars gone, isolating them from the rest of human space for more than a century. Then one day, a powerful warship materialized in the system without warning. Alarmed by the sudden appearance of such a behemoth, the commanders of the Altan Space Navy dispatched one of their most powerful ships to investigate. What ASNS Discovery finds when they finally catch the intruder is a battered hulk manned by a dead crew.

That is disturbing news for the Altans. For the dead battleship could easily have defeated the whole of the Altan navy. If it could find Alta, then so could whomever it was that beat it. Something must be done...

## 4. Antares Passage - US$4.50

After more than a century of isolation, the paths between stars are again open and the people of Alta in contact with their sister colony on Sandar. The opening of the foldlines has not been the unmixed blessing the Altans had supposed, however.

For the reestablishment of interstellar travel has brought with it news of the Ryall, an alien race whose goal is the extermination of humanity. If they are to avoid defeat at the hands of the aliens, Alta must seek out the military might of Earth. However, to reach Earth requires them to dive into the heart of a supernova.

## 5. Antares Victory – FIRST TIME IN PRINT US$7.00

After a century of warfare, humanity finally discovered the Achilles heel of the Ryall, their xenophobic reptilian foe. Spica – Alpha Virginis – is the key star system in enemy space. It is the hub through which all Ryall starships must pass, and if humanity can only capture and hold it, they will strangle the Ryall war machine and end their threat to humankind forever.

It all seemed so simple in the computer simulations: Advance by stealth, attack without warning, strike swiftly with overwhelming power. Unfortunately, conquering the Ryall proves the easy part. With the key to victory in hand, Richard and Bethany Drake discover that they must also conquer human nature if they are to bring down the alien foe ...

## 6. Thunderstrike! - US$6.00

The new comet found near Jupiter was an incredible treasure trove of water ice and rock. Immediately, the water-starved Luna Republic and the Sierra Corporation, a leader in asteroid mining, were squabbling over rights to the new resource. However, all thoughts of profit and fame were abandoned when a scientific expedition discovered that the comet's trajectory placed it on a collision course with Earth!

As scientists struggled to find a way to alter the comet's course, world leaders tried desperately to restrain mass panic, and two lovers quarreled over the direction the comet was to take, all Earth waited to see if humanity had any future at all...

## 7. The Clouds of Saturn - US$4.50

When the sun flared out of control and boiled Earth's oceans, humanity took refuge in a place that few would have predicted. In the greatest migration in history, the entire human race took up residence among the towering clouds and deep clear-air canyons of Saturn's upper atmosphere. Having survived the traitor star, they returned to the all-too-human tradition of internecine strife. The new city-states of Saturn began to resemble those of ancient Greece, with one group of cities taking on the role of militaristic Sparta...

## 8. The Sails of Tau Ceti – US$4.50

*Starhopper* was humanity's first interstellar probe. It was designed to search for intelligent life beyond the solar system. Before it could be launched, however, intelligent life found Earth. The discovery of an alien light sail inbound at the edge of the solar system generated considerable excitement in scientific circles. With the interstellar probe nearing completion, it gave scientists the opportunity to launch an expedition to meet the aliens while they were still in space. The second surprise came when *Starhopper's* crew boarded the alien craft. They found beings that, despite their alien physiques, were surprisingly compatible with humans. That two species so similar could have evolved a mere twelve light years from one another seemed too coincidental to be true.

One human being soon discovered that coincidence had nothing to do with it...

## 9. GIBRALTAR EARTH – First Time in Print — $6.00

It is the 24th Century and humanity is just gaining a toehold out among the stars. Stellar Survey Starship *Magellan* is exploring the New Eden system when they encounter two alien spacecraft. When the encounter is over, the score is one human scout ship and one alien aggressor destroyed. In exploring the wreck of the second alien ship, spacers discover a survivor with a fantastic story.

The alien comes from a million-star Galactic Empire ruled over by a mysterious race known as the Broa. These overlords are the masters of this region of the galaxy and they allow no competitors. This news presents Earth's rulers with a problem. As yet, the Broa are ignorant of humanity's existence. Does the human race retreat to its one small world, quaking in fear that the Broa will eventually discover Earth? Or do they take a more aggressive approach?

Whatever they do, they must do it quickly! Time is running out for the human race...

## 10. Gridlock and Other Stories - US$4.50

Where would you visit if you invented a time machine, but could not steer it? What if you went out for a six-pack of beer and never came back? If you think nuclear power is dangerous, you should try black holes as an energy source — or even scarier, solar energy! Visit the many worlds of Michael McCollum. I guarantee that you will be surprised!

## *Non-Fiction Books*

## 11. The Art of Writing, Volume I - US$10.00

Have you missed any of the articles in the Art of Writing Series? No problem. The first sixteen articles (October, 1996-December, 1997) have been collected into a book-length work of more than 72,000 words. Now you can learn about character, conflict, plot, pacing, dialogue, and the business of writing, all in one document.

## 12. The Art of Writing, Volume II - US$10.00

This collection covers the Art of Writing articles published during 1998. The book is 62,000 words in length and builds on the foundation of knowledge provided by Volume I of this popular series.

## 13. The Art of Science Fiction, Volume I - US$10.00

Have you missed any of the articles in the Art of Science Fiction Series? No problem. The first sixteen articles (October, 1996-December, 1997) have been collected into a book-length work of more than 70,000 words. Learn about science fiction techniques and technologies, including starships, time machines, and rocket propulsion. Tour the Solar System and learn astronomy from the science fiction writer's viewpoint. We don't care where the stars appear in the terrestrial sky. We want to know their true positions in space. If you are planning to write an interstellar romance, brushing up on your astronomy may be just what you need.

## 14. The Art of Science Fiction, Volume II - US$10.00

This collection covers the *Art of Science Fiction* articles published during 1998. The book is 67,000 words in length and builds on the foundation of knowledge provided by Volume I of this popular series.

## 15. The Astrogator's Handbook – Expanded Edition – Coming August, 1999

The Astrogator's Handbook has been very popular on Sci Fi – Arizona. The handbook has star maps that show science fiction writers where the stars are located in space rather than where they are located in Earth's sky. Because of the popularity, we are expanding the handbook to show nine times as much space and more than ten times as many stars. The expanded handbook includes the positions of 3500 stars as viewed from Polaris on 63 maps. This handbook is a useful resource for every science fiction writer and will appeal to anyone with an interest in astronomy.